COLD STEEL

COLD STEEL

Britain's Richest Man and the Multi-Billion-
Dollar Battle for a Global Industry

Tim Bouquet and Byron Ousey

Little, Brown

LITTLE, BROWN

First published in Great Britain in 2008 by Little, Brown

Copyright © Tim Bouquet and Byron Ousey 2008

A CIP catalogue record for this book
is available from the British Library.

ISBN HB 978-0-316-02799-1
ISBN CF 978-0-316-02807-3

Typeset in Caslon by M Rules
Printed and bound in Great Britain by
Clays Ltd, St Ives plc

Little, Brown
An imprint of
Little, Brown Book Group
100 Victoria Embankment
London EC4Y 0DY

An Hachette Livre UK Company
www.hachettelivre.co.uk

www.littlebrown.co.uk

To my wife, Sarah Mansell – TCB

To my partner, Marcia Delaney – BJO

Contents

Preface

The idea for this book came during a damp Sunday morning in February 2006 when the authors were attending a weekend school for writers held at West Dean College, a grand turreted mansion made of stone and flint and set in six thousand acres of park and farmland near Chichester in West Sussex. Before becoming a college devoted to the creative, decorative and performing arts, West Dean was the home of the late Edward James, a poet and writer who used his inherited wealth to become a passionate supporter of Surrealism and sponsored artists such as Salvador Dalí. The house is packed with paintings, sculpture, furniture and stuffed animals which all reflect the late owner's take on life.

Over a mid-morning coffee break the prospective authors, surrounded by the Sunday newspapers, got talking about the far more realistic intentions of steel billionaire Lakshmi Mittal, and Britain's richest man, who had just launched an audacious and hostile bid for the world's second-biggest steel company, Luxembourg-based Arcelor.

Tim (the tutor) and Byron (the pupil) discovered they had a common interest. Tim was hoping to be the first feature writer to profile Lakshmi Mittal, for an article for the *Telegraph Magazine*. Byron happened to have a bird's-eye view of this takeover battle raging in Luxembourg. He was advising the Luxembourg government, which was the biggest shareholder in Mittal's target, Arcelor, on its communications strategy, but was not directly involved with either Arcelor or Mittal Steel.

It was not until the early summer months that the idea for the book began to take shape. Tim had conducted exclusive interviews with Lakshmi, his son Aditya and their closest colleagues, advisers and friends for the *Telegraph* profile. He and Byron were convinced that although the Arcelor–Mittal Steel takeover battle had received massive international media coverage the inside story of the many extraordinary personalities involved had not been told. They also realised that this would not be a dry business textbook. This tale of epic twists and strange turns featured six billionaires, many of the world's top investment bankers, hundreds of international lawyers, seven governments and their presidents and prime ministers, secret meetings at private airports, accusations of skulduggery, many people who were not always quite what they seemed and above all massive amounts of money. It was a contest full of culture clashes and corporate espionage, and even some allegations of racism.

But to tell it like it was from the inside meant winning the cooperation of the senior managements of both companies as well as their galaxies of advisers. It would take more than two good contacts books. For many of the bankers, lawyers and public relations advisers Mittal v. Arcelor was the defining takeover battle that led to what they all called a 'destination deal'. They also referred to it reverentially as 'the Fight'. For scale, complexity and sheer aggression, there would never be another like it in their careers. Most of them, winners, losers, major players all, were now ready to talk.

The authors conducted more than fifty extensive face-to-face interviews during July and August 2006, an exhausting schedule that took them to London, Luxembourg, Paris, Milan, Brussels and the massive Sidmar steelworks near Ghent in Belgium. There were many other telephone calls to Hamilton, Ontario, the United States, Holland, India and Moscow. Their research took them to some of Europe's most esteemed boardrooms, fine hotels, exclusive restaurants, too many airports and a military graveyard. Many of the people interviewed for this book and appearing in it have never spoken in public before. Such is the confidential nature of their work, and of their clients' bonuses, it is unlikely that they will ever do so again.

Unlike business books *Cold Steel* is a truly international thriller played at pace and mirroring the impact of globalisation on one of the world's least known but most important industries. The outcome of the battle was to transform the landscape of the steel industry and bring a much needed victory for shareholder democracy in mainland Europe. It is written as a thriller because that is what it was. *Cold Steel* is a story of mounting jeopardy starring an international cast, many of them with exotic names and backgrounds. They all had motive and opportunity and were in the right places at the right and the wrong times. Some also got very rich in the process. In addition, the story is not without a touch of the fantasy, the illogical and the unexpected juxtapositions that are the true hallmarks of Surrealism.

Introduction

Imagine a world in which there are no airports, skyscrapers, motor-cars, railways, planes, bridges or football stadiums, or at least, not as we know them. To some this might be paradise. But this world would also be without surgical instruments and other medical equipment. There would be none of the computers, cookers, fridges, cutlery, scissors, saucepans, garden tools, ships, tractors, plough-shares, springs, wristwatches and heart pacemakers we take for granted.

Steel is all around us, and even if it is hidden by concrete, glass, brick or paint it forms the backbone of our built environment and governs the way we live. And yet, as we race across the Forth Railway Bridge, the world's first steel bridge, or San Francisco's Golden Gate, we forget that had it not been for a brilliant inventor and businessman confined to his bed during the Crimean War we would still be living in a cast-iron world and making those crossings and many other navigations the slow way.

At the age of forty-two the Englishman Henry Bessemer was a phenomenally successful inventor with hundreds of patents filed. He is the man who put lead in our pencils. He invented the embossed stamp. But as he lay on his sickbed Bessemer was pondering how he could improve the construction of artillery guns. Britain's cast-iron cannon were exploding at a worrying rate because they were not strong enough to withstand the pressure caused by the projectiles they were called upon to fire. The problem with iron was that it had too much carbon in it, making it prone to brittleness. Steel was the obvious alternative. It was stronger and more flexible and it had been around for two thousand years, but it was very expensive and time-consuming to produce and quality was variable. If only it could be mass-produced to a guaranteed high standard, Bessemer figured, then Britain's gunnery problems would be at an end.

He rose from his bed and returned to his workshops and began to experiment. The rest, as they say, is history – the kind of history most of us leave behind in the classroom with the exception of maybe a couple of words that, like the spinning jenny or Stephenson's *Rocket*, still ring a distant bell. In Henry Bessemer's case, it was two very significant words that he added to the lexicon of the Industrial Revolution: the 'Bessemer converter'.

Bessemer had discovered that if you blew cold air through molten iron ore heated in a pear-shaped cauldron or blast furnace to 1250 degrees centigrade it removed most of the impurities, reduced the carbon content to an acceptable level for hardness and created one of the world's strongest alloys: modern steel. Various other elements could be added to achieve different levels of ductility and tensile strength. With his 'converter' blast furnace Bessemer could produce thirty tons of reliable high-grade steel in one hour. In 1859 he opened a factory in Sheffield and started making guns and steel rails. Henry Bessemer became the world's first steel millionaire.

Typically of British history, homegrown entrepreneurs were slow to pick up on Bessemer's modern steel, but a poor boy from Dunfermline in Scotland who had emigrated to the United States and was making a name for himself in Pittsburgh, Pennsylvania, visited Sheffield and saw that here was a highly versatile material that was going to change the world. His name was Andrew Carnegie. Back in Pittsburgh he founded the Carnegie Steel Company – which would one day become US Steel – and started making huge amounts of the stuff that was to build the railroads, skyscrapers, bridges and ships that made the US economy dominant and him the richest man in the world. Carnegie was so successful his name was added to the list of 'robber barons' – a term for those businessmen and bankers, like John D. Rockefeller or Standard Oil's Henry Flagler, who dominated their respective industries and amassed huge personal fortunes, often as a result of pursuing allegedly anti-competitive or unfair business practices.

Steel proved itself increasingly versatile, from shipyard to dining table. In August 1913 forty-two-year-old Sheffield-born Harry Brearley created a steel with 12.8 per cent chromium and found it resistant to lemon juice and vinegar. He described his invention as 'rustless steel'. We know it better as 'stainless', forever synonymous with the city of Brearley's birth. In 1952 a new refinement in steel-making came out of Austria. Still using a converter blast furnace based on Bessemer's design, the new process used a water-cooled lance to blow oxygen at high velocity downwards on the surface of the hot metal. The carbon content of the alloy was lowered and changed the material into the even more versatile low-carbon steel.

Today steel is made in various types, shapes and sizes. 'Long' steel, also known as 'volume' steel, is used to reinforce concrete and for rail tracks, structural girders and bridges. Higher-quality 'flat' carbon steel is used for car bodies, trains and ships as well as washing-machines and other 'white goods'.

Unlike the rarefied world of the microchip, steel is tangible. It's dirty and noisy and hot. It spits, it smokes and it hisses. A steel plant could occupy ten square kilometres and more and be covered in a web of vertiginous belt conveyors speeding rich seams of rust-coloured ore, delivered by ship or rail from Brazil or Australia, to the huge scoops and the slow-moving rolling-machines that sift, grade and form it into symmetrical mountains half a mile long and sixty feet high. Other machines like dark praying mantises fashion huge stacks of coal, which will be turned into coke to melt the ore. The thick red liquid is then put into black 'torpedo ladles', each one carrying 170 tonnes, which are pulled by muscular trains to the blast furnaces where they are lifted, dipped and tipped into Bessemer-style converters higher than houses. To the recipe is added a carefully weighed portion of scrap – steel is the ultimate recyclable material – which causes the mix to spit and gurgle, throwing fountains of angry red and white sparks into the higher realms of the plant where the steelmen sit behind glare-proof glass surrounded by their computer screens like air-traffic controllers. From here they monitor and boss the process as long thick red slabs hit the rollers for a journey around the complex that will see them, if they are not intended for the construction industry, racing around machines like giant newspaper printing presses getting thinner and thinner until they emerge just a few millimetres thick, to be wrapped up and stored in huge coils or stacked in sheets. This 'flat' steel is highly prized and can also be galvanised, by being either hot-dipped or electroplated in zinc for protection against rust.

Because of the critical role played by steel in economic development, the steel industry is often considered, especially by governments, which traditionally owned it, to be an indicator of economic prowess. World production has grown exponentially, but there were big highs and equally big lows all through the 1900s and up to 2002. Recovery from two world wars and the great Depression of the 1930s caused massive disruption and lay-offs. Over-capacity and low steel prices continued to play havoc through the 1970s and 1980s and politicians began to lose their belief that the wealth of a nation was directly coupled to its steel production.

This led to a wave of privatisations, as state-owned enterprises shed their financial liabilities to hungry capitalists. A whole new breed of steel-makers came into being using a new technology, the mini-mill. This used a smaller electric-arc furnace fed that just melts down 'cold' scrap. It was a cheaper process than the traditional 'hot metal' 'integrated mills' with their mountains of ore and coal and monumental machinery, but it was used almost exclusively for lower-grade building and other 'long' products.

By the beginning of 2005, the world steel industry was on a high, after decades of moving from apocalypse to break-even and then back to apocalypse. Since 2003, when a staggering 960 million tonnes were produced – compared to 21.9 million tonnes for aluminium – there had been unprecedented demand, mainly from China and India. China was both the biggest producer, the first country to exceed 200 million tonnes of crude steel in a year, and also its biggest consumer at 244 million tonnes. The global economy was also booming, but this was creating production bottlenecks for all steel-makers and by 2004 steel had for the first time hit an average of $650 per tonne shipped. Profit margins were better, but where was the growth to come from? In tandem, the costs of essential raw materials for steel-making – iron ore and coking coal – had gone through the roof, along with bulk shipping costs. The key to future growth was to secure plants in emerging markets where ore and coal were close to production sites, labour costs were much lower and where technology transfer and investment could spur greater savings.

But the central issue was that globally the industry remained a very fragmented one. No single company was producing 100 million tonnes a year, or 10 per cent of total world production. The name of the game was consolidation into fewer, bigger players. With this would come the chance for steel-makers to gain greater pricing power, increasing their profitability and the value of their shares.

Two groups had begun to move ahead of the pack. One was Mittal Steel with its operational headquarters in London's prestigious Berkeley Square. Mittal Steel was the world's biggest producer, especially of 'long' products. It was young, aggressive, fast, and a big risk-taker, fuelled by its founder Lakshmi Mittal's visionary zeal to consolidate the industry. Its nearest rival, Arcelor – the world's most profitable steel company, focusing on 'flat' products – was headed by the Frenchman Guy Dollé, and was a combination of three former state-owned European steel plants: Arbed of Luxembourg, Usinor from France and Spain's Aceralia. These three were now merged, restructured and administered from the grandiose, chateau-like former Arbed headquarters on Luxembourg's Avenue de la Liberté.

Both groups were passionate about steel. Mittal, already dubbed 'the Carnegie from Calcutta', had a clearer vision of the need to streamline steel, but Arcelor was determined to become the biggest as well as the best. Dominating the market would enable either firm to increase its pricing position with customers, the car-makers, ship-builders and construction firms, as well as chasing growth in the new markets of Asia, South America and Eastern Europe.

Guy Dollé could hear the clump of Mittal's feet marching ahead, and it hurt. Arcelor was Europe's reigning steel champion and arrogantly proud of it. It had a commanding market share of the specialised high-strength steel supplied to European car-makers and a total overall production approaching 50 million tonnes a year, all with state-of-the-art technology. The group had repaired its consolidated balance sheet, ravished by decades of downturns and continual restructuring costs. It had invested heavily in the quest for the best technology and had also acquired companies in Brazil, set up joint ventures in Russia, Japan and China and was now eagerly eyeing gateways to the North American car market. And to its long-suffering shareholders, starved of decent dividends, Arcelor was at last moving in the right direction after the blood, sweat and tears of shifting from public to private sector. The Luxembourg group was clearly on a wake-up call, gunning to overtake Mittal Steel and keep it at bay.

By 2005 the battle for supremacy had begun to hot up. Two projected state sell-offs by public auction, in Turkey and Ukraine, were particularly attractive commercially. Both auctions were taking place in October, within three weeks of each other. The first, in Turkey, was for the 46.3 per cent of government-owned shares in Erdemir, a steel-maker producing 3.5 million tonnes a year for car-makers and other industrial clients in a country of seventy million people shaping up to join the European Union. Mittal and Arcelor both already owned minority stakes in the Turkish company and were eager to get majority control.

Representatives of Mittal Steel and of Arcelor rolled up at the Hilton hotel in Ankara to slug it out in a plush carpeted room with four other bidders, two from Russia and two local groups, Ergeli and Oyak. Lakshmi Mittal withdrew after the second round, having bid up to $2.3 billion. The whole dynamic of the auction then changed. The Russians pulled out, and then Arcelor followed in round three. Guy Dollé was relieved that he had not overpaid and even more comfortable that his arch-rival had walked away empty-handed. The two men dubbed 'the stallions of steel' left the locals to fight it out, Oyak paying a ritzy $2.77 billion, a price considered way over the odds.

This was the end of the phoney war. Lakshmi Mittal and Guy Dollé were saving themselves for a much bigger fight.

1

Monday 25 October 2005

Kiev, Ukraine

The unusually warm morning sun glistened on Kiev's renowned green mosaic domes and gold-encrusted minarets, creating a halo effect over the old part of the city overlooking the right bank of the River Dnipro. On the left bank, for three million citizens in the bustling newer sections of the Ukrainian capital, it was going to be another dramatic day under the nine-month-old 'Orange Revolution'. For many it was a day full of new-found optimism, as bold economic reforms and liberalisation policies swept away the iron-fist legacy of those who had once commanded the former Soviet Republic.

However, for other Ukrainians, the "Blues" who still leaned towards Mother Russia, it was a day of protest, underlining the continuing chaos in the country's political arena.

For Viktor Yushchenko it was show time. Ukraine's democratically elected head of state – whose now familiar pock-marked face was a sinister souvenir of a Kremlin-inspired attempt to kill him with dioxin poison prior to an election re-run under the auspices of international observers – made sure the capitalist world had ringside seats. Punctually at 9.45 a.m. the well-built shirt-sleeved President rose from his desk in the teak-panelled government offices in Bankova Street, flanked by the blue and yellow motifs of the national flag. He reached for his jacket and set off for his official engagement at the nearby state-owned Property Department. He was shepherded by an entourage of hefty bodyguards dressed in dark-grey suits with matching shirts.

After a brisk five-minute walk in the sunny but blustery weather, the President reached the side entrance to the department, consciously avoiding a large group of noisy protesters behind barricades erected around the front entrance chanting 'No, no, no' to privatisation. Aware that his every move was being caught on state television station Channel 5, Yushchenko waved to the rooftop cameraman whom he spotted high to his right just as he entered the building. Inside he was escorted quickly to a drab office on the fifth floor where he greeted two men at a small oval conference table in the middle of the room. Prime Minister Yuri Yekhanurov and Viktor Pynzenyk, the finance minister, were staring intently at a portable TV. To their right a Channel 5 camera captured their reactions to the scene unfolding on screen, beamed live from an adjoining room.

Yushchenko removed his jacket and sat to the left of his prime minister. He gulped down a glass of water and settled to watch the event. In his left hand he held a five-page document containing a list of numbers, big numbers expressed in the national currency, the *hryvnia*. He leaned forward, glancing quickly at the document, and turned to his two ministers. 'I have a clear conscience,' he said. 'This will do wonders to revitalise Ukraine's enterprise culture which we so badly need.' Then he added defiantly, 'And none of it would have been possible without the Orange Revolution.'

Yushchenko had come to witness an auction. But this was no Manhattan-style bidding festival for well heeled art lovers hoping to land a Monet or a Picasso. At stake was one job lot: Kryvorizstal, Ukraine's flagship steel mill.

The previous evening two men had been checked into Kiev's Premier Palace hotel by a local man who handed them the keys to an executive suite that had already been swept for security. They had arrived in their private jet and were using assumed names and temporary mobiles, which routed all calls on secure lines via the Netherlands. The elder of the two was Lakshmi Niwas Mittal, fifty-five, the biggest maker of steel in the world and fifth-richest man on the planet, with a personal wealth of £15 billion. With him was his very ambitious twenty-nine-year-old son Aditya, chief financial officer of Mittal Steel. In a breathtaking series of forty-seven acquisitions in fifteen years, costing a total of $15 billion, Lakshmi Mittal, born penniless in Rajasthan, had proved adept at leveraging bank finance to support his war chest as he swept east and west snapping up debt-ridden, poorly run state-owned assets, especially in the former Soviet bloc, and turning them to profit in record time. Mittal, a tall man with broad shoulders and youthful good looks, wanted Kryvorizstal very badly. It was another piece in his plan to create the biggest steel company the world had ever seen. He was especially determined, having been cheated out of Kryvorizstal once before in a bent auction handled by the corrupt regime Yushchenko had unseated with his revolution.

In 2004 Kryvorizstal had been sold for the equivalent of $800 million, a steep discount on its true worth. Foreign buyers, including Mittal, had been prepared to pay much more. Although he had bid the most, he had been outmanoeuvred by blatantly unfair insertions in the tender documents. One clause stipulated that the bidders must own local coal mines in Ukraine, producing at least one million tonnes of coking coal to feed the mill's furnaces. This neatly disenfranchised all foreign buyers. Kryvorizstal went to a group led by then President Kuchma's son-in-law.

Supporters of the Orange Revolution saw the Kryvorizstal sale as the last straw. Between August 1994 and February 1997 Ukraine's privatisation programme had seen many questionable sales of state-owned properties, with Kuchma's cronies the main beneficiaries. Yushchenko publicly accused him of corruption and in the battle for political change Kryvorizstal became an integral part of the Orange Revolution's appeal to a majority in the country. People took to the streets wanting an end to political and financial cronyism.

Yushchenko vowed to annul the deal and, once elected, he acted swiftly on his promise. Having survived intensive legal challenges from the Ukrainian Supreme Court, Yushchenko then announced a resale and invited the international community to bid in a public auction. He demanded it be televised so as to prove to the world that Ukraine was now transparent, anti-corrupt and open for foreign investment. He vowed it would be the turning point for Ukrainian enterprise. For Lakshmi Mittal the auction was the chance to right a wrong.

*

In a small private hotel in the centre of Kiev, another man had checked in who was equally determined to stop Mittal getting his hands on Kryvorizstal. This was Guy Dollé, the sixty-three-year-old French chief executive of Arcelor. Until Mittal came along Dollé, a lifelong steel-maker with pale-blue Caligula eyes, had been top man. He wanted the position back. For a while now Arcelor's senior managers had feared that Mittal might even come after them, so much so that they had created a small group to plan a defence. Its name was Project Tiger. A major Tiger goal was to acquire strategically important steel companies that would give Arcelor greater global reach, better able to compete against Mittal, improve the value of its shares and make Arcelor too expensive for the rapacious Indian. So clandestine was Tiger that it always referred to Mittal Steel by codenames. Lakshmi was known as 'Mr Moon', his son Aditya was 'Adam'.

Mittal Steel, dominated by the Mittal family, and Arcelor, the very model of European social democracy, were oceans apart culturally. Mittal Steel was unsentimental, dynamic and focused, with the short lines of decision-making that characterise a close-knit family-dominated business. Arcelor, with a hundred-year pedigree and high-quality assets and technology superior to Mittal's, was well engineered but far less nimble, its legs tied by concerns for its 'tripartite industrial stakeholder model' – a clunky piece of jargon coming out of the tough years when the company was being forged, meaning that the management, unions and government ran the show on costs, wages and funding and that shareholders took a back seat, or preferably sat in a different vehicle altogether. Arcelor was the very determined but slower-moving beast to Mittal's sleek and well oiled free-market acquisition machine. The contest between them promised to be as epic as Ali versus Frazier.

The first number at the top of the front page of President Yushchenko's document was 12.6 billion *hryvnia*, equivalent to $2.5 billion. Down the page, set left, the numbers were tabulated in increments of 100 million *hryvnia*, $20 million. To the right of each number was a lined space, left blank, to fill in the bids.

On screen he watched an official from the state Property Fund mount a podium and begin addressing his audience, explaining the legalities of the proceedings. On the wall immediately behind him was a large blue plasma screen emblazoned with the words 'State Property Auction – 2005'. All cameras and lights were on. The Kryvorizstal auction was so bound up in Ukraine's fight for democracy that an audience of six million viewers, higher than for a national football match, was watching or listening on a simultaneous radio transmission from homes, offices and coffee bars across the country. At the same time, the programme with translation in English was being uploaded to an SES Astra satellite, then downloaded to the political and financial capitals of the world.

Suddenly the cameras swerved to get a fix on the late entrance of the vivacious Yulia Tomashenko. The charismatic politician, with her Heidi-style plaits, was spearheading the Orange Revolution's controversial privatisation programme. Yulia was feared by her political rivals, who dubbed her 'the Orange Goddess'. She was in the room to maximise the public relations impact on her own political ambitions, which she pursued relentlessly. Fully aware of the cameras as they zoomed in, Yulia flashed a wide, disarming smile like a Hollywood movie star playing to her audience.

The ground rules for the auction had been set with a reserve price of $2 billion. Yushchenko's financial advisers had told him that the mill would comfortably fetch $3 billion. If he pulled this off, then he knew he could show the Ukrainian people how the original Kryvorizstal privatisation had been a blatant steal.

'The auction will commence at 10 a.m.,' the state official said coolly, and pressed the five-minute bell for the bidders to ready themselves.

Located in the east of the country, Kryvorizstal was one of Ukraine's most lucrative assets. The mill exported seven million tonnes of steel a year and was the nation's single biggest earner and its biggest employer, with fifty-six thousand Ukrainians all on a meagre payroll by Western standards. Amongst the workers of Kryvorizstal, toiling beside the glowing hot steel, there was also increasing nervousness about the future. The mill was about to change hands again.

Yushchenko's commercial timing was brilliant. The Kryvorizstal business was a richer prize than Erdemir. It was ideally placed geographically to feed the booming markets of Russia and Eastern Europe, with its own iron ore and coal mines close to the point of manufacture. Mittal and Dollé both wanted it badly. Under the right infusion of investment and management, the mill was capable of delivering a significant upgrade in performance. In other words, it was a once-in-a-lifetime opportunity on the road to becoming the Toyota of steel.

The previous evening Mittal had flown in a highly trusted colleague, Sudhir Maheshwari, his long-serving chief of staff, who arrived by commercial flight from London and checked in at the Radisson Hotel. Like the Mittals he carried a temporary mobile phone and had agreed to travel only by chauffeured car. The clandestine nature of his arrival was reminiscent of Cold War espionage, and spoke volumes on the need for precaution against eavesdropping by well trained local spooks, acting either for the Ukrainians or for Mittal's industry competitors.

Guy Dollé had also flown in with a heavyweight team, including his chairman Joseph Kinsch, Dollé's deputy Michel Wurth, who was heading up the Project Tiger team, and Paul Matthys, a Belgian on the Arcelor operating board who had been at the Erdemir auction. Alain Davezac, who had a freebooting role as Dollé's international emissary, completed the Arcelor quintet. Like the Mittals, the Arcelor team had dispersed to different hotels and then met up in the evening to talk tactics with their local partner, a private firm under the leadership of Sergey Taruta, a forty-eight-year-old billionaire Ukrainian, and pro-Yushchenko. Dollé reckoned that having a Ukrainian company alongside would help Arcelor's cause.

The Mittals had already done their homework, schmoozing the local politicians, getting advice and linking in with Ukraine's door openers, part and parcel of the steep learning curve of dealing with Eastern Europe. After years of tramping places like Bucharest, Warsaw and Sofia, no one did it better than Lakshmi Mittal.

Mittal also knew that Dollé was not to be underestimated. As they settled in on the Sunday evening, he told Aditya, 'This auction is going to be tough. I don't want to fail on this one, but I know Guy will go to the wire because he cannot afford to lose this either. Our limit is $5 billion. I believe their limit is between $3.5 and $4 billion, so we have more than an edge.'

'And the Russian bidder?' Aditya asked. Apart from Mittal Steel and the Arcelor consortium, there was the Smart Group, controlled by the Russian oligarch Vadim Novynski, who had strong ties to Viktor Chernomyrdin, now the Russian Federation's ambassador to Ukraine.

'He cannot match either of us,' Lakshmi Mittal said.

'We are going to have to pace this cleverly,' Aditya suggested.

'We need to stay the course,' Mittal agreed, 'but we must be aware that Dollé will force us to bid unrealistically higher.'

Dollé discussed tactics and strategy for the auction with his team over dinner at their hotel. Arcelor had been advised by its investment banker Merrill Lynch on valuations and agreed these with its local partner. Dollé said Wurth and Paul Matthys should front up the bidding in the auction room. But how high should they go? They set a limit of $3.5 billion. Dollé had full approval from the Arcelor board, but was nonetheless comforted by the presence of his chairman Kinsch, who had the authority to push higher if needed. Unlike Mittal, who ultimately took all the big decisions in his company, Guy Dollé worked for a bureaucracy and was not even a member of his board.

Arcelor's Plan B was to push Mittal sky high if he was bidding aggressively. If the Indian overpaid, then that would leave less in his kitty with which to attack Arcelor.

Lakshmi and Aditya Mittal dined early at the Premier Palace with Sudhir Maheshwari and two local lawyers from the Kiev office of Baker & McKenzie. At 11 p.m. Sudhir had returned to his hotel and was about to retire for the evening, when his mobile phone rang.

'Sudhir? This is Aditya. Can you come and join us? We need to revise our plans.'

Maheshwari dressed quickly and left his hotel. Out on the street he hailed a cab, breaking the undercover code they had agreed. He had no choice. There had been urgency in Aditya's voice and the hired limo was not available. Ten minutes later he joined the Mittals, who were relaxing in their executive suite.

'We think it is best that you front the bidding tomorrow,' Lakshmi told him. Maheshwari was taken aback. He had never done anything like this before. 'If we are in the room, it gives added impetus to the event, which we want to avoid,' Mittal explained, 'especially since we know that Dollé has asked Wurth to lead his team. Let's go through the tactics and double-check everything.'

Maheshwari hardly slept that night, his mind buzzing with the excitement and the enormity of the task ahead of him.

There had never been a public steel auction of this scale before, and the organisers hoped they had got their organisation right. Representatives of each bidding group were seated, classroom style, at three separate sets of tables at the back of the room, each with an open phone line to their respective base camps. In front of them sat the locals, led by high-ranking bureaucrats, an eclectic mix seated on green leather chairs around an oblong mahogany conference table set at a right-angle. Between them and the three bidding tables was an empty glass container, the size of an average fish tank.

The auctioneer invited the three bidders to come to the fish tank and deposit their opening bids. The TV camera zoomed in as three state officials approached. With some ceremony each took an envelope, slicing it open with a pair of scissors, and then returned to the podium to hand them over to the auctioneer, who with an exaggerated sense of theatre extracted the contents of each one. 'I sense lots of emotion right now,' he said, as his eyes scanned the bid documents for the opening prices. 'I do not know who suffers the most, the bidders or the members of the privatisation commission. We are not accustomed to such situations,' he added poignantly.

The eerie silence in the room was broken as the auctioneer shuffled the papers in front of him. The Arcelor team looked on passively. The Russians smiled nervously. Sudhir Maheshwari tried to look casual, as though he was not really there.

'The Arcelor consortium group has offered the highest starting price at $2.5 billion,' the auctioneer declared. The bureaucrats breathed out and looked pleased. It was a good start. The reserve price had already been reached. The bidding could get very competitive.

The auctioneer gestured to the three tables. 'We will now move to the open auction,' he told them. 'Who has the first bid?'

Each bidder had been given a small placard, with a number. Smart was allocated number 1, Arcelor had 2 and Mittal 3. The Smart Group was the first to open up with a rise to $2.6 billion. The numbers flashed up on the blue plasma screen. Arcelor followed: $2.7 billion. Bidding was slow, measured and quiet, like high rollers at a game of stud poker, weighing up their opponents. The bidders were also aware that they were taking part in a highly unusual event, so they paused frequently to take advice over the phone. Early on, minutes passed between bids.

Just as he had been told by the Mittals, Sudhir Maheshwari remained passive and motionless as Smart and Arcelor dominated the early running, each raising a white placard to hike the bidding in increments of $20 million. After half an hour, on the thirty-fourth bid, the price broke through the $3 billion barrier. The tension heightened. But there was still no sign of a bid from Lakshmi Mittal. Maheshwari appeared ambivalent, almost bored.

The Smart Group continued to make the running, with Arcelor in measured pursuit. Bid number 40 was $3.3 billion. Who would buy? Sudhir's expression now changed. 'Let's get serious,' he told himself. He had had the call from Mittal to enter the auction. He raised placard number 3 for the first time: $3.32 billion. Mittal Steel was coming up suddenly on the rails.

At the Arcelor table Michel Wurth called Dollé at base for his riding instructions.

'This is just what we expected,' Dollé told him. 'Keep bidding. We can go higher.'

The Smart Group suddenly pulled up, as if transfixed by their competitors' burst of financial firepower. Ukrainian citizens watched in awe, barely able to comprehend the numbers flashing on screen. In the trading rooms of the big investment banks in London, New York and Paris, the spread bets were already placed.

The atmosphere in the auction room grew uncomfortably tense as the Mittal and Arcelor teams chased up the bidding, working the phones back to base. In five brisk minutes they pushed the price through the $3.5 billion barrier. The bidding got so fast at one point that the auctioneer could hardly keep up.

At bid number 51, the Smart Group came back in with $3.75 billion, as if trying to close the game. It was to be their last throw of the dice. The auctioneer, recovering his composure, steered the bidding on. Arcelor and Mittal pushed through the $4 billion mark. At the Arcelor table, Wurth, a thin and pensive fifty-two-year-old who looked like a geography teacher, was furrowing his brow. He knew that his side was way over the original limit. Guy Dollé came on the line.

'Take it higher,' he told Wurth. 'We are looking to go to 4.5 billion.'

The bidding edged up by increments of $20 million, reaching $4.68 billion.

Aditya came on the line to Sudhir. 'You are doing fine,' he told Maheshwari.

'Now raise the game by 120 million.' After forty minutes of measured bidding, Sudhir now crashed through the gears and ramped up the stakes to $4.8 billion.

Dollé held his nerve. He asked Kinsch for more. The chairman gave him the nod. Arcelor came back immediately. Wurth told Matthys to raise his card: $4.82 billion.

Mittal fired again, taking the bidding to $4.84 billion. There was a pause. The auctioneer looked across to the Arcelor team. 'May we have the next bid?' he asked.

Wurth avoided eye contact. He heard Guy Dollé come on the line. 'We're done.' Wurth bowed his head on the news. The Arcelor table was motionless as the auctioneer's hammer fell.

'Sold to the Mittal Group! Congratulations, gentlemen.'

Sudhir Maheshwari punched the air, shook hands with his team, ignoring the other bidders. The cameras closed in, but Yulia Tomashenko beat them to it, right in the spotlight and the first to congratulate Lakshmi Mittal's men. In the adjoining office, the camera captured a beaming Yushchenko, shaking hands with his two ministers. At a princely $4.84 billion, Mittal's winning price was five times more than was paid for the original privatisation and almost double what had been anticipated by the advisers. In cash terms, it represented 20 per cent more than all the previous Ukrainian privatisations combined.

'The auction is a defining moment in Ukraine's modernisation,' Yushchenko declared triumphantly. 'Democracy has prevailed and I pledge the money will be put to good use for the benefit of all Ukrainians.'

Guy Dollé welcomed his dejected team back to their hotel. Like him they were stung by losing out to Mittal. Their only consolation was that they had forced their foe to pay significantly more than had been anticipated. 'At least Plan B has worked,' Dollé commiserated. Or had it?

2

18–19 Kensington Palace Gardens, London

'If Guy Dollé had not been bidding, we would have paid at least a billion dollars less for Kryvorizstal,' Aditya Mittal told his father as they reflected on their latest prize over breakfast at Lakshmi's palatial home. His father nodded. It was obvious to both of them that they would continue to face Arcelor in future bidding wars.

'It is not in our best interests, or the shareholders of Arcelor, for this battle to continue,' Aditya added. 'There are fewer opportunities for both of us going forward, so it can only get worse. We need to talk to Arcelor and come up with some form of collaboration, perhaps splitting some of the assets we are pursuing.'

'I agree,' Lakshmi said. 'Let's see if they will cooperate.'

Within days Aditya was putting out feelers. His chosen route was Alain Davezac, the fifty-five-year-old Frenchman who had worked closely with Dollé since the Usinor days. Davezac, a corporate strategist, had a special role, travelling the world on intelligence-gathering missions for Dollé, building relationships with key industry figures in China and Japan and identifying joint ventures, greenfield projects and takeover targets. A multilinguist who spoke English, Russian and Italian and 'notions of Thai', Davezac was seen by outsiders as an ambassadorial figure for Arcelor. But within the company the Knight of the Légion d'Honneur with the lustrous black hair was viewed with deep suspicion and resented by his Luxembourg colleagues, who saw him as the dark side of Dollé, a 'black ops' man who reported only to his chief.

Between 26 and 28 October Aditya talked several times with Davezac, with Dollé's blessing, and they met twice in Berkeley Square, where they talked about possible areas of collaboration and splitting assets. Then on the 29th Aditya bumped into Davezac in London at the Third Steel Success Strategies Europe conference. 'Mr Mittal is keen to speak with Mr Dollé,' Aditya said. 'Can a meeting be mutually agreed before Christmas?'

Davezac looked at him knowingly. 'I will try to arrange.'

Davezac reported Lakshmi Mittal's request to Dollé and the matter was debated at Arcelor's directorate general, known as the 'DG', its operational management board.

'Davezac should be taken off this role,' Paul Matthys told Dollé. 'As a member of the DG, it is I who should confer with Aditya.'

'That is the last thing I want,' Dollé said sharply. 'If you took over it would put the discussion on a whole different footing. Let's keep this low-key.'

Lakshmi Mittal was now pushing hard for a meeting with Guy Dollé. By early November Aditya was trying to pin Davezac down on diary dates, but with Dollé's heavy schedule and Christmas approaching it was difficult to find an agreed time and place. 'I think Guy is stalling,' Lakshmi told his son.

At the same time Aditya asked his director of investor relations, Julien Onillon, a former steel industry analyst with HSBC bank, to draw up a full analytical report on Arcelor's business, strategy and finances. 'I don't want you to discuss this with anybody internally,' he instructed the garrulous Frenchman.

While Onillon embarked on his secret mission, Aditya stayed in touch with Davezac as if they were on a permanent diary conference. In one conversation Aditya told him, 'My sales people tell me that your sales people are terrified we are going to come to take over Arcelor, but we never will.'

'I have no mandate to discuss that,' Davezac told him.

'I have not talked to my father about a takeover,' Aditya replied.

Davezac had no mandate because Guy Dollé was very busy trying to cultivate allies on the other side of the Atlantic.

Hamilton, Ontario

The tall, flaming chimneys burning off the gas produced by the coking ovens, the massive blackened plant leeching steam and smoke, rolling-mill sheds each a thousand feet long and the alpine tips of coal and iron ore being shifted by train trucks on a lattice of tracks could be seen from miles away. Founded in 1912 as the Dominion Foundries and Steel Company, Dofasco was more than a muscular landmark on Hamilton's horizon. The major employer in the town on the banks of Lake Ontario, it had won awards for being the most sustainable manufacturing company in North America and was a leading supplier of flat steel, used to make everything from car bodies to fridges, girders and reinforcing rods for the construction industry and pipes for the energy suppliers. It also prided itself on being a model employer. In 1938, Dofasco was the first Canadian company to introduce profit-sharing for all, and this now stood at a minimum 10 per cent of salary for every one of its 7400 workers, from the board down to the shop floor. In 2002 they had shared out $C51 million. The company had given the town the hundred-acre F.H. Sherman Recreation and Learning Center, where employees and their families could enjoy seven baseball diamonds, a soccer field, two National Hockey League-size ice arenas, a driving range, an eighteen-hole mini-putt golf course, a double gymnasium, tennis courts, six training rooms, and 'facilities to accommodate the forty-five separate clubs that fall under the recreational umbrella'.

A corporate culture known as the 'Dofasco way' had been the driving force in employee relations since the company was founded, meaning there was no need for trade unions at Dofasco, something that made a profitable, well run company extra-attractive to a predator.

Silver-haired CEO Donald A. Pether, who at fifty-seven had been with the company man and boy, had been fending off one such predator since May 2005 – Arcelor and Guy Dollé. Pether, who had started in the metallurgical department, had come up through the ranks just like Dollé, whom he had met back in the sixties. The relationship had continued and now Dofasco and Arcelor had a joint venture, DoSol Galva Inc., a hot-dip galvanising line producing high-quality flat-rolled steels for the automotive industry. Dofasco owned 80 per cent and Arcelor the rest.

Now, acquiring the Canadian company fitted Dollé's expansion strategy to shoehorn Arcelor into North America. Arcelor, partnered by Nucor, the Michigan-based steel group, had opened up discussions with Dofasco. Nucor's chief executive Dan DiMicco wanted to get into the higher-value areas of steel and had first made an approach to Dofasco on his own, but that plan was scuppered by the financial chaos precipitated by the 9/11 disaster in New York in 2001. In the early summer of 2005 Dollé and Nucor together pursued talks and were keen to get the Dofasco board to recommend a deal with them. On 27 May Arcelor/Nucor offered Dofasco $C43 dollars a share.

'This is no time to contemplate selling our company,' Pether told his directors.

Dofasco then did a smart thing. It bought Quebec Consolidated Mines (QCM) for $C350 million, which provided strategic new supplies of coal close to the Hamilton plant. It also entered into negotiations to acquire a business making tubular steel. Both acquisitions would significantly raise Dofasco's market valuation, but this was not transparent until later in the year when the deals were consummated. Dofasco planned an initial public offering (IPO) of shares for QCM. The money received for those shares would ensure that Dofasco's investment quickly turned into cash. Over the summer months, Dollé and DiMicco continued to plug away at Pether. In a conference call on 28 June they upped their bid from $C43 to $C46 a share, to take account of QCM, but subject to their being able to examine in detail the books of the enlarged company.

'The company is not for sale – and even if it was, your price is insufficient,' Pether told them pointedly.

On 6 July Guy Dollé tried again. Once more Pether rebuffed him. He was looking elsewhere in Europe for somebody to jump into bed with.

Dollé knew that Dofasco had been having discussions on and off with German steel and armaments group ThyssenKrupp. It happened all the time in the industry, but he had no reason to suspect that the talks were more than the usual exploratory rounds of possible technical cooperation. Earlier in 2005, on Valentine's Day,

Dofasco had held friendly talks in Hamilton with Thyssen on joint technology ventures, and there was a follow-up meeting in April. The two sides met again on 12 and 13 June, the very week after Pether had rebuffed Dollé and DiMicco. This time they were bunkered in Thyssen's secluded conference and seminar centre Schloss Landsberg, a hillside castle set in dense forest at Meiningen near Essen. It had been built by Adolf, Fifth Count of Burg, between 1276 and 1289 and bought and restored by industrialist and entrepreneur August Thyssen in 1903.

Inside its powerful battlements Dofasco and ThyssenKrupp scoped out areas of cooperation. Dofasco, being relatively small, needed technology partners in order to penetrate further into North America. But Pether made it clear to the Germans: 'Dofasco is interested in cooperation, but it is not up for sale.'

Dr Ekkehard Schulz, ThyssenKrupp's executive board chairman, wasn't giving up on the Canadians that easily. He was desperate to make a big deal. 'If you are ever put "in play" by an unsolicited offer,' he told Pether, 'we would be interested in making a counterbid for Dofasco.'

Having lost out in Turkey and Ukraine and eager to keep Mittal at bay, Guy Dollé called Don Pether again on 11 November. Dollé was convinced that Arcelor, enlarged with Dofasco and the added value it would bring in terms of its assets, market share and share price, would make it harder for the company to fall to Mittal. A key strand of Project Tiger was to make Arcelor too expensive for Mittal. Dollé was confident that Lakshmi's war chest was severely overstretched thanks to his getting him to bid higher than he wanted to at the Ukrainian auction. Dofasco was a big potential prize for both Arcelor and ThyssenKrupp because it would give them entry to the North American market. It was also outside the reach of Mittal – he had steel plant in the USA and by acquiring Dofasco he would break American competition constraints.

'Don, we believe that our joint offer is full and fair,' Dollé insisted. 'I expect you to table this with your board at the next meeting on November 14 and I look forward to you getting back to me. We want this to be friendly. We would hate to have to go direct to the market,' he added.

Pether read the threat. While his board worked to achieve a

friendly merger with ThyssenKrupp it was obvious that Guy Dollé was prepared to go over the heads of the directors straight to the shareholders with an unwanted hostile offer. Alarm bells started ringing all over Dofasco. This had never happened before in the steel industry. The board met and considered its response. The message was clear: No sale. Pether told Dollé the news on 16 November by transatlantic phone call. 'Your valuation criteria are insufficient since they hardly recognise the substantial value of QCM. It is our fiduciary duty to our shareholders not to entertain your proposal as it greatly undervalues the company. We also have to be very mindful of not upsetting the unique relationship between the workforce and the management. It is the key to the success of Dofasco. We value the relationship between our two companies and hope that this will continue,' Pether added, putting down the phone.

Then Dollé had a second rejection. Dan DiMicco called him. Nucor had cooled on doing a joint bid and was pulling out. DiMicco feared a deal on Dofasco would get too expensive and he did not want to go hostile. Again, unknown territory for steel.

Behind the scenes in Hamilton Don Pether was huddled with his management team and their long-standing banking advisers, Royal Bank of Canada. There was no doubt that Dollé was not going to go away. Dofasco would be put in play soon. It was time to bring in other interested parties. Pether called ThyssenKrupp and asked to be put through to Dr Ekkehard Schulz. He was praying for a German lifeline to save Dofasco from Guy Dollé.

In London, meanwhile, Lakshmi Mittal was becoming increasingly frustrated by the lack of progress in getting Arcelor's CEO to meet him. Then, on 23 November, he understood why Guy Dollé was being so elusive. Arcelor made its hostile offer of $C56 a share for Dofasco, valuing the company at $C4.3 billion.

Over afternoon tea at Mittal Steel's Berkeley Square offices, Aditya Mittal teased Alain Davezac. 'So you are bidding hostile for Dofasco. That's never been done before in our industry.'

A trademark half-smile broke on to the go-between's face. 'It's not hostile,' Davezac replied coolly, 'it is *unsolicited*.'

Five days later, ThyssenKrupp emerged as a white knight to save Dofasco from Arcelor. (In big takeover fights, 'white knights' merge with a target company in exchange for a large stake in a combined business, while a 'white squire' takes a smaller but significant position in a company to prevent its takeover by a hostile bidder, known as a 'black knight'.) ThyssenKrupp's friendly counter-bid was $C61.50 per share, or $C4.8 billion. Pether's board accepted it immediately.

The log fires were burning in Lakshmi Mittal's newly built €44 million villa at Chantarella, an upmarket clearing in the forest above St Moritz. Nearby was the exclusive Corviglia Ski Club, founded in 1930 by a largely aristocratic group that included several Rothschilds and Agnellis as well as the Duke of Alba. What better spot for one of the world's new economic nobility and his family – who had become members – to take their annual Christmas/New Year break? While Aditya skied downhill his father – seeking a tougher challenge than his son – *landlaufed* cross-country and went skating. The question of closer links with Arcelor continued to gnaw away at them both. There was still no date in the diary to meet Guy Dollé.

They pored over Julien Onillon's report on Arcelor. It was, he said, an extremely successful, technologically advanced steel-maker. There was no geographic overlap between its operations and Mittal Steel's. The two companies appeared to have plenty to share in terms of technology and market reach. But Onillon had identified that Arcelor also had two significant weaknesses. Its shares were very widely held, with the biggest shareholder, the government of Luxembourg, owning just 5.6 per cent of the company. And also, like Mittal Steel's, its shares were way undervalued at €22. 'I reckon its share price should be at least double,' Onillon reported. These were weaknesses that made Arcelor ripe for takeover.

Lakshmi Mittal was not interested in a takeover while there was still a chance of cooperation, even if he could get the company for half what it was really worth. 'I still think we should try and merge some of our operations,' he insisted to his son. 'We must try and keep it friendly.'

In Hamilton the Dofasco workers were unusually uneasy as they rolled up for the firm's all-day Christmas party on 18 December at Copps Coliseum, the sports and entertainment arena on Bay Street North and York Boulevard which is the home of the Hamilton

Bulldogs of the American Hockey League. On one of the ice rinks a seventy-foot fir tree twinkling with coloured lights greeted the thirty thousand employees, their families and retirees. In days gone by the company closed down one of the production lines in the plant in order to host what had gone on to become one of the biggest Christmas parties in the world. This year the gifts from Santa were bigger and better than ever. Scattered around the rinks were gift booths where children under sixteen scrambled for the goodies. For the grown-ups there were giant food hampers.

But this Christmas the workers could not hide their angst. Don Pether and his senior colleagues worked the crowds tirelessly, seeking to pacify the workforce and the town about the future of the company, about jobs and the profit share, which could hit 20 per cent of salary for the current year.

'Which company do you favour, Thyssen or Arcelor?' they asked Don Pether repeatedly.

'We think we can work well with either,' he said, hoping to mollify them. 'We know them well and have worked with both firms and we share the same culture.'

Then on 24 December Guy Dollé gave Don Pether a present the Canadian really did not want: a bid of $C63 for Dofasco shares.

Feeling bullish that he had seen off the Germans, Dollé now turned his attention to the Indians. He had responded at last to Lakshmi Mittal's invitation for a meeting.

'He's gone for 13 January,' Aditya told his father.

Lakshmi looked a little puzzled, then a familiar grin broke on his face. 'Adit, isn't the thirteenth a Friday?'

Guy Dollé was not a superstitious man. He was content that Project Tiger was on the verge of a very significant success in its campaign to fend off Mittal. He did not realise, therefore, that the tiger was highly auspicious for Lakshmi Mittal. The year of his birth, 1950, was the Chinese Year of the Tiger, a beast associated with good fortune and power. It was the star of the zodiac and its element was metal.

3

15 June 1950

Sadulpur, Rajasthan, India

Piped water and electricity were more than a decade away when Lakshmi Niwas Mittal, the eldest of five children, was born in this unremarkable town of eighty thousand people built on the shifting sands and among the thorn-trees of the Thar Desert in the Churu district of Rajasthan, north-west India, 155 miles and a world away from the pink palaces of Jaipur. With some prescience his parents Mohan Lal and Gita Devi named their son Lakshmi after the Hindu goddess of wealth, even though they had no regular income and lived in a modest house – built by his grandfather, a small-time broker from Karachi – where twenty extended-family members shared rooms, slept on rope beds and cooked in a brick oven in the yard. As soon as he could walk Lakshmi took his turn to help fetch water from the pump.

The Mittal family was of the Marwari caste – the name originating from the Sanskrit word for desert, *maru* – as were the majority of India's leading industrial families, such as the Birlas and the Jindals, who had moved from Rajasthan to Bengal to make their fortunes. When Lakshmi Mittal was six his family also moved, to Calcutta. 'Bengalis wanted only to enjoy the easy life,' Mohan Mittal said. 'Marwaris had come from Rajasthan and had nothing to eat.'

The Mittals rented a first-floor apartment at 2 Chitpur Road in a poor suburb in the north of Calcutta. As a small boy Lakshmi woke daily to the rattle of the city's trams. The electricity cable for the tramway was a few feet outside his window. The trams would start rolling at five in the morning. Not that he had enough money to take a tram – instead he walked to school, wading though knee-deep water during monsoon.

Lakshmi was a diligent and above-average student. He was also shy and introverted, but as a teenager he already had the desire to become somebody in life. On the reverse of his ruler he scratched in ink: 'Dr Niwas Mittal, BCom, MBA, PhD'. By now his father had become a working partner in the British India Rolling Mill, a small steel company in Calcutta, so after classes ended every morning Lakshmi would go and help his father in the business, working in the post room and running errands. The massive rollers driven by rubber belts and pulleys that flattened the red-hot steel into bars, rods and slabs inspired him. Traditionally and culturally, there was little doubt as to where his future lay. Marwaris, active in tea, textiles, manufacturing, mining and steel, believed that it was crucial that their companies be family-owned, with children, brothers, sons-in-law and daughters expected to help run operations, oversee factories or plot mergers and acquisitions. Holding a minority position in a company was anathema to most Marwari businesses. Mohan Lal's five brothers had also started a business trading in steel, and together in 1963 they won a licence to build a rolling mill in the southern state of Andhra Pradesh, the 'rice bowl of India'. It was his family's first manufacturing venture. They called the company Ispat, Sanskrit for steel. Lakshmi would visit during his vacations in May and June and stand in the mill, studying how it was run.

When he was sixteen he entered the prestigious St Xavier's College situated in an imposing white five-storey neo-colonial building on Park Street. At first the Jesuit college didn't want a Hindu boy, but relented when they saw his almost perfect marks in accounting and mathematics. Having attended a Hindi-language school, Lakshmi felt inferior in a college where most students were privileged, rich, spoke fluent English and were to be seen out and about at the city's fashionable locations. Lakshmi did not enter a restaurant until he was fifteen. His fellow students did not go and work in the family business, as he had to. Nor did they take extra evening classes in finance and marketing.

In 1969 Mittal graduated with the highest marks ever achieved by a St Xavier's student in accountancy and commercial mathematics and a Bachelor of Commerce degree in Business and Accounting. Hard work may have been the mantra of his success, but he still did not have the courage to book a trunk call to tell his distant father who was constantly out of town trying to build a fortune. Lakshmi sent him a telegram instead. Later Mohan Lal presented his son with a Sheaffer fountain pen by way of celebration.

Even though steel was in his veins, it was only a dislike of early-morning starts that prevented Lakshmi opting for a career in the classroom. When he went up to collect his degree St Xavier's principal said, 'Mittal, you start teaching accountancy from tomorrow.'

'OK, what time am I to come?'

'You have to begin with the first years at six in the morning.'

'Six o'clock? I will not do that again,' Mittal told him. 'I have done it enough in my three years as a student.'

So Mittal joined the family business full-time. By now Ispat was booming and Mohan Lal had moved his family to a mansion-like property in Alipore, one of Calcutta's most exclusive and expensive suburbs, located in the south of the city. With a sense of grandeur, he called the property Mittal House.

Three years later bespectacled Lakshmi, sporting a geeky fringe and a thick moustache, arrived at the Calcutta Club to take tea with three women. He was just twenty-one and about to meet his future wife. Usha Dalmia, an economics student from Benares, was sitting with her mother and her aunt. They talked to Lakshmi about her charms and questioned him about his intentions. As is traditional in an arranged marriage meeting, the potential bride and groom barely spoke to one another directly although Lakshmi was attracted to her open smile. Next, he met her father, who was in paper and engineering. Lakshmi was impressed, telling his own, 'He's a very smart guy. Even if Usha is only a fifth as intelligent as him I will marry her.'

He wrote a letter to her in Benares in which he said rather formally, 'I welcome you as my life partner.' Two weeks later the engagement was announced and Lakshmi and Usha spoke to one another for the first time by phone. She was impressed by his dedication to hard work. But beneath the rather serious exterior there was a surprise. He also made her laugh.

*

Although Lakshmi Mittal had been inspired by his father to 'accept challenges. Don't get scared by new prospects', Mohan Lal's other dictum, 'If my sons are not better than me, my business is finished', carried pressure. With an inspiring if dominating father and his two brothers, Vinod and Pramod, coming into the burgeoning business, Lakshmi hit his mid-twenties feeling hemmed in.

In 1975, aged twenty-five, he gazed out at the rice paddies in Surabaya, East Java, that his father had sent him to sell because his plans for building a steel mill there were beset with bureaucratic and government obstacles to gaining the necessary permits and electricity supply. Lakshmi had only planned to drop in while on a $250 bucket-shop holiday in South-east Asia, but instead he decided to adopt his father's creed while ignoring his instructions.

He went to the retail market to see the prices of bars (steel for making gears, tools and engineering products) and rods (used to reinforce concrete) and saw there was a good margin in the business. Here was also a chance to produce steel for the first time in Indonesia and strike a blow against the Japanese companies who used the country just for finishing products and were monopolising the local market. He would undercut them by building a mini-mill using an electric-arc furnace fed with enriched iron-ore pellets known as 'direct reduced iron' (DRI) rather than the bulky coking plants and blast furnaces, which were much more expensive to build and operate. A mini-mill would give him a cost advantage of up to 50 per cent. Then he called his father and told him, 'I am not going further on my vacation, I shall build this plant here.'

But he had no cash, and even if he had had, he would not have been allowed by the Indian government to take rupees abroad. But he discovered that India did have a scheme that would allow him to invest overseas. He could buy equipment and building materials in India, export them to Indonesia, and the Indian government would lend him up to 85 per cent of the cost of that equipment and building materials against the export. Mittal put together the deal: $2 million in Ispat shares, $1.75 million in cash from a local partner and a $3.7 million loan from the Bank of India in Singapore.

Mittal went back to the ministry and the power company he had been in contact with earlier. He got his permit and his power supply. He was in business.

At midnight on 21 November 1977 Usha was close beside him, clutching their baby son Aditya, as Lakshmi Mittal stood in the heat, breathing in the metal dust, blinking at the deep orange of a furnace burning at 1400 degrees centigrade. His expectation was stoked even higher by the muscular percussion of heavy metal rollers kicking in as the first wire rod came out of the rolling mill. With his brothers and his father also there, it was the happiest day of Mittal's life.

He might have been the first Indian to have started a steel mill abroad, but Lakshmi could only afford to pay himself $250 a month. He had bought a large second-hand silver Holden – an Australian car – which was not only family runabout but also works taxi as the mill was a two-kilometre walk from the nearest bus stop. To help him run the plant and train four hundred local staff Mittal had brought in twenty-four-year-old Bhikam Agarwal, whom he had met in Calcutta. Agarwal had been working as a bill-passing clerk in a mill processing jute used in the manufacture of sacking and rope. It did not take much persuading for him to join Mittal's adventure.

It was tough work. Mittal and Agarwal spent most of their time at the plant. Aditya's first memory was aged four going to sleep on the back seat of the Holden with his mother, while his father went inside to sort out another problem. For Usha life was just as challenging, having to bring up a child in a country and culture whose language she didn't speak, and without the support of a traditional extended Indian family. She too began spending more time at the plant. It was the only chance she had to get to know her husband. She also began to learn his business from the inside out.

In the first full year, 1978, Mittal made 26,000 tonnes of steel at Surabaya, generating a profit of $1 million on $10 million of sales even though the Indonesian currency devalued by 50 per cent, making imports of raw materials very expensive. The Japanese began to pull out. Mittal held his nerve and even started exporting small quantities to Japan. It took him eleven more years to get up to 330,000 tonnes. Now a father of two – his daughter Vanisha was born in 1981 – Lakshmi realised that if he could give birth to one successful steel mill, why not two? He also knew that at the age of thirty-nine he did not have enough years in front of him to build many more plants from scratch. '*Accept challenges. Don't get scared by new prospects.*' He decided there and then that instead of building new steel mills he would start buying up other people's.

Mittal was still vulnerable in raw materials. He was relying on one supplier in West Java for DRI and the scrap needed to feed his furnace. Now he turned to the Caribbean to find a supplier. The state-owned Iron & Steel Co. of Trinidad and Tobago (ISCOTT) was facing bankruptcy. It was co-managed by sixty Germans from the company Hamburger Stahlwerke, who cost $20 million a year. Its contract was due for renewal and the government in Port Louis decided to put it out to competitive tender. Mittal saw his chance to make his first acquisition. He told the politicians, 'Your company is losing $10 million a month. Give me the management and I will pay you $10 million every month.' He promised he could run the plant and ramp up profits by increasing production and slashing costs. He got his deal, but he added one condition. If he made it come true he would have the chance to buy the company in five years.

Cutting costs and continuity were already key in Mittal's mind. The Germans quit and were replaced with sixty Indian managers who cost $2 million. One of them was a calypso-loving young chartered accountant called Sudhir Maheshwari.

When Mittal took the lease at ISCOTT in 1989 the plant was producing 420,000 tonnes. In 1993 it was close to one million tonnes. Mittal bought the plant. ISCOTT became Ispat Caribbean.

The Mexican government had not been having much joy with its state-of-the-art plant at Lázaro Cárdenas, a port city in the southern part of the central western state of Michoacán, when Lakshmi Mittal came to call in 1991. It was designed to use DRI and electric-arc furnace technology to produce high-quality 'slab' that could not only be used in the construction industry and for gas and petrol pipes but was also suitable for sophisticated applications in the automobile and electrical appliance industries. Conventional wisdom in the steel industry said this could not be done – the high-quality and low-end markets were quite different. Mittal didn't believe them. He saw that the plant's real problem was that although it was designed to produce two million tonnes a year it was, thanks to the end of the oil boom causing a slump in steel prices, producing only 500,000 and losing $1 million a day. He returned to Indonesia and told Aditya: 'I

have just been to a graveyard.' The next year he bought the graveyard and made the plant a private company.

Mittal's first big-ticket acquisition had cost him just $200 million
and he had made one government very happy that it was free of a
millstone. Once again he slashed costs, retrained a young workforce
and ramped up their output. In the first month they produced 70,000
tonnes. Mittal congratulated them by setting a new monthly target –
200,000 tonnes. Of course it could be done, he told his chief operating officer Malay Mukherjee. Mukherjee was enjoying the
switchback ride with Mittal. It was completely the opposite of his
previous job as the youngest executive director of the largest government-owned steel plant in India. But he was not sure that this
plant could deliver so much so fast. The new target was not just a
number Mittal had plucked out of his head. 'Your down time is
30 per cent. It's too high,' Mukherjee said. 'If you trained more staff
and invested in spare parts the plant would not be idle.'

Mittal's big risk now was that he had too many eggs in too few
baskets. A vision began to take form in his mind. It was very simple.
State-run parochial steel companies had no place in the modern
world. Steel would have to go global just like the car manufacturers,
the shipbuilders and the iron and coal producers. It was game on,
and with a showman's flair for flying in the face of the improbable he
bought Sidbec-Dosco in Quebec in 1994. The next year he snapped
up Hamburger Stahlwerke, formed Ispat Shipping and bundled the
whole lot up into a new company called Ispat International.

But there had been a change in the Mittal family dynamic.
Lakshmi never spoke of it, but there had been ructions. Mohan Lal
and his other sons wanted to stay Indian-based. Mohan felt his
eldest son was moving too far and too fast. In previous acquisitions
Mohan had always come to merger and acquisition meetings as head
of the family company. When Lakshmi Mittal went to Canada to buy
Sidbec-Dosco he went alone.

Mittal was now moving at increasing speed. All these deals were
financed by Credit Suisse, where top analyst Jeremy Fletcher was
impressed and excited by Mittal, whom he regarded as a breath of
fresh air in an industry that in Europe had been scarred by years of
nationalisation and over-capacity and run by tired old executives
surviving on massive subsidies. In America the industry was now

rust belt, and anybody with any talent had left years before. As far as Fletcher was concerned Mittal had found a new model. He'd have no trouble getting future finance from Credit Suisse. Fletcher produced a major piece of research on how Mittal was turning steel upside down, which he entitled 'Arguably the Best Steel Company on the Planet'.

It was 1995 and Lakshmi Mittal had still not registered on the radar of steel's aristocracy. Then came Kazakhstan.

Landlocked Kazakhstan is the ninth-biggest country in the world, greater in size than Western Europe, bordered by Russia, Kyrgyzstan, Turkmenistan, Uzbekistan and China. It was the last of the Soviet republics to declare independence in December 1991, under its reformist leader Nursultan Nazarbayev. Although rich in natural resources – with the second-largest reserves of uranium, chromium and lead in the world plus ample supplies of natural gas, petrol, coal, gold and diamonds – its economy was completely ruptured following the dismantling of the Soviet Union's centrally planned economy. Gross national income per capita was just $2930 – almost $30,000 less than that other steel-making nation, the United States – and life expectancy for men was fifty-eight years. Kazakhstan was up for grabs, a free-for-all, a modern-day Klondike.

And nowhere more so than at the massive Karmet Steel works in Temirtau, covering more than twelve hundred acres on the banks of the Nura River in the mineral-rich Karaganda region in the north of the country. Traders would turn up daily on donkeys with panniers stuffed with bundles of plummeting local currency, the *tenge*, to buy steel. Others placed more faith in barter, enquiring at the gates how many black-market TV sets it would take to buy a tonne of steel.

Enter Lakshmi Mittal. Where his competitors saw a basket-case economy, he had spotted an opportunity. China was booming. It needed steel to build the high-rises, highways and airports of a glistening new world economic order. What better place to make it, he reasoned, than in neighbouring Kazakhstan? And in hulking, sprawling, smoking Temirtau, built originally by Soviet prisoners of war, he saw just the place. It was one of the world's biggest single-site integrated steel plants, with its own captive coal (1.5 billion tonnes) and iron ore (1.7 billion tonnes) and a 435-megawatt thermal power station to fire its three massive blast furnaces, coke ovens, slabbing mill, hot- and cold-rolling mills and coating lines for electrolytic tin-plating and hot-dip galvanising. The mini-mill maestro could join the big blast-furnace boys.

Interestingly it was in Temirtau that President Nazarbayev had begun his career as a metallurgist before rising through the political ranks. Given the economic climate, he decided to privatise.

Mittal went to the banks. None of them had offices in Kazakh-stan, or knew anything of the country. They refused to back him through Ispat. So Mittal financed a deal via the LNM Group, a private company he had set up with tangible family capital and which therefore enjoyed greater confidence from lending banks. He won the prize at a knock-down $400 million. Not only did he get a bargain, he also wrung huge concessions including a moratorium on the payment of taxes and an agreement that no new environmental laws would apply to the plant for ten years from the date of privatisation.

Mittal described the President as a visionary for his decision, and got down to work. The 250,000 inhabitants of the town relied on the plant for their livelihood, and the workers had not been paid for six months. He promised to pay them their arrears, some $9 million. But none of the workers had bank accounts. Salaries were not even paid in cash but in coupons issued by the plant in lieu of real money. Mittal started to convert hard currency into local, but within days he had a call from the Central Bank. If he put that much hard currency into the local banking system all at once and then withdrew it in *tenge*, it would stoke such inflation that the economy would collapse beyond repair. Mittal was in a bind. He had a promise to keep. He opted to drip the money in at a rate the system could accept, and every fifteen days he chartered a plane which flew from the then capital Almaty, six hundred miles to the south, loaded with suitcases of cash.

Mittal brought in Indian management, many of whom had been educated in the former Soviet Union – India's ally when America had been arming up Pakistan in the seventies and eighties. They could speak Russian and knew the mentality of the people they were dealing with. Mittal wasn't finished yet. Next, he bought the local tram and railway services, which were threatened with closure; the power plant that heated the mill and the city, where temperatures sank to –40 degrees centigrade in winter; the TV station and the local coal and iron ore mines, ensuring jobs for twenty-seven thousand miners. 'There's something quite compelling about buying an entire city,' he told a journalist. He was also wise to the millions that the European Bank for Reconstruction and Development had in its coffers to fund the improvement of steel plants.

Within a year Temirtau was profitable. Steel production had doubled to 250,000 tonnes a month. Many in Kazakhstan revered Mittal as a saviour, second only in popularity to the President. When he visited, policemen stood to attention. The ten thousand miners and steel workers that would be laid off were not so sure.

It was also in 1995 that Mittal, against the wishes of his father and brothers, separated his own steel interests from the family's Indian businesses, and went his own way with two tandem companies. These were Ispat International, registered in the Netherlands, into which he put more reliable companies like those he possessed in Trinidad, Mexico and Canada; and his private company, LNM Holdings, which included riskier ventures such as the one in Kazakhstan and his original Indonesian operation, now being run by Usha as he spent more and more time buying up plant. The decision to split was the hardest of his life. And the family bonding was so strong that it took him a year to complete. It was a separation with many tears on both sides. Usha, having been a mother figure to Lakshmi's younger brothers Vinod and Pramod, was distraught. The two halves of the extended Mittal clan would not speak to each other for another two years.

Lakshmi Mittal gathered ever more speed. He shifted his family from Indonesia to London, no doubt lured by the huge tax breaks offered to foreign billionaires based here – who like Mittal could claim 'non-domicile status', which meant that they paid no tax on their overseas earnings – and its ideal geographical positioning between Asia and the United States. Usha bought a house for them called the Summer Palace on The Bishops Avenue, the gilded ghetto of Saudi princes and Russian oligarchs that runs northwards from Hampstead Heath.

By 1995 Mittal was producing 11.2 million tonnes of steel a year. In a conference speech in Hamburg in August of that year, he said his goal was to produce 20 million tonnes, this at a time when the world's biggest manufacturer, Nippon Steel, was making 27 million. The upstart was laughed at. The industry felt no need to go global. Executive imaginations could not make the leap. They never thought that steel could be transported to customers around the globe. They did not see the advantages of scale. Even some loyalists thought it was all a bit too breakneck. After Kazakhstan Malay Mukherjee said to Mittal: 'LN, shouldn't we pause for a year and take stock?' The answer was the same as it always was: 'No, we must grow, we must move on.'

In 1997 Credit Suisse and Jeremy Fletcher helped launch Ispat International's initial public offer (IPO) of 20 per cent of its shares to the public on the New York and Amsterdam stock exchanges. The IPO, valued at nearly $780 million, was the largest ever in the steel industry. Mittal retained the other 80 per cent through LNM Holdings. By then Mittal, who had boosted company revenues to nearly $2.5 billion, with profits of some $140 million, had so impressed the industry that the IPO was eight times oversubscribed, and its shares opened at $28.50. That year the *Sunday Times* Rich List reckoned that Mittal was one of Britain's richest tycoons, worth around £2.2 billion.

In 1998 Mittal stood before the industry elders at an international conference in New York and spelt out his vision of consolidation and globalisation so as to flatten out the ruinous cycles of boom and bust. Fewer, bigger players would also have bigger clout, just as they did in the automotive and mining industries. 'This industry is made up of too many small regional players. It is still too highly nationalised,' he said. 'For the long-term health of the industry it has to change.'

He was greeted by silence. The majority argued that steel must remain an industry of smaller, regionally focused players. A year later, following another massive slump in prices, a third of all steel companies in America filed for bankruptcy.

Mittal's buying spree continued. He decided he needed a footprint in the Americas and flew to Venezuela to try and buy the Sidor steelworks from the Venezuelan government. But his acquisition strategy had started to catch on within the industry. Previously, Ispat had been able to make unrivalled bids for its acquisitions. In the second half of the 1990s, however, as more and more governments began looking to sell off their often money-losing steel operations, others began to see the opportunity for relatively low-cost entry into the industry. Mittal was on the verge of winning Sidor for $2.045 billion when suddenly a consortium of local investors came in with $2.4 billion. To Mittal's mind there was more than a hint of second-guessing about the winning bid. Deeply frustrated, he didn't even stay to the end of the auction. As he headed for his private plane he was already thinking of other irons he had in the acquisition fire. From Carácas airport he rang a man called Bob Darnell, who ran Inland Steel, based in Chicago, one of the world's largest single operations, and said, 'Do you want to do a deal?' He named a price. After months of listening to Mittal's persuasive tongue, Darnell was ready to talk.

Mittal ordered his pilot to fly him to the States and put his negotiating team on a commercial flight back to London. He bought Inland for $1.43 billion. Never mind a bunch of Venezuelans, he had his American footprint and was now in charge of a steel empire with an annual production of some 19 million tonnes. But when he called his bankers at Credit Suisse to do the financing, they were not impressed. 'You've paid too much,' they told him. 'Steel's heading for recession. Get it cheaper.'

Most Western businessmen would have gone back to the acquired company and renegotiated the price in the light of a gathering downturn, blaming the bankers for not financing the deal. But Mittal saw a good company with scope for huge per tonne cost savings. He was not in the mood for caution. He had also shaken Darnell's hand. In his eyes that could not be renegotiated. 'That is the deal I have struck, execute it,' he told Credit Suisse. 'If you don't want to do it I will get another bank that will.'

When he got back to his office the failed Venezuelan bid was still bothering him. He ordered a security sweep. Sure enough, his phones were bugged. Steel was turning dirty. The industry that had not wanted to know him and had dismissed him as a crazy maverick now seemed very keen to know his every move.

But he had bigger problems to face. Just as his bankers had told him, he had bought Inland Steel at exactly the wrong point of the cycle and loaded Ispat with too much debt. Steel had slumped. The global price of slabs had fallen around 40 per cent. Unable to finance any more acquisitions, Ispat International's stock quickly slipped. It hovered around $9, then as the industry recession became worse it tumbled to a low of $1.90. Mittal was on the edge, in charge of a 'penny stock' company, with the shareholders that remained feeling that he had messed with their trust and with their cash. The mutual funds that owned him had never before owned something so small. His competitors sat back to enjoy a meltdown more dramatic than Icarus.

Still in his early twenties, Aditya Mittal had an almost telepathic understanding with his father. The pair were so close that when Aditya left home to attend the prestigious Wharton School of Business at the University of Pennsylvania – established by Joseph Wharton, the co-founder of Bethlehem Steel, based in that state – Lakshmi was so upset he couldn't go to the airport to see him off. Three years later, having graduated with flying colours, Aditya then cut his teeth working as an analyst at Credit Suisse. It was not a happy experience and lasted only six months. Some regard analysts – who work a hundred hours a week assessing the performance of industry and the markets and its players and predict future trends – as the lowest form of life. Being the good-looking, well mannered and extremely well connected son of a very wealthy man made life even worse for Aditya. He was given all the menial assignments that nobody else wanted. Instead of reacting adversely, he got his head down and worked harder than anybody else, learning everything he could about the financial markets and how bankers' minds worked. Lakshmi spotted in his son a natural deal-maker and brought Aditya back into the family business for the Ispat initial public offering. Groomed in steel by his father, Aditya was now in charge of mergers and acquisitions (M&A).

As the recession in steel wore on through 2000, 2001 and 2002 most companies kept their powder dry on the acquisition front. The Mittals bucked the trend. Lakshmi had the vision: he saw that thanks to the recession the cost of plant was at an all-time low. It was time to carry on acquiring. Aditya, using the profits now being generated by Kazakhstan through LNM, put the deals together. Sharp as flint, they bought mills in Algeria, Poland, Romania, Macedonia and the Czech Republic, in South Africa and France, adding hundreds of millions of dollars in sales. Not everyone in the steel business liked the Mittals' aggressive acquisition policy. When Aditya, who still looked about seventeen, was doing a deal with Guy Dollé's old French company Usinor, a counterpart studied his business card and quipped sarcastically, 'But it says you are head of M&A – surely it should just be A.'

Negotiations in the cash-strapped former Soviet bloc were never easy. Sudhir Maheshwari alone made sixty trips to Romania before Mittal finally won the nationalised steel firm Sidex. The pattern was always the same. 'The Indians', as they were referred to by local apparatchiks on the make, would be kept waiting for hours – days even – in bare rooms, waiting to do a deal with senior management who hoped that if they kept them waiting long enough their visitors would go away. They never did. Speed, surprise and variety were Mittal watchwords. There was another: patience. Mittal took on each company's debt and refinanced it through his banks, Credit Suisse and HSBC (which he had come to work with regularly and closely), which meant that in most cases he had bought the plant for a song. In came the Indian management and up went the productivity.

Along with the acquisitions came the flak. In 2001 Lakshmi gave the Labour Party £125,000, a donation which coincided with a letter Tony Blair wrote to the Prime Minister of Romania supporting Mittal's takeover of Sidex. Mittal insisted that Blair had written the letter at the request of the British ambassador in Romania, 'after we had already been informed that our offer had been accepted. I gave to Labour because of my love of the party and its leader. I never asked for anything, never expected anything in return.' Blair dismissed accusations that he had undermined British companies like Corus by supporting a non-British competitor like Mittal as 'Garbagegate'. The storm blew over and Mittal was clearly irritated, but it did not stop him gifting the party £2 million more in July 2005 and kicking off another controversy. Armed with a $100 million loan from the European Bank for Reconstruction and Development, Mittal started cutting jobs at Sidex and began to turn the plant around.

In Kazakhstan and in Poland Mittal used lobbyists and middlemen to broker takeovers who later became the subject of scrutiny by the media and investigators. The BBC's *The Money Programme* alleged that a man called Patokh Chodiev, the subject of corruption investigations in Belgium, was paid $100 million by Mittal to make contact with and lobby President Nazarbayev on the Temirtau deal. Key members of the Chodiev group, said the programme, were alleged to have links with organised crime in the former Soviet Union but nothing has ever been proved. In May 2007 the *Financial Times* reported that 'Chodiev and his two associates might have to step down from ENRC's board in order to acquire a listing, due to money-laundering charges against the three, currently outstanding in Belgium'. The trio have denied the charges.

Then there was polo-playing Marek Dochnal, one of Poland's premier lobbyists. He worked for Mittal on securing the deal to buy a 69 per cent holding in the Polish steel manufacturers Polskie Huty Stali in March 2004, with an option to acquire an additional 25 per cent. Dochnal was then arrested over allegations of bribery and corruption on non-Mittal privatisation deals and is in jail awaiting trial. Once more Mittal defended himself. 'You need people to guide you, advise you, make contacts in these countries. None of the major investment banks know anything about Kazakhstan and could not advise. They don't even know where it is on a map. I had to use local people, just like anybody else trying to do business there.'

Then there was the issue of the safety record in his mines in Kazakhstan, where in December 2004 twenty-three miners died in explosions caused by faulty gas detectors. Mittal rushed to be with the bereaved. Standing alongside President Nazarbayev, he expressed his concern and agreed to pay speedy compensation and to spend millions on upgrading safety equipment.

In Ireland, Mittal's Midas touch finally deserted him. In 2001 he pulled out of the former Irish Steel Haulbowline plant in Cork, which he had bought five years before for £IR1, at a few hours' notice, leaving behind debts of over €57 million and four hundred people jobless. It was the first company he had ever shut down. Although workers received most of the millions owed to them in wages, holiday pay and other entitlements via the state redundancy scheme, the unions criticised Mittal for his instant exit. 'We agreed to run it for five years, we did run it for five years and fulfilled all our

commitments in terms of investment, in terms of jobs and in terms
of social commitment,' Mittal responded. 'After five years and
investing £IR35 million my advisers tell me that they can see no way
to make it profitable. So, we did not do it very quickly.'

While critics had questioned some of his methods, none of their
mud had stuck to Lakshmi Mittal. Always smiling, he just went on
making money. The Nova Hut mill in the Czech Republic, for
which he had paid $10 million in 2003, was well on the way to being
worth $2 billion. Kazakhstan was the engine room of the expanding
Mittal empire – spanning four continents and with steelworks in
fourteen countries – satisfying the insatiable demand for steel from
China. Its output had gone through the roof, from 150,000 tonnes to
well-nigh more than four million. In April 2005 the *Sunday Times*
Rich List put Lakshmi Mittal's personal wealth at £15 billion,
making him the richest man in Britain and pushing Roman
Abramovich into second place.

Throughout these turbulent early years of the new century Mittal
was served well by a close-knit team of long-standing loyalists. But
one person was always at his side. Aditya, his protégé and son, was
now his father's business partner too.

In 2001 Lakshmi Mittal's family was brought together by tragedy,
the fatal illness of his mother. His parents and brothers had moved to
London in 1998, and now they met in the hospital at Gita Devi's
bedside as chronic heart disease drove her into a coma. In the corridors outside it was Usha – who, after the rift that had developed
between the two sides of the family back in 1995, was missing her
brothers-in-law, just as Aditya and his sister Vanisha longed to see
their cousins again – who began the bridge-building. Then, after his
mother's death, Lakshmi chartered an aircraft for the reunited family
to take her body back to India for cremation.

Lakshmi Mittal was as proud of his twenty-three-year-old daughter
Vanisha as he was of his son. Having gained a BA in Business
Administration from the European Business School, Vanisha now
had a seat on the board after corporate internships at his shipping
line, a steel mill in Germany and an Internet-based venture capital
fund.

In June 2004 Mittal famously splashed a reported £34 million on her wedding in France to Amit Bhatia, a Delhi-born investment banker. A thousand guests, put up at Mittal's expense at the Grand Hôtel Intercontinental in Paris, flew in for five days of events including an engagement party at Versailles, Usha Mittal's favourite place, and a wedding ceremony at Vaux-le-Vicomte, reckoned to be the finest chateau in France. Mittal, resplendent like all the men present in a flowing pink Rajasthani turban, banned the press, but that did not stop the breathless reporting. According to Indian website WeddingSutra.com, 'three top Indian designers were roped in to do the trousseau'. The twenty-page hand-painted invitation – some said it was only fourteen – was 'commissioned by Mittal from the well known watercolour artist Florine Asch . . . [and had] pictures of the happy couple entwined in elliptical frames'. It also included romantic poems by Shelley and a set of verses by Aditya's wife Megha.

For the newly-weds and their guests, there was an hour-long drama with song and dance staged under canvas. With music specially written by Bollywood composer and singing star Shankar Mahadevan and choreography and script by Indian film director Farah Khan, it told the story of how Amit and Vanisha had met and fallen in love. The production featured professional Bollywood dancers, but starred some unusual actors. Aditya played Amit and Megha took the role of Vanisha. The roles of Mr and Mrs Mittal were played by Lakshmi and Usha, 'who had rehearsed in London for three weeks'. Tents were made by Rajasthani craftsmen and the dinner, served in the Jardin des Tuileries, was cooked by chefs flown in from Calcutta. There was a disco at the Lido de Paris, opera at the Versailles Opera House and, to top it all off, Lakshmi Mittal's favourite Bollywood stars and Kylie Minogue serenaded them.

'Papa, Buy Me an Eiffel,' headlined the Indian magazine *Outlook*. Contrasting the wedding expenditure with the financial situation of the redundant steelworkers of Cork, the London *Evening Standard* headlined its story of the wedding 'Obscene!' 'I do not comment on family matters,' Mittal insisted. 'All the figures are speculation. Any father wants to give his daughter a very special day.' On the palm of his right hand Vanisha had written in henna in English and in Hindi: 'Papa, I love you.'

*

That summer, Lakshmi and his family were holidaying in Los Angeles and Las Vegas. As he relaxed, he mused on the fact that he still had several pieces missing from his global jigsaw. One of them was a bigger presence in North America than just owning Inland Steel in Chicago.

At the end of the vacation, he and Aditya flew to New York and to a meeting with a diminutive sixty-six-year-old billionaire in his office at 600 Lexington Avenue. Wilbur Ross Jr, the Manhattan-based connoisseur of left-for-dead companies, had plunged $450 million into America's failed industrial heartland to emerge triumphant and with a place on the Forbes 400, the US Rich List, and a fortune of $3 billion. In a series of bold financial gambles Ross, who for twenty-six years was executive managing director of Rothschild, had used his private investment and hedge funds, worth more than £2 billion, to take over mothballed Southern textile mills and bankrupted Appalachian coal mines and turned them to profit. Because these had filed for Chapter 11 bankruptcy* Ross could take over assets on the cheap and the collapsed companies could walk away from their burdens of debt, pension obligations and healthcare packages. Freed of such obligations, fallen companies suddenly looked prime candidates for a renaissance on the cheap.

Some called Ross a vulture capitalist. He preferred the term 'industrial saviour'. But the tag that stuck was 'the bottom-feeder king' as he out-muscled even the likes of heavyweight American investor and philanthropist Warren Buffett, the third-richest man in the world, in the acquisition stakes. In 2002 Ross began picking up rust-bucket steel companies, including the icon of American steel-making, the Bethlehem Steel Corporation, to form the International Steel Group. ISG was now one of the biggest steel-makers in the

---

* Chapter 11 bankruptcy is the usual choice for large American businesses seeking to restructure their debt, reorganise and make a fresh start. This is done under the supervision of the federal bankruptcy court, acting on behalf of the creditors and which can grant complete or partial relief from most of the company's debts and its contracts. Often, if the company's debts exceed its assets, then at the completion of bankruptcy the company's owners (stockholders) all end up with nothing; all their rights and interests are terminated and the company's creditors end up with ownership of the newly reorganised company.

USA. But like world series baseball, which is not 'world' at all, ISG was international in name only. Ross looked to go global and join the consolidation game, but every target he identified had already been snapped up by the even more rapacious Lakshmi Mittal.

Ross decided he must take a closer look at this phenomenon. For his part, Mittal knew that if he could acquire ISG it would give him a massive footprint in North America. Their meeting had been scheduled to last half an hour. Two hours later, the Mittals and Wilbur Ross were still chatting away about steel and the need for globalisation. On the surface Lakshmi, tall, quiet and calculating, and Wilbur, small, balding, bespectacled and never afraid to lace his opinions with a volley of quotable adjectives, seemed to have little in common. But both men were outsiders. Both had come up the hard way, buying the kind of assets others laughed at and turning them into cash cows. Both were adept at outmanoeuvring the opposition and admired each other's lack of pretence. Both were pragmatic, unsentimental realists. Ross was also impressed by the calibre and intelligence of Aditya. Here was the kind of man he'd like to hand his company over to.

'Why don't you come and work for me?' Wilbur said.

'I don't think you can afford him,' Lakshmi teased.

As Wilbur said, 'it was an immediate love affair'. The two men agreed in principle that ISG should merge with Ispat International. Love or not, Wilbur was already due at the altar on 23 October 2002 to marry his third wife, the twice-married platinum blonde Hilary Geary, fifteen years his junior and a popular fixture on the social sets of New York, Southampton NY and Palm Beach, where the about-to-be-weds planned to buy a house. As one newspaper put it: 'Anyone wishing to know Hilary Geary's take on life need only gaze at the inscription on a needlepoint pillow in the living room of her home in Southampton, New York. It reads: "Eat, Drink and Remarry".'

Mittal and Ross continued to forge their deal by conference call. Two days before Ross's wedding the two men met again in a New York hotel. They were just $50 million apart on agreeing a value for ISG. Suddenly Ross pulled a coin from his pocket and said, 'Lakshmi, we're so close – let's toss for it.' Although he had a fifty-fifty chance of winning, this was a gesture worthy of legendary steelman John

Warne Gates, who in a horse race in England in 1900 scooped $600,000 on a $70,000 bet – which rumours increased to over $1 million, earning him the nickname 'Bet-a-Million' Gates.

Unlike Gates and Ross, Mittal was not a gambling man. When it came to deals he had the mentality of the market trader. 'Wilbur,' he said, 'everybody knows that the head is heavier than the tail.' They continued haggling.

'Are you going to invite us to your wedding reception?' Mittal asked Ross. Two days after their wedding, on Monday 25 October, the new Mr and Mrs Ross would be entertaining two hundred guests at a dinner dance at the Rainbow Room high above the Rockefeller Center, where they were to be serenaded by the sequinned Valerie Romanoff and her Starlight Orchestra. But Mittal wasn't going to get on the ticket. 'Until all the details are finalised I want to keep this confidential,' Ross said. 'If you were there, the wrong people would start to talk.'

Instead, the third Mr and Mrs Ross delayed their honeymoon and invited the Mittals to dine with them the following day at Le Cirque, the famed restaurant on Madison Avenue, where after more than three decades patron Sirio Maccioni still reigned supreme, pre-siding over his soufflés and stroking egos. Ross and Mittal raised their glasses to a deal that was now done. ISG was sold to Lakshmi Mittal for $4.5 billion. Ross cashed out with $267 million in stock profits from his shareholding, taking half in cash and half in Mittal stock. He had also made his ISG shareholders $545 million richer since the stock market had closed the previous Friday.

Lakshmi Mittal had not only bought himself a front-row seat at the North American steel game. In appointing Wilbur Ross Jr to his board he had acquired a loyal friend and a tenacious ally.

Mittal now put Ispat, LNM and ISG into one big company: Mittal Steel. The rest of the steel world now had no choice but to take notice. In just twenty years Mittal had amassed a $27.7 billion fortune. Only Microsoft's Bill Gates, Warren Buffett and IKEA's Ingvar Kamprad were richer. Mittal Steel now employed 179,000 people worldwide and supplied 30 per cent of all the steel used by Ameri-can car companies. *Fortune* magazine named him 'Businessman of the Year in Europe' for his ability to 'combine managerial savvy with superb acquisitive instincts'.

From paperclips to suspension bridge cables, shipbuilding to car bodies, hi-fi chassis, oil and gas pipes, muscular girders and high-spec galvanised goods, Mittal's steel was everywhere. Tenacious and tough, the boy from Sadulpur had cajoled, sweet-talked and outwitted legions of steel executives from every corner of the planet. But unlike most of them Mittal knew his business from the inside out. Unlike other steel magnates he could actually work the control panel of a blast furnace or a rolling mill. The shy young man with the big moustache and the fringe had become a clean-shaven global citizen as at home on the shop floor and in the canteen – 'the only place to really feel the pulse of a company' – as he was in boardrooms and bankers' dining rooms. Yes, he had the houses, the yachts and all the trappings of wealth, but the only asset that really mattered to him was his 60 million tonnes. He was by 10 million tonnes the biggest steel-maker in the world.

Lakshmi Niwas Mittal received a terse congratulatory email. It was from the man he had just deposed – Guy Dollé, chief executive of Luxembourg-based Arcelor.

4

Friday 13 January 2006, 6 p.m.

18–19 Kensington Palace Gardens, London

'His house is so big you need to catch a bus to visit the bathroom,' Guy Dollé smirked. Alain Davezac gazed across and saw that the humour was gallows. Dollé had not wanted this meeting. Not now. His mind was miles away in Hamilton and the battle with ThyssenKrupp. Ten days before, the battle for Dofasco had reached stalemate when ThyssenKrupp had matched Arcelor's 24 December bid of $C63 a share, pushing the value of the company up to just under $C5 billion. Now things looked even worse for Dollé. The Dofasco board was unanimously recommending that its shareholders accept the revised German offer and tender their shares to Thyssen before the expiry date of 24 January. 'The ThyssenKrupp offer is less conditional than the Arcelor offer, while offering the same cash to shareholders,' they said. Neither Don Pether of Dofasco nor Guy Dollé would be drawn on what the Arcelor conditions were.

Dollé had just eleven days before the expiry date to intervene again and swing Dofasco his way. He would have to persuade Joseph Kinsch and the Arcelor board to raise their offer, and he wasn't going to do it from the back of a car as it swept through the elegant gates of Lakshmi Mittal's gleaming white three-storey neo-Palladian home.

In Guy Dollé, Arcelor had inherited from the founder company Usinor a brilliant but irascible engineer. He had been born in Compiègne, eighty kilometres north of Paris, the eldest of four children. When he was four just after the end of the Second World War his family moved to Metz in eastern France, where his father, who made stained glass, was kept busy restoring bombed cathedrals and churches. Metz is the capital of the Lorraine region, the heart of the French steel industry. The young Dollé became a boy scout and grew up in the cloth-cap environment of an industry that he would one day join. He excelled at maths and science, but life was tough. When his mother died, Dollé was ten, and he found it hard to study. But local people encouraged him and in 1963 he was one of two hundred out of three thousand applicants to win a place at the elitist École Polytechnique in Paris, a special military school, a two-hundred-year-old Napoleonic institution that had bred the occasional general. After three years Dollé left for the city of Trier, across the border in Germany on the banks of the Moselle River, where he continued to study mathematics and physics, emerging as a trained engineer.

He married Michele, a schoolteacher from Metz, in 1966, but he had yet to find a job. The steel industry beckoned. Dollé joined the French Steel Institute, located near Metz. Ten steel companies in France financed the institute, and for thirteen years he steeped himself in computer applications for controlling the steel process, working on pioneering mainframes ten metres long and a thousand times less powerful than a BlackBerry.

In 1979 Dollé was recruited by Usinor, one of the flagship French steel companies, where he rose through the ranks to become a senior vice president. He worked tirelessly to drive the integration of Usinor with Luxembourg's Arbed, which had already subsumed Aceralia of Spain, and was rewarded with the job of chief executive of the combined group, newly named Arcelor to reflect the Luxembourger, French and Spanish parentage. He worked even harder at the integration of the three companies, maintaining high standards of production and research and development, in which he always excelled.

Balding and with a clipped military moustache, Guy Dollé was a quick-thinking and highly respected steel veteran. Wherever he went he carried with him a magnetic pencil which when placed against any item of steel could tell him its carbon content and even where it was manufactured. He was inclined to be stubborn and at times could become emotionally volatile. Privately, he lived modestly, one of the lowest-paid chief executives of the CAC 40, France's index of top companies. Unlike his counterparts, he read the sports daily *L'Équipe* avidly before turning to the *Financial Times*, the French financial daily *Les Échos* and then *Le Monde*. He had also come to love opera. His favourite was Mozart's *The Magic Flute*, in which the hero Tamino is given the flute to stave off the hate and anger in his heart and told to remain fearless, patient and silent while he rescues his loved one Pamina from the traitorous Monostatos.

Dollé and Davezac pulled up outside Lakshmi Mittal's large front door, where the two men were greeted and welcomed discreetly inside by a servant. Dollé had visited Mittal's home once before and felt uncomfortable in its overt splendour, just as he did when forced to attend functions in the plush drawing rooms of Paris, where he was happier renting a modest flat.

Numbers 18 and 19 Kensington Palace Gardens had once housed the Russian and Egyptian embassies. It was David Khalili, the Iranian-born Jewish property developer and renowned Islamic art collector, who turned the two dilapidated buildings into one of the most remarkable houses in London. The fifty-five thousand square feet of floor space included twelve bedrooms, a ballroom, a picture gallery, parking for twenty cars, Turkish baths and a jewelled swimming pool in the basement. Ranked four places behind Mittal on the *Sunday Times* Rich List at £4.5 billion, Khalili imported marble from the same quarries as used for the Taj Mahal and swathed the palm-tree pillars in gold leaf. In 1998 Mittal tried to buy it, but Khalili wanted too much money. In 2001 he sold it to diminutive Formula One supremo Bernie Ecclestone for £45 million. Mittal bought it from him for £57 million in 2005, London's costliest house.

Of all the houses the Mittals had bought this was the only one that Lakshmi had chosen. Usha had not been keen to move from the Summer Palace, where she felt happy and settled. Then the children started to lobby. 'Mummy, you always have your say in houses,' they said. 'If Papa likes it, just say yes.'

Mittal chose to move because this house with its mixture of large formal rooms for greeting and entertaining and private family quarters was ideal for a man whose two great loves, his only loves, were his work and his family. In a garden room a sculpture of six arms with upturned palms cradled a steel globe. The piece was commissioned by Mittal. A close look revealed its true symbolism. Each arm and hand was different. One was moulded from Lakshmi. Another was Usha's. The four remaining arms were those of Aditya and his wife Megha, and Vanisha and her husband Amit.

As Davezac complimented him on his ormolu furniture, fine porcelain and Impressionist paintings – the kind of artefacts that most people only see cordoned off by silk ropes and security beams – Mittal explained: 'I chose the house but Usha furnished it. Everything you see in this house has a history, so it would take me years to understand the history of everything she has done.'

Guy Dollé glanced up at one of the massive chandeliers twinkling like a constellation, and blinked. He was not in the mood for interior design.

Lakshmi and Aditya invited their guests to sit. Drinks were ordered. The four men sat facing one another on large formal sofas by the fireplace, nursing their champagne. They kicked off with steel industry small-talk, second-guessing the market, iron ore supply, personalities on the move, politicians on the make or the meddle, and how the consolidation of the industry was going to pan out. When it came to the facts and figures of their business Davezac found that he was increasingly captivated by Aditya Mittal's grasp of a complex and globally fragmented industry. For somebody so relatively inexperienced he seemed to know deals inside out.

Guy Dollé had no time for Aditya. As far as he was concerned he had just been born rich and lucky. But, even if they were poles apart as people and he did not trust his charm, he admired Lakshmi as a steelman. Aditya had not worked his way up as he and his father had. What Davezac took for brilliance Dollé regarded as an irritating brashness. Sometimes, like right now, he found it hard to be in the same room as him. He could not even call Aditya by his name, always referring to him as 'the son'.

Then suddenly Lakshmi said to Dollé: 'If you bid $C5.6 billion for Dofasco you will get it.' As always, Mittal's avuncular smile came into play, along with the colder gimlet brown eyes, which always seemed to be on an intelligence-gathering mission.

'Excuse me?' Dollé bristled. He was not in the market for acquisition advice from Mittal.

'You must bid higher than Thyssen,' Mittal smiled again.

Dollé tried to steer the conversation back to the business of the next meeting of the International Iron and Steel Institute (IISI), which he chaired, scheduled for Paris early in February.

Mittal's eyes were focusing on a much bigger agenda. 'Guy,' he said.

Dollé stopped short.

'I have something very important to tell you. Our two companies are both undervalued in the market. We share the same consolidation goals. We should discuss how we could work more closely together. Let's discuss on a friendly basis.'

'The cultures of our two companies are entirely different,' Dollé said, barely able to hide his disdain.

Mittal shrugged and smiled patiently. 'There is only one thing we can do for the benefit of both companies and the steel industry, and that is to merge. Where we are strong you are weak, and you have great strengths that we don't have. If we joined forces we could be a great steel champion.'

Davezac looked at Dollé and grew concerned. The normally assured Frenchman had slumped into the sofa. This was the man who had told Wilbur Ross after the combative billionaire had given a keynote conference speech in Paris on the consolidation of the steel industry: 'That wasn't bad for somebody who knows so little about the industry.' He was determined to cap his distinguished career by regaining his crown from Mittal as the King of Steel. He was not going to be relegated to a footnote.

'Seventy-five per cent of such mergers fail because the cultures of the two companies don't mix,' Dollé said. 'There is too much friction. Three-way mergers work much better,' he insisted, going off into a long account of how Usinor, Arbed and Aceralia had come together to form Arcelor and what a strong and competitive company it had become, focusing on the high end of the market. 'Arcelor has been a success story for the simple reason that we have developed a new model, balanced between profit, employee relations, customers . . .'

Mittal pressed him again.

As Dollé played for time and tried to recover his composure, his English began to get ragged. Davezac stepped in to translate for him. 'Our companies are not compatible,' Dollé continued. 'Arcelor specialises in high-end steel for the automobile and packaging industries, while you focus on emerging-market volume steel for the construction industry.'

So why are you bidding for the same emerging-market volume steel companies in places like Ukraine? Mittal thought. But he didn't pursue it.

'Lakshmi, you are the owner of your company. I am just an employee. I cannot take such decisions. I have to talk to my board, and to others. And even if we were to merge you would become the dominant shareholder. My board would not appreciate that. They have their own strategy.'

'OK,' Mittal said. 'We will meet to discuss this again.'

The large dining table was covered in an armada of Indian dishes. On the wall was a large painting of a Mughal emperor with a hawk on his arm. Dollé was a devotee of Indian food, and of the country, which he had visited several times. The big glasses were filled with the best French red. 'We should make Guy feel at home,' Lakshmi Mittal had instructed. As the four men ate, he set about putting Dollé at his ease. Never less than relaxed, Mittal was always happy to listen and let his guests steer the conversation, touching the tiller here and there himself with a well placed joke or observation. 'I see my team is doing better than yours,' he laughed.

'Yes, it's too bad,' Dollé smiled wanly.

Mittal was a Chelsea fan. Dollé had the No. 10 shirt of the French national side hanging above his desk at Arcelor headquarters and was an avid follower of mid-table FC Metz.

As a young man Guy Dollé had been a talented footballer, playing libero, or sweeper, for amateur side ARC Metz. As captain he enjoyed the free role, plugging breaches in his defence and always putting away the penalties. He played seventeen seasons, but he was no Franz Beckenbauer or Franco Baresi. Sometimes he regretted that he had never been quite good enough to turn pro, but he had kept involved with the playing side, coaching a local amateur team. Mittal, on the other hand, was more of a directors' box man.

'How is the labour situation in your company?' Aditya asked, switching the subject. Intelligence reports told him that there had been friction between workforce and management in some Arcelor plants.

'Very optimistic,' Dollé told him formally. 'There is no significant need for any concern.'

Aditya nodded. As far as he was concerned Guy Dollé had ticked the last box. Arcelor was a profitable company with widely held shares and few labour problems.

The concept of Mittal Steel and Arcelor teaming up was not mentioned again as the dinner stretched out over three hours. At 9.15 Dollé and Davezac took their leave. Having arrived by cab, they were offered Mrs Mittal's car and driver to return them to their hotel near City Airport from where they would fly back to Luxembourg in the Arcelor jet the next morning.

Sitting in the back of Mrs Mittal's car, Guy Dollé was non-committal. There was a silent surliness about him. He had visions of his host's smiling face, the food, the opulent surroundings, and of being pole-axed. He did not want to talk any more about getting into bed with Lakshmi Mittal.

As Lakshmi and Aditya watched the car pull away into the night, father turned to son. 'Adit,' he said, 'we must acquire that company.'

5

Arcelor headquarters, Luxembourg City

'Guy, this is Ekkehard Schulz.' Dollé sensed the temperature dropping.

'ThyssenKrupp is increasing its offer for Dofasco to $C68,' Thyssen's executive board chairman told him. Thyssen had also increased its break fee to $C215 million, the penalty it was prepared to pay if it pulled out of the $C5.26 billion deal. It was a major statement of intent.

'Thank you for telling me,' Dollé said and put down his phone.

'It's a potential knock-out blow,' Chuck Bradford, an analyst with New York's Soleil Securities, told steel reporter Naomi Powell of the *Hamilton Spectator*. 'You don't usually make a higher bid when you've already won. It sends a message that these guys at ThyssenKrupp are very serious.' According to regulatory documents Don Pether was on stream to make a personal profit of more than $C17 million from the deal if he exercised his stock options and sold his shares. It was no surprise when the Dofasco board issued a statement 'unanimously recommending to shareholders that they accept the offer and reject the Arcelor offer'.

Dollé wondered at the strange timing of the new Thyssen offer. Last night Mittal had told him to increase his bid; the next morning Thyssen had ramped up its offer. Dollé was deeply troubled. Without Dofasco, Arcelor was vulnerable to Mittal. If Thyssen got Dofasco it would have its hands on Arcelor's galvanising technology, making it a keener competitor. The libero sensed fissures appearing in his defence. He recalled Alain Davezac's words as they were driven away from the Mittal dinner: 'Guy, you have no idea how long the Mittals are prepared to wait.'

He had to get to Joseph Kinsch.

The chairman was at home. 'As the board has given me the authorisation, I am going to overbid Thyssen immediately this evening,' Dollé told him. He and Kinsch agreed the amount. Arcelor increased its bid to $C71 per share, a massive $C5.5 billion. It also covered Thyssen's break fee.

It was a high-risk throw of the dice. As a hostile black knight, Arcelor had still not gained access to Dofasco's confidential data on its assets and other commercial information, and without that detailed assessment of the company's value it could be difficult to justify such a costly takeover to shareholders – not that *they* figured high on the priority list of either Dollé or Kinsch. As a friendly white knight, ThyssenKrupp had studied the books and had based its bidding accordingly. The market wasn't bothered by Arcelor's gambling. In this latest twist of the big steel poker game Dofasco stock soared to $C72.40. Two months before, its share price had been $C44.

Because the conditions of both offers were now exactly the same Don Pether and his board had no alternative but to announce that Arcelor's was a superior bid in cash terms. It would now have to open its books to Dollé. Hoping against hope, Pether gave ThyssenKrupp until 23 January to match.

At Thyssen's headquarters in Düsseldorf Dr Ekkehard Schulz knew he was beaten. If he went to $C71 it would threaten the company's credit rating and reduce a German industrial institution – in the words of Standard & Poor's, the world's foremost provider of independent credit ratings – to 'junk status'. Thyssen was already heavily indebted, thanks to financing its huge pension deficit, and matching Arcelor would have added to that burden of debt, jeopardising its future credit-worthiness in financial markets.

Wednesday 18 January

Luton Airport

Lakshmi Mittal looked at his watch. He had just flown with Aditya in his helicopter from Battersea heliport to catch his private jet. It would be mid-afternoon in New York. He pressed out the numbers on his phone and waited for Lloyd Blankfein, the president and chief operating officer of the Goldman Sachs Group, one of the largest global investment banks, to take his call.

'I would like Goldman's to be my lead advisers on a major takeover transaction by Mittal Steel,' he explained.

'Lakshmi, a pleasure,' Blankfein replied from his office at 85 Broad Street, Lower Manhattan, a muscular twenty-nine-storey eighties block clad in brownstone – a nod to the historic buildings it looms over in the heart of the city's financial district. Mittal had never used Goldman Sachs before, but he had met Blankfein several times and they had become friends. Employing more than twenty-six thousand worldwide and raking in net revenues of $37.7 billion, Goldman Sachs prided itself on its 'culture of success', even if traditionally it had advised Mittal's losing opponents in other deals. But it was a class act when it came to mergers and acquisitions, and acted as financial advisers to some of the most important companies, largest governments and wealthiest families in the world.

Blankfein, a balding man with an astronaut's smile, was thrilled personally that he was about to add Mittal to his roster. Working a big deal with the world's number one steel-maker would also keep Goldman in coveted top spot of the merger-and-acquisition adviser league table, ahead of arch-rivals Morgan Stanley and Merrill Lynch. In the high-testosterone, high-billing world of investment banking top dog always got to charge its clients top dollar.

'I want you to explore strategic options and analyse the feasibility,' Mittal told Blankfein. 'How soon can you do it?'

'As soon as you like,' Blankfein said. 'Who's the target?'

'Arcelor.'

'How are you spelling that?' the Bronx-born Blankfein asked.

'A-r-c-e-l-o-r.'

That evening the Mittals were the dinner guests of Dr Ekkehard Schulz at ThyssenKrupp's hideaway, Schloss Landsberg. Lakshmi Mittal wanted to explore a second option to Arcelor, a coming-together with the Germans.

Thursday 19 January, 9.30 a.m.

Berkeley Square House, London

The dappled, peeling trunks of the gnarled two-hundred-year-old plane trees in the heart of Mayfair, famous for its society nightclubs and private casinos, were reflected in the sheer glass atrium of Berkeley Square House, where Lakshmi Mittal had headquartered his company since 1995.

Gambling was furthest from Mittal's mind as he shook hands with Richard Gnodde, Goldman's co-chief executive officer in London, and Shahriar Tadjbakhsh, the forty-three-year-old managing director of mergers and acquisitions at Goldman's office in Paris. Tadjbakhsh, studious, well tailored and soigné, had been up most of the night on the Internet, gleaning all he could about an industry that was being transformed by the inexorable rise of Lakshmi Niwas Mittal. The Swiss-born, French-educated son of an Iranian diplomat, Tadjbakhsh was now a US citizen and had trained at Harvard as a lawyer before making his name in mergers and acquisitions, but he was not a steel expert. M&A advisers in investment banks are not specialists in any one industry or sector; what they are good at is listening to the client, structuring deals and swinging the shareholders of target companies.

As he welcomed the two men to his utilitarian suite of offices on the seventh floor, Lakshmi Mittal was even more convinced that when it came to industrial logic a merging of Mittal Steel and Arcelor was a rock-solid banker. The previous evening he had tested the waters with Schulz for a merger with ThyssenKrupp, but there were too many problems. ThyssenKrupp was not just a steel-maker, it was an industrial conglomerate; so merging just its steel operations was fraught with problems. And then, any deal would face major competition difficulties in Europe and the States.

Joining Gnodde and Tadjbakhsh for what Mittal called a 'kick-off' meeting were Aditya, Mittal's director of investor relations Julien Onillon and chief of staff Sudhir Maheshwari. Mittal set out the logic of his deal. It was simple and it was short. 'Now you tell me how to do it.'

'Have you considered trying to do a friendly deal?' asked Gnodde, a strongly built, sporty South African who had spent eight years in Asia running Goldman's business there.

Mittal shrugged. 'Of course. A friendly deal is always best, but Mr Dollé tells me the cultures of our companies are not compatible and refuses to meet to discuss. One of the reasons Arcelor is trying so hard to acquire Dofasco is to escape from us.' In Lakshmi Mittal's life timing was everything and he was not prepared to wait for months to get Dollé back to the table. There was no alternative. 'We will make an offer direct to Arcelor shareholders over the heads of its board and management.'

Could they do a full cash offer? Tadjbakhsh counselled against. 'This is still fundamentally a cyclical industry, even if the cycles have flattened out, and to load up so much debt on to your company would be very risky.'

As they brainstormed the issues the sheer complexity of bidding for Arcelor came into sharp relief. A cabal of banks would be needed to help finance what promised to be the biggest steel deal in history. The EU Competition Commissioner, concerned about monopoly, would have to be brought on side along with politicians and trade unions worried about potential job cuts and plant closures. Then there would have to be a valuation of Arcelor on which to base an offer that was attractive to its shareholders and the market. That in itself would be difficult because Arcelor would refuse to open its books to a hostile raider.

Although he had Goldman as lead advisers to craft the bid and build the assault team of bankers, lawyers, political advisers and PR spinners, Lakshmi Mittal wanted one of his most trusted lieutenants at the very hub of it as a kind of über project-manager. 'Sudhir will take that role,' he said, nodding to Maheshwari. Aditya called Maheshwari 'the split rock', a bit of American political jargon he liked to use in presentations. 'As in any successful political campaign you need one person who is the focal point,' he explained.

'Sudhir will manage the war room, coordinate communications strategy, work with existing communications to craft the message and develop daily themes, and identify potential avenues of influence on Arcelor board members and individual shareholders.'

While Lakshmi and Aditya Mittal were on the road selling their bid to politicians and to Arcelor's investors, Maheshwari was to be the ringmaster. The trickiest arena of all in which the Mittals would have to perform was that of the market regulators in France, Luxembourg, Spain and Belgium, where Arcelor operated, and those in the Netherlands and the United States, where Mittal Steel was listed. In what would be a legal minefield, every single one of them would have to clear Mittal's offer before he could open it formally to Arcelor's shareholders. If he had been bidding in the UK for a British company this process would have taken no more than two months.

Mittal needed lawyers fast. By 11.30 Maheshwari and Tadjbakhsh had hired the Paris office of US legal firm Cleary Gottlieb Steen & Hamilton, whose lead counsel Pierre-Yves Chabert immediately called Bonn Schmitt Steichen in Luxembourg, one of the country's oldest, largest and most prominent law firms, to advise on Luxembourg legal issues. Simultaneously one of his colleagues was signing up a senior partner in the Barcelona office of Garrigues, the Iberian peninsula's biggest law firm, to act as counsel on issues there.

At 5.30 that afternoon an energetic olive-skinned, finely boned man with an impressive nose and sporting trademark Bulgari cufflinks checked in at reception. 'Yoel Zaoui to see Lakshmi Mittal,' he said. He looked like Ben Stiller, but he talked like Al Pacino.

Yoel Zaoui (pronounced Zowie) was one of Goldman Sachs's most prolific deal-makers, a guru of merger and acquisitions and one of Europe's most influential financiers. As head of European investment banking he was always on the move, frequently starting a conversation in one country and finishing it in another. Zaoui had landed in Mayfair to lead the Goldman team.

A French citizen, born in Casablanca, raised in Rome, and a graduate of Stanford Business School, the forty-five-year-old Zaoui had joined Goldman Sachs in 1989. Almost immediately he brought his talents for acquisition back to Europe, which was freeing itself of its economic shackles and allowing American banks to sweep in and turn the slower-paced, clubbier world of European investment banking upside down. Taking advantage of the euro, they set about expanding and redefining Europe's capital markets. As Old Europe went global and became 'Euro Inc.' the fastidiously calculating and precise Zaoui masterminded a wave of mergers, spin-offs and buy-outs involving major brand icons. His campaign honours included the battles between banking giants HSBC and Crédit Commercial de France (2000), energy and utilities companies ItalEnergia and Montedison (2001), metals and mining outfits Pechiney and Alcan (2003) and in 2004 the takeover tussle between pharmaceutical companies Aventis and Sanofi.

When Goldman opened its London office it had forty staff. Now Zaoui managed a team of nine hundred across Europe, with more fanning out into the Middle East, Turkey and Russia. Just like steel, investment banking – along with Zaoui's lucrative share and bonus package – knew no boundaries. As he walked quickly towards the serried ranks of lifts he was excited at the prospect of working with Lakshmi Mittal. Like Mittal, he enjoyed being number one. The only person who enjoyed it even more and stood a chance of pushing him down to number two on the merger adviser league table was his M&A counterpart at Morgan Stanley. And his name was Michael Zaoui, Yoel's elder brother.

Yoel Zaoui joined the second kick-off meeting and listened to Mittal describing his grand vision. Although he did not speak at great length, over the course of the meeting it seemed clear that he had grasped every implication and nuance of what he was about to unleash. And unlike many clients he had worked for, Lakshmi Mittal hid his ego well.

'The mission is how do you get something done – right?' Zaoui summarised.

'Right,' Mittal said.

'And the how is really up to us to figure out in discussions with you.'

'Of course,' Mittal smiled. 'That is your job.'

Zaoui insisted on one thing: 'With a deal as big as this, Arcelor are going be sniffing around for any intelligence so they can throw roadblocks in our path. We must keep this core team as small as we can to minimise leaks.'

'Yes,' Mittal agreed, 'but everyone in the core team must know everything that is going on at all times. We have no time for bureaucracy and long communication lines.'

Security in big deals was vital. Following the Sidor bugging scare Mittal had had his offices swept weekly by the security spooks from Control Risks Group. Control Risks describes itself as 'a leader in strategic internal audit partnering, protecting organisations from an external hacker attack, and the risks posed by internal parties' from cleaners to consultants.

'This is going to be the battle of the century,' Yoel Zaoui announced. 'Be very careful what you say to whom and when. From now until the offer is tabled we will call this transaction Project Olympus. Mittal Steel will be referred to by the codename Mars, and Arcelor will be Atlas,' he said, mixing up his Greek and Roman myths. Everybody knew that poor Atlas was condemned by Zeus to bear the heavens upon his shoulders. Yoel Zaoui was probably not aware that according to some mythologists Atlas was originally known as a cunning god of 'dangerous wisdom'.

Friday 20 January

Lyon

Guy Dollé was driving en route to a short skiing break when his phone rang.

'Guy, this is Lakshmi. I would like to come to Luxembourg tomorrow so we can carry on with our discussions about a global strategy.'

'It is impossible.' Dollé flinched for a moment, then he relaxed. After all, Dofasco was looking promising. ThyssenKrupp had not responded to his bid. They now had only three days to do so. 'I could be back in Luxembourg on Tuesday,' he told Mittal.

'Let's meet then. The twenty-fourth. In the late afternoon.'

As soon as Mittal hung up Dollé phoned Alain Davezac. 'Call Aditya and find out what Lakshmi really wants to talk about.'

Davezac called Aditya instantly to establish what was in Lakshmi Mittal's mind. 'Aditya says they want to talk to you about Dofasco, and as soon as possible,' he reported back to Dollé.

'Why the rush? We are due to meet them in Paris at the next IISI meeting in a couple of weeks.' And by then he might have Dofasco and be immune from Mittal's attentions.

While Dollé took to his skis Yoel Zaoui and his team merged strategy and numbers into an offer. Over the weekend Lakshmi Mittal realised that there was no way Guy Dollé was ever going to sit down and discuss friendly mergers with him. He also realised that if he bid for an Arcelor that had just won Dofasco this would pose him major problems with American regulators, who could block him on monopoly grounds. Always thinking laterally, Mittal had seen that there was a way around this problem.

On 22 January he called Ekkehard Schulz. By the time he had finished talking, Schulz was stunned. Despite a distinguished career he had relatively little experience of big deals. And he could not believe that he was to have another chance to bag a Canadian jewel for the Thyssen crown.

6

Monday 23 January

Berkeley Square House, London

Lakshmi Mittal, Aditya and Sudhir Maheshwari took up station on one side of Mittal Steel's very long, narrow boardroom table. Modern repro walnut, it looked as though it had been inspired by an aircraft carrier deck and escaped from a hotel. On the other side were a dozen lawyers and bankers. Alongside Yoel Zaoui was Goldman Sachs's number one number-cruncher Gilberto Pozzi, a willowy aristocratic-looking Italian. Leading the posse of Cleary Gottlieb lawyers was lanky, handsome, bespectacled and Harvard-educated Pierre-Yves Chabert, who had flown in from Paris to mesh in the legal planning.

Lakshmi Mittal began the meeting. 'I want to hear everyone and we need to cover all the points.'

Each of them had fifteen minutes to present a report to the Mittals on the feasibility and structure of the deal, on the corporate financing, market reaction, anti-trust issues, minimum-acceptance thresholds, plus a whole range of technical, legal and financial challenges of an offer that would have to be piloted through the six separate regulatory authorities under which the two companies operated.

'Our main concern is that the government of Luxembourg has very good relationships with the former Arbed,' Chabert reported. 'It's obvious we are going to have a lot of tension and resistance from them. Luxembourg is also due to implement the EU competition directive by May of this year and they may frame their law in such a way as to block any takeover, so we have challenges there. As we are operating in a global legal framework there will also be a lot of uncertainties that we will have to overcome. On the plus side Arcelor has no key shareholders that can block this at the end of the day, so we believe that the market will ultimately prevail whatever poison pills or roadblocks they might throw in our way.'

'Are you sure the market will prevail?' Mittal asked him.

'As long as you have the right price,' Chabert said, 'the market will give you a deal. In my experience it is very difficult to organise a successful defence against a deal if the price is right.'

There was no answer on price from this meeting, which was done and dusted in three hours. Chabert was amazed. In all the takeovers he had worked on this kind of meeting took weeks, interspersed with fly-pasts of emails.

Putting the two companies together would bring cost-saving synergies of more than $1 billion by 2009 without need for redundancies or plant closures. There was no geographical overlap between Arcelor and Mittal Steel, beyond Dofasco. Maheshwari now signed up Credit Suisse, Citigroup and HSBC to help finance the deal. With Goldman they would hammer out Mittal's opening offer share price. That day Arcelor's shares stood at €22. Mittal would pitch higher, but how much higher?

The next day Aditya Mittal called Nicola Davidson, Mittal Steel's general manager of communications, into his office. 'We are thinking about making an offer for Arcelor,' he told her. 'I want you to go away and think about PR.' It was the first the dashing polo-playing Scot had heard of it. 'Winning the communications battle is going to be every bit as important as wooing politicians and Arcelor shareholders,' she replied. 'We'll need outside help.'

As she assessed the PR requirement, Davidson knew that her in-house team – that pretty much amounted to her and a secretary – needed an external communications capability that extended beyond the UK. Mittal Steel had links with Maitland, a London agency headed by its founder Angus Maitland, a wily, shrewd Scot who was a doyen in the cut and thrust of takeover battles and whose clients included Tesco, Cadbury Schweppes and GlaxoSmithKline. Maitland had sold off part of his consultancy to EuroRSG, which had tentacles in other parts of the world. His small, slim frame neatly attired in short-sleeved shirt and shorts, Maitland was relaxing on the proceeds, cruising the Caribbean on his chartered yacht, when the call from London came through on the satellite phone.

'In confidence,' Nicola Davidson told him, 'Mittal Steel is about to launch an unsolicited major cross-border transaction which will be very high-profile. I need a lead agency with strong external support in a number of different countries. Can you help?'

'Of course – when is this happening?'

'In the next week,' Davidson said.

Maitland almost lost his glass of thirteen-year-old malt over the side. In the world of PR, such calls came infrequently, but when they did the large dollar signs started flashing immediately. A consultancy would drop everything and rush to the aid of its client, with a dedicated team pulled off other client work, and join forces with the bankers and lawyers on the deal. PR fees on this type of mandate were huge, from a minimum of $100,000 a week plus expenses and with a chunky success fee thrown in if the client won.

In normal circumstances, assuming he was not conflicted with another client, Angus Maitland would have rushed to Davidson's office, terms of business in his hand. But he was miles away, stranded in the sun. He could rely on his deputy Philip Gawith. The PR guru returned to his malt knowing that the Maitland name, his name, would be up in lights on one of the most fiercely fought takeover battles Europe had ever seen.

As the planning gathered speed, Yoel Zaoui had another issue he needed to raise with the Mittals. 'I think corporate governance is going to be a problem,' he told them. The Mittal family owned 88 per cent of the shares in Mittal Steel and enjoyed multiple voting rights. Mittal Steel's share structure comprised two categories: A shares and B shares. A shares were for external holders, B shares for the Mittal family. Under Mittal Steel's articles of association, the B shares were granted voting rights that gave them greater control. The voting rights were: one B share had ten votes, while one A share had one vote. Shareholders had two levels of interest – economic, which concerned the value of the share and the dividends attached to it, and voting rights, which meant their ability to vote at general meetings and to influence events. The Mittal share structure was typical of a close-knit family-controlled business. The previous August, Goldman Sachs had done its first research notes on the newly combined Mittal Steel and had said that any valuation of the group should include a 15 per cent discount because of the strength of family control.

'You are going to have to give way on that,' Zaoui urged.

'Most of the most successful businesses are family businesses,' Lakshmi reminded him. 'When we went public our advisers said that this voting right was acceptable. We have always run our company very professionally to the standards required by the Securities and Exchange Commission in America and on the New York stock exchange, where the company is listed. There are no significant differences between Mittal Steel's current corporate governance practices and those required to be followed by US domestic companies under the NYSE listing standards.'

'The Europeans will not see it that way,' Zaoui said.

Mittal looked incredulous. 'But Mittal Steel is governed by the laws of the Netherlands. We are a European company with our corporate headquarters in Rotterdam.'

'This bid will have enough problems as it is without you creating problems for yourself,' Zaoui said. 'We must try to remove these obstacles quickly.'

Mittal listened intently, as he always did, nodding from time to time to indicate where he agreed or disagreed, but never interrupting Zaoui.

When his adviser had finished, he said: 'The culture of this company is that we are prepared to change the culture of the company. Adit and I, the family, we will discuss.'

Tuesday 24 January, 11.30 a.m.

19 Avenue de la Liberté, Luxembourg City

In his office in the chateau headquarters of Arcelor, Guy Dollé could not disguise his happiness as he called Mittal. 'We cannot meet today as planned,' he said. 'I have to go to Hamilton to meet the managers of Dofasco. Our bid has been successful.'

'Congratulations,' Mittal said, a smile on his face.

'There is no urgency for you and me to discuss this business any more,' Dollé added dismissively. 'We shall see each other in Paris.'

Dollé and his team headed for Frankfurt airport to catch a Lufthansa flight to Toronto. Mittal gazed down from his window at the black cabs circling Berkeley Square. He returned to his desk and called Düsseldorf. He had to get an answer from Ekkehard Schulz.

Dr Schulz was welcoming the press to ThyssenKrupp's headquarters in the Dreischeibenhaus building in Düsseldorf. 'In its meeting yesterday evening, the executive board decided not to submit a higher offer to acquire Dofasco,' he began. 'Despite the strategic significance of Dofasco we will not become involved in a value-destroying bidding contest. We are firmly convinced that any offer over \$C68 would go beyond the point of profitability.'

'What happens next?' Dr Schulz asked rhetorically, then spelled out that Thyssen would strengthen its market position on North America by increasing production in Brazil and building new plants or alliances. What he did not say was that Mittal had offered him a side deal on Dofasco. 'I am going to make an offer for Arcelor,' he had told Schulz. 'If I am successful I will sell Dofasco to you at your final bid price of \$C68.'

Would Schulz take the bait? Mittal could tell from his voice that the German was very tempted. He said he had to consult his board. Mittal had to have a yes soon. That way he would sidestep the regulator and pocket a large sum with which to finance his deal for Arcelor, which was now shaping up nicely on the seventh floor of Berkeley Square House. The likely launch date for Mittal's offer was to be either 27 January or 3 February.

'I'm not in favour of the twenty-seventh,' Mittal told Yoel Zaoui at one of their daily briefings. 'Time is too short to fix every detail and this is a big deal. Any unexpected issue could delay or derail the whole process.'

'OK, sure,' said Zaoui, 'but my main concern is the longer we leave it the bigger the chance of leaks, which could also derail the deal.'

While Zaoui went back to his core team and the mechanics of the deal, Lakshmi Mittal was getting some tips on the diplomatic charm offensive he would have to launch to get it through potentially hostile governments once it was announced.

'The first person you must call is EU Competition Commissioner Neelie Kroes and let her know the scope of what's coming,' Goldman Sachs's government affairs adviser Lisa Rabbe suggested. 'We've been following her for some time and we know that she is not against big deals per se, so it is absolutely crucial that she sends out the right signal to other commissioners and other politicians around Europe.'

'I can tell her that there will not be any problems on the competition front,' Mittal said.

'That's just what you mustn't do,' Rabbe said. 'Keep it neutral. Just do the courtesy thing. Don't make the Jack Welch mistake.'

'Yes,' Mittal nodded, 'I understand what you are saying.' Mittal knew all about the legendary Jack Welch, chairman and CEO of General Electric. Each year, Welch, who had a reputation for brutal candour in his meetings with executives, would fire the bottom 10 per cent of his managers and reward the top 20 per cent with lavish bonuses and stock options. Displaying an uncanny business acumen, eradicating inefficiencies and trimming bureaucracy, Welch had increased GE's market capitalisation by $400 billion. It was all music to Mittal's ears, and he had even quoted the legendary Jack in his speeches. But in 2001 Welch was trying to take over the industrial supplies manufacturer Honeywell in a $45 billion deal when he ran head on into the European Commission. He had profoundly irritated the commissioners by going around saying there were no problems, that the acquisition was a piece of cake, and that he didn't see any competition difficulties. 'They blocked the deal,' Rabbe said.

Mittal smiled. 'Neutron' Jack, so called for his reputation for destroying whatever stood in his path, had stumbled upon an obstacle even more persistent than himself. He now planned for his retirement that summer and his eagerly awaited autobiography, *Straight from the Gut*.

'You are going to get a rough ride in France,' Rabbe warned him. 'You have to see Thierry Breton, Minister of Economy, Finance and Industry.'

'It's fixed,' Mittal said. 'I called one of my friends in Paris and said I wanted to see the finance minister for a get-to-know meeting. He called me back yesterday and said, "Breton will be really happy to meet you. He has heard about you, he would like to meet you for breakfast on the thirtieth."'

'Excellent,' Rabbe said.

'He doesn't know about this big news, but I wanted to inform him before we launch the bid.'

Lakshmi Mittal and Rabbe then plotted out a political sweep that would include the prime ministers of Luxembourg and Belgium and leading political figures in Spain. He would also meet mayors and other elected officials in those areas where Arcelor had steel plants. All that was missing were the final dates.

Mittal welcomed another visitor to his office that week – Anne Méaux, president of Image 7. Brought in by Yoel Zaoui, Méaux was the leading PR fixer in France with one of the heaviest contacts books in Europe. Once media relations honcho to President Giscard d'Estaing at the Élysée, she now employed Giscard's niece Constance on the staff of her 'independent cabinet of communication', which focused its influence on politicians, journalists, industrialists and all those involved in hostile takeovers. Méaux was now in her early fifties and understatedly elegant with a liking for trouser suits, good antique rings and chandelier earrings. She had a dry conspiratorial wit, an espresso voice, and her eyes twinkled when she laughed. Méaux was also famous for speaking her mind, causing humbled cabinet ministers or captains of industry to look nervously for the exit.

'I think we should invite a few French journalists over to a press conference when we announce the bid,' Mittal said. 'What do you think?'

Méaux raised a sculpted eyebrow. 'You cannot do this just from London,' she said with characteristic frankness. 'France may not have any ownership of the company but Arcelor is seen like a national treasure. The reaction will be amazing, really amazing. You will not believe it. You will have all the politicians against you because you are not French,' explained Méaux, who had known Thierry Breton for twenty years. 'Mr Mittal, let me tell you, all they know of you in France is that you are the very rich Indian guy who spent a lot of money on his daughter's wedding in Paris. Mittal Steel is completely unknown. So you have to go there and explain your bid, that you have a real project. Explain to them why this industry must be globalised, that you will be very careful about employment, that you are not a raider.'

'But Breton has been in private enterprise,' Mittal argued. 'That's why I have fixed a meeting to see him. Surely he understands?'

'In the Anglo-Saxon world you speak of money and say the shareholders will decide. In France the first thing we speak of is employment, and you will have to explain what you will do with the company once you have bought it.'

While they were talking Méaux's mobile rang. 'I'm sorry, do you mind?'

'Of course not,' Mittal said, absorbing what she had just told him. If France, which had no shares in Arcelor, was going to be a very tough nut to crack, what about Luxembourg, which had the biggest shareholding in the target company?

Méaux cupped her phone. 'I'm sorry but it is François Pinault. He was expecting to see me in Venice.'

The self-made retail billionaire was a leading client of Méaux's and had won a famous and nasty battle to take over Gucci in the late nineties, preventing its acquisition by LVMH, the world's largest luxury goods company headed by fellow French billionaire Bernard Arnault. Pinault, who had no educational qualifications and was not universally loved by the French elite, had also become one of the most powerful people in the international art market. In 1998 he bought auction house Christie's for £721 million and was also one of the world's most important collectors. He had hoped to build a £150 million contemporary art museum to house his collection on an island on the River Seine three miles from the centre of Paris, but frustrated by French planning bureaucracy he bought instead an 80 per cent share in the eighteenth-century Palazzo Grassi in Venice, previously owned by the Fiat motor company, and had embarked on a hectic five-month renovation programme. The French establishment was outraged.

Now Pinault was irritated. He was not used to being kept waiting. His first exhibition was due to open at the end of April and deadlines were slipping back. He wanted to know what was so important in London that it was keeping Anne Méaux from joining him to sort out his problems.

Mittal watched Méaux running her fingers through her blonde highlights as she tried to placate Pinault.

'Yes, I am still in London. No, I cannot tell you about it, but it is very important,' she said, glancing at Mittal.

'Please,' Mittal said, 'may I borrow your phone?'

Méaux handed over her mobile.

'Mr Pinault, this is Lakshmi Mittal,' he began. 'If I could have Anne for just a few more days – she is working with me on a major project.' He could not tell Pinault anything before going public as that would have made the Frenchman an 'insider', but he added with typical Mittal astuteness, 'I have heard so much about you and how you are the top businessman in France. I would be very happy and grateful if you would support me when the time comes.'

After a few more words, he handed the phone back to Méaux.

'And what did he say?' she asked.

'He said, "Please come over and see me",' Mittal smiled.

'Already building a French fan club?' Méaux laughed.

'OK,' Mittal said, rubbing his hands together. 'Let's go to Paris. You tell us what we have to do and we shall do it.'

7

Wednesday 25 January, 8 p.m.

Jonathan's Restaurant, Oakville, Ontario

'We have always had great respect for Arcelor and the people we have gotten to know over the years, Guy included,' Don Pether said, raising his glass to his guests in the Platinum Room of the award-winning Jonathan's, frequented by Prince Andrew and King Constantine of Greece. Pether had chosen to celebrate Dofasco's merger with Arcelor in a private room of the restaurant in the sleepy commuter town of Oakville, halfway between Hamilton and Toronto. After so many months supporting ThyssenKrupp's bid, he wanted to keep this marriage low-key. 'Arcelor's business strategy and values are very consistent with Dofasco's and we are looking forward to our future together,' he said, proposing a toast to their collaboration.

'We are obviously very pleased in acquiring Dofasco,' Dollé responded. 'We value this company greatly and we see it as the platform for our growth in North America. As part of the Arcelor group we see Dofasco becoming a stronger, more competitive steel producer in an increasingly competitive North American steel market. I would also like to express our ongoing support for Dofasco's management team,' he concluded, smiling in turn at eight of them, who were sitting with Pether in high-backed armchairs around the rich walnut dining table. Here was a company whose attentions they had fought so hard to resist, but their bulging share options certainly made up for missing out on the anticipated German alliance.

The Dofasco deal was done. For Guy Dollé this was a moment to savour, as he tucked in to his celebratory dinner with his team: chief financial officer Gonzalo Urquijo, deputy CEO Michel Wurth and Patrick Seyler, humorous head of corporate communications. Dollé felt like a reprieved prisoner, saved at the last minute from a life sentence with Mittal. Now he could finish his career back at the top.

Thursday 26 January, 2 p.m.

Mittal Steel, Berkeley Square House

The message light was flickering on her phone. Nicola Davidson sat down at her desk and replayed the voicemail.

'Hi, Nicola, this is Bob Jones from *Metal Bulletin*. Can you ring me urgently? I have heard a rumour that you might be making a bid for Arcelor.' As she walked briskly from her office to find the Mittals, she bumped into Sudhir Maheshwari. 'I've just had a voice message from Bob Jones,' he said.

Then she spotted Aditya just outside his office. 'Aditya, I have just had a message . . .' But before she could finish Aditya Mittal's mobile started ringing. He looked down at the screen. 'It's Bob Jones.'

'We have to bring this forward to tomorrow,' Yoel Zaoui told the team.

'We can't afford any more leaks,' Lakshmi Mittal agreed. 'It will give the other side extra time to prepare their defence.' Throughout his career, once Mittal had agreed a target he moved in on it extremely fast. But he regretted that he would not now get to Thierry Breton until after the offer had been announced.

The advisers looked at each other. Several days of outstanding work would have to be done overnight. Once the figures had been finalised by Gilberto Pozzi and the banking team, Aditya Mittal, Pierre-Yves Chabert and Julien Onillon began working on a draft press release announcing the tender offer and an appendix explaining its rationale which they would send to all the regulators in France, Luxembourg, Belgium, Spain, the Netherlands and the United States, having already warned them of its arrival by phone. To prevent any more leaks if the release fell into the wrong hands, they used the agreed codenames throughout for Arcelor and Mittal Steel.

At 3 p.m. Lakshmi Mittal, with Aditya by his side and his Goldman bankers and Cleary lawyers in attendance, hosted a full meeting of the board by telephone, in which he outlined the deal and the financing and other arrangements that were in place to support it. The meeting took minutes to rubber-stamp the offer. It delegated to the Mittals and to Wilbur Ross, acting jointly, the authority to change and/or finalise the terms and conditions of the offer.

The pressure was building to lock up the small print. Goldman Sachs now brought in the support bankers who would underpin the deal by £6 billion and target key Arcelor shareholders to buy into Mittal's offer. They had already walked miles up and down the carpeted corridors talking to their colleagues and share buyers on their mobiles and mashing their BlackBerrys with emails, building up a slate of support for the deal. Of all these big beasts Jeremy Fletcher from Credit Suisse was probably the biggest of all. A chain-smoking bear of a man with a rasping humour and never afraid to say exactly what he thought, Fletcher bore more than a passing resemblance to the hell-raising Shakespearian actor Robert Stephens. He was no stranger to drama in real life. In the early 1990s when Yeltsin's drive to democratise Russia's corrupt command economy had turned his country into a madhouse, Fletcher, one of the first Western bankers to invest, was frog-marched at machine-gunpoint off a Soviet steel plant he was financing for daring to show up as a representative of the newly arrived capitalist evil. Before kicking him out into 'the middle of fucking nowhere, miles from the nearest town and a passing car every hour', the security guards told him that if he ever came back he would be shot.

Fletcher had worked with Mittal as a lead adviser to Ispat International since the Trinidad takeover. But this was the first Mittal deal on which he had been asked to play a supporting role. The big man was not happy. Not happy at all. Fletcher had stuffed his frequently escaping shirt back into his trousers and marched into Berkeley Square earlier in the day, telling Yoel Zaoui: 'I'm not going to pretend that our noses have not been seriously put out of joint by you taking the lead on this one and I fully expect us to lock horns.'

'I'm not here to mess around with your relationship with the Mittals,' Zaoui replied calmly. 'And you know far more about the steel business than I do. There'll be no need for locking horns. And we don't have time.'

Beirut-born Spiro Youakim of Citigroup had also brought his considerable testosterone to the party, wrapped up in Savile Row blue pinstripe and topped off with a trademark silk pocket-handkerchief and one of his four hundred ties. Citigroup had been lending the Mittals M&A money since the mid-nineties and had advised on the merger with Wilbur Ross's International Steel Group. Inspired by the Mittals' get-up-and-go, Spiro was ready to roll. Completing the trio was Adrian Coates of HSBC, which had backed and advised Mittal's private company LNM before the creation of Mittal Steel. But his normal 'let's spook the market' approach to deals seemed to have deserted him when he had arrived at Mittal HQ that day.

'This is a nice idea, a good investment banker's pitch,' he told Lakshmi and Aditya, 'but it's too ugly, too difficult to do. It's going to get very nasty and very dirty. The real question you should be asking yourselves is not how to do it but whether you shouldn't stop this.'

'Adrian, you know where the door is,' Aditya had told him. But Coates was still here. Who would want to miss out on a massive deal like this?

'But Goldman Sachs don't even know anything about steel,' Coates said to Jeremy Fletcher.

'Maybe that's an advantage in a deal as ballsy as this,' Fletcher replied sardonically, retreating outside to chew on a cigarette.

Ever since they had entered the building Fletcher, Youakim and Coates had been jockeying for face time with the client. After all, they reasoned, we are underpinning this deal to the tune of £6 billion. But Lakshmi Mittal had made his choice and replied to every advance: 'The Goldmans,' as he now referred to them, 'are running the show. We must all work with them.'

9.35 p.m.

Aditya Mittal's office

Lakshmi Mittal sat, Aditya at his side, taking one last look at a series of bullet points on a piece of paper. In front of him was the phone. This was to be one of the most important calls of his life. He felt calm. He was certain that what he was doing was absolutely right.

'Good luck,' Aditya said as his father buttoned out the number: 00 33. . . .

Five hours behind, Guy Dollé was in the Lufthansa business-class departure lounge at Terminal 1 of Toronto's Lester B. Pearson International Airport when his mobile rang. He fished it out of his pocket and looked at it quizzically. He didn't recognise the number.

'Yes?'

'Guy, this is Lakshmi Mittal. I am calling you as a matter of courtesy to tell you that tomorrow Mittal Steel will be announcing an offer directly to your shareholders for all the shares of Arcelor.'

At that very moment Patrick Seyler happened to look up at Dollé. The CEO looked like a man who was about to fall off a building.

'I can't believe it,' Mittal said to his son. 'He hung up on me.' He redialled the number. This time all he got was Dollé's voicemail. He left a message: 'We share the same vision regarding consolidation in the steel business and I hope that this can still be friendly. I do not want this to be hostile.'

Aditya took the phone from his father and put in a call of his own. It flashed up on a mobile phone in a Renault Vel Satis that had just zipped into the fast lane of the A4 Strasbourg–Paris motorway at Metz.

'It's a call from Aditya Mittal,' Chloë Davezac told her father. Chloë had just finished her internship at Arcelor and was desperate to get back to Paris to see her boyfriend. 'He'll leave a message,' she said, hoping her father would not take the call and slow them down.

'I've got to talk to him,' Alain Davezac said. He switched lanes, cut his speed and listened.

'Alain. We have a problem,' Aditya said. 'We are trying to speak to Guy – where is he?'

'Guy is in Toronto.'

'We know, but we can't talk to him. His line is dead.'

'He must be in the air,' Davezac said. He heard Aditya pause. He was talking to someone else at his end.

'Alain, tomorrow morning Mittal Steel will be announcing an offer for all the shares of Arcelor,' Aditya told him.

'Guy, you have no idea how long they are prepared to wait' – the words minted so recently in Mrs Mittal's car now began to echo around his own. Davezac could all too easily imagine Dollé frustrated beyond belief, stuck on the wrong side of the Atlantic while Mittal tried to make off with his company.

Over in Toronto the Arcelor team had one hour before taking off for Frankfurt, and they had to decide what must be done first in their defence against Mittal. There would be no chance to talk as a group on the long flight back to Europe. Because their tickets had been booked so late they were not even all sitting together on the plane. They soon lost count of how many calls they had made to Luxembourg. The first had been to Arcelor chairman Joseph Kinsch, who had been dumbfounded when told the news.

As he took his seat on the plane, Guy Dollé remembered some sound advice he had been given by an investment banker: One of the most important things to do when you are defending a hostile bid is to sleep. It will be very gruelling. Arcelor's in-house lawyer had also told him that Arcelor's by-laws said that nobody could bid for the company unless it was a full cash offer. There was no way Mittal, stretched by the Ukraine auction, could afford to do that without the risk of bankrupting himself in the process.

Guy Dollé let his eyelids drop shut.

As the plane took off Gonzalo Urquijo turned to Michel Wurth and said, 'You know, Michel, whatever happens from now on, life at Arcelor is never going to be the same again.'

On the seventh floor of Berkeley Square House the lights blazed through the night. At midnight on 26 January Lakshmi Mittal addressed fifty-five managers of Mittal Steel worldwide by teleconference to tell them that the offer for Arcelor was about go live.

'This is a very big deal,' he began. 'You will be bombarded with questions from journalists, but my message is that we will handle this fight and I have every confidence in all of you not to lose focus on our operations, on our business.' While the Mittals went after Arcelor, Malay Mukherjee would be holding the fort.

To a man and woman they were excited, congratulating Mr Mittal from all parts of the Mittal globe. None of them seemed to really understand what it meant to be making a hostile offer.

At 4.30 a.m. Aditya, who was working on his presentation for the next day's press conference, came into Nicola Davidson's office, where she and Goldman's number-crunching Gilberto Pozzi were refining the press release. He picked up a copy and studied it. 'But these are the wrong figures,' he said. Tiredness was taking its toll. In contrast, Aditya was all youthful exuberance. He turned to Davidson and said, 'Should I include a slide in my presentation showing the two company logos together, the new company Mittal Arcelor?'

For a moment Davidson thought he was joking, but then she realised that he was serious. 'I think that would be most unwise,' she said. 'It might look a little too presumptuous.'

By now rumours were flying among journalists and steel industry analysts. One said that Arcelor was about to launch a bid for Mittal Steel.

8

'Mittal Steel N.V. . . . today announces that it has launched an offer to the shareholders of Arcelor SA . . . which will create the world's first 100 million tonne-plus steel producer', making it four times larger than its nearest rival, Nippon Steel.

The eleven-page release was finally issued at 6.30 that morning (7.30 a.m. Luxembourg time). In the very early hours the regulators had been informed by Mittal of its impending publication: the AMF (Autorité des Marchés Financiers) in France, the Commission de Surveillance du Secteur Financier (CSSF) in Luxembourg, the Comisión Nacional del Mercado de Valores (CNMV) in Spain and the Commission Bancaire, Financière et des Assurances (CBFA) in Belgium. On the Mittal side the Dutch regulators Autoriteit Financiële Markten (AFM) were also contacted, and a registration statement had been filed with the US Securities and Exchange Commission (SEC) in Washington DC. Trading in Arcelor shares had been suspended on the stock markets in Belgium, France, Luxembourg and Spain, while trading in Mittal Steel shares had been suspended on Euronext Amsterdam, 'pending a statement'.

Lakshmi Mittal had already made his first courtesy call to EU Competition Commissioner Kroes. He did not ask for her support and he kept his comments short, explaining what he was doing and why, ensuring that she was safely in the loop. He also called the Luxembourg Prime Minister Jean-Claude Juncker, who was on an official visit to Africa. Ominously, the PM refused to take his call. Next, Mittal contacted the CEOs of every major competitor, starting with China's Shanghai Baosteel Group Corporation, asking for their support. There was also an implicit warning: Don't get involved as a white knight for Arcelor. From China, Japan, Brazil and Russia the world's top steelmen promised their support. Lakshmi Mittal never forgot what people promised him.

'The offer values each Arcelor share at €28.21,' the release explained. 'This represents a 27 per cent premium over the closing price and an all-time high on Euronext Paris of Arcelor shares on 26 January 2006 . . . This offer values Arcelor at an equity value of €18.6 billion.'

The new company would have predicted annual revenues of $69 billion and earnings before interest, taxes, depreciation and amortisation (EBITDA) of $12.6 billion. Mittal was offering to acquire all of Arcelor's shares currently trading in three ways: a primary mixed cash and exchange offer for Arcelor shares, consisting of four new Mittal Steel shares (referred to as 'paper') and €35.25 in cash for every five Arcelor shares; a secondary cash offer consisting of a straight €28.21 for each Arcelor share; and a secondary share exchange offer consisting of sixteen new Mittal shares for every fifteen Arcelor shares. It reflected the fact that Mittal could not finance a deal with more than 25 per cent in cash and was having to use his paper for the bulk of the offer.

Mittal's exhausted team trudged the short distance from Berkeley Square House down to the British Academy of Film and Television Arts on Piccadilly. Most of them had not slept for the best part of two days, sending home for shaving kits and changes of clothes. Lakshmi and Aditya arrived by car and were surprised to see 150 journalists in the auditorium. 'Nicola told me there would only be thirty-five,' Lakshmi said as he made his way to the podium, a spring in his step. He looked relaxed, as though he had just come back from holiday. His wife, his children and his father were sitting in the front row, as they always did. He put on his glasses and peered out over them at his audience, like a preacher, before delivering his text.

'The last ten years have seen a major shift towards consolidation of the steel industry, helping to create sustainable value for all stakeholders,' he began. 'Both Mittal Steel and Arcelor have been at the forefront of this consolidation and share a similar vision for the future of our industry. This combination accelerates the process and leaves us uniquely positioned to benefit from the opportunities created.'

The mood among the journalists was upbeat. There had not been anything on this scale in steel ever. Mittal's takeover team had almost defied gravity to put the offer together in just four days. But apart from the Mittals none of them looked particularly triumphant, just very tired after working so hard. Some heads had dropped. Several of the bankers were nodding off as up on stage Lakshmi Mittal continued to unveil his vision.

'We believe the offer provides a very attractive premium and has been structured so that Arcelor shareholders have the opportunity to participate in the exciting growth potential of the combined company, whilst also receiving a generous cash element. We would encourage them to consider the merits of our compelling offer and play a part in the future of the world's only global steel company.'

Mittal had also agreed to ease his family's stranglehold on the company's shareholding. 'Should the offer be successful, the family will reduce its multiple voting rights on the company's class B common shares from ten to one to two to one.' Pragmatic as always, he had taken Yoel Zaoui's advice. He was even considering relocating the headquarters of the merged company to Luxembourg if his offer was successful.

And then came a bombshell. 'Mittal Steel has entered into an agreement with ThyssenKrupp to resell all the common shares of Dofasco Inc at a price equal to the euro equivalent of 68 Canadian dollars per share.'

Mittal had done his deal with Schulz, who had signed the day before. Schulz had his prize and Mittal was free of a potential regulatory millstone. And what made it all the sweeter was that Thyssen was getting Dofasco for three dollars a share less than Dollé was prepared to pay. Given that he and Kinsch had ramped up the bidding in Ukraine to make Mittal pay a billion more, Guy Dollé would not fail to see the double irony of being urged by Mittal to pay more for Dofasco, only to lose it for less.

'Dofasco is a great company, so why sell it?' a journalist asked.

Mittal paused. 'I am saying to Arcelor shareholders: Look, you want North American exposure, we can give you four times what you get from the Dofasco deal, plus the benefits of our fast-growing emerging market operations.'

'Dofasco is a significantly smaller producer than our assets in the

United States,' explained Aditya, who was sitting alongside his father. 'It's the number five producer, we're number one. It's number four in automotive, we're number one. Dofasco, for us, is redundant and subscale. We do not need these facilities.'

A stickler for routine, Don Pether left his home in Dundas, Ontario, a small community of some twenty thousand on the western edge of Hamilton, which was famous for its annual cactus festival. He climbed into his 2003 Cadillac STS bang on time for the thirty-minute drive to Dofasco. Normally he tuned into local station 102.9 FM to catch the news, but today he left the car radio off. He had a problem at work he wanted to think through.

He strode into the Dofasco building, and was waiting by the lifts when he heard a shrill female voice calling behind him. 'Mr Pether! Mr Pether! Hold the elevator.'

It was a colleague from sales running breathlessly towards him. To Pether's neat and ordered eye she looked in quite a state of dishevelment. 'Have you heard?' she said, her head shaking.

'Heard what?'

'Mittal has just bought Arcelor.'

'No, I think you're mistaken,' Pether reassured her. 'That's not the case. *We* are merging with Arcelor.'

'But it was on the radio.'

Pether saw despair in her eyes as the doors closed between them.

At his desk Pether logged on, went through his emails, then went online and read the news. His stomach followed the lift all the way back down to the ground floor.

That afternoon Aditya Mittal was driving home feeling extremely confident that the deal was now as good as done. Early press and investor reaction was positive to 'Mittal's ballsy bid'. Chicago-based analyst Michelle Applebaum was impressed by the audacity of it. 'For the steel industry, this is like Microsoft buying Apple,' she said.

With Guy Dollé about to land back in Europe, Alain Davezac called friends and contacts in India to see if they could shed light on why Mittal had moved even more dramatically and devastatingly than usual. 'Mittal has the kind of hunger that you Europeans will never understand,' they told him.

While Lakshmi went home to reflect with Usha on a momentous week, Aditya took a call in his car. It was Yoel Zaoui.

'Great launch, Yoel,' he said. 'We're on the way.'

'Yes, a great launch,' Yoel agreed. Aditya could hear the 'but' in Zaoui's voice. 'But don't expect this thing to be over any day soon.'

9

The Grand Duchy of Luxembourg

The tiny landlocked country of Luxembourg knows all about wars and hostile invaders. Centuries of marauding by Austrian, French, German and Spanish warlords have left their mark on this minuscule country which occupies an area some 140 kilometres by 70, about the size of the county of Surrey, or half the size of Rhode Island in the USA. Ask anyone outside mainland Europe where Luxembourg can be found on the map, and they will not have much of a clue. The Grand Duchy sits in the north-west, cramped between Germany to the east, France to the south and Belgium to the north and west, where the land is a continuation of the heavily forested and slightly mountainous Ardennes.

Military historians still write with fascination about the country's central terrain, with its challenging high-walled city fortresses, surrounded by the impregnable natural escarpments of the Pétrusse and Alzette valleys. At one point Luxembourg had forty fortified buildings and a complex of deep underground tunnels covering twenty-three kilometres, designed by top military engineers from France, Germany and Austria. It was dubbed the 'Gibraltar of the North'.

In 1839 under the Treaty of London Luxembourg finally won independent status under Grand Duke William, who was also King of the Netherlands. Encapsulated within the House of Orange, the Grand Duchy of Luxembourg was guaranteed perpetual neutrality. But after being occupied by Germany in two world wars, it abandoned this as a bad idea and in 1949 Luxembourg signed up as a charter member of NATO.

In a secluded area five kilometres west of the centre of

Luxembourg City is the most poignant reminder of all Luxembourg's wars. Rows of white crosses in the immaculately kept American Military Cemetery commemorate the lives of 5076 soldiers of the 5th Armored Division of the US 3rd Army who fought and died in a fierce three-month battle against the daring German Panzers on the north Luxembourg hinterland during the winter months of 1944. Luxembourg was liberated in February 1945 and the man who commanded the US 3rd Army, the legendary General George Patton, is also buried in the military cemetery in a centrally positioned lone plot at the head of his men. Ahead of him stands a thirty-metre-high sentinel, engraved with the names of every soldier who gave his life in the battle famously depicted in the film *Battle of the Bulge*.

At the very end of the war Patton, nicknamed 'Old Blood and Guts', died rather tamely of a broken neck in a car accident in Germany. He had willed that he be buried alongside his men in Luxembourg. The small nation of 450,000 people so revered the General that if they had had their way he would have been buried in the Cathédrale Notre-Dame de Luxembourg, in the heart of the Grand Duchy's capital, alongside a grand line of Grand Dukes.

Luxembourg has a lot to thank General Patton and his men for. Today, the country is the most prosperous of any industrialised democracy, and at $67,000 has the highest per capita income in the world. The Grand Duchy has also learned to punch above its weight, especially in all things European. A founding member of the European Economic Community, due in part to Robert Schuman, the eminent Luxembourg-born politician, Luxembourg was the official seat for the continent's politicians until that passed to Brussels in 1965. It remains the seat of the European Court of Justice, the European Court of Auditors and the European Investment Bank, and it acts as the secretariat of the European Parliament.

The Prime Minister Jean-Claude Juncker, the longest-serving national leader in Western Europe, is a highly respected politician, often the broker on weighty domestic matters to big brothers in neighbouring Germany and France. Small in stature but big in political nous, at fifty-two Juncker has one of the best diplomatic black books on the planet.

The country fights hard to dispel the image that it is just one street full of banks. But it is indeed a leading financial centre, with 150 of the world's best-known financial institutions employing 23,500 people housed in modern, high-tech offices who now account for 70 per cent of the national GDP. In 2006 total banking assets were $1 trillion. In mutual funds Luxembourg is second only to the USA, with $ 2.15 trillion in domiciled funds (those that are domestically registered or home-based).

But Luxembourg is also big in media; it is the home of RTL, a global broadcasting group, and of SES, the world's largest provider of direct-to-home satellite television. In terms of logistics the Luxembourg company Cargolux is the biggest all-cargo business in Europe, and the government promotes the country for its central access to key cities in Europe. The government is also successfully pursuing the diversification of light and medium-sized high-tech industry in addition to Luxembourg being a centre for electronically supplied services.

Each weekday, over a hundred thousand commute to Luxembourg across the Belgian, French and German borders to work for higher pay in financial services or for the EU. Most can speak at least three languages but only the natives speak Luxembourgish, a strange mix of German dialect and French. French is the language of government and law; German is the language of the media, and English mostly the language of business. There is also a growing population of Portuguese and Italians.

A bank secrecy law, tax incentives and the lowest VAT rate in Europe are a big draw for financiers and ultra-high net-worth individuals. In the 1980s the German government decided to impose an annual 10 per cent tax on people's domestic bank deposits. Before the law bringing in this 'withholding tax' had time to be put in place, a huge wall of private money fled overnight to Luxembourg and never returned. The Luxembourg banks were so elated that they clubbed together and sent ten cases of champagne to the German Chancellor, Helmut Kohl, ensuring that the German press witnessed its delivery. Luxembourg and its convivial people do have a sense of humour.

However, the country is also the butt of jokes, especially French jokes. A favourite was circulating among French colleagues at Arcelor headquarters about how Luxembourgers see their place in the world: 'The Luxembourg cabinet is in session and is very bored because nothing exciting has happened for ages. One member says, "Let's start a war." The cabinet gets very excited, studies an atlas and settles on China. They write a letter to Beijing, saying "You are a bunch of idiots, we are declaring war on you." China responds, "We accept your declaration but don't you realise the disparity in the sizes of our two countries?" The Luxembourg cabinet goes back to the atlas and then after great debate responds, "We rescind our declaration of war because we do not have enough cells in our jails for all the prisoners we are going to take."'

There is something else for which Luxembourg is famous. Entering the City of Luxembourg from the airport, you see on the edge of the Kirchberg Plateau six thirty-metre-high slabs of steel upended and mounted side by side next to a roundabout. The sculpture is a rusting reminder that Luxembourg has always been at the forefront of steel production.

Steel is in every Luxembourg family, father to son, because for more than seventy-five years it was the country's main source of income and employment. The Prime Minister's father worked in steel, and you hear similar stories of all strata of this small society. The emotional attachment is understandably huge.

At the end of the nineteenth century iron ore was discovered in the south of the country, an area of open, rolling countryside which is part of the Lorraine plateau where the French steel industry came to be based. In 1911 the steel company Arbed was founded in Luxembourg. At its peak in the 1960s Arbed was producing over six million tonnes of steel in southern towns with such curious-sounding names as Esch-sur-Alzette, Esch-Belval, Differdange and Dudelange. The company employed twenty-seven thousand workers, roughly half of the total industrial workforce. It was a national flagship, a big organisation growing up fast in a small country on the back of regular 5 per cent growth rates. It had survived through periods of great difficulty: the First World War, deep social unrest in 1919–20 and then the Depression, when massive lay-offs occurred. It was during this time that the country laid the foundation for a unique consensual tripartite agreement between government, the Arbed management and the trade unions.

By 1950 steel was at the heart of postwar Europe, from the German Ruhr to the French Lorraine, with Belgium and Luxembourg between. The European Coal and Steel Community, an initiative based on the work of the French politician Jean Monnet, came into being in 1951. It was the forerunner of the European Union. By the 1960s Arbed represented 46.5 per cent of the Luxembourg economy. But in the 1970s steel began to lose its strategic significance. Several European governments grew frustrated at the cost of supporting state-owned companies battered by years of stagnation, not helped by the 1972 oil shock when producers hiked prices. Arbed again went through very tough times, but was faithfully supported by the government, which held a 40 per cent stake.

In the 1990s governments began to privatise their steel interests. One of the first to take this route was Spain, which decided to sell its interest in the steel-maker Aceralia, based in the Basque country. Arbed saw its chance, wooing the Spanish despite a protracted battle with its French rival, the Usinor steel group led by Francis Mer. A former mining engineer and, like Dollé, a graduate of the École Polytechnique, Mer was a formidable former senior executive at Saint-Gobain, a major French industrial group, who was tasked with privatising Usinor and leading the consolidation charge.

Economic reality kicked in again in 2002 when Arbed merged with the privatised Usinor, after protracted discussion with the competition authorities in Brussels, to become Arcelor, Europe's steel champion, with the Luxembourg government still the largest shareholder at 5.6 per cent.

Arbed always had good leaders, and their portraits feature prominently around the walls of the company boardroom on the ground floor of its majestic administrative headquarters on Luxembourg's main thoroughfare, the Avenue de la Liberté. One of them is of Émile Mayrisch, who entered the Dudelange works at twenty-three and by thirty-five was managing it. It was Mayrisch – a man of imagination and ideas, a skilled diplomat and shrewd negotiator who strove to develop the company beyond its cramped borders – who helped create Arbed. He constantly pursued efficiency, and the development of the business. It was Mayrisch's imagination that led to Arbed buying coastal land by the Ghent Canal, which became the home of Sidmar, one of the company's state-of-the-art steelworks in Belgium.

In 1961 a young Luxembourger called Joseph Kinsch entered
Arbed. His father and his grandfather had both worked in the steel
industry. Kinsch was to rise rapidly through the ranks, becoming
chief executive in 1972, chairman of the group management board
in 1992, and the following year executive chairman of the board of
directors. Kinsch had many of Mayrisch's diplomatic and shrewd
negotiating skills. Some colleagues called him 'the Silver Fox', but only
behind his back. The local workforce had shrunk to five thousand
but abroad Arcelor employed forty-nine thousand, spread among
516 companies and subsidiaries. It was now the second-largest steel
company in the world. More importantly, the decision-making centre
was in Luxembourg, and it was Kinsch who had ensured that this
endured during the wooing of Aceralia and then the merger in 2002
with Usinor. The alliance with the French was never easy. Kinsch
was co-chairman with Francis Mer and the deal was that Mer, six
years the younger, would succeed him as sole chairman when Kinsch
retired. Then, one day later in 2002 Mer phoned Kinsch to tell him
that he was accepting the post of Minister of Finance in Jacques
Chirac's government and would have to step down. Kinsch congratulated him heartily, delighted that he now had a free rein.

By way of celebrating Mer's removal from the script, sole chairman Kinsch, who was also becoming something of a collector of fine
art, had placed a triptych by the renowned Luxembourg artist and
sculptor Auguste Trémont (1892–1980) on the wall outside his office.
Trémont had been employed at Arbed during the First World War.
His painting depicted muscular steelworkers toiling nobly in the
heat of the furnaces. They were Luxembourger steelworkers, of
course.

Tall and distinguished with a salt-and-pepper moustache, Kinsch
was now a Luxembourg grandee and had a hot line to Prime
Minister Juncker. But as a man of advancing years – he liked to
describe himself now as 'an old man of steel' – Kinsch was not
advancing with them. Even though No Smoking signs had popped
up all over Arcelor headquarters, the pungent tell-tale smell of the
chairman's chain-smoked Maryland cigarettes – a well known
Luxembourg brand – still seeped out from underneath the door of
his office, a smell evocative of a Turkish café. Now approaching sev-
enty-two, Kinsch, known to his close friends as 'Jupp', but to

everyone else as 'Chairman' or 'Mr Chairman', was due for a two-year extension as chairman of the board, if shareholders agreed. They would agree. They always agreed with the Chairman. Some said he was just marking time while they designed a statue of him – made of steel, of course – to be placed in the square facing Arcelor HQ.

Given his Prussian-like bearing, it surprised nobody that Joseph Kinsch loved to quote the nineteenth-century German philosopher Hegel: 'Nothing great in the world has been accomplished without passion.'

On the evening of Thursday 26 January 2006, Kinsch, a keen golfer with a handicap of eleven, was looking forward to some week-end rounds at the Club Grand-Ducal de Luxembourg, a lushly scenic golf course that had once been owned by Arbed. Late that night, he took a phone call from Guy Dollé that made his passion for Arcelor burn like never before.

10

Friday 27 January 2006, 8.30 a.m.

Frankfurt-am-Main Airport

Lufthansa's overnight flight from Toronto touched down on time. After disembarking, Dollé, Wurth, Urquijo and Seyler hurried through passport control, trundling their hand luggage. Red-eyed on account of having managed only occasional snatches of sleep on the eight-hour flight, they looked weary and worried as they tried to come to terms with the harsh reality of Lakshmi Mittal's sudden hostile move, and fearful of the impact it would have on their own futures. Even if they kept their jobs, they could lose status. They were facing a crisis, and it showed on their faces in the depressing grey light of the winter morning.

The Arcelor group headed across the arrivals concourse to two waiting BMW 7-series company cars that would take them on to Luxembourg. Dollé, Wurth and Urquijo travelled together in the first car. As they sped down the Koblenz–Trier autobahn on the two-and-a-half-hour, 250-kilometre drive, Guy Dollé checked his mobile for overnight messages and grimaced as he listened to the message from Lakshmi Mittal.

'Mittal says he wants to do a friendly deal,' Dollé told his colleagues. 'He says that he was forced to move early because there had been a leak.'

'Did he reveal the bid details?' Urquijo asked.

'No, and I cannot believe he has the financial ability to make an all-cash bid for Arcelor, and that's what our by-laws stipulate.'

'We urgently need to check the detail in Article Seven of

the by-laws,' Wurth said, nervously. 'I have no precise recollection.'

In late December 2005 Michel Wurth had been appointed deputy to Dollé under a series of changes that streamlined the directorate general. Dollé cut the DG from eight to four men – himself, Wurth, Gonzalo Urquijo, who was appointed chief financial officer, and Roland Junck, another lifelong Luxembourg steelman.

As a Luxembourger, Wurth came from an establishment family and was an influential figure locally. He joined Arbed after qualifying as an accountant and worked his way through the ranks, becoming chief financial officer in 2002 when he took on the task of trying to raise Arcelor's share price as part of a broader image-building exercise to create greater awareness and a better understanding of the steps that the company was taking to transform itself. If he could spread the good news share prices would go up, and a robustly healthy share price was the best defence there was against takeover.

In April 2005 Wurth had made a presentation to the board. He was accompanied by Brett Olsher, global co-head of industry and natural resources with Deutsche Bank, based in London, a long-standing investment adviser to the company. Olsher, an American, had specialist knowledge of the global steel industry and was a former analyst with JPMorgan Chase. Olsher and his team produced a detailed analysis of the threats to Arcelor and offered potential defence themes. The bottom line was that there was a risk of an industrial predator descending, especially Lakshmi Mittal, even though Dollé kept telling the board that no steel company had €15 billion-plus of ready cash to put on the table. In addition, several private equity houses, which certainly had the cash, had made tentative approaches, scenting an Arcelor recovery. But they had difficulty making the financials work for them.

Arcelor's share price was still sitting at a lowly €13. It had to be pushed to above €20 at least. The board also decided to boost the company's corporate image through a communications blitz, telling shareholders, customers, suppliers and employees of the solid progress they were making following the three-way merger. Arcelor prepared to jazz up the website, freshen up the corporate literature, upgrade presentations to shareholders and staff and, scheduled for February 2006 on the back of stunning financial results in 2005, to go live with a global advertising campaign, extolling the company's achievements.

This was also part of Project Tiger, referred to earlier, run by Wurth and aimed at killing off all lurking predators, especially the ever more likely Lakshmi Mittal. The board was comfortable that Tiger was making progress when in early January Arcelor's share price touched €22, but it still lagged behind what Dollé, Kinsch and others thought was the true worth of the company.

At 10.30 a.m., as the chauffeured cars reached Trier, near the Luxembourg border, Dollé recalled his sixth-month stay studying mathematics and physics at Trier University, one of the oldest in Germany and where Karl Marx had grown up and studied. He had fond memories of the town because it was where he finally qualified as an engineer. Trier was a pretty place, he recalled, an ancient town remarkably untouched by the Second World War, which had flattened so many other German towns and cities.

His recollections were abruptly ended by a call on his mobile. It was Kinsch. 'There will be an emergency board meeting on Sunday,' the chairman said. 'We will need an overview of our options from the DG.'

'I have already called for a DG meeting with all advisers for 11 a.m. tomorrow, Saturday,' Dollé told him. 'I will debrief you immediately afterwards and we can prepare for the board meeting.'

Members of the DG always attended the board meetings, but it irked Dollé that he was not yet formally appointed to the board, especially given his success in integrating the Arcelor merger, making big efficiency gains across the enlarged group, markedly improving site safety and spurring entrepreneurship among the top 350 men and women in the upper echelon of Arcelor's management. It was very unusual for a publicly listed European company with such a global reach not to have the chief executive as a fully fledged member of the board. Deep down, it was felt as a personal affront by the accomplished Frenchman.

Radio RTL, the main Luxembourg station, had already broken the news, reporting that with shares in Arcelor and Mittal still suspended there was intense speculation in the financial trading rooms across

Europe. With RTL's radio and television stations both carrying extended news coverage, one question was being asked – 'What is Mittal Steel?'

Philippe Capron, number two to Urquijo in Luxembourg, soon had the answer. He printed off the Mittal Steel press release and, swiftly taking in the financial highlights, emailed the front page to Urquijo's BlackBerry and then rang his mobile to discuss the detail. The Spaniard listened intently, recounting the key aspects to Dollé and Wurth.

'It's not a full-cash offer,' Dollé scoffed. 'It will never fly.' But as the Arcelor party neared Luxembourg City the anger and hostility were welling up inside him. He, more than anyone, had always suspected that one day Lakshmi Mittal might try and do a deal with Arcelor, but the immediacy of his aggressive move hit home hard. News of the Dofasco side deal with Thyssen was particularly painful and unnerving. He quickly began to recount the conversation at Lakshmi's house two weeks before, when Lakshmi encouraged him to raise his bid for Dofasco. Now he knew why: he was convinced that Lakshmi had already been plotting against him. By forcing Arcelor to bid higher, Mittal was giving himself room to negotiate with Thyssen. He could sell Dofasco to the Germans at $C68 – which was what Thyssen was prepared to pay in the first place, so he knew he had a deal in the bag at that price. He would also pocket the difference between what Thyssen could pay and what Arcelor had paid for Dofasco, thus boosting his campaign funds for taking over his Luxembourg rival. But you could never absolutely tell what was going on in Lakshmi Mittal's mind.

The share suspensions were lifted shortly after 11 a.m. Dealings in Arcelor on the European exchanges were frenetic. The night before (26 January), Arcelor's share price had closed at €22 on the Luxembourg, Paris and Madrid exchanges. In Amsterdam, Mittal Steel closed at €27 (equivalent to $32 on the New York market, where Mittal was also listed). Now Arcelor's shares soared in seconds to €30, more than 8 per cent above the value of Mittal's bid, which itself was a 27 per cent increase on Thursday's closing publicly available market price on the Paris stock exchange before Mittal Steel announced its intended offer for Arcelor. Savvy institutional shareholders, who a year earlier had bought shares in Arcelor at between

€13 and €15, sensing the recovery story, could not resist the immediate desire to cash in and double their money. In fast and furious
trading on the Paris stock exchange, where Arcelor was most actively
traded, more than 70 million publicly traded shares out of 600 million in issue changed hands in the first two hours after trading
resumed – almost 12 per cent of the total issued stock.

Normally, after formally announcing his intentions, a hostile
bidder will enter the market to acquire shares in the target in order
to secure a strategic base – often between 10 and 20 per cent – and
to demonstrate its commitment. Mittal decided not to take that step
for one very good reason. He would have to commit to a full-cash
alternative under Arcelor by-laws and, financially, that was more
than challenging.

In the Arcelor–Mittal trading blitz other types of investor now came
over the hill: the hedge funds. These are global investors with billions of pounds of investments at their disposal and privately
managed by smart former investment bankers who can deliver sus-
tained superior returns for their clients, often above 20 per cent a
year, unlike the more pedestrian fund managers who feel good if
they make 10 per cent. The hedge funds take bigger risks with
bigger amounts of investment. They often supplement money they
attract from investors with money borrowed from banks so as to
leverage their positions for massive short-term gain. The investment positions they take are big, gambling between €200 and €500
million a deal. Brash and ballsy, they use very sophisticated computer analysis to track their investments in a wide range of asset
classes; their fund managers are skilled at using a variety of tech-
niques to 'hedge' their investment strategy in a company's shares.
Often, they do not hedge, but take strong views as to where markets are heading, then bet on their judgement, just like George
Soros, the Hungarian-born American financial speculator who
famously made billions on the demise of sterling in the currency
markets in 1992.

Hedge funds can also become substantial owners of a company
that they believe will perform well in the future. In other instances
they buy into a company that is not doing well and use their influence to force management to make changes in strategy or assist their

removal. These types of hedge funds are known as 'activists'. The Germans prefer to call them 'locusts'.

One widely accepted market method, used by all hedge fund managers, involves borrowing shares in a company from an existing institutional owner for a small premium over the prevailing share price, a process called 'stock-lending'. The ownership rights transfer across to the borrower; these include the voting rights at shareholder meetings, which allow the hedge funds to influence bid outcomes because of the big blocks of shares they temporarily own in the target company. Another method is one in which an investor takes out a 'contract for differences', a financial instrument that enables him or her to speculate in a company's shares without having the underlying ownership. Hedge funds provide big revenues for the investment banks with whom they deal in these instruments. Like any business, the banks tend to look after their big customers, offering them preferential deals or other favours. Critics see this as incestuous. They are right!

Just like locusts, the hedge funds were now hunting for every Arcelor share they could devour. They could see the logic of the deal and they quickly spotted that the financial markets liked it too. More importantly, they also sensed that Mittal would have to bid higher, especially if there could be a counter-bid by a third party, such as another steel company, eager to join the consolidation game. But most of all the hedge funds smelt whopping profits, to be delivered probably in a matter of weeks if, as they suspected, the Arcelor share price continued to move up. They knew also that Arcelor would put up a strong defence, which could work in two ways: it could force the bidder to raise his bid, maximising shareholder value. Or, not such good news for hedge funds, Arcelor might invoke a 'poison pill' defence to stave off a bid. One poison-pill defence would be, for example, the decision on Arcelor's part to issue new shares to the Luxembourg government to ensure it had a 30 per cent blocking stake in the company. This would be seen by all investors and particularly by the hedge funds as deliberately obstructionist and anti-market, which would immediately send the shares crashing, meaning big losses for the speculators.

Saturday 28 January

Berkeley Square House

Tracking the message, making sure it was getting to the right people in the right places, was almost as important as the message itself. Philip Gawith of the Maitland Group had joined Nicola Davidson to review the early press coverage of Lakshmi Mittal's offer. While the bankers and lawyers caught up with their sleep, Davidson and Gawith pored happily over the column inches.

'In all the deals I have been involved with, I don't ever recall such positive coverage as this,' said Gawith, the bluff South African not famous for peppering his observations with superlatives. Tall, balding and brooding, Gawith had spent eight years on the *Financial Times* including two on the Lex column before jumping ship to the international PR outfit run by Angus Maitland. '"This is a beautiful deal – a stroke of genius,"' Gawith said, reading aloud the words of Tommy Taccone at the US consultancy First River. '"The investment community likes the strategy of the deal, which is not something to be taken for granted."'

'The *Wall Street Journal* has a great quote from Peter Marcus,' said Davidson. 'He says: "Mittal would be in a position to create and have an influence on the industry environment which is beneficial both to them and their competitors."' Marcus was a leading steel analyst who headed up World Steel Dynamics, an organisation based in Englewood Cliffs, New Jersey, five minutes from the George Washington Bridge, which was hugely influential in the industry. WSD described itself as a 'strategic information service, providing critical and new perspectives of possible and probable steel industry developments'. WSD organised the world's biggest international steel conference, for which all steelmen, particularly Lakshmi Mittal and Guy Dollé, and their bankers, blanked out their diaries. For Mittal to have the combative and always critical Marcus tucked safely in the deal's fan club so early on was a big coup.

The UK press, meanwhile, was picking up on all the Mittal messages put out by the deal team in the press release and at the offer-launch press conference. Aditya had already given an interview to *The Times*, around which the paper had built its story with the headline 'Mittal to Target $1 Billion of Savings without Closures'. 'The benefits of the Arcelor deal would come from purchasing strength,' it went on, 'not job cuts.' There would be no plant closures beyond anything that Arcelor was already committed to. Nicola Davidson could have written the story herself.

But Mittal's communications team was not bowled over. 'Remember,' Gawith counselled, 'this is just day two, week one.' He pointed out two columns in the *Guardian* and the *Daily Telegraph*. They were lukewarm about Mittal's governance arrangements. Would Arcelor shareholders really want to hold shares in a company they did not control? they asked.

Saturday 28 January

Arcelor headquarters, 19 Avenue de la Liberté, Luxembourg City

From the outside, the headquarters of Arcelor resembled a grand French chateau, with its high, pointed, blue-slate mansard roof and classic sculptured stone façade. The only things missing were the sweeping lawns and the moat. At night under floodlight, the building took on a more magisterial look. Built in 1920 with thickly cut, beige-coloured stone from Comblanchien and Savonnières, normally reserved for cathedrals, the chateau was a symbol of solidity and power. Above the main entrance dramatic sculptures depicted the noble triumph of science, industry and trade.

It was a different picture inside the building. Here everything was chaos. Staff with stern faces scurried through the wide, high-ceilinged corridors. At the reception desk, staff were increasingly stretched by the security-badge process as the queue of arrivals showed no sign of shortening. These were the investment bank and the law and accountancy people, the public relations consultants, all desperate to get a mandate to join Arcelor's defence team as advisers. They were behaving like gold prospectors. The waiting room, just to the right of the reception desk, was brimful of unfamiliar faces expecting to be escorted to one of the many meeting rooms. The telephone lines were hot as the media and the financial markets scrambled to get clarification of how Arcelor was going to respond to Lakshmi Mittal's offer.

The DG was already in conference and Gonzalo Urquijo had some bad news for Guy Dollé. 'Michel and I have checked the by-laws, particularly Article Seven. It's not as we thought,' the Spaniard revealed.

'What *is* the situation, then?' Dollé demanded.

'Anyone who bids outright for the whole of the company's shares does not have to make a full offer in cash,' Urquijo told him.

Dollé looked as though he had been punched hard and low in the stomach. A surging anger brought him back up to his full height. 'How is it that I can't get decent advice in this place?'

By 9.30 a.m. a line had formed at the Arcelor main entrance, stretching back twenty yards to the pavement. These were mostly the appointed advisers, waiting to register. In the queue were also two lawyers from the top US firm Skadden, Arps, Slate, Meagher & Flom, appointed by Arcelor the day before as the main legal advisers in the fight against Mittal. Heading up the team was lead counsel Pierre Servan-Schreiber, a partner in Skadden's Paris office, located in the fashionable rue du Faubourg Saint-Honoré, opposite the Élysée Palace. Servan-Schreiber, a combative former French cavalry officer with a penchant for exotic touring and off-road motorbikes, was accompanied by his right-hand man Scott Simpson, whose five-feet-two-inch frame belied one of the best hired guns in international takeover battles. Simpson, a pugnacious American, headed Skadden's London office. In terms of creative defences the two of them were the hottest legal team around.

As they collected their security badges, Servan-Schreiber, every inch living up to his top-drawer billing, looked at the flustered staff trying to deal with the impatient crowd milling around the reception desk and grinned. 'Looks like a beehive that's been run over by a truck,' he remarked to Simpson. But the Skadden pair were astonished to find themselves shepherded like lowly paralegals to an attic room on the furthest reaches of the top floor.

'Hell, this is a shack,' Servan-Schreiber said, gazing around the attic. 'They may do steel better than anyone else, but we do takeover defences like no one else and they are going to have to realise that we need to be physically in the centre of this thing.'

'Once we are around the table with them, they will get the message,' Simpson said earnestly.

The Skadden duo were now joined by Philippe Hoss, a tall Luxembourger with precise and polite manners, who was Arcelor's local external legal adviser. He worked as a partner for Elvinger, Hoss & Prussen, one of Luxembourg's top corporate law firms, based in a smart cream-walled townhouse in the city centre. This was exciting new ground for him.

At 11 a.m. the three lawyers were called to a meeting of all advisers. In the room was Brett Olsher from Deutsche Bank and Marc Pandraud, the jovial, seasoned head of the Paris office of Merrill Lynch, two of Arcelor's longest-serving strategic investment advisers. New to the team was Christophe Moulin from BNP Paribas's corporate finance unit in Paris. Thanks to the tenacity of BNP's chairman Michel Pébereau, who had relentlessly pursued Kinsch over the previous twenty-four hours, BNP had won a seat at the lucrative advisory table at the expense of its fierce French rival Société Générale, another long-standing Arcelor adviser. The appointment caused considerable mirth in the bitchy Parisian banking community, especially since Daniel Bouton, chairman and CEO of Société Générale, had up to eighteen months previously served on the Arcelor board as one of the main independent non-executives. What added more spice to the BNP appointment was that, seven years before, the two French banks had fought a fierce battle in which Société Générale had fought off a predatory attack by BNP. As Moulin settled into his seat, Bouton was back in Paris, still waiting for the call from Kinsch.

Representing the Arcelor internal team was Belgian lawyer Frederik Van Bladel, a former chief executive at the Sidmar plant in Ghent, and with him were the Project Tiger team including Wurth, Urquijo and a support group comprising Philippe Capron and Rémi Boyer, a young Frenchman pulled in from human resources to sort out the administrative chaos.

At 11.15 Guy Dollé swept into the room. His mood was black. He still could not fathom how the legal advice on a full-cash-offer takeover had been so wrong. He skipped all pleasantries and started jabbing his finger around the room, but especially at Michel Wurth. 'What the hell has the Project Tiger team been doing all this time? Whoever is responsible for this will pay for it,' Dollé snarled.

Then he spotted Servan-Schreiber. 'Who are you?' he said.

'I am Pierre Servan-Schreiber from Skadden, Arps in Paris and this is my London colleague Scott Simpson. We, Mr Dollé, are your lead counsel.'

'Whatever you advise, make sure you get it clear, concise and right first time. I don't want to be informed that legal advice is changing.'

Simpson and Servan-Schreiber tried to look smart, focused and in control, but the remainder of the meeting was chaotic and unstructured. People kept leaving the room and then re-entering. Endless cross-talk, mobile phones ringing constantly and the clatter of coffee cups all added to the symphony of discord. To Servan-Schreiber there appeared to be no central chain of command.

'One of the things you need to do in any takeover defence is to slow the bid process down,' he explained.

'Slow it down?' Dollé snapped. 'I want this bid stopped in its tracks right now.'

'We will play for time while we figure out a way to shut down the Mittal bid,' Servan-Schreiber added quickly. God, this guy is jumpy, he thought.

Servan-Schreiber could see a complex and ever-changing legal environment. There were five different European regulators who would have a say in the Mittals' takeover bid: Luxembourg's CSSF, the AMF in France, Spain's CNMV and the CBFA in Belgium. Each asserted jurisdiction on the takeover but deferred to Luxembourg on basic corporate law. On the Mittal Steel side there was AFM in the Netherlands for the Euronext Amsterdam exchange and then in the USA the Securities Exchange Commission. In all, six sets of regulators, all of whom would have to be consulted to ensure that Mittal's formal offer documentation – in the form of a 515-page prospectus comprising the rationale of the bid, the potential risks and a substantial amount of financial information on both companies – was acceptable. Each one would also have to include local regulations in the respective local language. The Dutch AFM had the authority to clear the prospectus under a new harmonised EU law. Once cleared, it would be 'passported' into the other jurisdictions.

This would be preceded by weeks of consultation with lawyers in each country. Mittal Steel had elected to extend its offer for Arcelor into the USA, where a high percentage of the shares were owned by US institutional investors. Completing the regulatory landscape were the EU competition authority in Brussels and the anti-trust regulators in Washington, the Department of Justice (DOJ) and the Foreign Trade Commission (FTC) as well as the Canadian Competition Bureau, all of whom would have to make judgements as to whether the bid in any way contravened local competition policies. The timing of the EU decision would be critical. If Mittal's bid passed muster quickly then the competition authority would give the go-ahead within a month. If there were more serious competition issues, it could take up to three months. In the USA the process faced even more complex issues since there were two regulators with different remits.

Every Arcelor shareholder would also receive the prospectus. It could take a week for any serious-minded investor to plough through the fine print.

'There is also the question of anti-trust scrutiny, both in Europe and the USA, where Mittal and Arcelor operations overlap,' Scott Simpson continued. Anti-trust legislation in the States and competition law in Europe are designed to prevent mergers and acquisitions that lead to monopoly, cartels and predatory pricing. 'We can play regulatory arbitrage, because of the different regulatory schemes.' Regulatory arbitrage was a favourite piece of Simpson jargon. It was a game where every legal trick in the book was played in order to stall and play one legal system off against another while the bidder got more and more frustrated.

Servan-Schreiber then raised the question of the geographical overlap between the two companies and competition policy issues. The banking advisers looked across at each other. These hotshot lawyers cannot have done their homework, Van Bladel thought. 'Despite the fact that Mittal and Arcelor rank number one and two in the world, they do not overlap geographically,' he informed them politely. 'There is only one overlap and it is not a significant one. It's our acquisition of Dofasco. Other than that, Arcelor does not see any substantive anti-trust issues.'

Van Bladel steered the discussion to other possible defence themes. First, Arcelor had the power in its by-laws to issue a lot more shares, up to 30 per cent of the value of the company, without recourse to its shareholders. This potentially powerful tool, which would not be permitted in an Anglo-Saxon context, could be used to head off an attacker by ensuring these newly minted shares were placed in friendly hands. This would enable Arcelor to create a powerful blocking vote. Second, the new takeover law, complying with the EU directive enforcing harmonised rules across the member states, had to be on the Luxembourg government's statute book by May. This meant that the Mittal Steel bid would fall within its jurisdiction. If Arcelor could successfully influence the makeup of the law with protectionist poison-pill wording it would stop Mittal in his tracks. Third, the weakest link in Lakshmi Mittal's offer was the governance of his company. Even though he had reduced his family's shareholding and voting power there were still relatively few shares to be bought on the Amsterdam and New York stock exchanges. His shares were illiquid, a term used to describe a company that had a publicly traded float of shares amounting to less than 25 per cent of its market value for at least twelve months. If so few shares were available their marketability was uncertain, and they were prone to volatility in value. Hence the universal ruling by the regulators that in any offer combining illiquid shares and cash, the bidder had to provide an all-cash alternative to his bid to compensate.

Arcelor quickly wised up to the fact that if the new Luxembourg takeover law encompassed such a stipulation it would be game over for Mittal. Despite his ability to leverage debt-financing, a full cash offer was beyond his reach. But Servan-Schreiber warned them: 'You cannot take any measure that would automatically prevent Mittal's offer from proceeding.' Anti-market poison pills, like sudden massive share issues, designed just to scupper a deal irrespective of what the market and investors wanted, were out of the question. But Serban-Schreiber had put heavy stress on the word 'automatically'. Being bloody awkward to stop Mittal getting Arcelor for a song was something else altogether.

There were other defence tactics to consider, including the search for a potential white knight who could counter-bid, or a white squire to make Arcelor Mittal-proof. Arcelor already had many connections with big steel companies in China, Japan, Russia, Brazil and throughout Europe who would want to thwart Mittal, while taking advantage of consolidation. The only problem for Arcelor was that they would be regarded as negotiating from a position of weakness and potential partners would be aware of their leverage. The other issue was keeping such talks confidential; the steel industry was a small, leaky universe, as Guy Dollé and Lakshmi Mittal knew well.

Of course, there was another alternative, which only one person in the room had spotted. 'We should at least look at the merits of the proposed Mittal Steel offer,' Philippe Capron said. Servan-Schreiber thought for a moment that Guy Dollé was going to implode.

'I pay you to shut up,' Dollé told Capron.

Capron, a former chief financial officer of Usinor, had been top of his class when he emerged from the École Nationale d'Administration, France's elite school of learning and the breeding ground for many of the country's political leaders and top civil servants. Heavy-set and none too diplomatic, Capron was witty and held right-wing views. When somebody told him he was a right-wing anarchist, he replied, rapier-like: 'As I strive to be.' But not all Capron's colleagues admired his undoubted intelligence as much as he himself did. 'Philippe is too clever, he is too French, he's too everything,' said one.

As the meeting began to break up, Servan-Schreiber, Simpson, Hoss and Van Bladel retreated upstairs to the attic room. 'We need a calendar because we need to know the time frame we are going to be operating in,' Van Bladel said.

'This is going to be a very complex battle,' Servan-Schreiber replied. 'It's difficult to gauge, with six regulators in the frame, a lot of moving parts and our strategy of buying time.' As he sketched an outline timetable he pencilled in 28 June as the end game, exactly five months away.

'Your regulatory arbitrage point is the best thing to emerge from our meeting,' Van Bladel said. 'I really feel we can take advantage of that. If we can figure out a way to break the agreement between Mittal Steel and Thyssen, then there is at least a big regulatory problem for Mittal in the USA because of his existing dominant domestic position in steel production.'

The lawyers sensed an intriguing new plot line. 'If he is unable to offload Dofasco to Thyssen it would deprive him immediately of $4 billion to finance his cash component in the Arcelor offer,' Servan-Schreiber said. 'And he would be forced to sell other assets in the USA to comply with the Department of Justice's competition rules, which would take time.'

'It might make him just withdraw,' Van Bladel said wishfully. Everybody else shook their heads.

'Frederik,' Scott Simpson said, clearing his throat, 'if you really want to block the sale of Dofasco to Thyssen, I think I have a way to do it.'

Van Bladel suddenly looked a whole lot happier.

'Just give me a week,' Simpson said.

Pierre Servan-Schreiber knew exactly what Simpson was hatching. He smiled. They had been this way before.

After the meeting Dollé flew by private plane to Paris with Alain Davezac and Philippe Capron. Thierry Breton had summoned him to a meeting at his private residence. En route Dollé reread the six-page brief he had prepared for the minister. He was also preparing himself for a dressing-down.

'I have to confess, Minister,' Dollé began as Breton served soft drinks and cookies, 'I made a mistake in believing that Mittal Steel would not be able to acquire Arcelor without having to make an all-cash bid, which, financially, we believed would be beyond him.'

'What?' Breton fumed. 'But you told me when we spoke on the phone on Friday that that was the case.'

'I was misinformed by our legal team,' Dollé said. 'The truth is that the Arcelor by-laws do not prevent him from making a cash-and-shares offer. There is a proviso that if a company acquires more than 30 per cent on a creeping basis, then it has to make a cash offer. An offer to buy all the shares in one go, as Mittal proposes, is not covered.'

'How can this be?' Breton exclaimed. 'How can you have put us in such a situation?'

'I was wrongly advised, I regret to say.'

'So what are you going to do about it?' Breton asked.

Dollé rattled off plans for an aggressive defence strategy, then added, 'We need the full support of the French government, and the establishment, to create a political storm.'

Breton had already talked to his counterpart Jeannot Krecké in Luxembourg. Although Arcelor was not a French company, the government having sold off all its shares, Breton felt that it still was psychologically. With thirty thousand Arcelor employees working in Lorraine, he had no fear about expressing a sense of Gallic outrage to Krecké.

Breton took Dollé's crib sheet. 'I am meeting Lakshmi Mittal at 9 a.m. on Monday. I intend to be very firm with him.'

11

Sunday 29 January, 2.30 p.m.

19 Avenue de la Liberté

The cigar smoke wafted across the large anteroom as members of Arcelor's board and the DG gathered for coffee and *digestifs* after the usual sumptuous lunch in one of the elegant dining rooms on the second floor. It was well known that Arcelor had the best dining table in the steel industry. Staff joked that the wine cellar was worth more than the entire company. Unlike Mittal Steel, where Aditya Mittal might eat a fruit salad at his desk, Arcelor was a company that lunched the proper way. Every meal, served discreetly by the waiting staff, began with the finest champagne and finished with a visit to the humidor.

The main boardroom adjoined the office of Joseph Kinsch at the end of a long corridor and was a resplendent reminder of a bygone era. A magnificently crafted chandelier hung from the ornate ceiling over the centre of the immensely long mahogany table, around which were placed forty-three antique armchairs, a microphone in front of every one. Heavy sculptured wall lights and mottled brown marble pillars dominated each end of the room, which over the decades had witnessed the steel barons of the day ranging over both the big strategic issues and more mundane matters like pricing, tariffs, quotas, labour rates and raw material costs.

Dark, life-size oil portraits of the great men of Arbed adorned the walls, including Émile Mayrisch with his Santa Claus beard and penetrating blue eyes, gazing down expectantly as Joseph Kinsch had presided at noon that day with his usual consummate skill over a crisis meeting of Arcelor's directors – an eclectic mix of Europeans and a Brazilian together with the four DG members, two secretaries who kept the minutes, and translators from Spanish, Portuguese and German.

Kinsch had a seat in the middle of the table. To his immediate left sat Prince Guillaume of Luxembourg, brother of the Grand Duke Henri and representing the Grand Duchy's interests. He barely spoke at any meeting. Further left around the table were a galaxy of European corporate heavyweights, including Ulrich Hartmann of the German energy group E.on, and Noël Forgeard, a director of EADS, the French defence group which had a big stake in Airbus. Representing Spanish interests were José Ramón Álvarez Rendueles, who was deputy to Kinsch, Ramón Hermosilla Martín, a Madrid-based lawyer who acted for the Aristrain family, one of the founders of Aceralia and an Arcelor shareholder with 3.6 per cent stake. The only non-European was Sergio Silva de Freitas, former vice president of Banco Itaú in São Paulo, who was there for a Brazilian view, given Arcelor's strong presence in that country. To the immediate right of Kinsch, a secretary sat taking the minutes. Down the line sat trade union representative Manuel Fernández López of the Spanish union UGT, and the Spanish businessman Francisco Javier de la Riva Garriga, vice president of Fertiberia, a chemicals conglomerate. Then came Belgian industrialist Hedwig de Koker, chairman of Van der Veken Vastgoed, representing Flemish business interests, followed by Jean-Yves Durance, chairman of Marsh France, the international insurance broker. For Luxembourg there was Georges Schmit, a top civil servant from the Ministry of Economy and Foreign Trade and, representing the trade union OGB-L, John Castegnaro, who was also a Socialist Party MP from the steel region of the south. Edmond Pachura, president of the French steel products trading group UNAS, sat next to him.

Dollé was sitting directly opposite Kinsch and flanked by the other members of the DG. The seating was completed with two Frenchmen and a Belgian. They were Daniel Melin, a director of EDS, Michel Marti, former secretary general of the CFDT trade union in France, and Jean-Pierre Hansen, a director of Electrabel, the Belgian energy group which is part of the all-powerful French energy conglomerate Suez.

The Arcelor board was renowned for its tranquillity. Kinsch and Dollé did all the spadework in advance and the board by and large rubber-stamped their decisions. But today they were all in shock.

'This is war,' John Castegnaro declared. 'We must fight this bid to the last drop of blood.'

The board was unanimous in rejecting Lakshmi Mittal. Kinsch understandably felt good, the entire board behind him. In a press statement issued shortly after the meeting, Arcelor declared defiantly: 'The two companies do not share the same strategic vision, business plan or values. [The move] will have severe consequences on the group, its shareholders, employees and customers. We urge all shareholders to take no action.'

After lunch, as Guy Dollé drove out of the rear courtyard of the Arcelor chateau to catch a plane back to Paris he was caught by the hovering local press. He opened his window and said, 'The Mittal Steel offer is 150 per cent hostile. We will fight it and win.'

3 p.m.

Ministry of Economy and Foreign Trade, Luxembourg City

Unusually for a Sunday afternoon, Jeannot Krecké, Minister of Economy and Foreign Trade in the Luxembourg government, was at his desk on the top floor of an uninspiring 1970s prefabricated concrete office block on the Boulevard Royal, one block away from the capital's main shopping square and al fresco cafés. In this tiny prosperous capital there was deep unease in political circles because of Lakshmi Mittal's bid for the Grand Duchy's crown jewel. It was equally disturbing news for ordinary citizens, the voters, of whom the country's five thousand steelworkers, mainly located in the south, their families, their communities and all the companies that supplied and serviced the steel plants, were a significant lobby that could not be dismissed by the politicians.

Mittal had called Krecké the morning the bid had been announced.

'Frankly, I am a little bit surprised that you didn't give us any indication of this,' Krecké told him, with more than a hint of under-statement.

Mittal explained that he had had to move earlier than planned because of a leak.

'Well, this is not the way we normally handle things like this,' Krecké said.

'But this is a good story for Luxembourg, a good story for the company,' Mittal said.

Krecké wasn't enjoying the story any more than when he had heard it the first time. He had just finished a tense satellite phone call with his Prime Minister Jean-Claude Juncker, who was returning hurriedly from a government-aid mission to Mali and Niger to deal with the crisis that had erupted at home. 'Mittal must be stopped,' the Prime Minister had said simply.

Krecké's cabinet colleague Luc Frieden, the forty-three-year-old budget minister who also doubled as Minister of Justice, had joined Krecké in his office for an important drafting session. There was one agenda item: how should the government respond formally to the Mittal bid?

Krecké knew it was a critical moment for his country and also for his career, because the four hundred and fifty thousand Luxembourgers as well as the political and financial world would be watching his every move. He felt vulnerable on three counts. First, Luxembourg was the legal domicile for Arcelor. If Mittal were to win, Krecké must ensure that the Arcelor headquarters remain in the Grand Duchy: for political reasons, through the preservation of jobs and both direct and indirect investment around the domestic steel industry; for reputational reasons, in keeping a global champion listed on the country's stock exchange, thereby underpinning Luxembourg as a financial centre; and, more cynically, for the millions which the government obtained through the withholding taxes on the dividends paid out to Arcelor's widely held register of domestic and international shareholders. Mittal Steel's legal domicile was in neighbouring Rotterdam, where multinational corporations also enjoyed generous tax breaks. Krecké reckoned it was going to be tough to negotiate the switch.

Second, both Krecké and Frieden knew that if they bungled the assignment through brazen discriminatory tactics against Mittal they

would incur the wrath of the EU competition directorate, led by
Commissioner Neelie Kroes. Luxembourg's reputation was also on
the line with the international financial community, which detested
any kind of governmental intervention in the private sector. The two
ministers knew they could not put the country's reputation at risk for
fear of upsetting international investors and financial service firms,
which could cut off vast capital inflows to the country in a fit of
angst.

Third, the government had been having detailed discussions with
Arcelor over future investment plans for the steel plants in the country and about preserving jobs. Over the years Arcelor had grown
internationally, and it employed more workers overseas than at
home. Additionally, Arcelor's board of directors, always in a
love–hate relationship with the Luxembourg government, had committed to investing over €100 million over the next five years to
update technology at the steel plants and to maintain jobs. Arcelor
believed that its five-year plan would keep the government off its
back, but the relationship was about to be stress-tested even more
than during the abyss years of 1970–80.

Krecké's office was a roomy L-shaped space. At one end, facing
the door, were an ordinary-looking desk stacked with government
papers and a side table holding his computer terminal. A four-seater
black leather sofa and two matching chairs, set around a low glass
coffee table, occupied the centre of the office. Along the back wall to
his desk were shelves of government and EU reference books. At
the far end of the room was a large conference table with eight black
leather chairs, looking out through large framed windows on to a
myriad of rooftops. Around the side wall were pictures of a fifty-
metre sailing yacht, Krecké's favourite toy, on which he enjoyed the
waters of the Mediterranean.

The socialist Krecké, a fifty-six-year-old former schoolteacher with
strong trade union links, felt at the peak of his career. He had worked
his way up the political ladder, faithfully espousing the hard-won
industrial and social working model which characterised the country's
ethos and which was enshrined in its constitution. It was here that
labour unions, management and government worked as equal-ranking
stakeholders. The Anglo-Saxon maxim of preferential treatment for
shareholders was total anathema to the Grand Duchy.

All Luxembourg ministers had dual portfolios. Krecké was also sports minister, a role he enjoyed, given his former career as a professional footballer who had made it to the Luxembourg national team. In spite of his relatively expensive sailing hobby Krecké still regarded himself as a man of the people. He enjoyed popularity not only at home, but also in Brussels, where his wry sense of humour and convivial nature had enabled him to engage successfully with the highly diverse political and economic community. There was always advantage in being a small country's minister in a big political pond like the EU. Luxembourg had played its cards well and, like the Republic of Ireland, had benefited disproportionately to bigger nations in the Community. Krecké was a master at exploiting this while retaining comradely access to his counterparts in the other member states

But thanks to Lakshmi Mittal, he now nursed a deep fear. The minister's popularity ratings were on the line. But there was a bigger concern: if he mishandled his role this time he could also become the scapegoat for the Prime Minister. Politics is a dirty business, he reminded himself.

Luc Frieden was a Harvard- and Cambridge-educated lawyer with impeccable credentials. Slim, bespectacled and pinch-faced, he could have been mistaken for a serious-minded accountant. His dual portfolio combined the justice ministry with that of treasury budget, which, day to day, put him closer to Prime Minister Juncker, who doubled as finance minister. Frieden was fiercely ambitious and coveted the premiership, nurturing his personal profile skilfully in the local media. Politically, he came from the Christian Democratic Party wing, which dominated the coalition with the Socialist Party in Luxembourg's Chamber of Deputies.

Krecké and Frieden didn't have long. The government's formal statement had to be emailed at 4 p.m. to the news wires and the print and broadcast media in order to secure publication and broadcast coverage the next morning. They kept it short and carefully worded, with no trace of emotion or hint of potential state discrimination. It ran to just four paragraphs and was meant as a holding statement to win time, but there is no doubting the underlying message.

The Luxembourg government has 'strong concerns about the

hostile nature of the bid by Mittal Steel', it began. 'In the absence of a preliminary dialogue, the current project lacks commitments, concerning notably the role of the Luxembourg state, maintaining the main headquarters of the steel group in Luxembourg, as well as respecting commitments made by Arcelor in the area of jobs and investments in Luxembourg.' In other words Luxembourg, as the single largest shareholder in Arcelor with its deep-rooted social model, was deeply offended by the lack of any prior consultation by Mittal. But the statement also demonstrated how European governments caught in the slipstream of globalisation failed to understand the raw capitalism of hostile mergers and takeovers. In the brutal Anglo-Saxon business world, could Mittal have consulted privately before launching its bid? It had been leaked more than once. The whole dynamic of Mittal's audacious bid would have been engulfed in political meddling, the momentum would have been lost, and Arcelor would have had infinite time to marshal its defence.

This is why Mittal went hostile, Krecké told himself, but he was determined to unnerve the Indian.

Krecké was now joined by his eager press attaché Luc Decker, a tall, well scrubbed, youthful-looking twenty-nine-year-old who swam butterfly for Luxembourg at the Sydney Olympics and was in his first ministerial advisory post. They spoke in French. The statement was to be issued in French, the language of government, but also translated into English for distribution to the media globally.

'We have to give a clearer indication of what our options are as a government and as the single largest shareholder in Arcelor,' Decker said patriotically.

'We have to be careful not to make the PM a hostage to fortune before his speech to the Chamber of Deputies this Tuesday,' Krecké told him.

'Understood, Minister, but we cannot look weak and woolly in the face of our people, the media and Mittal.'

'We are constrained in what we can say because of the EU's competition regulatory framework,' Frieden explained, wearing his legal hat. 'We can only address this issue as the single largest shareholder of Arcelor, not as the government wishing to intervene over an asset which is not wholly owned by us. The EU is making us adopt a new, harmonised pan-Europe takeover law in line with the principles of an open, transparent marketplace. That law has to be on our statute books in Luxembourg by the end of May.'

It would be Frieden's job to draft the new law. 'The irony is that the Mittal Steel bid will be in full swing during this period. Arcelor, for their own vested reasons, will want us to delay, because they can drive a coach and horses full of poison pills through the current law, such as it is. We must comply with Brussels. This is going to be tricky for us to manage.'

'Luxembourg, then, is caught between a rock and a hard place,' Decker exclaimed.

Krecké and Frieden glanced at each other in agreement.

'Luc, you have to understand. We have to play the game long,' Krecké assured Decker. 'This is a battle that will run for months. We must keep our powder dry, but let me be clear to you: our intention is to use all means at our disposal to influence the outcome in favour of Luxembourg.'

By 3.30 p.m. Krecké's statement was in its final draft: 'To date, Arcelor's industrial and social model has completely satisfied the Luxembourg government. The government will use all means at its disposal to ensure that, while respecting European law, the industrial, social and financial interests of the Grand Duchy, as the host country and as a strategic shareholder in Arcelor, are maintained,' it concluded.

They then emailed it to Juncker for approval. It was returned within five minutes. 'Excellent,' said the Prime Minister. 'Proceed.'

Project Louise, the government's codename for the defence of Luxembourg's interests in the battle with Mittal, was off the launch pad. Mittal was codenamed Marc, Arcelor, André; and the Grand Duchy was David. The news was out by 4 p.m. Within minutes Luc Decker was being swamped with media calls seeking clarification on the use of the phrase 'by all means at its disposal'.

4.30 p.m.

18–19 Kensington Palace Gardens, London

With Project Olympus already in orbit, Lakshmi Mittal was enjoying some time with his family before embarking on a rigorous diplomatic round of European capitals to explain his bid to government ministers in France, Belgium, Spain and Luxembourg and to the regional media.

His phone rang. It was Sudhir Maheshwari. 'The Luxembourg government has just put out a brief statement, and posted it on their website,' he said. 'As you would expect, their response is critical of our approach. They are offended by us not consulting them in advance. There is also in the statement code for a robust defence of Arcelor.'

'Please read me the full statement,' Mittal asked. He listened intently as Maheshwari read it out to him and then said, 'Please have this emailed now to the senior management and itemise it for discussion with project advisers in the morning conference call tomorrow.'

Mittal consulted his schedule for the week and decided to prioritise a call to Krecké. There would be many conversations between them, two of which would be face-to-face encounters in secret.

133 Avenue des Champs Élysées, Paris

Guy Dollé arrived in the early evening of the 29th at the big glass-fronted offices of Publicis, one of France's premier advertising and communications consultancies, overlooking the Arc de Triomphe. Led by the legendary Maurice Lévy, known as 'the Napoleon of advertising', Publicis had an international network of 251 offices in eighty-two countries, including Saatchi & Saatchi, competing with other communications giants such as Omnicom of the USA and WPP of the UK. Its nine thousand staff serviced a client roll-call of global capitalism, advising the likes of Heinz, Samsung, Sony, L'Oréal, Renault and British Airways on advertising, branding, marketing, public relations and event management.

Dollé had called in Jean-Yves Naouri, one of Lévy's key lieutenants, for the Sunday afternoon meeting to prepare Arcelor's
defence. Naouri was external communications adviser to Arcelor,
before which he had been fully immersed with Mer and Dollé on
the privatisation of Usinor and the subsequent merger with Arbed.
Also at the meeting were Patrick Seyler and Martine Hue, Arcelor's
head of investor relations.

'How did the interview go?' Naouri asked Dollé. That afternoon
Naouri had arranged for Dollé to be interviewed by *Le Monde*, who
would publish on Monday. It would be a powerful trailer for the
day, setting the tone for Arcelor's response.

'Very well,' Dollé said, rubbing his hands together and ready to
get down to work for his press conference and analyst presentation
the next day at the Hilton Arc de Triomphe. On the surface, the
camaraderie was strong, but as the meeting evolved Dollé began to
sense that preparations for the campaign were not up to scratch. He
needed a dynamic presentation with key messages and powerful
slides to combat Mittal's Paris conference, which would precede his.
He also needed detailed question-and-answer documents and a
basic fact sheet comparing Arcelor with Mittal. Key interviews had
been planned with other French mainstream daily newspapers and
the broadcast media, but everything else was a total mess. What the
hell had the Project Tiger team been doing all these months? They
should have been able to cover all the issues and the dynamics
involved. Dollé was caught out by the lack of preparation and his
frustration showed.

'Do you suppose that Mittal Steel is as well prepared as we are?'
he asked his colleagues facetiously. Deep down, Dollé did not trust
his communications advisers. It was a world in which he was not
comfortable. It was also a world where he could be his own worst
enemy, as Jean-Yves Naouri was about to discover. The communications team had set to, planning the next day's events with the
media and the Paris financial community and preparing to work
through the night, when Naouri's BlackBerry rang. He had an email.
In return for exclusive access to Dollé, he had insisted that the *Le
Monde* journalist should run his story past him. Now here it was. As
he scrolled down he saw that it was all good stuff, arguing Arcelor's
strength and superiority over Mittal Steel. Then he stopped dead. The

story contained a quote by Dollé referring to Mittal's shares and his cash offer as *monnaie de singe*. That would have to go.

Naouri emailed the journalist and told him to take the phrase out.

In English *monnaie de singe* literally means 'monkey money'. It also means 'funny money' (tainted money) or 'Monopoly money' (ridiculously large but worthless sums). Naouri knew that if any of these definitions was used in connection with the Indian billionaire it would be a public relations disaster for Arcelor.

'You must avoid using the phrase in all further communications,' he told Dollé.

12

Monday 30 January, 8.21 a.m.

Radio Europe 1, Paris

Guy Dollé settled into his headphones at radio station Europe 1, pleased that the French press was swinging its weight behind Arcelor. Later that day *Le Monde* would be running his interview, now cleansed of the offending 'monkey money' quote, but also publishing a strident editorial which said, 'If this raid succeeds, it will bring down one of the rare edifices of industrial Europe, proving that no position is secure any longer in a world of global competition.' Dollé was about to be interviewed on the breakfast show by veteran journalist Jean-Pierre Elkabbach. This was not Elkabbach's normal slot – after all, he was also president of the station – but such was the furore already being caused by Mittal's bid for Arcelor that this man who had interviewed Chirac and made a movie with Mitterrand had decided to bring his gravitas to the debate.

Beyond wired, Dollé was determined to get his big shots in first, while Mittal prepared in the luxury of his suite at the George V before his meeting later that morning with Thierry Breton, in which he would reiterate his offer for Arcelor just as he had in that morning's edition of business daily *Les Échos*.

'Will you accept it?' Elkabbach kicked off.

'The answer is clearly no,' Dollé insisted. 'We explained our position yesterday. The offer is bad for our shareholders, and bad for all other stakeholders in the company – employees, customers – and for the larger community in which we live. Clearly, none of this will change.'

Dollé agreed that there was no geographic overlap between Arcelor and Mittal but he was outraged at those who said that putting the two companies together was the perfect industrial fit. 'There are two categories of steel,' he said, winding up to the line he had rehearsed with Naouri. 'There is premium-quality steel and there is commodity steel. It's like, there's perfume, that Arcelor specialises in, and then there's a sort of eau de cologne, which is Mittal's domain. We sell a little less tonnage, but we sell it at much higher prices because a lot more technology and grey matter goes into each tonne we sell.'

Dollé had delivered it well.

Elkabbach prodded some more. 'And if he sweetens his offer, you'll still say no?'

'There are always limits,' Dollé smiled, 'but the offer he has made to shareholders is a bit ridiculous.' Dollé had heard a rumour that after winning in Ukraine Mittal had had trouble finding the $4.6 billion to finance the deal. He could not raise it from inside Ukraine because the agreement stated that it must be foreign money. That was one of the reasons why in discussion with his bankers he had come up with the idea of offering a lot of paper for Arcelor, which otherwise was way beyond his means.

'Part of Mittal's offer consists, if you'll excuse the expression,' Dollé added, 'of *monnaie de singe*.'

Whether or not Elkabbach was aware of the offensive meaning of this expression, he let it go.

'Funny money,' Dollé continued, 'that is, of shares in the Mittal Steel group of which he controls ninety-eight per cent of the voting rights and whose share performance since its flotation has been mediocre. In the last eighteen months Arcelor's share price has risen by more than 50 per cent, whereas that of Mittal Steel has been flat or has declined.'

'But he promises to reduce the family's percentage ownership,' Elkabbach said.

'Yes, but you know that he plans to keep 64 per cent of the voting rights, which means he will decide everything himself. Arcelor shares are widely held, Mittal Steel is untouchable.'

'But it's not the Indian government or Indian laws that make the playing field uneven,' Elkabbach suggested, 'it's the way the company is structured and in this case it's a European-law company.'

'That's true,' Dollé said, taking another big step out on to dangerous ground. 'It's not an Indian company per se, it's a company of Indians. The majority of the seats on the Board are held by Indians, in particular by Mr Mittal's family; most of the positions on the management committee are held by Indians, and the company's speciality, when it makes an acquisition, is generally to send in a dozen or so Indians to improve plant operations.'

Dollé ploughed on. Mittal was a job-cutter, he said, buying up obsolete rust-bucket plant and running a company with a 'last-century' structure. 'People should go and look at the Mittal Steel plant at Gandrange in the Lorraine region, between Metz and Thionville*, and then go ten kilometres north and visit Arcelor's Florange installations and compare the modernness and the capital he has invested, employee morale and efficiency.'

But wasn't Mittal a success story?

Dollé agreed. 'He's a charmer.'

'He's a smooth talker,' Elkabbach suggested.

'He's a smooth talker who doesn't always tell the truth . . .'

'Wait a minute,' Elkabbach cut in. 'He's going to walk into the office of the Minister of the Economy in forty-five minutes and you're calling him a liar? Careful now.'

Dollé spat back. 'I say he doesn't tell the truth, that's not quite the same thing.'

'You have already met with Mr Breton.'

'I explained to him.' Dollé described the meeting he had with Breton as 'comforting'.

'What are you asking of Breton, of the French government?'

'I am not asking for anything specifically, just moral support,' Dollé smiled.

Elkabbach returned to the Indian theme. 'You don't think that saying no to a group of Indians will spark – will lead to – reprisals from the Indian government, at a time when French companies are going after the Indian market?'

'I repeat that the Mittal Steel group does not have operations in India.'

---

* Bought by Mittal from Usinor six years earlier.

'You think that this takeover bid does not risk having consequences for President Chirac's forthcoming trip to India in a fortnight's time?'

'Absolutely not.'

'And you don't think there is a risk they will send the hull of the *Clemenceau* – which is approaching Indian waters right now – back to us, either?'

For a moment Dollé was taken aback by this question slipped in suddenly by Elkabbach. What had this highly sensitive international incident got to do with him? A few weeks previously the decommissioned 27,000-tonne French aircraft carrier had set sail from Toulon for a scrapyard in Alang in the north-western Indian state of Gujarat. Greenpeace had tried to block the *Clemenceau*'s departure, claiming that France was violating international conventions and should herself deal with the asbestos, PCBs, lead, mercury and other toxic chemicals in her superstructure instead of shipping it to India where poorly paid workers in a badly managed shipbreaking industry would be put at risk of injury and death.

'I remind you that it is made of steel,' Dollé recovered, pride surging into his voice, 'manufactured, for that matter, by Arcelor.'

Elkabbach switched from the diplomatic battle over a toxic warship to Arcelor's campaign to stave off Mittal. Dollé predicted that the fight would last four to six months at least.

'You have the resources to resist?'

'We can resist. We are strong. We are marathon runners,' insisted the CEO, who liked to jog outdoors while Mittal was happier stimulating his circulation on the gymnasium treadmill. 'We are ready,' Dollé declared. 'We have measures to see this thing off,' he promised. 'You have seen the statement from our board. It was unanimous and vehement.'

'One last time, Mr Dollé,' Elkabbach concluded, 'wouldn't the wisest path be to negotiate a friendly merger, replete with guarantees, rather than see certain shareholders abandon ship and suffer a defeat?'

Dollé gazed at his interviewer perplexed, as though he were speaking Martian.

'The battle has begun and we are going to win it.'

'Thank you, Guy Dollé. The battle has begun.'

Dollé left the studio buoyed up, ready to fight tough. At the Arcelor headquarters dozens of emails were flying around, headed 'Cheerio Mittal'. The Mittal team had been listening in to his broadcast too. They were stunned by Guy Dollé's performance. They could not believe that their adversary had just made a public relations monkey for his own back.

9.15 a.m.

Ministry of Economy, Finance and Industry, 139 rue de Bercy

Home to sixty thousand civil servants, the Ministry of Finance had been built out over the Seine like a great white post-modernist aqueduct and was one of François Mitterrand's *grands projets* of the late eighties. Lakshmi Mittal pulled up outside after a fifteen-minute drive from the George V and went inside for what had been billed as a meeting over breakfast with Thierry Breton.

After the reaction of the Luxembourg government and Guy Dollé's radio rant, he knew he was in for a rough ride. From his briefing with Goldman Sachs's government affairs adviser Lisa Rabbe Mittal knew it had been a tough start to the year for Breton. The French government was trying to deal with a raft of corporate issues. There was a growing turbulence at the defence giant EADS, and France's flagship Airbus was strapped by costly delays. France was trying to preserve national champions, but had to navigate the EU competition authorities and negotiate with private shareholders.

Breton's ministry had traditionally laid down the rules in industry and finance, yet he was being constantly undermined by a divided right wing, by factions inside the government, and by a weakened President Chirac. A siege mentality had set in. It was also likely that Breton had been shoved front of stage by Chirac and his Prime Minister Dominique de Villepin. If the Mittal bid was to turn nasty for France it was Breton who would catch the flak.

As he waited to be shown in to the minister Mittal remembered the last thing Lisa Rabbe had said to him when she had briefed him – 'Remember to say "we".'

If I could just talk to Breton entrepreneur to entrepreneur, Mittal thought. As the minister knew all about rescuing failed companies he should appreciate Mittal's vision. Before going into politics Breton, who had just celebrated his fifty-first birthday, had dragged the French consumer electronics company Thomson Multimedia away from death's door. Before Breton took over as chairman, Thomson was such a basket case that the French government almost gave it away for one franc. By 2001 Breton had made it the world's number one producer of digital set-top boxes. He had then become chairman of the board at Orange and CEO of France Télécom. Equally famous for his Beethoven hair, Breton had also written an international sci-fi bestseller called *Softwar*.

As soon as he walked into the room Mittal knew there would be nothing soft about this meeting. The minister, wearing a grey suit with crisp blue shirt and matching tie, greeted him coolly. 'Mr Mittal, it will not surprise you that this morning you are not the most popular visitor to Paris,' he said, ushering him into a chair, 'but I am grateful that we have an opportunity to give you our views on your bid.'

As soon as he sat down Mittal saw on the minister's desk the six-page briefing document prepared by Guy Dollé (not that he guessed its author). When the coffee arrived it was lukewarm. To his right Mittal spotted a plate of croissants, but they were tantalisingly out of reach. The minister, barely able to mask his anger, showed no sign of offering him one. Mittal wished now he had breakfasted at the hotel.

'I do not wish to be protectionist,' Breton continued.

But? Mittal thought.

'But in Europe it is important for you to understand the concept of stakeholders and the need to consult and provide a clear industrial plan to all parties concerned. That's how we like to do things in mainland Europe. Mr Mittal, I do not think you respect what we in France call *la grammaire des affaires*, the grammar of business. What's more, I have zero information to go on. I need your industrial plan. Can you share it with me?'

Mittal did not have an industrial plan. The offer documents detailed the strategy, scope, logic and financing of the deal but there was no way they could be issued to somebody who was not even an Arcelor shareholder before they went to the regulators – without whose blessing the offer could not be formally made public – even if the person doing the asking was the French Minister of Economy, Finance and Industry. In a free-market world, providing governments with industrial plans in takeovers between public companies was unheard of.

'We have a plan but the work has not been fully completed,' Mittal said, playing for time. 'I am away from the office and travelling a lot but I will get it to you.'

'Good,' said Breton, relaxing a little.

Mittal looked at the croissants. They stayed where they were.

'Meanwhile,' Breton continued, referring to Dollé's briefing notes, 'you must withdraw your offer.'

'That is one thing I cannot do,' Mittal told him.

'This is not the way,' Breton said. 'You should have come to me before, talked to me.'

'That is what we had arranged, but things moved so fast.' Mittal tried to explain why the offer announcement had been brought forward.

Breton waved him away. 'After we receive the plan, we will analyse it and send you our questions, and then we will see the full scope and reality.'

Up against an emotional brick wall, Mittal decided not to pursue the strategic rationale for the bid or to get into details about job preservation, investment and scope for growth. There was going to be no 'we' this morning. An hour had gone by. Mittal's time was up.

'We are ready and waiting for your plan,' Minister Breton said, shaking his hand.

'One piece of advice,' Mittal said, smiling.

'Yes?'

'Whatever happens, let's please not have any more of these unfortunate remarks.'

He could see in Breton's eyes that even if he had not heard the Dollé broadcast personally it had been reported to him.

'Mr Mittal, on this point I agree.'

Mittal emerged from the minister's office and shot a self-conscious half-smile at Lisa Rabbe, like a small boy emerging from the headmaster's office after a caning. She read the translation: That was tough. Anne Méaux had been right. This deal was going to be very political and it would not stop at France.

11.30 a.m.

Pavillon Gabriel, 5 Avenue Gabriel, Paris

As the Mittals drew up outside the renovated 1840 exhibition hall that overlooked the Jardins des Champs Élysées, near the Place de la Concorde, they could not believe what they were seeing. Pavillon Gabriel, which Anne Méaux had chosen for their Paris launch press conference, was often used to hold corporate announcements as well as fashion shows and concerts, but even they didn't draw two hundred journalists and the fifty-strong pack of photographers jostling for first glimpse of the Indian steel billionaire and his son.

'Mr Mittal, over here!' the snappers called out, 'Mr Mittal, over here!' Paris had not seen anything like it since Posh Spice had been in town.

'The bird flu scare in Europe is far from over, but is the European Union facing a danger altogether more menacing?' an Indian TV journalist asked his viewers. 'It's Mittal Mania.'

The two men were eased through the scrum by the muscular presence of Philip Gawith. Once inside, Lakshmi and Aditya took five minutes to make their way to the platform, such was the eagerness of people to get a good close look at them. Unlike Lakshmi Mittal, Anne Méaux had not underestimated the impact he was having on the French capital. On Friday Mittal had still been largely unknown in France. Forty-eight hours later, and with the full weight of continental establishment opinion mounting against him, the French were captivated and horrified in equal measure by the Indian interloper who had landed in their midst.

While Aditya led the presentation, showing how the merged company would hit the big profit numbers without the loss of a single job or plant closure, Lakshmi stared down at his notes, calm and composed. Every time he looked up at his son, the camera shutters fired in unison. The flash made him blink. Then he began to play a game with them. He half raised his head, and when he sensed that the snappers were getting ready to fire, he lowered it again. Several times he did this, until he could resist no longer. Suddenly he looked up and gave them a big beaming smile.

Breton, meanwhile, had rushed out comments via Agence France-Presse. 'I doubt that the cultures of the two groups could function and live together,' he said. 'But Mittal is free to do what it wants. We can only reiterate the deep concern of the French government.' Was he suggesting that the French leaders were refraining from actively seeking protection for Arcelor?

1 p.m.

Hilton Arc de Triomphe, Paris

As Guy Dollé took to the stage for his press conference Arcelor shares were now trading at €30, approximately 8 per cent more than the value of the bid. Nicola Davidson was putting an even greater gloss on it. On the year Arcelor stock had now gained more than 41 per cent in value, largely because of Mittal's bid.

While Mittal had been giving his press conference, Dollé had been closeted with his bankers putting the final touches to the slides that would present his case in the best light. Gonzalo Urquijo and Michel Wurth were concerned that Dollé was becoming over-excitable as the press conference drew near. He was twitchy, responding in monosyllables, his mind elsewhere.

'Whatever you do, don't make this personal,' Urquijo urged.

As they took their places alongside their CEO on the stage, Dollé began crisply enough. 'Thanks to so many for coming today. I would like to introduce my colleagues from the management board.' Then he gazed from his lectern around the large basement conference room, which was packed wall to wall. '*My* son is *not* on the management board,' he said. Urquijo's heart sank. Michel Wurth and Roland Junck smiled nervously as laughter bubbled around the journalists, many of whom had rushed straight from the Mittal event a short cab ride down the Champs Élysées. Mittal's men had also crept into the room. Behind Dollé was the Arcelor logo and the legend, 'The World #1 Steel Manufacturer'.

'We are the Airbus of the European metals industry,' Dollé said, now working though his slides. 'Although we have ventures in Brazil and now in Canada, we have certain values deeply rooted in the

European way of doing things. Mittal's business model is not based on state-of-the-art technology. His is mainly commodity products, which are subject to greater cyclical activity than Arcelor's. We have a bigger turnover with fewer tonnes produced.'

He repeated his perfume/eau de cologne line. It went down well.

'Mittal heads up a group of less than average companies,' said Dollé, rattling on like a train gathering speed. 'Apart from Kazakhstan he has not turned them around. Mittal took over ISG, itself a conglomerate of failed companies that need major investment. Mittal will cut forty-six thousand jobs in the years to come. We have world leadership with automotive customers and an unmatched distribution network. We invest thirty-two euros per tonne of steel and Mittal only seventeen, and he's threatening to cut that.' The only reason Mittal wanted Arcelor, Dollé said, was to strip out billions of its value to prop up his failing rust-bucket plants in Eastern Europe.

He hammered away at what he had identified as the weakest link in Mittal's hostile offer. He said that Mittal Steel was opaque and family-dominated. If Mittal had been offering all cash, then its governance standards would be irrelevant. But three-quarters of its offer was in the form of its own paper. By contrast, Arcelor's shares were widely held and its board was democratic and representative of many nationalities and interest groups. 'We have trades unionists on *our* board,' he said. Arcelor's high standard of transparent corporate governance was on 'a different planet' to Mittal's.

'Even though sometimes apples and oranges can mix, there is no strategic fit between the companies,' Dollé declared. 'We will not share our future with Mittal Steel.'

A journalist put to him, 'At his press conference this morning Mittal said that you are falsifying the results of his group.'

Dollé bristled. 'This data is all in the public domain,' he fired back. 'You too can see if he's telling the truth.'

Asked if he planned to talk to Mittal, Dollé finally lost his composure. 'Four minutes' conversation at his house about a merger, when I said neither yes, nor no. Now this. That's Mr Mittal's definition of a friendly bid. There's nothing left to say.'

Guy Dollé needed help, and he knew exactly where to get it.

13

SeverStal, Cherepovets, north-west Russia

Describing his career in steel to a visitor, Alexey Mordashov, Russia's youngest billionaire, had said, 'I was at the rear of the camel train, crossing the desert when suddenly things changed. The train turned on itself and I found myself at the front.' The visitor, back in 2005, was Alain Davezac, and Mordashov, forty, and number sixty-four on the *Forbes* Rich List with $7.6 billion-plus and still climbing, looked every bit the smart, clean-cut businessman that you would find in a Manhattan or Mayfair executive office.

As chairman and chief executive of SeverStal, Russia's third-largest steel company, Mordashov loved to use the camel-train analogy to explain his sharp rise to fame as one of the more Westernised oligarchs. In essence, he was summarising in his competent English, learned studying for an MBA at Northumbria University, that he had been in the right place at the right time; and, in a game of pure chance, he just took what there was to take, a controlling interest in the SeverStal industrial group of steelworks, plus its coal and iron ore mines, with the railways, a university and a professional ice hockey team thrown in.

Cherepovets, a grey industrial city with few redeeming features, is 475 kilometres east of St Petersburg and 620 north of Moscow, on the crossroads of the Volga–Baltic waterway and on the west–east St Petersburg–Ekaterinburg railway, allowing the continuous delivery of raw materials and fuel to the plant. Mordashov employed a hundred thousand people and his company had revenue of $11.57 billion.

Westerners suffering from Russia phobia tend to believe that

oligarch means gangster. There was nothing gangsterish about
Alexey Mordashov, but there were intriguing stories about his management style and how he became top dog in Cherepovets. One
version described the Slavic-looking father of three as 'a tank', a
self-styled 'iron man' not to be messed with. Others said he was an
unassuming, thoughtful, hard-working entrepreneur, fluent in
German and English and one of Russia's showcase industrialists,
able to sit at any table in the West.

When he was twelve years old, growing up under constant leaden
clouds and the billowing smokestacks of the steel city, Mordashov
dreamed of becoming a professional manager. After graduating from
the Leningrad Engineering Economic Institute in 1988, he got his
first job, as an economist for the Cherepovets steelworks, where his
mother and father both worked for a pittance. While in Leningrad
the young Mordashov got to know a man who would have a distinct
influence on his life – Anatoly Choubais, the future champion of
Russia's privatisation programme.

Mordashov did well in his first few years at the steelworks, which
was still operating under the Soviet model. His hard-work ethic, his
charm and his outwardly compliant nature quickly won him recognition, and he was singled out for further career development. Two
years later, as the Soviet regime collapsed, Mordashov went on a
training course to Austria, working for the steel-maker Voest Alpine,
where he learned Western-style financial modelling. On his return,
aged twenty-seven, he found himself the right-hand man to his boss
Louri Lipoukhine, who let the now financially smart Mordashov
handle the privatisation of SeverStal. These were the early days of
the Yeltsin era, when Russians were given their first taste of capitalism by the allocation of vouchers entitling them to shares in the
privatised businesses where they worked.

In 1996 at the age of thirty-one, Mordashov emerged as chief
executive of SeverStal, which did not go unnoticed in the West.
The late US investigative journalist Paul Klebnikov suggested in
Forbes magazine that Mordashov secured ownership of SeverStal by
ousting his boss. Klebnikov also alleged that Mordashov used
SeverStal's huge earnings to buy out the free shares allocated to the
staff that they were entitled to sell if they wished and were more
than happy to turn into hard cash for short-term gain. The visionary

Mordashov had a greater ambition: the shares' long-term increase in value on the back of a global steel boom. Sleight of hand? No, pure opportunism, Mordashov insisted in the same article. 'We never seized anything, we never twisted anyone's arm, we never used state organs or corruption,' he told *Forbes*.

Mordashov set about transforming SeverStal. He saw tremendous opportunities to grow the business in a booming Russian economy, but he faced considerable competition in his home market. Other major producers such as Evraz, where Roman Abramovich was homing in, and NLMK (Novolipetsk Metallurgical Combine) between them controlled over 50 per cent of the Russian production of rolled-steel products.

To compete with them SeverStal had to modernise, boost technology and make acquisitions to supplement its feedstock of coking coal. It was a low-cost producer, with its own supply of coal via its wholly owned mines and railways. Mordashov moved quickly on all fronts. Being stuck between Moscow and St Petersburg made commuting difficult, so he bought an airline and began to branch out overseas through joint ventures with other steel companies. One of his first contacts was Guy Dollé.

Mordashov had first got to know Dollé in 1996 when the Frenchman was planning manager at Usinor. An instant rapport was established as the two men shared their respective visions of the steel industry of the future. Mordashov saw explosive growth, Dollé a deeper strategic alliance with SeverStal that would plug a big gap in his armoury – entry to Russia's car-makers. Usinor had little spare cash so Dollé knew he would have to wait, but he kept close to Mordashov, whom he regarded as a protégé.

In 2002, as boss of the newly created Arcelor and with more cash at his disposal, Dollé got to work on his Russian friend. First, they established two joint ventures in Russia – one in high-quality flat steel for the car industry, called Severgal, and the other in wire-drawing. The Severgal joint venture mirrored what Arcelor had achieved with Dofasco in Canada: the infusion of Arcelor's galvanising technology in exchange for a 20 per cent stake; and it was the precursor to an entry into the lucrative car market.

Later that year Dollé began to lay the ground for a more concerted link with SeverStal. 'Our relationship has developed considerably, and I would like to suggest that Arcelor acquire a direct stake in SeverStal,' he said, keeping the conversation informal. Other Western companies were beginning to build stakes in Russian companies, particularly in oil and gas, and it seemed that a Russia under Putin favoured more direct investment from the West. There were still big risks – the lack of full accounting transparency and corporate governance – but Guy Dollé saw that the opportunity was there for Arcelor to make a move.

He kept the courtship slow but steady. As they met at steel industry gatherings, he would tell Mordashov, 'Look, we are very similar businesses. We both focus on high-quality steel and there are no geographical overlaps between us. I know that my Luxembourg colleagues will agree.'

Mordashov, keen to be seen on the global stage, wanted to take the bait. 'I think we should try and outline the potential areas for putting the two companies together,' he told Dollé.

In his 'what might be' scenario Dollé favoured Arcelor taking a 2 per cent equity stake in SeverStal, then moving incrementally to between 5 and 10 per cent. By then, both sides would know whether a full marriage made sense. As Dollé had his mergers and acquisitions team crunch the numbers, it was immediately obvious that getting a fair valuation on SeverStal as a private company, crucial to cementing any formal alliance, was going to be a major problem. The steel assets were straightforward but the company's mines were far more difficult to value and would require a full independent audit.

By 2004, SeverStal had posted a net profit of $1.4 billion on sales of $6.6 billion, and Dollé encouraged Mordashov 'to follow in the footsteps of other pioneering Russian companies and to float part of your shares on the London stock market. That would anchor a valuation on SeverStal that would be acceptable to Arcelor's institutional shareholders.'

Mordashov could not, or would not, do it. 'I do not think the timing is right,' he said, 'but let's keep the idea under review.'

Dollé suspected there could be many reasons for Mordashov holding back. First, he owned over 90 per cent of SeverStal and might be reluctant to dilute his holding. SeverStal needed funds for further investment, but Mordashov had more than hinted that he had other acquisitions in mind to make him more international. Sure enough, he went on a buying spree. First he outbid US Steel to buy the bankrupt Rouge Steel for $285 million, then at the beginning of 2005 he bought a 70 per cent stake in the financially troubled Gruppo Lucchini, Italy's second-largest steel manufacturer.

Guy Dollé looked on with admiration. A young Mittal in the making, he mused. But why would Mordashov not list his company in London, making an alliance a real possibility and Arcelor much harder for Mittal Steel to capture? By now Mittal was a big threat and looming larger.

Mordashov, advised at all times by the canny Vadim Makov, his deputy director of strategy, was still not listening. Instead he began to diversify into banking and insurance. He also bought a big stake in the last private state-owned TV channel in Russia, REN-TV, which suddenly hit the international news when it cancelled the former athlete Olga Romanova's programme allegedly because she reported that the son of Deputy Prime Minister Sergei Ivanov would not be charged for running over and killing an elderly woman with his car. Was Alexey Mordashov now dabbling in politics, something he had studiously avoided? Russian politics were something to stay out of even if you were, like him, considered one of Vladimir Putin's favourites.

SeverStal enjoyed another buoyant trading year in 2005, and as the New Year dawned Mordashov was relishing life on the world stage. Not only was he acknowledged as one of Putin's clean-cut industrial sons, as he strutted his way across the diplomatic communities he was pushing for Russia to be accepted into the World Trade Organisation.

On Friday 27 January news of Lakshmi Mittal's bid for Arcelor reached Moscow fast, where Mordashov was attending to a clutch of business matters in SeverStal's office at 2–3 K. Tsetkin Street. His opportunistic mind went into overdrive. He looked at his phone and smiled. It's only a matter of time, he thought. Sure enough, three days later he got the call he had been expecting. He picked up his phone. It was Alain Davezac.

'Of course I would like to meet Guy.' Dollé was once more talking about alliances, but this time the protégé had the upper hand. I have got them by the balls, Mordashov congratulated himself.

14

Tuesday 31 January, 9.30 a.m.

Berkeley Square House, London

As Sudhir Maheshwari chaired the first of the twice-weekly core team meetings of bankers, lawyers and communications advisers the press was awash with Guy Dollé's remarks about monkey money and a company of Indians, and the obvious indications of his personal disdain for Aditya Mittal. The Mittal team pored over summaries of newspaper coverage in Britain and across Europe, deciding how they should respond.

Desperate to smokescreen Dollé's outbursts, the Arcelor press team – twenty-strong but for some reason housed away from the chateau in another building – had that morning fired its first shots in the PR war: 'For the second time in a row, Arcelor has been included in the Global 100, an annual ranking of the world's 100 most sustainable corporations. Arcelor, the only steelmaker in the Global 100, considers this inclusion as excellent news for its sustainability endeavours and an important reward for all its employees that have contributed to the success of Arcelor's sustainable development strategy.'

Are we going to let Dollé get away with these remarks? the Mittal bankers chorused, meanwhile.

'Mr Mittal does not want to respond,' Nicola Davidson said. At that moment Lakshmi Mittal and Aditya were heading out to Luxembourg and to a meeting with Prime Minister Jean-Claude Juncker.

'To do so would be to sink to Dollé's level,' Gawith agreed.

With Maitland, Nicola Davidson had set up a daily message track so that every member of the media team, with the bankers taking press calls too, would have an agreed and uniform script with which to respond to every statement coming out of Arcelor, and a form of words with which to correct every Arcelor 'fact' and bit of spin that they perceived to be an error. Nobody would deviate.

There were already many topics on which they could counterattack Dollé without resorting to insults. For example, a leader in the *Financial Times*, 'Stainless Steel Deal', had been primed with a Mittal-provided fact to counter Dollé's accusation that Mittal's offer meant job losses: 'Arcelor has cut 10,000 jobs in the past couple of years.' Helpfully, the piece also noted that in all other countries where he had invested Mittal had been 'an appealing buyer for the governments concerned, because he has maintained production and invested in modernisation'.

The *Wall Street Journal Europe* chipped in: 'HQ'd in London and listed in Amsterdam, Mittal is as "European" as the other guys.' Above all the share prices of the two companies were good. Mittal Steel was up to $36.20 from $34.26 on 27 January. Arcelor was holding steady at $28.9, from $28.54 the day Mittal made his offer. And even better, Guy Dollé was now being taken to task by the French eau de cologne manufacturers, hugely insulted at being likened to second-rate steel. The core team found that one very funny. Poor old Guy – nothing was going his way. But Nicola Davidson was not laughing. 'The perfume/eau de cologne remark is very smart,' she said. 'It's a good soundbite, very graphic.'

'But it's not true,' Jeremy Fletcher said.

'Even so, we are going to have to be very clever in how we respond to it,' Davidson said.

Discussion now turned to Arcelor's legal team. 'They have hired Skadden, Arps – what are we up against?' Maheshwari asked Pierre-Yves Chabert.

'Very strong on mergers and acquisitions,' Chabert said. 'If Scott Simpson is involved this is going to be very, very aggressive.'

1.30 p.m.

Prime Minister's office, Luxembourg City

Jean-Claude Juncker, in his third term as Prime Minister of Luxembourg, was trying to control his emotions. Voted European politician of the year in 2005 by his EU counterparts, Juncker had been enjoying this accolade from his European buddies, further enhanced by a very public run-in with Tony Blair on the UK's rebate from Brussels. But now he was facing a serious issue on his home patch. He was about to address his parliamentary colleagues with an explanation of the government's stance on Mittal Steel. For Juncker, the son of a steelworker and born in the small commune of Rédange-sur-Attert in the west of the country near the border with Belgium, this was personal. Steel was in his blood.

It was a point he had made to Lakshmi Mittal and to Aditya at a brief meeting held earlier in the day at Senningen Castle. Juncker had met the Mittals with Ministers Krecké and Frieden and had chosen a venue set in secluded woodland away from the centre of the city so that nobody could see him even greeting the Mittals. The meeting was brief and courteous and the Prime Minister was anxious to articulate the government's antipathy to the way Mittal had delivered his bid.

'We don't understand it and we don't want it,' he said pointedly.

Lakshmi Mittal responded by underlining his desire for a friendly deal and attempted to press home the importance of his strategic vision and how Europe and Luxembourg in particular would benefit. At the same time he felt that he was running into further political backlash. He was right.

For Juncker, smart politician that he was, the emotion could spill over. As he conferred with his press officer Guy Schuller, who shadowed him on international diplomatic visits, there was a lot at stake for the tiny country. The coalition government had a clear lead at home, but the Prime Minister knew that a Mittal victory could produce a humbling swing factor among his supporters. The nation was not only being asked to sell the family silver, but all its other property as well. What was the government going to do about it?

Juncker rose to speak at 2 p.m. Krecké and Frieden were side by side in the Chamber as the sixty MPs settled into their seats. The speech was being televised, and watching the broadcast was Georges Schmit, one of four directly reporting to Krecké, and who also sat on the Arcelor board as a non-executive representative of the government, a role he had held since 1992 when he was appointed to the board of Arbed and then to the board of Arcelor upon the merger with Usinor in 2002. The bespectacled fifty-two-year-old had, like most Luxembourgers, been badly shaken by the events of the last forty-eight hours. Behind his calm exterior there was an inner defiance to beat off Mittal.

The Prime Minister spoke without notes. It was a measured performance, philosophical in tone and delivered in the Luxembourgish language. Throughout his delivery, he made it very obvious where he stood. As they hung on his every word, the deputies sensed the government had a rough ride ahead because it had no ultimate control in the new world of free markets. What hurt them most was that for years before the advent of Arcelor, Luxembourg had nursed the Arbed company, pumping in millions of Luxembourg francs. Then it had participated in the restructuring and formation of Arcelor and secured its HQ in Luxembourg. Now one of the country's prime assets was on the block, and neither the government nor big brother Brussels was legally able to intervene, even on competition grounds.

'It is not about the money,' Juncker told his parliamentarians. At the current bid price, Luxembourg could pocket €1 billion profit, exactly double the state budget, if it sold its shares to Mittal. 'But that is not what we want to do . . . We do not want a quick solution by taking measures dictated by speculative logic,' he said, cranking up through the gears. 'No, we want to remain a strategic partner in a European company with a European social dimension, in a European environment and a European concept of governance, with its headquarters in Luxembourg.'

Juncker explained how after numerous turns and challenges the government had become a strategic partner in a steel group that was a European champion competing on a world stage. Arcelor's industrial concept of stakeholder democracy differed greatly from Mittal Steel, he said, which was impervious to external thinking.

'We say no to Mittal!' he concluded, to applause from the Chamber, and then went off to build a bridgehead of like-minded European leaders to stop the Indian.

Juncker's speech heartened Krecké, Frieden and Schmit, especially Georges Schmit. A sense of excitement was lifting him out of the humdrum of mountainous paperwork, endless departmental committees and report-writing. This was going to be a big fight and he would have a ringside seat in the boardroom on Avenue de la Liberté.

Later that day Lakshmi Mittal flew back into Paris Le Bourget and to a meeting at the Élysée Palace with President Chirac. He had just heard that he had scored his first diplomatic point. Competition Commissioner Neelie Kroes had told the European Parliament that the deal was likely to fall under her jurisdiction and that she was not opposed in principle to a large steel merger. 'We need to give it a severe eye,' Ms Kroes added. 'It's too early to say that if it's on my desk it will be an easy walk. It's likely that we'll look at it carefully.' It was not ringing support, but at least it was neutral.

As his car swept through the Élysée Palace gates Mittal knew that the prospect of Chirac being neutral was about as likely as Guy Dollé buying him a birthday present. The meeting was short and very formal. Mittal could see that his argument about Europe needing a stronger steel sector to compete with China, and promises to locate the combined company headquarters in Luxembourg and ensure strong independent representation on its board, were cutting no ice with a president whose hatred of hostile takeovers and the Anglo-Saxon free market was matched only by his well known dislike of foreigners.

'This is a purely financial operation, devoid of any industrial objective,' Chirac said after their meeting.

Mittal responded: 'I am not scared about the politicians' reaction. I feel saddened about it. It is a process of educating and informing them about the importance of this merger.'

The diplomatic charm offensive would go on. The row, though, was gathering force.

15

Wednesday 1 February

Élysée Palace, rue du Faubourg Saint-Honoré, Paris

Jean-Claude Juncker bounced out on to the palace steps to greet the press and photographers. He was very buoyed up after his meeting with his mentor and political confidant, Jacques Chirac. 'There is no way that this deal can be allowed to happen,' Chirac had told Juncker. 'You have my full support.'

Earlier in the day Juncker had had an equally positive meeting with Prime Minister de Villepin, after which he had said France and Luxembourg 'are on the same wavelength regarding the necessary response' to Mittal. Once more de Villepin had used the phrase 'economic patriotism' in response to Mittal's offer, as he had done the previous year when he railed against a rumoured hostile takeover of the leading French food group Danone by the US soft drink giant PepsiCo. After meeting Juncker, de Villepin described Mittal's bid as 'a very unfriendly offer'.

Now also able to call on presidential muscle in the fight against Mittal, Juncker was armed with full and unquestioning French support. He gave a short statement: 'To put it clearly, the Luxembourg government is not in favour of the hostile takeover bid for Arcelor. We do not want it because we do not understand it. We have no plausible, rational or coherent explanation. As a consequence, we respond with hostility to this hostile bid.'

It was a headline-grabbing moment for the Luxembourg leader, but he would rue the day he ever said it.

*

In Brussels there was no doubt what topped Trade Commissioner Peter Mandelson's in-tray. It was a blunt letter of protest from India's Minister of Commerce and Industry, Kamal Nath. The combative Nath, at sixty, was a champion of inward investment to India and of Indian companies operating abroad, and was, like Mittal, a graduate of St Xavier's College. In his letter he hinted that the continuing World Trade Organisation multilateral negotiations on cross-border investments such as the Mittal–Arcelor deal could be derailed if members of the European Union blocked market opportunities for Mittal Steel.

Guy Dollé's 'monkey money' remarks and talk of 'companies of Indians' had caused a predictable outcry in India, as people in very high places rushed to defend the nation's favourite non-resident Indian from bigoted and racist abuse. 'This is an era of globalisation, cross-border investment and liberalisation,' Nath told reporters, 'not one in which investors are judged by the colour of their skin in breach of . . . national treatment rules. France has to recognise that the centre of gravity is shifting from the Atlantic Ocean to the Indian Ocean. This kind of reaction shows that maybe Europe is not ready for the globalisation they are trumpeting.' He accused European governments of not giving citizens of other countries the same breaks as their own nationals.

To the delight of Mittal's communications team and to the horror of Arcelor's image-makers desperate to reburnish a tarnished reputation, Nath's words were now common currency across European newspapers and websites.

The same day, the European Metalworkers' Federation rattled a different sword: 'Trade unions from Belgium, France, Germany, Spain, Luxembourg and Italy have declared unanimously that they are very strongly opposed to the hostile takeover bid of Arcelor by Mittal.' The group said it would lobby EU policy-makers against the plan, while national unions would contact politicians to 'try to elaborate with them ways to prevent the takeover'.

They were out of luck with Mandelson. He rushed out a statement saying any Commission inquiry into the deal would be decided on competition grounds alone. Two days later he flew to London for urgent placatory talks with Nath, after which the two men agreed a press release. 'India is a very important partner for the EU and vice versa,' it stated. 'So while our priority for now is the Doha Development Agenda* and we are fully focused on that, we want to think creatively about how to boost our commercial relations.'

And as the takeover temperature soared, Nath was not the only one outraged. Anne Méaux took a call from the president of a company she had just won the contract to represent. He was withdrawing his business from her PR company Image 7. When she asked why, he apologised and told her that he had come under pressure from a high-ranking French government official to take his account to a 'more patriotic' agency. 'He told me, "Anne Méaux is working against her country."'

Enraged, Méaux phoned Thierry Breton. 'Thierry, what is happening? We are good French people. This is not the Second World War and I'm not selling butter to the Germans.'

---

* The DDA was created in November 2001 at the World Trade Organisation's conference in Doha, Qatar. It launched a new round of initiatives to improve world trade.

16

Thursday 2 February, 9.30 a.m.

Berkeley Square House

As Sudhir Maheshwari assembled the core team for the second of the twice-weekly war-room meetings that would carry on throughout the deal, Mittal's supporting bankers were getting twitchy. This was brewing up into a very big fight, and Fletcher, Coates and Spiro Youakim wanted to get stuck into Arcelor and Guy Dollé.

'How long are we going to allow Dollé to get away with his histrionics?' Jeremy Fletcher demanded.

'Mr Mittal is taking up all those issues with the politicians,' Maheshwari said, his hand firmly holding on to the corporate line. 'Wilbur Ross is the only person who will comment directly on personal attacks.' Failed companies' saviour Ross had already waded into Dollé, accusing him 'of going right off the chart with his racial epithets'.

Although the French and the Luxembourgers were still overtly hostile, the Mittals' charm offensive was bearing fruit. Aditya had come smiling out of a meeting the previous day with officials from Spain's Asturias region. Overlooking the Bay of Biscay, and having been the centre of Spain's steel industry under Franco's dictatorship, Asturias now had fifteen thousand people employed by Arcelor. There the initial reaction to the bid had been almost like a call to the barricades to defend the region's steel from Mittal. Now it was a different story. 'They have expressed their support for this transaction,' Aditya Mittal reported. 'They appreciate the industrial logic. They like the value creation that the transaction offers. The best example of their support is the stock market, where Arcelor's stock price has appreciated almost 30 per cent since we announced this transaction.' The two companies' share prices were now at level pegging, Arcelor's €29.35 and Mittal's up to €29.70.

Lakshmi Mittal had been in Madrid trying to reassure Deputy Prime Minister Pedro Solbes and the industry minister José Montilla, who were terrified of job cuts, that his move on Arcelor was positive, and that he could save jobs threatened by Arcelor. 'We are purchasers of large volumes of raw materials. Arcelor has a strong distribution network which we don't have, so this would produce major synergies,' he told *El País*. Even though the previous October he had announced forty thousand job losses in his Eastern European plants – 'the result of agreements with unions and with governments' – there would be no need for redundancies in Spain.

'The charm offensive is all well and good,' Jeremy Fletcher insisted, 'but it is Arcelor's individual shareholders and institutional investors we need to be convincing. They'll decide this thing.' Even if he wasn't locking horns with Yoel Zaoui, there were times when Fletcher could have cheerfully strangled Maheshwari and the Goldman gang.

'We have to do these things in sequence,' Zaoui argued. 'Because this offer has to go through six different regulators it will be months before we can formally open it to Arcelor shareholders. We have three or four months to talk to them – and anyway, right now, they are just watching this space to see what happens.'

'Too much political noise puts doubt in the minds of investors about our ability to get the deal done,' Lisa Rabbe added. 'Once we have got the governments out of the way we can get on with selling the commercial side of the transaction to shareholders.'

Maheshwari continued down the agenda. 'About this industrial plan,' he said. 'Thierry Breton has demanded to see an industrial plan.'

'It's highly unusual,' said genial Australian Bill Scotting, who was Mittal's softly spoken group director of continuous improvement, hired by Mittal from international management consultants McKinsey. If there was ever a man who liked to have a plan it was Bill Scotting. His usually relaxed demeanour hid a ruthless grail-like quest for best practice. Of course Mittal's M&A team had a plan, a strategy and a legal schedule for this deal, but it was an internal document and not prepared for the scrutiny of a government that had no shares in Arcelor.

Maheshwari asked him if he had ever put together an industrial plan. Scotting frowned. Zaoui asked what needed to go into an industrial plan. Garbage in, garbage out, Fletcher fumed silently. Window dressing for politicians.

'It should include the strategic rationale for the merger,' Scotting said, 'the complementarity between the two companies, the operational model for the enlarged group and the synergies and cost savings that could be achieved.' It might run to hundreds of pages and the team was already stretched with countless other demands.

'If we do it,' Fletcher replied, 'there is the risk that in all future deals you guys do you are going to have to slap an industrial plan on the table every time some stakeholder shows their head above the parapet.'

'It's just a hoop we are going to have to jump through,' Scotting said. 'The most important thing to prove is that synergies do not equal redundancies – that this is all about growth for Mittal and Arcelor, together shaping the future of steel.'

As soon as he said this, it set Bill Scotting's juices flowing. It sounded like an excellent sales pitch. Maybe they could turn this annoying government request tossed in their path to their advantage, and win over the stakeholder mentality.

At that moment no more than a mile away, Guy Dollé and Gonzalo Urquijo, in London to drum up support from investors, were walking into a suite of offices on the sixteenth floor of a block looking north over Cavendish Square. They were greeted by Benoît d'Angelin, the energetic and bustling forty-five-year-old managing director of hedge fund Centaurus Capital. Centaurus, managing a fund of around €4.5 billion of investor cash, had a relatively small interest in Arcelor, investing some €100 million in shares for its private clients, but it had supported a distressed Arbed in a series of money-raising rescue exercises and also helped in the financing during the three-way merger in 2002 that had created Arcelor. D'Angelin and his French chairman Bernard Oppetit were frequent visitors at Avenue de la Liberté.

'We know your story very well and you can count on our continued support,' d'Angelin told them. 'As far as we are concerned Arcelor is a much better company and a much better performing company than Mittal Steel. That is why we are increasing our position to 3 per cent.' When Mittal's bid was announced and d'Angelin and Oppetit saw the immediate €10 increase in the share price, they wished they had moved sooner. But d'Angelin also had a warning for his visitors. 'I have to tell you one important thing about this battle; as long as you let the shareholders decide and you don't frustrate the deal with silly games, we will stay one hundred per cent behind you.'

'Look, we will not frustrate the bid,' Dollé told him, 'but we will do whatever we can to convince shareholders that this offer by Mittal is no good for Arcelor.'

There was something in the manner of Dollé and Urquijo that made d'Angelin feel uneasy after the two of them had left. They never said it to him but it was very clear what they were thinking: Who does that Indian think he is, trying to take our company?

That evening, Mittal flew into Paris to attend the dinner of the executive committee of the International Iron and Steel Institute. As he arrived, he was once more encircled by photographers. He was the last of the committee members to get there, and all of the eleven others were already seated.

'I apologise for my lateness,' he said. The room was pin-drop silent, the way rooms are when the person the occupants have all been talking about walks in through the door. Mittal went around the table shaking their hands one by one, until he got to the chairman. 'Good, evening, Guy,' he said. Dollé barely nodded. Mittal took his seat for a stilted meal that seemed to take an age to get through.

As the committee members finally left the room after dinner, Mittal was surprised to see Guy Dollé being greeted by two large men in dark suits who walked either side of him as he left the building. At the committee's meeting next day they were there again. There was no doubting it. Guy Dollé had hired bodyguards.

'Who does he think we are?' Mittal joked. 'We're not Russians.' It was a remark that mirrored Guy Dollé's apparent intolerance of Indians.

Monday 6 February

Arcelor headquarters, 19 Avenue de la Liberté

'How many banks do we have today? Is it seven? Oh, it's eight! I'm losing count,' Pierre Servan-Schreiber said facetiously on seeing the swelling ranks of banking advisers at the chateau as he prepared for the daily conference call with Arcelor's core defence team, what they were calling 'the Bengal Crisis Cell'.

Apart from Merrill Lynch, Deutsche Bank and BNP Paribas – which not only advised on strategy but also worked to stop existing Arcelor shareholders defecting to Mittal and encouraged their other clients to buy Arcelor shares so as to put the target out of his reach – Arcelor had shored up its defence with UBS, a strong European house with roots in Switzerland, together with Calyon, France's biggest bank, Banco Santander and Banco Bilbao Vizcaya, Spain's two leading banking groups.

Servan-Schreiber had heard one of the senior management team say, 'I need an eighth bank about as much as I need a second ass-hole', but these additional banks had outreach to Arcelor's widely scattered investors. Relationships with them could prove crucial in the days ahead. In terms of combined financial firepower they more than matched Mittal's armoury. Some conspiracy theorists said Arcelor was muzzling the banks' steel analysts from becoming hostile. Any research reports were immediately disenfranchised under house rules once a bank was acting for either side of the Arcelor–Mittal trench war. The same applied to Mittal Steel, with its four banks.

Arcelor was beginning to overcome some of the initial chaos and was getting to grips with its defence options. The Bengal Crisis Cell was the counterpart of Mittal's war room and was charged with daily strategy and pulse-taking. It was led by Gonzalo Urquijo, coordinated by Rémi Boyer, and included Philippe Capron, Alain Davezac, Frederik Van Bladel and Martine Hue. External members included Marc Pandraud, Jean-Yves Naouri, Christophe Moulin for BNP Paribas, and Servan-Schreiber. Philippe Hoss completed the group. Noticeably excluded was Patrick Seyler, Arcelor's head of communications, a move that was already causing constant friction between his in-house team and the communications giant Publicis preferred by Guy Dollé.

'Our motto is to win time and we have a situation that can work to our advantage,' Servan-Schreiber told the Cell. He was referring to the five European regulatory regimes with which both Arcelor and Mittal had to consult on all matters connected with the takeover. The key question was: which jurisdiction was best equipped to take the lead?

'The obvious choice is France, where the Autorité des Marchés Financiers has the largest experience of dealing with hostile takeovers compared to the other three, Belgium, Luxembourg and Spain. It is also likely to be influenced politically by the French authorities to favour Arcelor,' Servan-Schreiber explained. 'In the Netherlands, where Mittal is listed, it is much the same, except that the authorities would be responsible for any new shares brought to the market as part of Mittal Steel's proposed deal.'

So France would take the lead, then?

'No,' Servan-Schreiber said. 'We are not going to propose that any jurisdiction takes the lead because that will give us considerable scope to cause confusion, since there is no common ground between the regulators.' The only certainty was that in corporate law Luxembourg would lead, but the takeover law was not yet in place.

Servan-Schreiber and his team would frustrate Mittal with a blizzard of paperwork. One of the best feeding grounds was the 515-page prospectus that Mittal Steel was putting together, setting out in minute detail the terms of its offer, complete with a mass of supporting business data on both itself and the target company. To do this it would need information from Arcelor. In an agreed takeover, the bidder would have the full cooperation of the target company. In a hostile bid, the target would normally not agree, but the bidder was obliged to ask. If it failed to get cooperation it would have to trawl publicly available information, which might not be to the satisfaction of the European regulators or the SEC in America. Servan-Schreiber and his team of Skadden, Arps lawyers, which had already grown to fifteen, would never refuse to cooperate, but neither would he say yes. Every time he was asked for information by

Mittal he would respond with detailed small-print questions and clarifications by mail and email, forcing constant cross-referrals between the regulators as they sought to find consistency of application across the jurisdictions.

The Bengal Crisis Cell liked the sound of this approach very much.

'It works very well,' Servan-Schreiber said. 'We call them bedbug letters.'

The bedbugs would delay the opening of Mittal's offer. They would buy time to find potential white knights or white squires identified by Arcelor. Either would save it from takeover by Lakshmi Mittal. The bugs would also buy time to shape the takeover law to Arcelor's advantage, which was now a priority.

In addition, the bedbugs would irritate the hell out of Lakshmi Mittal, even more than the article he was now reading in that day's *Financial Times* by Thierry Breton, who reminded his readers that the term stakeholder 'is familiar to leaders of international companies with high corporate governance standards'. Breton also said that his government's concerns about Mittal's 'lack of adequate preparation' in addressing non-shareholder concerns were 'not prompted by efforts to protect or discriminate against a large and emerging country. India is neither directly nor indirectly concerned with this bid, which only involves European countries.'

We'll see about that, Mittal thought as he made another call to Luxembourg.

Ministry of Economy and Foreign Trade, Luxembourg City

'Lakshmi Mittal is ringing me every day – what do I say?' Jeannot Krecké asked as he sat with his advisers in a strategy session. 'He keeps asking to see the Prime Minister,' he added, knowing that Jean-Claude Juncker was in no mood to entertain Mittal again. Krecké felt as besieged as the Arcelor castle as depicted in a full-page cartoon in *Tribune*, which showed Mittal's Napoleonic armies advancing to overpower the citadel of Luxembourg. How they needed a General Patton, an 'Old Blood and Guts', to repel this latest invader.

'It is important we keep a line of communication open with him, Minister,' said Georges Schmit; although he, more than anyone in the ministry, had a delicate balance to strike as the government's representative on the Arcelor board and adviser to his minister on contact with the enemy. 'Strategically, it makes sense for you to meet with him, Minister,' Schmit added. 'But this will have to be done very discreetly.'

At that moment Thierry Breton rang Krecké, who interrupted his meeting to take the call. The two ministers compared notes on their governments' action to stop Mittal. Krecké got a distinct sense from their conversation that Breton, aware that his President was about to visit India, was on some sort of retreat from his earlier pronouncements. Krecké did not mention to Breton that he was setting up a meeting with Lakshmi Mittal.

Krecké's strategists continued to address three linked questions: where should this meeting take place, what should the minister say, and who should accompany him? A neutral airport, outside Luxembourg, was the obvious choice.

'What about Brussels?' Krecké said.

'No,' Schmit said knowingly. 'Too close to the European political community.'

'Then it has to be Charleroi,' said Krecké. They agreed that the relatively small airport, situated on the border between Belgium and Luxembourg, would provide the perfect cover. The Conrad Hotel, close by the airport perimeter, would be the best place for the secret summit.

Who should accompany the minister? It was out of the question for either Schmit as an Arcelor board member, or any external advisers, to be in on the discussion. If they were present, it would look to Mittal as if there was official sanction of the meeting. But, as part of government policy, no minister was ever to be left alone in such circumstances. It was agreed that Schmit would consult Luc Frieden. Between them they would nominate a government official to accompany Krecké. Gaston Reinesch from the Ministry of Finance got the job of note-taker.

'What should I say to Mr Mittal?' Krecké asked nervously.

'As little as possible,' said his advisers. 'Just listen.'

*

In the offices of the Luxembourg regulator, the Commission de Surveillance du Secteur Financier, no one seemed to be listening to Pierre-Yves Chabert. As he presented Mittal's draft shareholder prospectus, outlining the offer, to Jean-Nicolas Schaus, the CSSF's director general, and his takeover watchdog Françoise Kauthen, he could feel their hostility. As he spoke, they mostly stared at the ceiling. What little conversation they did have with him could have been summarised as follows: 'Good morning. Thank you. Goodbye.'

He was to get the same reaction from every regulator he visited.

17

Thursday 7 February, 10.30 a.m.

Hôtel Le Royal, Luxembourg City

Jean-Luc Pignier, revenue manager of the Royal, Luxembourg's plushest five-star hotel, checked the bookings for the remainder of February and noticed something odd was happening. February was always a quiet month and his forward budgeting had calculated that occupancy rates in his 190 guest-rooms on six floors and his twenty executive suites would fall below 50 per cent, as was normal for the early months of the year. But 90 per cent were booked for the whole month, and advance bookings for March were also way ahead of budget. Business was brisk, too, in the spa and in the small gymnasium. As he ran his finger down the bookings he noticed an unusually high number of exotic names – Chinese, Japanese, Russian, Brazilian. There is no major convention in town, he reasoned. Another unusual name caught his eye: Zaoui. He had not checked in yet. The reservation had been made that morning from London.

In the high-octane world of investment banking, two names were perennially obsessed with each other – Goldman Sachs and Morgan Stanley. They were always head to head in the big fee-earning takeover battles especially, on both sides of the Atlantic, where billing for advice, underwriting and success on one deal alone could run to £10 million. The competitive nature of the business brought on a fierce sense of rivalry between Goldman and Morgan. They frequently jostled for the top spot on the leader board of deals. Such was their omnipotence that if spotted at the opera clients had been known to crawl over the seats to shake the hand of their favourite banker in either house. Michael Zaoui was one such banker. Stylish and very successful, he worked for Morgan Stanley as chairman of European mergers and acquisitions.

Michael, as mentioned earlier, was Yoel's elder brother. Corporate finance was in the Zaoui genes. Both brothers were at the top of their game and earning million-dollar bonuses. They were frequently on opposite sides of a battle, but occasionally worked together for a client, mostly in France or Italy. Where Yoel was the quiet, instinctive strategist, Michael was flamboyant, a great inventive communicator. As brothers they were very close, speaking to each other most days, and dining their mother once a week. Fatigued by constant late nights in boardrooms, Michael, with his wife Anna and their two children, would go holidaying in the south of France with Yoel and his wife and two children. But when they were working on opposite sides there was one thing they never spoke about to one another: the deal.

'I hate not being involved in the big fights,' Michael once confided in a rare interview. 'Any top professional has to be in there.'

Which is why at that moment Michael Zaoui was sitting with Joseph Kinsch in his private meeting room, situated directly across from his office, the one place where the Arcelor chairman could light up a cigarette at will. A smoky atmosphere suited Zaoui too. Chicly Parisian in all other ways, his teeth betrayed a heavy cigar habit – Punch Habana (Manuel López) or Hoyo de Monterrey Habana were his preferred brands.

Having seen the list of banks already signed up by both sides of the proposed transaction, Michael Zaoui recognised that Morgan Stanley was conspicuous by its absence. To keep up its reputation he knew that his bank had to get into the game, and as a leading player. He did not do supporting cast.

'In a big fight like this you need me, and here's why,' Zaoui said, spreading six sheets of A4 down on the table. On each one was a value graph of six very big 'fights' where he had either successfully defended a target company or dramatically forced the bidder to offer far in excess of what they had originally planned. The week before, Zaoui had presented his six-graph trick to an impressed Guy Dollé in an office in Paris next to the La Défense headquarters of Société

Générale, which he had defended from takeover by its cross-town rival BNP Paribas in a five-month battle in 1999 that netted shareholders $20 billion.

'Then there was Crédit Commercial de France,' he said, showing Kinsch another graph and taking him through it in impressive and almost inspiring detail. 'In their successful $20 billion battle against ING of Holland I brought in HSBC as a white knight.' He moved to another sheet. 'In this transaction I defended Elf against Total,' he explained. 'Total won, but I got the deal up to $60 billion, way more than Total had been prepared to pay at the start. It was the same story with Aventis, a pharmaceutical company, in the hostile attack by Sanofi. Sanofi won, but we forced it to pay $70 billion – again, far in excess of its own assessment of the target's valuation.'

'Mr Zaoui,' Kinsch said, blowing smoke out through his nostrils and engaging Zaoui in one of his typically long stares: 'Arcelor is *not* for sale.'

'In any situation where you receive an unsolicited offer, the company is not for sale,' Zaoui agreed. He did not explain that hanging up the Not for Sale sign generally resulted in a higher price being achieved. Zaoui, who had graduated from Harvard Business School in 1983 and had travelled the world first class ever since, could tell that the Luxembourger Kinsch, who had never been a takeover target before, was in unknown territory. He noticed a slight tremor in the chairman's hand as he stubbed out one cigarette and lit another.

'Chairman Kinsch, in this fight you need to have someone who can speak in front of the board on the options generated by the eight other bankers who are working to the directorate general. Somebody who can tell you whether they make sense, whether they could be improved upon, whether other negotiations with other white knights should take place, how they compare to the existing offer and the prospect of getting a better offer from the first bidder. Basically, working for the shareholders.'

As Dollé had the week before, Kinsch grudgingly accepted that it was the Arcelor board's fiduciary role to maximise shareholder value. Kinsch looked at Zaoui favourably. He seemed to know what he was doing. He had authority and he explained things very simply. Kinsch was finding it difficult to navigate his way through this armada of banks and their advisory teams moored in numerous offices off the lofty cathedral-like corridors, many of them highly excited by the spreading news of Michael Zaoui's presence in the chateau. Kinsch realised that for the board to have its very own adviser had many advantages.

'I can promise you the mother of all defences,' Zaoui told him.

Kinsch smiled. His flinty eyes softened. 'I will have to get my board's approval. I will let you know in three days,' he said.

The chairman returned to his office. Joseph Kinsch was not by nature a spontaneous man, but now he sat down at his large black marble desk and sent an email to Dollé and Urquijo: 'I am engaging Michael Zaoui.' Board approval would be a formality. It would be unanimous.

Michael Zaoui left the Arcelor chateau and took in the crisp Luxembourg air. 'I think we are in the fight,' he told his banking colleague Bernard Gault, a portly Frenchman who had long-standing connections with Kinsch and who had set up the meeting. 'Bernard,' he added cheerfully, 'when we arrived one of the other bankers came up to me and said, pointing at you, "Who's the Russian?" They thought I had brought in a white knight from Moscow.' Gault, proudly French, was not amused.

Where Gault was slightly unkempt and with a waistline that betrayed a fondness for fine dining, Michael Zaoui, a French national like brother Yoel, was dressed impeccably in a tailored dark-blue suit and a crisp blue shirt. Right down to his Gucci shoes he looked like a matinée idol cruising elegantly into early middle age with his looks intact. He liked Gucci clothes for more than just the sartorial elegance they brought. Michael Zaoui had an unrivalled track record, but if there was one transaction that resonated more than most it was his role in defending Italy's Gucci against a hostile attack from the French luxury goods rival Louis Vuitton Moët Hennessy (LVMH) during a two-year battle in 1999–2001. Zaoui had defended Gucci with an inventiveness that caused controversy and some judicial disapproval. The main fight took place in the Netherlands, where Zaoui brought Gucci a white knight in the shape of Pinault-Printemps-Redoute, headed by François Pinault.

Gucci's holding company was incorporated in the Netherlands for tax reasons. Few employees worked there, but it owned the operating companies of the worldwide Gucci group. The Dutch authorities frowned on hostile takeovers and had introduced some interesting and unique devices for companies to fend off attackers with. Unlike other European jurisdictions, the Netherlands allowed companies to create a foundation – *stichting* in Dutch – that held shares with special voting rights or sheltered assets from corporate predators. The trustees of the foundation exercised the voting rights of the shares, giving them effective control of the company, while the owner of the receipts got all the economic benefit. It was a bit like making a vulnerable target company a ward of court.

Some of the country's lawmakers and lawyers feared that these foundations, like Amsterdam's brothels and marijuana shops, were a feature of a permissive society that persisted for the pleasure of foreigners. 'Anyone can come here, find a notary, and – boom – in ten minutes you have a *stichting*,' said Judge Huub Willems, who headed the Enterprise Chamber of the Amsterdam Court of Appeals, which heard disputes. Pinault, coming to the rescue of Gucci, agreed to put the company into a *stichting* to protect it from LVMH's clutches in a battle that was already raging in the Dutch courts. At first Zaoui had thought that the *stichting* would be seen as overtly protectionist and damaging to Morgan Stanley's jealously guarded reputation. He had a big late-night row with his legal adviser before agreeing to do it. That adviser was Scott Simpson of Skadden, Arps.

Zaoui had just finished checking in at the Royal when he spotted Simpson and Pierre Servan-Schreiber talking in the foyer amid a gaggle of lawyers and bankers from the various Arcelor defence teams.

'Guys!' Zaoui called out, rushing over to them. 'Tell me what I should know.'

Servan-Schreiber and Simpson exchanged nervous glances, but said nothing. This was not a conversation they wanted to take place in the foyer of the hotel, especially as they had been brought into the battle by Deutsche Bank, another fierce rival of Morgan Stanley.

'We can't talk here,' said Simpson, heading for the lift. 'Let's go upstairs.'

'So tell me what you guys are about to do,' Zaoui said, when they got to Simpson's room.

'Are you in on this?' Servan-Schreiber asked.

'Not quite,' Zaoui grinned, but he was bursting to know.

'We have just got the OK on a defence option from Arcelor counsel Frederik Van Bladel,' Simpson told him.

Zaoui saw a smile break on to Scott Simpson's face.

'Don't tell me,' he said, clapping his hands, 'you're not going to do that *stichting* thing again?'

'You know what,' the lawyers chorused, 'that's exactly what we are going to do.'

While the external lawyers plotted happily, not all was well within the Arcelor chateau. A disgruntled member of the company's senior management team was taking a swipe at the way Messrs Dollé, Kinsch, Wurth and Urquijo, especially Wurth, were handling the fight against Mittal. As far as he was concerned they hadn't the first clue, whereas he did, and he was not being listened to. Never mind. He was cheering himself up by beginning an account of a similar takeover battle being fought out in the parallel fantasy world of Taxembourg. He took the nom de plume 'Monsieur Shrek', and was using only the thinnest of veils for his cast of warring characters. The company CEO was warlike Astérix, its Spanish chief financial officer was Juan, hugely ambitious and with a 'movie star physique', and the deputy CEO who had been leading the undercover surveillance operation against their invader, Mister Moon, and his company of Indians for the past nine months was the garrulous Marcel Dumber, 'one of those people who needs to talk to find out what they are thinking'.

"We may be under attack from Indians," Dumber told Juan and Astérix, "but they won't get us, because while they may stick us full of arrows, we'll fight back with guns."'

Sure enough, in Chapter 1, 'Welcome, Mister Moon', Moon was accorded a special Taxembourg welcome as he drew up outside the regal building on Avenue de la Liberté in his black Mercedes to stake his claim to the crown of Arcelor. In the scrum that followed, Shrek heard *'the hard sound of a detonation. La tache rouge apparut soudain sur la belle chemise blanche de Mister Moon . . . the red spot suddenly appeared on Mr Moon's impeccable white shirt, just as he stepped out of the car, all smiles and hand extended, just before he fell to the sidewalk.'*

18

Brussels Airport

Back in the real world there was a spring in the step of Lakshmi
Mittal as he headed for his helicopter. 'Roland, are you OK for a helicopter trip to Paris?' Mittal asked Roland Verstappen, his newly
appointed director of government affairs. The Belgian, who for
twenty years had worked in the calmer confines and silo thinking of
the Ford Motor Company, now found himself smack in the middle
of the bitterest takeover battle in many years.

'Mr Mittal, I have never been in a helicopter,' Verstappen admitted, looking none too sure as they climbed into Mittal's
French-made black nine-seater Eurocopter.

'What?' Mittal, who had made hundreds of trips, couldn't believe
it.

Verstappen shook his head. As the five-bladed main rotor began to
turn, then whirr into a blur, Verstappen strapped himself in and
calmed his nerves to brief Mittal about the meeting he was due to
have that afternoon with fifty French MPs in Paris. Verstappen had
persuaded Mittal and Lisa Rabbe that here was another good chance
to tackle French concerns head on.

An hour later it was with some relief that Verstappen spotted the
Eiffel Tower to his right. It couldn't be long before they touched
down at Le Bourget. But the aircraft was now held, waiting for a
landing slot. It began to circle. Suddenly to his left Lakshmi Mittal
spotted another helicopter. It was circling too. Then he realised it
was tailing him, and getting closer. It was close enough for him to see

that somebody inside was holding up a sheet on which was printed what looked like a row of numbers. 'Maybe it's an offer that Arcelor will accept,' he joked, to keep Verstappen from passing out. The chasing helicopter edged closer. That's when Lakshmi Mittal saw the machine-guns.

He grabbed the intercom to speak to the pilot, Nik Bowe. It wasn't working. He started banging on the door. Now he was very afraid. The other helicopter seemed close enough to touch. What was going on? He banged some more. Eventually the door opened.

'They say we've strayed into military airspace,' Bowe called back to him over the noise of the twin engines. 'They're forcing us down.' Bowe could hear the other pilot ordering the control tower to give Mittal's helicopter a landing slot immediately. He was bringing in a suspicious aircraft.

Mittal could see the headlines now. 'Billionaire Indian Industrialist Arrested for Espionage', 'Mittal Now Being Questioned by Security Services'.

Once they landed it was Bowe who was taken away for questioning as the military helicopter flew away. As soon as the immigration official saw Mittal's passport, he said, 'You're Lakshmi Mittal. We know who you are, you can go.'

'Thank goodness this isn't America, where they shoot first and ask questions later,' Mittal smiled.

'But France is a civilised country, Mr Mittal.'

'The most civilised,' Mittal agreed, ushering Roland Verstappen to a waiting car.

At the French Parliament there were so many journalists and rubber-neckers inside and outside the building that the security guards had to shove them back to clear a path for Mittal. Following in his wake, Verstappen saw that this was what it must be like to be a celebrity, or even royalty. Everybody was slavering to get a close-up of the Rajah of Steel.

Inside, the reaction of MPs ran from cool to hostile. 'Will there be job losses?' they asked. 'Will you guarantee the investment in French plants already promised by Arcelor?' 'What is your plan?' 'What exactly is going on?' If the translator was charging for speed as well as accuracy, he could have afforded to retire by the time Mittal had described his plan in detail, told them that he wanted to stick to issues, not prejudices; assured them that there would be no job cuts beyond those already put in place by Arcelor, and that investments would be honoured. 'France is very crucial to this merger,' he told them.

Mittal left to a standing ovation. As he drove away into the city, he turned to Verstappen. 'Roland, are you enjoying yourself?'

'Yes, I think so,' Verstappen answered, still relieved to be back on solid ground.

'Good,' Mittal said. 'It is important to always enjoy.'

The next day, helicopter pilot Nik Bowe resigned. After several hours' interrogation by the French security services, he felt that there had to be easier ways of earning a living.

Although Mittal was having success wooing French national and regional politicians, Anne Méaux was busy in her office on the rue Copernic, a few minutes' walk from the Arc de Triomphe, organising what she called 'a climate of sympathy' in France for him. She had opened her cast-iron address book and invited some of France's leading business figures to meet Mittal at a series of dinners. 'Away from the storm they can meet you and realise that you are really one of them,' she had advised him. She also urged him to bolster his advisory team with a French bank. That would also send out powerful signals to the business community. And what better venue to host the first discreet meeting with France's entrepreneurial elite than François Pinault's house?

Pinault had already come out against his country's 'economic patriots'. 'I didn't like the welcome he received in France, nor the xenophobic, even racist character of certain comments about "the Indian",' he said.

Welcoming Lakshmi Mittal to his house, Pinault apologised 'for what some people have been saying. It reminds me of the way I was received when I began to succeed, because in France we are very snobbish and if you don't come from an old family, if you have not made very good graduate school, then you are considered dangerous, an outsider.' Introducing Mittal to his other guests, Pinault said – something he would go on to repeat many times – 'If you have a strong rationale and industrial logic, you will win.'

For Mittal it was a major boost. Unlike Thierry Breton, Pinault was a man who spoke the same language as him. He suddenly saw that France was not one country, but two in conflict. And the one that had not welcomed him was even more outraged when, a few days later, Mittal announced that he had added Société Générale to his banking team. Breton sprang back into print, telling *Le Figaro* and CNN that he supported 'economic patriotism' and that the government's plans to give the nation's companies extra defences against hostile takeover bids would have a 'dissuasive effect' on predators. The government would help shield French companies from bids that were totally hostile and undertaken without prior consultation, he said.

'This is a big political decision for Société Générale, and shows that some in the French establishment are happy to support Mittal,' a banker close to the deal said.

At Arcelor the news had rendered Joseph Kinsch speechless. As soon as he heard he had flown to Paris to meet Société Générale's chairman and CEO Daniel Bouton. You could not get much more French than fifty-six-year-old Bouton. He was a graduate of the École Nationale d'Administration, he had started his career in the Ministry of Finance and he was a Knight of the Légion d'Honneur.

'Daniel, how can you go to the other side?' Kinsch pleaded with him. 'Our two companies have excellent relations; until recently you were on our board.'

Bouton explained that he had not handled the arrangement personally – it had been done by his departments. His leaving the Arcelor board had nothing to do with Mittal, he said.

Kinsch did not find his arguments very convincing. Maybe if he had realised the resentment that Arcelor had generated at Société Générale by hiring arch-rivals BNP he might have understood. Bouton had waited and waited for the call that never came. Kinsch certainly would have understood Société Générale's decision to join Mittal if he had also known that Daniel Bouton was on Anne Méaux's list of must-meet dinner guests for her client.

19

Chamber of Deputies, Luxembourg City

Justice minister Luc Frieden rose on leaden legs before the Chamber of Deputies to present the draft takeover law. It was key territory for Arcelor's defence.

Frieden's advisers had drafted the document over a weekend, and it showed flaws. Whereas in France and the United Kingdom there were mature regulations already in place, Luxembourg had never had a takeover law. It had never needed one. Takeovers, especially hostile ones, just didn't happen in the Grand Duchy. Before the end of May a tortuous path lay ahead, when comments would be invited from business, trade unions, legal and academic circles. There would then be suggested amendments tabled before the Finance Committee, before the final bill was put to the parliamentary vote.

Already the lobbying on Frieden was intense. Pressure was building on him and, by implication, on Juncker and Krecké. In a press conference to announce the draft law, Frieden tried to manage expectations. 'Mittal Steel's bid for Arcelor has speeded up our work and we must adopt the Bill as soon as possible,' he declared. 'Once voted in, it will apply to all current public tender offers. It will allow a board of directors involved in a hostile takeover to defend themselves, as long as their actions are authorised by the shareholders.

'This is no more an anti-Mittal or pro-Arcelor law than an anti-Arcelor or pro-Mittal law,' he went on, enjoying the political double-speak. Then he added that, given the bid by Mittal for Arcelor, the 'process of adopting the new takeover legislation will be expedited and is expected to take place before 20 May'.

Dollé and Joseph Kinsch were furious. An anti-Mittal law was exactly what they wanted. Kinsch, who had fought so hard to keep Luxembourg as the headquarters during the ground-breaking deals with Aceralia and Usinor, had talked up the favourability of the Luxembourg laws as a big benefit.

Although Frieden had speeded up the timetable the government had invited submissions on the new law from interested parties, so Pierre Servan-Schreiber and Scott Simpson, working with four local law professors for academic gravity, set to work drafting amendments that while not overtly stopping Mittal would seriously hinder him. They put in a clause stating that if the bidder was proposing an offer in shares and cash and those shares were not liquid enough, then he would also have to propose a full-cash alternative. Mittal Steel, with its huge family shareholding, had a free float of 'liquid' shares that could be traded publicly of no more than 13 per cent. The other 87 per cent were owned by the Mittals, and were not on the market. The Arcelor lawyers knew full well that Mittal could not do a full-cash alternative for those who did not like his paper.

Servan-Schreiber and Simpson also requested that in the new law there should be a stipulation that in all takeovers there had to be, for a formal offer, a minimal acceptance level of at least 50 per cent of all the target shareholders. This was a convention followed by the UK and other European countries. This stipulation, if adopted by Luxembourg, would deny any bidder the flexibility of waiving the 50 per cent acceptance condition and accepting a lower level of 40–45 per cent, which is where they sensed Mittal might eventually finish, if he were to revise his offer. Putting the hurdle at 50 per cent could potentially scupper him.

Their third amendment said that if within six months of an offer the bidder had not attained sufficient acceptances, then the offer would lapse and the bidder could not return to bid again for a full twelve months, a rule in line with Britain's highly regarded self-regulatory code.

They submitted their amendments to Frieden, and hoped.

Frieden's brow grew increasingly furrowed as he was pulled this way, then that. He also knew that the Luxembourg Chamber of Commerce, the Grand Duchy's official business lobby, was working away on its proposals for the law; and just to make his day complete, he received a visit from socialist MP, and the trade union representative on Arcelor's board, John Castegnaro, who stormed into his office and told him: 'If you do not write a law that saves Arcelor from Mittal you are a traitor to your country.'

News of the great takeover-law drafting frenzy had reached Berkeley Square House. There was no such thing as a secret in steel or in government in a small country like Luxembourg, where ministers could be got on their direct lines by anybody with a cause to promote. 'Arcelor's lawyers are likely to try and get the government to introduce initiatives that could seriously harm us,' Pierre-Yves Chabert told Lakshmi Mittal.

'Can we stop them?' Mittal asked. His war room was worried.

'There is somebody I could call,' Chabert said, in typical understatement, 'but we will have to tread softly.'

Pierre-Yves Chabert had been at Harvard with Luc Frieden and they had kept in touch ever since. They had a mutual professional respect. Chabert dialled his number.

'We recognise that this takeover law is a problem for you,' Chabert told Frieden. 'We also recognise that you have to safeguard Luxembourg's position as a financial centre.'

'My country has become rich because it is an open one, and it is always internationally focused in its outlook,' Frieden replied.

'There are things that are acceptable and there are things which are not only going to be a problem for us but will damage Luxembourg, and you cannot allow a protectionist law to go forward,' Chabert said.

'I have no intention of putting the country in jeopardy by being protectionist,' Frieden agreed.

Chabert also homed in on the personal level. He knew that Luc Frieden was conscious of his own image beyond Luxembourg and concerned for his future political career. 'For fifteen years you have promoted your country as an open financial marketplace,' Chabert said, 'and to introduce the kind of law you are being urged to draft would be totally inconsistent. If you stay within the confines of the EU directive that allows you to be relatively neutral, that's your best position. And,' he added, 'think about how that will impact on our future relationship if we win.'

The conversations and emails between Chabert and Frieden continued quietly over the next weeks, and despite the encouraging noises coming from the justice minister a flurry of amendments assailed him from all directions.

'There is no certainty that the government has sufficient strength and persuasion to resist any amendments which are distinctly helpful to Arcelor,' Chabert reported back.

'There are just sixty MPs in the Parliament. To get thirty-one to vote an amendment in favour of Arcelor must be really easy,' Sudhir Maheshwari said.

'It could seriously narrow our options,' Aditya added. 'My father is in touch with Minister Krecké. I must try to get to Frieden. Can you arrange that?' he asked Chabert.

Thursday 9 February, 5.30 p.m.

Charleroi Airport

In the darkness of a dank February evening, Jeannot Krecké sat with his colleagues Georges Schmit and Gaston Reinesch as they drove up to the entrance of a small hotel after the one-hour drive from Luxembourg City. They were rehearsing the meeting with Mittal when Krecké's mobile rang. It was Lakshmi Mittal, still in the air, seeking directions. There had been some miscommunication. His Gulfstream was approaching Brussels.

'But I am at Charleroi,' Krecké explained. The Mittal jet banked steeply and headed due east, requesting a revised routing from the air traffic beacon.

Finally at 6.30, Krecké greeted Lakshmi and Aditya Mittal in the hotel lobby and they headed for a private room on the ground floor. Georges Schmit sat at the bar, looking like a delegate to an Inspector Maigret look-alike convention in his raincoat and hat. He gazed across to the private room and was alarmed. He could see clearly the Mittals and Krecké engaging in conversation. He quickly punched out a text to Krecké. 'The whole world can see you!' Within seconds, he saw Krecké rise, come to the window and close the curtains.

Krecké listened intently for two hours as the two Mittals explained in some detail the strategic rationale for their proposed deal with Arcelor. It was a polished and persuasive performance. Krecké could not help but be impressed, especially with the younger Mittal. As he listened, his mind was cross-checking with the boxes that his advisers had laid out as the negotiating territory for any government-backed deal with Mittal Steel, should that occasion arise. It was a long list, getting longer by the minute.

It was also dawning on him that, almost against his will, he was starting to like Mr Mittal.

Friday 10 February, 11.30 a.m.

Via Condotti, Rome

It was a beautiful sunlit morning as Michael Zaoui took a stroll along the capital's most elegant shopping street, lined on both sides by a fashion parade of boutiques. Bulgari, Cartier, Prada, Christian Dior, Valentino, Dolce & Gabbana – on and on they came relentlessly, and then of course his beloved Gucci. He was just wondering if he had swung the Arcelor ticket when his phone rang. It was his colleague Bernard Gault.

'Michael, I've just had a call from Kinsch. He's hiring Morgan Stanley.'

Much too couth to punch the air, Zaoui contented himself with his favourite phrase, 'Great! We're in the fight.'

Back in Luxembourg, 'Monsieur Shrek' was just as thrilled. Here was some muscle at last, come to save Arcelor. He christened Zaoui 'the Great Zoudini' after his daring escape acts from corporate predators. He wrote almost lyrically, if touched with a little hyperbole, which betrayed his excitement.

'Of all the types of people you meet in the world of hostile takeover bids, none is more fascinating than the investment banker. As predators of the

financial steppes, they prowl their hunting area, always on the lookout, always looking for prey; they have the muscles of a tiger, the eye of a lynx, and sometimes the laugh of a hyena. Compared to them, the other inhabitants of the corporate jungle play only token roles.

Commercial bankers, for instance, often look more imposing because of their size, but they are usually not particularly dangerous – rather like ele-phants and buffaloes, and indeed they have the same gregarious habits. Lawyers are more like birds, waders quoting the law in a learned fashion or brightly coloured parrots with no real influence over events despite their constant babble. Communicators are more like zebras – amusing and attrac-tive to start with, but impossible to tame because of their nasty nature, which means they are no use to anyone.

And then there are the representatives of the government, the local author-ities and the trade unions – they all make you think instantly of various types of monkey. You hear the noise they make, but it's no real threat – their antics scarcely conceal their impotence, although they provide a good deal of enter-tainment.

We should not forget those animals that are least visible although most numerous, those who always win and will prosper in any operation – the great cohort of shareholders, investors and fund managers, the huge mass of people retired from the Californian civil service, widows from Carpentras and Edinburgh, Belgian dentists, all those small shareholders, savers and pensioners who are the ultimate holders of capital in today's economy. They ensure decomposition – they are the insects, larvae, worms and higher microbes that will make it possible to recycle, distribute and re-use organic matter, because capitalism is life that goes on with no purpose.

And finally, hovering above the scene, there are the journalists, informa-tion vultures, constantly drawn by a sure-fire instinct to the smell of blood, even if they don't understand much about the events they are going to feast on.

No one understood this race of major business bankers better than the Great Zoudini. He was the archetype of his profession, its ultimate incarna-tion. He was a star. And it's no doubt because of that that he managed – against all expectations – to get on board our already overloaded ship.'

20

Sunday 12 February

Arcelor boardroom

Pierre Servan-Schreiber glanced around the imposing room. It was his first time at an Arcelor board meeting, and he kept reminding himself that those seated around the table represented the essence of the company's vaunted industrial model. A totally non-executive board, drawn from all the constituent parts of the Arcelor group including trade unions as well as the Luxembourg government, all dutifully represented. Even the Grand Duke had his brother there to represent the Grand Duchy's interests. Who could argue that Arcelor did not have supreme corporate governance principles in place?

However, the PR battle was becoming a potential rout. As Servan-Schreiber had said to Scott Simpson, 'On their side they have the world's fourth-richest man with good looks to match and a son who looks like a Bollywood star. What do we have on our side? Two old guys with moustaches.' If Arcelor stood any chance of winning this fight he knew the lawyers would have to pull out all the stops . The board all sat expectantly as Servan-Schreiber updated them on the defence strategies to combat Mittal. First, he talked about the impending Luxembourg law and their attempts to influence the process. 'We feel we are not winning the arguments here and we sense the government is under a lot of pressure, especially from Brussels, to stay close to the directive.'

The faces looked glum. Servan-Schreiber moved on quickly to Dofasco.

'Mittal needs to deal with his problems with *his* assets, not Arcelor's,' he said. 'We have to force him to that position and we can do this by ring-fencing Dofasco out of his grasp through a legal device available in the Netherlands. It's called a *stichting.*' Some members looked puzzled by this new word thrust suddenly into their vocabulary by the eloquent Servan-Schreiber.

'My colleague Scott Simpson is working on the detail as we speak. He has used this device with great success on a previous transaction relating to Gucci, saving them from a hostile takeover. Scott will give you a detailed presentation at your next meeting.'

For the first time since Mittal's strike they sensed they had something to look forward to.

'The legal justification for putting Dofasco in a *stichting* is that we are protecting an Arcelor asset which Mittal intends to sell below what you paid for it. If what he is doing is not illegal, it is certainly immoral. By preventing the sale we safeguard the interests of your shareholders and force him to deal with his assets, not yours, in compliance with US anti-trust rules. We also immediately deprive him of the cash he would receive in selling Dofasco, which we believe he needs to buy Arcelor.'

All the heads were nodding now.

'There is another point we have to be mindful of in connection with Mittal Steel's proposed deal with ThyssenKrupp on Dofasco. Intentionally or not, it puts the Germans off-limits as a white knight for Arcelor. Food for thought, gentlemen?' Servan-Schreiber suggested, as he moved on to discuss the white knight strategy.

Arcelor had a trump card, the authority to issue up to 30 per cent of new capital, without the approval of its shareholders – to combine in a deal with another major steel company, creating a new grouping that could see off Mittal. As Servan-Schreiber knew personally from the medley of languages to be heard over the dining tables and bar of the Hôtel Le Royal, Luxembourg was now swarming with alternative suitors to Mittal. Senior Arcelor management were jumping on planes and heading out as far as China and Brazil, racking up the airmiles in a desperate search for saviours. 'If none of these efforts are coordinated they might even be counterproductive,' he advised the board. 'You will need legal support.' He had already told Van Bladel, 'You are talking of deals between five and ten billion euros.

There's a danger that it will take off in an unstructured way and confidence will be breached.'

Just as Chairman Kinsch was thanking Servan-Schreiber for his most constructive report, one of the directors chirped: 'This *stichting* of yours – is there anything else we can put in it?'

By now Servan-Schreiber had his team installed in a much nicer room than the attic 'shack' they had been allocated on day one. Just along from Chairman Kinsch's office and the boardroom, it overlooked the inner courtyard and was already known as 'the Skadden Room'. An early visitor next day was Frederik Van Bladel. 'Bearing in mind what you said to me and the board yesterday,' he said, 'we would like you to help us in negotiations with two sets of potential partners.'

21

Tuesday 14 February

San Felice, Milan

'I live in Italy and I prefer only to invest in Italian companies,' Romain Zaleski said. The seventy-three-year-old billionaire was sitting at his antique desk in the windowless basement office of his town house in the Milan suburb of San Felice, one of three districts in Milan regarded by taxi drivers as 'Berlusconi country' because of the residents' voting loyalty to Italy's colourful Prime Minister and media mogul. The district contained unpretentious houses with terracotta frontages. Wooden lattice entrance gates opened to steep steps leading up to varnished front doors. The ground-floor windows were protected by white security railings, and after 8 p.m. the area became a gated community. Inside his house the French-born, bridge-loving billionaire was finessing a question put to him on the telephone by Patrick Ponsolle, president of Morgan Stanley in France.

Tall and slim, with pastel-blue eyes set in a pallid face looking starved of sunlight, Zaleski seemed at odds with his surroundings. Around the bright-yellow walls were gilt-framed pictures of the Madonna and child – there were twelve in the sitting room alone, along with two fine medieval sculptures of the Virgin Mary. There were also many pictures of angels and his shelves were crammed with books on Italian art and Italian cities. Antique carpets in soft blues and reds, and stunning blue, yellow and red glassware blown by the glassworkers of Murano in the Venice lagoon completed the kaleidoscope of colours.

'Romain, you know the steel industry well,' Ponsolle said, from his office in Paris. 'There's a very interesting investment situation developing at Arcelor in Luxembourg.'

Zaleski smiled, his eyes slanting to accentuate the lines on his face, giving way to an impish grin. He felt flattered by his fellow Frenchman, but he preferred to concentrate on what he did best: spotting money-making opportunities in Italy's nepotistic industrial and financial landscape, and collecting religious works of art, antiques and rugs.

'You should take a close look at the opportunity,' Ponsolle urged him. 'Arcelor needs your support.'

Romain Zaleski had amassed more than €2.5 billion by playing the catalyst in Italy's complex web of cross-shareholdings controlled by Mediobanca, a financial institution that had dominated corporate deal-making in Italy under its omnipotent chairman, Enrico Cuccia. But since Cuccia's death in 2000, Mediobanca had become the object of intense in-fighting, and that had presented new opportunities for Zaleski. He was a shrewd entrepreneur with a maverick streak, and played outside Italy's *salotto buono*, an Agnelli-led group of powerbrokers drawn from industrial, financial and political circles who since the Second World War had virtually controlled Italian industry.

Zaleski's early life had been full of adversity. He grew up in Paris, the son of Polish parents who fled to France before the war. In 1944, when he was eleven, his parents took him on a fleeting and dangerous visit to see relatives in Warsaw, but his family became trapped there. According to close friends, the young Zaleski risked his life delivering information to Polish Resistance workers on behalf of his mother. He returned to see his mother arrested before his eyes by the Gestapo. He went back to Paris, his family divided and under great strain. Eventually, they were reunited and Zaleski went on to perform brilliantly at his studies. He graduated from the École Polytechnique – ten years before Guy Dollé – and then the École des Mines in Paris, a school for mining engineers. The French civil service called for him and he served as technical consultant in the Ministry of Industry, working closely with Valéry Giscard d'Estaing. While in Paris he married his second wife Hélène de Pritwitz, who was of Russian and German extraction and a descendant of Peter the Great. Together they had two sons, Wladimir and Konstantin. Zaleski had had a daughter, also Hélène, with his first wife Anna. History remains silent on what happened to that marriage.

Zaleski developed a love for bridge and hoped to become French champion, but in 1961 at the age of twenty-eight, he was committed to earning a living and bringing up a family, so he decided to leave the card tables. He enjoyed being involved in heavy industry – steel, iron, metallurgy and the production of electric power – and increasingly entertained the thought of working in the private sector. He crossed the Rubicon in the 1970s, working as a company turnaround specialist and then became managing director of the Paris-based conglomerate Révillon. He inherited his father's business Eramet, a hundred-year-old company which specialised in non-ferrous metals and owned a nickel mine in the French overseas territory of New Caledonia. Quietly and efficiently, Romain Zaleski began to create wealth through a series of well timed deals.

In 1984 he made a big change in his life. While retaining his business interests in France, he moved to Italy to become managing director of Carlo Tassara, a near-bankrupt steel company based in Breno in the foothills of the Italian Alps. If he succeeded in rescuing the company he would receive a 25 per cent stake. The Frenchman loved the challenge, and over the next five years he modernised the business and made it profitable, backed by regional banks such as Banca Lombarda. Ever grateful, the Tassara family allowed him to take majority control in 1989. By now Zaleski was enjoying the Italian way of life and his daughter Hélène was showing a distinct liking for her father's business, which thrilled him.

Still relatively unknown in Italian business circles, Zaleski suddenly burst into prominence when in 1996 he acquired a 38.5 per cent stake in a troubled Milan-based engineering group called Gruppo Falck. He had calculated that the market valuation of Falck, trading at €1.30 per share, was so low that it was worth buying it and then selling off its individual parts for more than the whole. He was right, cashing out with €350 million – a 300 per cent gain.

A man who shunned profile, Zaleski now suddenly found himself in the news, romanced by Milan's gossipy business press. He also began to win admiration from the city's banking cognoscenti. The deal with Falck had concentrated his mind on Montedison, and that is where he struck next.

In the autumn of 2000 Zaleski announced to a stunned Milan business community that he had acquired a 15 per cent stake in the utilities company Montedison, equalling Mediobanca's own stake in the company. He told the press, 'Montedison is a jewel of a company with enormous future potential.' The jewel was Edison, Italy's number two gas and electricity utility, well placed to take on Enel, the number one Italian energy distributor. In May the following year, the state-owned French utility Électricité de France (EDF) shocked the political and financial establishment of Italy by announcing it had acquired a 20 per cent stake in Montedison, 5 per cent of it bought from Zaleski, making him €50 million on one-third of his original investment.

All governments become protectionist over the security of domestic energy supplies. The thought that Edison might pass to a French state-owned company sent the Italians into a rage. Zaleski was now under fire for trying to help France break into Italy under cover. The Italian government retaliated with a temporary decree that froze all voting rights in Montedison at 2 per cent. A long-drawn-out fight followed, in which EDF and Milan's municipal utility AEMSpa became partners in a holding company that owned 71 per cent of Edison. EDF owned another 17 per cent directly in Edison. Zaleski ended up with warrants in Edison which gave him the right to buy shares in the company at €1 per share up to a total of €500 million. It was classic Zaleski, spinning money-making deals out of complex bid battles.

'Now I have to wait. I launched the game, but it has gone way beyond me,' Zaleski told the local media in his inimitable self-effacing manner. The media's consensus view was that the French-born maverick had turned the tables on Italy's old-fashioned style of capitalism. *Business Week* had a more dramatic headline. 'Romain Zaleski: The Frenchman Who Is Shaking Up Italy Inc'.

With a 2 per cent stake in Italy's biggest insurer Assicurazioni Generali, worth almost €1 billion, and his investments in Banca Intesa, Italy's second-largest bank, and in Montedison as well as a clutch of other Italian industrial companies, Zaleski had become a major investment player in Italy.

Then, curiously, after a thirty-year break he took up bridge again, delegating more of the day-to-day business side to his daughter and to his smart lieutenant, Mario Cocchi. 'It is like learning a new language,' he said, but having finished in the top ten of a world bridge seniors convention in his first week back at the tables, he showed that he had not lost his Midas touch.

Two days after his conversation with Ponsolle, Zaleski received a call from BNP Paribas, whom he knew well from his business days in France. On the line was Christophe Moulin, newly appointed adviser to Arcelor. All nine of Arcelor's banking advisers had been urged by Kinsch and Dollé to help put together a fan club of investors who between them could create a blocking stake against Mittal. BNP had singled out Zaleski as a prime candidate.

'Would you be interested in a private presentation on Arcelor and its strategy?' Moulin asked him. 'We would be happy to arrange this for you at a mutually agreed time with Gonzalo Urquijo, the chief financial officer of Arcelor. Would you mind coming to Paris?'

Within twenty-four hours the date had been fixed for 21 March.

In the financial calendar of the corporate world, February and March are known as the 'results' season. It's when listed corporations report to their shareholders on the results of their financial and operating performance for the preceding year. It can be a time of high tension, depending on which way the trade winds are blowing for the company in question.

All listed companies have to provide periodic guidance to the financial market ahead of time, and this is particularly important for analysts, who follow the company closely and provide their own projections in advance of the official numbers. The art is for companies to offer guidance without breaking inside-information rules and then to deliver results slightly ahead of market expectations. Everyone looks good that way, the markets like the numbers, the analysts' professional judgements do not appear out of line, the media reports are favourable and the shareholders generally rejoice.

For Arcelor, after the media battering over Dollé's outbursts and the political furore in Paris and Luxembourg, there was real hope that a more favourable wind might be heading their way.

On 15 February Mittal Steel announced a net income for 2005 of $3.36 billion. It was a decline of 28 per cent. Its operating margin was also down, from 28 per cent in the corresponding period the year before to 12 per cent, mirroring the fact that steel 'spot' prices had fallen more than a third during 2005. Mittal was more vulnerable to 'spot' prices, since it had far fewer of the more lucrative annual contracts where prices were locked in. The fourth quarter of 2005 had been particularly tough, with profits of $650 million, down 58 per cent from $1.6 billion in the fourth quarter of 2004.

On the upside, Mittal had boosted both production and sales volume during 2005, having integrated ISG, and had begun to get to grips with Ukraine, a valuable new low-cost provider. Total turnover was up from $22 billion to $28 billion and the guidance was that earnings would rise in 2006. Market observers were impressed by a 22 per cent return on equity – the percentage ratio of total shareholders' equity (shares) divided into the net income of the company – but Mittal Steel shares fell on the Amsterdam exchange, a point quickly seized on by Arcelor. Their shareholders would not want to accept weakened Mittal shares, which constituted 75 per cent of the cash/shares mix in the tender offers. It was a destabilising point.

The next day Arcelor came out in a blaze of glory, announcing a dramatic financial and trading improvement in 2005, posting a net profit of €3.84 billion, up 66 per cent from 2004, with turnover exceeding €32 billion. In an overt move to keep its shareholders sweet, Arcelor's board chose to double up its dividend from €0.65 to €1.20 per share. There was more to come, it promised. Gross operating profit in 2006 would reach €7 billion, versus €5.6 billion in 2005, and cash flow would exceed €4.4 billion. Add in predicted savings of €2.2 billion through the integration of Dofasco, and Arcelor was looking like the veritable cash cow, generating large volumes of excess money.

The results spoke for themselves and were a big boost for Guy Dollé's leadership, and more than a ray of hope for the defence team. 'These fantastic results prove the efficiency of the Arcelor model,' the company's chief declared proudly. 'Arcelor is transforming itself into a world champion. We have brilliant development and value perspectives over the next four years.'

As Dollé and Urquijo hit the road to woo shareholders in Europe and North America with the same upbeat messages, market observers were combing through the detailed financial figures of both Arcelor and Mittal and trying to come up with a considered view. In soccer parlance it was a score draw. Both companies were in good shape, and the debate was shifting from political rancour to the all-important question: the value of Arcelor. 'Mittal is trying to grab Arcelor on the cheap,' said breakingviews.com, the world's leading source of online financial comment, producing a cold analysis of the strengths of both companies. Both sides were exaggerating their cases, it stated.

'Essentially by saying that he doesn't need to pay more, Lakshmi Mittal is implying that his paper is 34 per cent more valuable than Arcelor's. All in all, the Mittal paper is worth more. But not 34 per cent more. Exactly what would be a fairer exchange ratio is hard to say and will become clearer as the battle proceeds,' said the breakingviews commentator Edward Hadas. By splitting the difference, there was an implied increase in Mittal's offer of about 17 per cent. 'But to extract that – let alone more – Arcelor will have to produce a proper defence,' Hadas concluded.

For both sides there would be a lot of fights in many different arenas.

If Lakshmi Mittal was piling on the mileage, sweet-talking politicians and shareholders, others of his team were putting in punishing travel hours. His French advisers Shahriar Tadjbakhsh, Pierre-Yves Chabert and Anne Méaux were frequent visitors to London, but it was Laurent Meyer, the tall, good-looking managing director of mergers and acquisitions at Société Générale, who had just joined the team, who was having to commute every single day. His job was crucial. He would handle all the French financial connections for Mittal and organise roadshows for him to swing the support of Arcelor shareholders in France. Mittal and Maheshwari knew Société Générale was crucial to establishing a French bridgehead, so every day Meyer got up at 5 a.m., took a flight from Charles de Gaulle to City Airport which landed at 7.25, then jumped into a taxi for the forty-five-minute – traffic permitting – ride to Berkeley Square House for an 8.30 meeting, where he would report on progress. Then he would head back in the afternoon to continue his work in Paris, often long into the night.

By the time Meyer got to Mittal Steel, the London-based bankers had been huddling in their respective coffee shops comparing notes over their skinny lattes with an extra shot. Company allegiances still held sway, as each bank colonised a different cappuccino outlet in and around Curzon Street. Jeremy Fletcher cut a lone figure under the plane trees of Berkeley Square, sucking the life out of a final cigarette before his day got under way. One morning as he stubbed out and was walking into Berkeley Square House he bumped into Aditya Mittal.

'You know, Jeremy, Arcelor is a fantastic company,' Aditya enthused.

'It *is* an excellent company,' agreed Fletcher, who in the past had had a minor advisory role to Guy Dollé. 'In fact,' he laughed, 'it's possibly a much better company than your company.'

'That's true,' Aditya laughed back.

But who, if either of them, was joking?

22

19–21 February

New Delhi

If President Jacques Chirac felt he had ridden out the storm over Mittal and staved off a further international diplomatic disaster with India by ordering the toxic ship the *Clemenceau* to turn round and return to France two days before his state visit, he was sadly ill advised. As the presidential jet carrying him, five ministers including Thierry Breton, and thirty-two business and industrial leaders neared Delhi's Indira Gandhi International Airport, the patrician politician was focusing hard on how France and her sluggish economy could get a bigger slice of India's economic boom. For every $1000 that India imported, France sold it just $18 worth, as the subcontinental superpower turned its attention away from Old Europe towards the New World.

He landed to the latest issue of the *Tribune*, an Indian daily published out of Chandigarh. It warned: 'Aside from any fallout from the *Clemenceau* dispute, another possible sore spot is last month's bid by Lakshmi N. Mittal to buy Arcelor SA.' Indian business leaders were still calling France's reaction to the bid xenophobic.

Lakshmi Mittal also happened to be in Delhi to attend the wedding of the son of his old friend Sant Singh Chatwal, the Sikh international hotel magnate based in New York and a major fundraiser for the Democrat Party. His son Vikram – also an hotelier, who had combined M&A work for Morgan Stanley with a modelling career – had like Aditya Mittal attended the Wharton School of Business. But there any similarity with Mittal's home-loving boy, also in India with his wife Megha for the wedding, ended. Sant Chatwal was out to tame his hard-living, jet-setting, model-dating son, known in Manhattan as the Turban Cowboy, with a wedding that would outshine even the lavish nuptials of Vanisha Mittal.

Lakshmi Mittal had caused a near-media riot when he and Usha had arrived in Delhi on the evening of 18 February. Disappearing into a melee of journalists and cameramen, he refused to comment on Arcelor, merely telling them that he was taking a break from a series of 'roadshows' that were now under way, where he had been meeting Arcelor shareholders. This was a purely private visit, he said, although he did give a television interview, remarking, 'I am sure that the Prime Minister Dr Manmohan Singh will take up this issue' with President Chirac. Singh's office, however, had said that the Prime Minister was unlikely to broach the subject with Chirac.

Any disappointment Mittal felt was short-lived. He was delighted when he then got a call from Prime Minister Singh, India's first Sikh premier, asking if he would attend an official lunch he was giving for Chirac on Sunday 19 February. 'I am delighted to accept,' said Mittal, who had always enjoyed rubbing shoulders with major world figures like Tony Blair and Bill Clinton, with whom he had had a meeting the previous evening. Clinton was also a guest at the Chatwal wedding. Mittal was keen to share his thoughts with political leaders, and Singh, the man he always referred to as 'my prime minister', was no exception. He also took notice of what they said, sometimes dramatically.

Three years before at a meeting in the Indian capital, Singh's predecessor Atal Bihari Vajpayee had asked him: 'Mr Mittal, where do you live when you are in India?'

'I live in the hotel,' said Mittal, who although he had no steel interests in India often visited the country as a board member of ICICI, India's biggest private-sector bank and the country's second-largest lender, with twenty-four million customers.

'Mr Mittal, it is not right that a man of your standing should be living in the hotel,' the Prime Minister implored him. 'You must have a house here.'

As soon as the meeting was over, Mittal had rushed to call his wife. 'Usha, we must buy some land and build a house.' Usha swept into action, spending a reported £7.5 million on an old colonial bungalow at 22 Aurangzeb Road, the capital's most exclusive street, occupied by embassies and millionaires, and rebuilt it as a house. The next-door neighbours were those other successful Rajasthani exports, the Birla family, whose multibillion-dollar interests ranged from textiles and commodities to automobiles and telecommunications.

Singh's lunch could also give Mittal the chance to meet another world leader and maybe persuade Jacques Chirac that his bid for Arcelor posed no threat to anybody's job, that no plants would be closed. Before setting off from his new house, Mittal went through the all-familiar arguments in his mind, the synergies, the industrial logic . . . His thoughts were suddenly interrupted. His phone was ringing. The voice on the other end of the line was not Indian.

'Mr Mittal,' the high-ranking French government official said, 'we request that you do not attend the lunch today.' Mittal demanded that he explain himself. The 'request' had come from the very top, he was told. Chirac did not want to meet him. His presence there would be considered 'unfortunate'.

Mittal was in a dilemma. He could either risk upsetting his Prime Minister by not attending the lunch or he could turn up and cause a diplomatic rumpus with the French, whom, in spite of governmental intransigence, he still believed he could woo to his bid for Arcelor. He put business before political patronage, and chose the latter.

That evening he was at a drinks reception when he saw the seventy-four-year-old Manmohan Singh making a beeline for him. 'You did not come for the lunch,' the Prime Minister said. Mittal apologised profusely and hinted at the French phone call. Ever the stealth diplomat, he also saw an opportunity. 'I would like to meet you officially sometime tomorrow and explain everything,' he said.

He had his wish. The PM would see him just before his official bilateral talks with Chirac at Hyderabad House, the palace built by Edwin Lutyens in 1926 and now used by the government of India for banquets and meetings with visiting foreign dignitaries.

Mittal was there promptly. He met Singh for just a few minutes but it gave him the chance to present his case for taking over Arcelor, to brief the Prime Minister on his meeting with Thierry Breton, and to explain that his non-attendance at the lunch was just the latest episode in the French government's hostile reaction to his bid. Singh agreed that he would indeed raise the issues with Chirac. At the beginning of their meeting Mittal had thought that at least if he could not get to Chirac directly to discuss his bid, this was the next-best thing. Now when he shook hands with Singh and prepared to leave he had changed his mind. Having a prime minister do it for you was an even better thing.

He called London and updated Nicola Davidson. Within minutes her communications hounds were hunting down the Delhi press corps just to make sure that Chirac suffered maximum payback for Mittal's cancelled lunch.

On Monday 20 February a beaming President Chirac sat beside Prime Minister Singh in front of the world's press. After signing nine agreements including one on defence cooperation and issuing a declaration on 'the development of nuclear energy for peaceful purposes', the two leaders opened up for questions on their 'land-mark' meeting. But the journalists already had another script.

'On the Arcelor case and your reaction to that,' the first questioner asked, 'isn't there something of a contradiction between your willingness to develop commercial relations with us and your reservations about this takeover?'

The President's smile disappeared quicker than the *Clemenceau* steaming back to Toulon on full throttle. 'I would not put it quite in these terms,' Chirac replied haughtily. 'First of all, the company which is willing to take over Arcelor is not an Indian company. It is a Dutch company.'

'But it is owned and operated by a person of Indian origin?' came the follow-up.

'Certainly, but the problem has nothing to do with L.N. Mittal. It is a Dutch company and Arcelor is a Luxembourg company. It has nothing to do with France and India.'

Still the questions came.

'But what does your government think of the bid?'

'The French authorities are concerned about the shareholders and the company. Again, there is room for debate on questions like differences in corporate cultures between Arcelor and Mittal, or the conditions of the bid.'

'If shareholders' interests were better understood, would you not have any objection to the bid?'

Chirac raised himself up. He was irritated. He had been well and truly mugged. It might have been possible to avoid having lunch with Lakshmi Mittal but his influence was at work everywhere. 'Again, the French government is a stakeholder, not a shareholder,' he said. 'Given the circumstances of the case, it would appear that it is not in the best interest of the company. It is up to the two companies involved to agree on the terms. It has got nothing to do with India.'

'In this somewhat strained situation, wouldn't you like to meet him, to clear up the misunderstanding, if there is a misunderstanding?'

Chirac's temper was fraying. 'I have to say that I find it hard to understand this dispute. First of all, clearly, two parties are involved here. A British resident of Indian origin at the head of a Dutch company who wishes to buy a Luxembourg company. As things stand at the moment, this is a so-called hostile bid, purely financial in character, without any known industrial project and without any prior consultation, contrary to normal practice.'

Chirac admitted that he had not looked at the offer document and claimed, 'We don't know what the plans are at the moment, we are waiting to find out – we'd like to know what's involved, what the plans are, so that we can take a view on this point. There's no question of any dispute; it's a natural and legitimate reaction.'

Any triumph Chirac had been expecting had just vanished. He looked across at Singh to help him out. There was nothing doing. Another journalist stepped up to the platform.

'Mr President, will your government take direct or indirect action to ensure it doesn't succeed?'

'I repeat, we haven't initiated any action against any company, or even against any procedure,' Chirac insisted via his interpreter. 'We are facing a situation where one major group has launched a hostile bid against another one, contrary to all normal practice, without us having the slightest knowledge of the reasons for it or the programme proposed. We're waiting, which is normal, to find out about the plans from the Mittal company and, when we know what they are, we'll form an opinion, in accordance with the traditions and laws and independence of the economic sector.'

Finally Prime Minister Singh came to his rescue, directing journalists now to ask some questions about their talks, but not before adding, 'I have held discussions with President Chirac on Mr Mittal's bid and I hope for a fair decision.'

As Chirac was still fluffing around, Mittal was on his way back to Indira Gandhi International to catch his plane back to Luton. Next day he had a date with an influential Spaniard in Madrid.

Guy Dollé, meanwhile, had received a nasty letter from American hedge fund Atticus Capital, which had $10 billion of assets under management and was one of Arcelor's largest shareholders. And just to make sure that the world knew about it, the Atticus chairman Timothy R. Barakett and vice chairman David Slager had published their letter on the newswires.

'We were very disappointed by the Board's initial reaction to the tender offer made by Mittal Steel and by your continued refusal to meet with them to discuss their offer for *our* company,' it began. 'We believe in the compelling industrial and financial merits of the transaction [which] would be in the best interests of Arcelor shareholders and stakeholders. We urge you to engage in negotiations in order to maximise their offer.' Then came the sting: 'We would like to remind you of the Board of Directors' obligations and fiduciary duty to your shareholders, and we reserve the right to protect our interests through voting at the April 28 AGM and/or through the courts.'

Arcelor insisted that it had received no such request for a meeting from other investors, but Lakshmi Mittal heaped on the pressure in an interview with Peter Marsh of the *Financial Times*. 'I hope that Arcelor management will agree to our idea of having a meeting to discuss our ideas and explain the logic. But if they don't agree to this in the end it will be the shareholders who must decide.'

'What's been the reaction of the Arcelor shareholders you have contacted?' Marsh asked.

'We estimate that we have talked to the shareholders, who account for 40 per cent of the "free float" of Arcelor, excluding the Luxembourg government and other groups with large shares that are relatively fixed and account for about 10 per cent of the total. We've generally encountered enthusiastic support.'

Tuesday 21 February

Madrid–Torrejón Airport

Spanish billionaire José María Aristrain was Arcelor's second-biggest shareholder, with a 3.6 per cent stake, but he never attended board meetings, sending instead a representative, his Madrid-based lawyer Ramón Hermosilla Martín, to do his bidding. According to *Forbes* magazine, which listed him as the world's 557th richest man, Aristrain never went out in public without a bodyguard to protect him and his family from kidnapping attempts that he feared could come any day from Basque separatists. Others said the bodyguards were an exaggeration. Aristrain also owned a cattle ranch in Seville, where he raised bulls for bullfighting.

His father, a giant in the Spanish steel industry who had founded the Corporación JMAC, based in Madrid and with steelworks in the Basque country, had been killed in a helicopter crash when José María was just twenty-two. José María did not have his father's touch; he sold his plants to newly privatised Aceralia in exchange for 10 per cent of the new company, a stake that was reduced to 3.6 per cent when Aceralia was folded into Arcelor. Even though 10 per cent of Aceralia was worth the same as 3.6 per cent of Arcelor, Aristrain had always felt short-changed in the deal and he held Joseph Kinsch and Gonzalo Urquijo, who had once worked for him, responsible. His relationships with both men were never easy, which was why, when all at Arcelor were gnashing their teeth at the Indian predator at their gate, Aristrain had said to his assistant: 'I would like an introduction to Lakshmi Mittal.' As the Mittal jet touched down, he viewed his guest's imminent arrival with great anticipation.

Staring out through his window, Mittal wondered if Aristrain might be a key to unlocking some support on the Arcelor board.

3 p.m.

Ministry of Economy and Foreign Trade, Luxembourg City

'Gentlemen, the salient point is that Arcelor may not remain independent at the end of this battle.'

Jeannot Krecké flinched. These unwelcome words had been uttered by Thierry d'Argent, corporate financier with JPMorgan Chase & Co. in Paris, who had just been hired by Georges Schmit to advise the Luxembourg government on how to manage their part in the bid battle.

'Are you saying that whatever happens in this battle, Arcelor cannot survive on its own?' Schmit asked.

'Much will depend on the government's stance, whether it wants to be overtly protectionist by legal means, or remain neutral, allowing all the shareholders to determine the outcome,' the banker replied.

D'Argent knew he was on sensitive ground. These were early days and he would need to spend a considerable amount of time helping Krecké and other government officials think through the key issues: Arcelor's true financial worth, regulatory matters in Luxembourg, the EU and the USA, corporate governance, the dynamics of the investors, especially the hedge funds and the financial markets, and above all timing and knowing when to exert its influence.

It had not been easy for Schmit to find an investment-banking house with the necessary credentials, since most had already been hired to work for either Arcelor or Mittal. JPMorgan was big, global and had a strong team at its lavish and gilded offices on the Place Vendôme in Paris, the other end of the architectural rainbow from Krecké's humdrum HQ. Furthermore, JPMorgan had demonstrated an acute understanding of the issues facing the government, and Schmit was greatly relieved to have them on board. Schmit was also closing the loop on his last advisory appointments, having hired Dechert, a leading international firm with a Luxembourg presence, as legal advisers and international communications company Gavin Anderson to handle the PR.

In an elaborate presentation, d'Argent had spelt out the issues
with a comprehensive run-through of the value considerations for
Arcelor, a preliminary assessment of the company's defence themes,
an explanation of the concept of building a fan club of core shareholders, and an overview of the potential partners who might come
in and save the company from a marriage with Mittal. Here the government had several cards of its own to play, in China and Russia,
especially.

More importantly, d'Argent had assessed the key issues for the
government's overall objectives. For tactical reasons, it included a
phase in which dialogue and negotiations with Arcelor and other
potential stakeholders should start as soon as possible. In terms of
timing, he said, the government had to oppose Mittal's opening
offer, fully leverage its position as a regulator and support Arcelor in
its stand-alone plan, which included a value-enhancing partnership
in which both the state and the company grew, with profits being
reinvested to secure jobs and provide dividends for the Luxembourg
Treasury.

'One thing is for sure: Mittal will not win with this current offer,'
d'Argent said confidently. 'It grossly undervalues Arcelor.'
Intuitively, the banker knew that when the battle had reached its
climax, the government might have to sit down with Mittal and
power-bargain.

'The government has to be very single-minded about its priorities. They will not necessarily converge with those of Arcelor,' he
said. Krecké looked anxious. 'The government has a multiple role: as
the legislator in Luxembourg, as a large shareholder, as a protector
of jobs and investment and as supplier of electricity to the country's
steel plants,' d'Argent summarised. It was important to ensure that
on these matters the government was not pre-empted by Arcelor.
But he knew there was another very important issue to the government – so important that when Schmit had first mentioned it to
d'Argent he had taken him into his office, locked the door and
unplugged the phone.

'We really would like Arcelor to remain Luxembourg-based,'
Schmit had whispered.

D'Argent took that as code for 'at any costs'.

Servan-Schreiber and Simpson were not the only ones suggesting to Luc Frieden ways in which he could draft the takeover law to hinder Mittal's advance into Luxembourg. Thierry d'Argent, armed with a bottle of first-growth claret, had sat down the previous weekend and played lawmaker. As he worked, he thought, This is probably one of the things that I will remember when I'm an old guy and tell my grandchildren – that I had the unique opportunity for a banker to write, physically write, the law with a pen and a piece of paper. Unlike Arcelor's gun-slinging lawyers, d'Argent, as the government's man, was concerned that Frieden should introduce a law that helped Arcelor but was not so protectionist that Luxembourg lost its reputation as the leading world financial centre. 'We must be clear about the government's own objectives in this,' d'Argent told Frieden, repeating the message he had now given more than once to Minister Krecké.

While Lakshmi Mittal waited for his lawyers to jump through the regulatory hoops before they could open his offer, Nicola Davidson and Philip Gawith made sure momentum was maintained by keeping the story top of the news agenda. They challenged every item coming out of Arcelor for accuracy, journalists were courted and briefed, and at 9 a.m. and 6 p.m. every day during the global PR network calls the bankers were available to talk to the media with their carefully crafted scripts. Spiro Youakim was so keen on his media-relations role that Nicola Davidson made him an honorary member of the communications team.

The off-record briefing was just as important. Snippets of intelligence gleaned from within the Arcelor chateau were dropped into the conversation to guide journalists' questions next time they interviewed the opposition. Some might have called this activity 'leaking'. The Mittal communications team called it 'heads up'. The team also had a media intelligence file it called the Mars Mudpack – Mars, after Goldman Sachs's codename for Mittal, and mudpack for all the negative mud that Arcelor was likely to hurl Mittal's way. The challenge was to hurl it back again before it stuck.

Sudhir Maheshwari provided a valuable addition to the mudpack when he placed a brown envelope on the Berkeley Square House boardroom table at one of the twice-weekly strategy meetings. 'This is the Finsbury dossier,' he said, passing it around. Inside were a number of published articles hostile to Lakshmi Mittal and Mittal

Steel, many of them to do with the health and safety record at his plants and mines in Eastern Europe. The dossier had been produced for journalists, to encourage and to help them write unfavourable Mittal articles, by Finsbury, a communications consultancy in London hired by Arcelor.

'How did you get this?' Nicola Davidson asked him.

'Ways and means,' Maheshwari smiled. Every time Finsbury produced a dossier, Maheshwari got his hands on it. None of the allegations was new and they had been rebutted a hundred times, but it was a useful insight into which way the opposition was spinning.

Then journalists from the *Wall Street Journal* complained to Davidson, alleging that they had been asked to sign undertakings by Finsbury that they would write specific anti-Mittal stories on certain dates. They had refused. 'There's only one way to respond to that,' Davidson decided. 'We will make Mr Mittal and Aditya even more available to the media, and without any conditions.'

23

Skadden, Arps, 68 rue du Faubourg Saint-Honoré, Paris

Pierre-Servan Schreiber felt more like a racing commentator than an international lawyer as he opened up a conference call with partners from Skadden offices around the globe. 'So which of the white knights is in the lead in the great Arcelor race?' he began.

Arcelor was collecting white knights like it collected banks. Now there were seven confirmed runners, and half a dozen more that had been spoken to. Two were in Brazil, two in Russia, and one each in Korea, Japan and Ukraine. Each Arcelor negotiating team had the support of a Skadden team, a total of a hundred lawyers.

For security reasons each one was always referred to by a code-name. The choice of names for potential suitors brought a moment of light relief to the advisers. Servan-Schreiber, when not astride one of his powerful motorcycles, liked to relax with a glass of wine in his hand at his country home in the balmy air of Provence. It was more than fitting, then, that he had awarded the knights codenames linked to grape varieties, but there were so many knights riding to Arcelor's rescue that the Frenchman had run out of wines. Into the running came 'Barracuda' and 'Newport'.

The early runners were those with whom Arcelor had a close working relationship. From Japan there was the Nippon Steel Corporation ('Nuits'), and from China the Shanghai Baosteel Group ('Barracuda'), the country's largest producer. A publicly listed company, Bao was nevertheless controlled by the Chinese government, and talks could be bureaucratically time-consuming and as intricate as a game of mah-jong. China was tricky in more senses than one. The US government had blocked an attempt by the China National Offshore Oil Corporation (CNOOC), 70 per cent owned by the Chinese government, to grab a mid-sized Californian oil producer, Unocol Corp. Washington said the deal could threaten US national security and violate the rules of fair trade. The Chinese found it a steep learning curve in terms of reputation and the publicity it caused. As a result the Chinese government was now a little more tentative about stepping out into the international corporate arena. If Baosteel was to win Arcelor's hand, it said, it wanted signed declarations of support from Jacques Chirac and Jean-Claude Juncker. Baosteel was handicapping itself out of the race.

In Japan, the cultural differences were immense, and corporately Nippon Steel could be very insular. The Japanese were notoriously long-winded in negotiations, and Arcelor, however much it admired the Japanese, did not have the time to hang around. In Michel Wurth's view it could have been the perfect partnership. Elsewhere in Asia, Posco, South Korea's biggest steel producer, was an attractive partner with a public listing and a widely held investor base, but it did not want to come under starter's orders for fear of becoming a target for Mittal.

From Brazil, where Arcelor operated, came Gerdau ('Georges') and CSN ('Cabernet'), two steel producers with big tonnages. From Ukraine Arcelor could not leave out Donbass ('Moselle'), the company it had linked with in its failed bid for Kryvorizstal. Then, for Russia there were two names in the frame: NLMK ('Newport') and SeverStal ('Sauvignon').

There was no doubt where Guy Dollé was placing his bets. Given their existing joint venture and Alexey Mordashov's rising international profile, it had to be SeverStal in the lead, although the Brazilians were giving him a run for his money. But progress was slow, and all the knights were getting greedy in their demands. Gonzalo Urquijo suggested that the field should be narrowed down to three.

Guy Dollé dismissed the idea instantly. 'I want to keep the tension. It's important that no one potential partner feels they have an advantage. White knights do not come into play until near the end. String 'em out,' he told his advisers.

Chicago

'I have read various comments about the product mix of the two companies being incompatible,' said Wilbur Ross, resuscitator of moribund steel outfits, gazing upon the dinner guests at a press junket of journalists he was leading to Mittal's plant at Burns Harbor, eighty kilometres south-east of Chicago on the banks of Lake Michigan, to counter Guy Dollé's 'perfume and eau de cologne' remarks. 'This is not true,' Ross insisted. 'We are producing exactly the same steels here in the United States as those Arcelor is producing in Europe.'

One of Mittal Steel's largest facilities in the USA, Burns Harbor was built in 1964 for Bethlehem Steel, subsequently bought by Wilbur Ross, who then sold it to Mittal as part of the ISG merger. Burns Harbor was a fully integrated plant, its two blast furnaces and plate mills producing 4.7 million tonnes of raw steel, making hot-rolled, cold-rolled and coated-sheet products primarily for the automotive industry. After singing the praises of Mittal's industrial model and explaining how merging with ISG had helped create 'a truly unique, dynamic and entrepreneurial company', Ross turned his guns on those, like Guy Dollé, who criticised Mittal's corporate governance. 'For the record,' he said, 'I am personally responsible for about two hundred million dollars' worth of Mittal stock, and you can be sure that if I felt corporate governance were an issue, I'd be off the board and out of the stock.'

Off the record, but within earshot, Ross said: 'Guy Dollé is arrogant and not too much in touch with today's world.'

While the journalists were being bussed to Burns Harbor next day, the Luxembourg Chamber of Commerce was busy submitting its opinion on the proposed takeover law to Luc Frieden's justice ministry. Like Servan-Schreiber and Scott Simpson, the Chamber argued that the law should stipulate that a cash alternative be mandatory for any takeover offer from a company with shares that were illiquid or that had unequal voting rights from the shares in the target company. The Chamber also suggested that the new law should apply to offers already in motion. Overtly protectionist – who could the Chamber be thinking of? quizzed the Anglo-Saxon press, as the French establishment liked to call it. If Frieden enshrined the Chamber's demands into law, Lakshmi Mittal would have to offer a cash alternative for all Arcelor shares. He would also have to provide a bank guarantee that he could find the necessary funds. In the unlikely event of his managing to do that, he would fail on the share test.

The Chamber of Commerce had no connection with Arcelor, but the fact that its chairman was Arcelor deputy CEO Michel Wurth allowed the press to have a field day. Although he said he had stood down from the Chamber's discussions, Philip Gawith was fond of saying to Lakshmi Mittal's core team, that Michel, like much of the rest of Arcelor, 'was not passing the smell test'.

Still hammering away on the perfume/eau de cologne front, while he waited for his offer to go public, Lakshmi Mittal knew that it was important not to lose the communications battle. And now an absolute gem fell into his communications team's lap. With so many banks and their analysts tied to either Arcelor or Mittal, there was very little analysis available on the prospects for a merged company. But French outfit Exane now published its view. 'Mittal Steel–Arcelor, the perfect combination . . . size, market impact, vertical integration, high growth, faster re-rating and synergies announced by Mittal Steel make this an attractive value proposition for Arcelor shareholders,' it said. This was a nightmare for Arcelor. Exane was part-owned, but not controlled, by BNP Paribas, one of its key banking advisers in its fight against Mittal.

From the point of view of the Anglo-Saxons, Lakshmi Mittal's proposed takeover was being seen increasingly as a very bright torch shining its way into the deepest, darkest recesses of state-owned Europe.

'Of course, you're sceptical – you're British,' Thierry Breton told Hugo Dixon of breakingviews.com. 'If the British weren't sceptical, we'd be living on Mars,' the minister counter-punched. No, he wasn't anti the free market, nor was he against cross-border takeovers, Breton insisted, but 'if you don't understand the notion of stakeholders, one day or another you'll miss something that will be very damaging to your shareholders. It's not a threat,' he added, 'it's a reality.'

Breton was now twitchy. No sooner had he got off the plane after

Chirac's Mittal-dominated state visit to India than he discovered that Italy's largest power company, Enel, was about to park its takeover tanks on the lawns of the French flagship energy and services giant Suez. The French government tried to avert this by fixing a rusted merger between state-owned Gaz de France and Suez. Italy's economy minister Giulio Tremonti was now calling on Brussels to intervene, accusing France of protectionism.

If that was not enough, Lakshmi Mittal's industrial plan was now sitting on Thierry Breton's glass-topped desk. It came in the form of a confidential six-page key-features summary. Mittal assured Breton that the full report was being worked on and that he would like to discuss it with him shortly, in detail, face to face. How long 'shortly' was, nobody knew, least of all Mittal's Bill Scotting. Back in Berkeley Square House the report seemed to be getting bigger by the day. Mittal was therefore surprised to see when he opened up his daily press review for 2 March that the contents of the report's executive summary had been leaked in full to *La Tribune*. Breton was saying that the plan was insufficient. 'It is much too thin,' he said. 'It's just an executive summary.' He must have the full plan, he insisted. It was indispensable.

Mark Reutter of MakingSteel.com said, 'It reads like Lucy Kellaway's tongue-in-cheek column of corporate prattle for the London *Financial Times*.' Mittal's anonymous spokesman volleyed back: 'This breach illustrates the concern that Mittal Steel has had in sharing non-public details of the industrial plan with selected stakeholders.' His media team moved to counter-brief. Nicola Davidson urged the bankers to stick to the script: 'Do not stray from our on-record comments, already issued, summarising the essence of the plan,' she instructed. 'If asked to comment specifically on Mr Breton's comments today, please decline to do so. Finally, if really pushed on whether or not we will provide Mr Breton with the full plan, please use the following answer: "We believe that a face-to-face meeting is the most appropriate platform to share such details."'

And now, in spite of making encouraging noises earlier on, the Spanish government was joining in, coming out in full opposition to Mittal. Like the French, the Spanish had no shares in Arcelor.

24

Friday 10 March

18–19 Kensington Palace Gardens

As the battle raged around him Lakshmi Mittal had a rendezvous with Simi Garewal, India's gentle interrogator of the rich and famous. The Bollywood star turned chat-show hostess looked even more regal than that other famed Indian beauty the Rajmata of Jaipur, as she arrived with her retinue at Mittal's house and parked her pristine white-silken-clothed self on one of his lavish armchairs. This was the first time that Garewal, known as 'the Woman in White', had taken her genteel vowels out of a TV studio to do a celebrity interview out on location for her show *A Rendezvous with Simi Garewal*.

Mittal had agreed to do an hour's interview, which would be broadcast in two parts on Star TV in India. Even more significantly, Usha had agreed a rare audience. Lakshmi had said yes without telling his communications team at Berkeley Square House, partly because as a fan of everything Bollywood it took his fancy, but mainly because he was conscious of the desirability of boosting his profile in his home country where he had no business interests and at a time when he was under attack simply for being an Indian.

There was no danger of the Mittals getting a hard ride from Simi. 'You are invited to a special evening!' her website trilled. 'An intimate evening of warm smiles and shared confidences . . . of rekindled memories and recounted experiences . . . of unashamed tears and infectious laughter. You are invited to a rendezvous. *A Rendezvous with Simi Garewal*.'

Mittal took the first set of questions solo. 'Which is the most important camera?' he asked, adjusting his tie.

'All,' said Garewal, 'but just look at me.'

'All?'

'Would you have been able to achieve all this if you had continued to live in India?' Garewal asked him.

'Perhaps. It would have been difficult, to be honest,' Mittal said. Government policies were too restrictive and tied entrepreneurs up in red tape. 'At the age of twenty-five, I got exposure to the world. And this helped me to think globally. Now government policies are very positive. If I would be twenty-five today, I wouldn't have to leave India. They encourage businessmen to go abroad, acquire foreign companies. Now I see that all Indian businessmen want to go abroad. They want to be global. And this gives me a lot of happiness that at least we led the process and everyone sees the value in doing that.'

He was first and foremost an Indian, but also a global citizen, proud to be travelling on an Indian passport, he said. Relaxed, considered and affable, there was no sign that Lakshmi Mittal was working sixteen hours a day and flying thousands of miles a week in the biggest battle of his career. He looked like a man who had just come back from the holiday of a lifetime. Even more so, when his wife joined him. Usha sat next to him, looking regal in a light-blue and white sari. It was the first time they had ever talked in public together and given a glimpse of their sumptuous house.

'She knows this business very well,' Lakshmi said of his wife. 'I respect her greatly.' Usha was his rock, sounding-board and confidante. Surrounded by family photographs, he admitted that 'within the family she is the stronger and I am emotional'. As they became more relaxed, Mr and Mrs Mittal frequently teased one another. Lakshmi revealed that he had pampered his children. 'What I did not get in my life, I gave them in advance', like allowing Aditya to drive at fourteen, 'but I made him promise you will only drive with me'. He also explained how he took his kids to visit all the places he had lived in in Calcutta. 'It was also important to keep them grounded,' he explained.

He admitted that he had an obsessive side. 'I once took up golf. I started playing it every day. Then one day I was driving to the golf club and it worried me that I was becoming addicted, losing my focus, so I turned the car round and came home. I have never picked up a club since.'

One of the takes was interrupted by the noise of a helicopter overhead.

'Prince Charles must be taking off,' Usha confided.

'I think ours is a different kind of marriage where you don't communicate too much before the marriage and it's a building of relations, a building of love,' Mittal continued. 'I wrote a letter to her immediately after the engagement because she went back to Benares and that's where I said to her I welcome you as a partner, and I'm sure I must have expressed a lot of love.'

'Yes,' Usha agreed, 'and one sentence that he wrote, that touched my heart was, he ended the letter with, "Kissed by smiling always". And that touched my heart the most.'

'Weren't you touched by my also saying that I welcome you as my life partner?' Mittal asked her in mock shock.

'Yes,' she giggled. 'But I was young then, you know.'

A huge audience of up to three hundred million viewers would tune in at the end of April to get a 'a sneak peek into the world's most expensive home [and] meet the woman he shares his success with . . . his inspiration, his adviser, his homemaker, his one great enduring love – his wife, Usha Mittal'. The interview might have made Parkinson look like Paxman, but it was a softly, softly tour de force, reaching out beyond the media cynics to aspirational India and a power base that would back his continuing fight with the Old Europe of Guy Dollé and Joseph Kinsch.

Friday 17 March

European Business Summit, Picardstraat, Brussels

'It is easy to buy companies – but hard to improve them,' Lakshmi Mittal told his audience. Four thousand eyes stared back at him. 'This, however, is something that Mittal Steel has done with success over the years, and it is precisely through developing successful ways of transferring best practice around the group that we have been able to achieve what we have done. But let me not get ahead of myself!'

Once again, Mittal was taking his vision right to the heart of Europe. The message to the fourth annual European Business Summit, held in the Thurn & Taxis exhibition and cultural complex in Brussels, had been crafted with Roland Verstappen and Lisa Rabbe to show that Mittal knew his history: he was paying his respects to the European Iron and Steel Community and its founder members in whose countries Arcelor and its predecessors operated. In front of him was an audience of two thousand including European Commission President José Manuel Barroso, all his commissioners and a healthy sprinkling of national government ministers and business leaders.

Originally Guy Dollé had been due to speak on day one and Mittal had been asked by the organisers to take part in a panel discussion. Verstappen had cautioned Mittal against taking second billing to Dollé. He told the organisers, 'I'd like Mr Mittal to be on the platform to give a keynote speech because this is a good story for Europe.'

There was not room for two keynote speakers. Then a classic Euro compromise was offered. 'Mr Verstappen, maybe we could have a discussion between Mr Dollé and Mr Mittal,' the organisers suggested.

'Mr Mittal wants to share his story with the audience,' Verstappen said – and not, by implication, with Guy Dollé. Then for some reason Dollé cancelled. Mittal grabbed the slot. When Dollé realised, he tried to get back on the bill only to find himself relegated to a panel discussion on day two.

'European steel companies are amongst the best in the world,' Mittal was now telling his audience. 'They have deep roots and enormous heritage. These represent considerable strengths – but they do not constitute an entitlement. The challenge is to harness these strengths to a globalising economy.'

At the end of the speech a hundred journalists rushed to the podium shouting out questions about the Arcelor bid.

'Do you really want to do this?' Verstappen asked Mittal.

'It's OK,' he said.

The same topics came up: jobs, investment and his vision of the future. Not once was he wrong-footed. There would be no job losses; but, he reminded them, 'the economic order is changing, the centre of gravity is shifting and this is something that businesses must respond to'. Mittal then went into a series of side meetings with politicians, commissioners and fellow entrepreneurs, airing his vision to an ever-expanding network and warning against a return to nationalistic reflexes.

As he left the complex, he turned to Verstappen and said: 'Roland, this event is very good. Next year we should sponsor it.'

Tuesday 21 March, 11 a.m.

BNP Paribas headquarters, rue d'Antin, Paris

Romain Zaleski and Mario Cocchi listened intently as Gonzalo Urquijo delivered a one-and-a-half-hour presentation on the merits of Arcelor, showing how Mittal Steel's cash and shares offer significantly undervalued the Luxembourg company. With him was Christophe Moulin of BNP Paribas. The presentation followed Arcelor's excellent results performance for the fiscal year 2005. Under market rules Urquijo could now talk freely about the company since it was outside the customary one-month 'quiet' period which was imposed before such announcements.

What impressed Zaleski were Arcelor's strong forward-looking prospects. It had a quality of earnings far superior to what he, as a steelman, had seen over the years. In addition, drawing on his own experience at Carlo Tassara, he had a strong feel for the way the industry was developing in terms of the emerging markets and how it was pushing up asset values. But should he invest?

As Moulin and Urquijo pressed for his reaction, Zaleski asked for a time out. He and Cocchi went and sat in an adjoining room.

'Arcelor is an impressive company but have we been priced out?' Cocchi asked. 'The shares are trading at between thirty-one and thirty-three euros – how much more upside is there?'

'It depends on how badly Mittal wants to win and whether or not we could see an interloper,' Zaleski responded, showing his shrewd sense of the dynamics of contested takeovers. 'This battle will run and run.'

Zaleski's intuitive powers were at full throttle. He recognised the scope for consolidation, but he knew little of Lakshmi Mittal or his company. He reckoned that whatever happened Arcelor had good long-term potential, even as a stand-alone company. As he returned to the meeting, he pondered on the fact that there was just one problem: Carlo Tassara International, his primary investment vehicle, was fully invested in Italy.

'We are very impressed with the presentation and we find the story very compelling from an investment point of view,' Zaleski commented as he and Cocchi rejoined Moulin and Urquijo.

Moulin and Urquijo exchanged glances.

'Mario and I will consider whether we will invest. At the moment the Carlo Tassara International portfolio is fully extended and we would like time to consider our options, since we have plenty of assets but no ready cash. We may have to borrow to fund the investment,' Zaleski added tantalisingly.

Two days after he returned to Milan, Christophe Moulin phoned him. He went straight to the point. 'We're happy to finance you, Mr Zaleski. How much do you need?'

'We would like five hundred million euros, as a first step,' Zaleski replied. 'This will give us a holding in Arcelor of between 2 and 3 per cent, but we may want to go higher, perhaps to 5 per cent. We think an overall facility of around eight hundred million to one billion euros will cover our requirements.'

Moulin did not even blink. Given Zaleski's strong asset backing, lending €1 billion to the entrepreneur was no issue for BNP Paribas. In any case, the French bank had the security of the underlying Arcelor shares, which were likely to increase in value. Just as important, they were securing a shareholder friendly to Arcelor and being paid extra for it, plus the loan interest. In the space of five minutes, Zaleski had a €1 billion facility. The money would be deposited in two tranches at a Carlo Tassara International account in Luxembourg, where a company subsidiary was registered.

If Tuesday 21 March was pay-day for Romain Zaleski, riding to Arcelor's rescue as a fan-club shareholder, it was a major let-down for Michel Wurth on the legal front. He had just discovered that the Luxembourg government appeared to have ignored all the suggestions from the Chamber of Commerce on the proposed takeover law. 'It is obviously difficult for us these days . . . to take part in the debate,' he told *Tageblatt*, one of Luxembourg's two dailies. 'Nevertheless . . . I am personally surprised to hear the justice minister talking about the Council of State's opinion as though the opinions of other economic partners did not exist.'

Later that week Jacques Chirac too was in a strop. On Friday the 24th, he walked out of the opening session of the EU's annual spring summit when fellow Frenchman Ernest-Antoine Seillière, the head of the European employers' group UNICE, committed the grave offence of speaking in English. When Seillière abandoned his mother tongue – claiming that English 'is the language of business' – Chirac picked up his papers and left with his foreign minister and Thierry Breton in tow. Gallic pride was soon restored when Jean-Claude Trichet, the French head of the European Central Bank, spoke to the meeting in French. Chirac then led his ministers back.

Watching from the sidelines, Lakshmi Mittal was still surprised that his bid for Arcelor had become such a huge rock in the EU pond. France and Germany were now at loggerheads over the economic future of Europe, with the German chancellor Angela Merkel criticising French attempts to limit foreign investment. In the name of 'economic patriotism' Dominique de Villepin had named eleven French business sectors that should be shielded from foreign bidders like Mittal.

'We can only have an internal market when electricity flows freely and when we accept European champions and do not just think nationally,' Mrs Merkel had said when she arrived at the summit. Lakshmi Mittal could not have put it better himself.

Jean-Claude Juncker, also at the summit, remained resolute and defended his attempts to resist Mittal's bid for Arcelor. 'Sometimes governments have good arguments,' he insisted.

But Pier Ferdinando Casini, the Speaker of the Italian parliament – still smarting at France's blocking Enel's takeover of Suez – mocked any government that restricted cross-border takeovers. 'Either you are a pretend European, and therefore in favour of protectionism and nationalism,' he said, 'or else you are a real European and want to stimulate competition.'

*

Just as the Arcelor Stakes was shaping up nicely, one of the white knights, 'Newport', broke cover. Vladimir Lissin, the boss of NLMK, announced to the media that he was interested in acquiring 15 per cent of Arcelor. Pierre Servan-Schreiber and the other Skadden grooms could not believe what Russia's third-richest man was playing at. The news caught the imagination of breakingviews.com. 'Arcelor may have no intention of committing a crime against its own shareholders. But it has the motive and the murder weapon. Now it looks like it might have the accomplice,' it commented, referring to reports of Lissin's interest.

Arcelor had been rumbled. The motive, according to the news service, was the possibility of selling a powerful block of shares to a third party in order to block Mittal. The weapon was to issue the shares, as provided in the by-laws, and sell them to a third party without consulting the shareholders. 'Do not go there,' it lectured. 'It would make a mockery of Arcelor's stated desire to mount a value defence. With luck, it hasn't even crossed its board's mind. If it has, it should scrub it out immediately.'

The board had been kept up to speed on the riders and runners, but it knew them by codename only. Joseph Kinsch was not going to be very happy next time he bumped into Mr Vladimir Lissin, and nor was Lakshmi Mittal.

Guy Dollé was another who seemed to be having trouble keeping his mouth shut. On 24 March, as the preparations for the *stichting* were nearing completion, the Arcelor CEO was reported to have told the *Wall Street Journal* that Arcelor could restructure Dofasco to prevent Mittal from selling it. 'Arcelor could forge a joint venture between Dofasco and another steel company. That would make it hard for Mittal to sell Dofasco if the joint-venture contract contained a clause requiring a punitive payment in the case of a change of control.'

Romain Zaleski, meanwhile, was moving altogether more shrewdly. When Carlo Tassara International SA held its board meeting in Luxembourg on 27 March it took the decision to invest the first €500 million of the BNP billion in Arcelor. It also voted to carry on buying up stock as soon as it became available between €33.50 and €34.11 for each share, as other investors cashed out. Because he held over 3 per cent of the total shares outstanding on Arcelor's register Zaleski had to disclose all trading in a series of regulatory filings to the Paris stock exchange, which then made the information public on its website. Zaleski's share-buying spree was switching on lights all over Lakshmi Mittal's radar screen, until he could bear it no longer.

In Zaleski's house the phone rang. As usual his desk was submerged under a pile of faxes from banks all around the world. Zaleski took it.

'Mr Mittal would like to meet you immediately,' Yoel Zaoui said. 'When are you free?

25

Tuesday 28 March, 1.30 a.m.

Indira Gandhi International Airport, New Delhi

During his nine hours in the air Jeannot Krecké had read through his briefing notes and prepped himself one last time. His thoughts were focused not only on the stalled double taxation agreement with India – a complex bilateral arrangement whereby two countries allowed companies and private individuals operating or living between the two not to have to pay tax twice, and the key reason for his visit – but also on Lakshmi Mittal's bid.

Krecké was determined not to suffer the same fate as Jacques Chirac the previous month and have his talks with Kamal Nath and Finance Minister Palaniappan Chidambaram – the suave, articulate politician from the southern state of Tamil Nadu who was well known for his pro-market reforms and for his bold steps to abolish red tape – hijacked over the Mittal issue. The Indian press was still in a frenzy over the way Europe was seen to be treating India's favourite non-resident Indian. Chirac and the gang had succeeded in transforming Mittal from a successful but distant industrialist into a 'son of the soil' icon in the country of his birth.

Stick to the issues, Krecké reminded himself. First, the new takeover law to be introduced into Luxembourg by the end of May was based on a 2004 EU directive for all twenty-five member states to adopt the principles of international best practice in takeovers. It was not, repeat not, some protectionist device suddenly introduced to stop Mittal. Second, on the merits of Mittal's bid the answer was simple: Arcelor shareholders would decide, not his government alone, although they were a key shareholder and also a stakeholder, anxious to preserve jobs and investment and keep Luxembourg as the headquarters.

But most important of all, he had come to remove any sense of discrimination or racism caused by Dollé's 'monkey money' and 'company of Indians' remarks. Luxembourg was free and open, he would tell Nath. Some 40 per cent of the workforce were international and were welcomed in the multicultural society. There were more than a hundred Indian companies listed on the Luxembourg stock exchange, helped by favourable bank laws and taxes. Luxembourg was bringing in new systems to ease the issue of visas and work permits for Indians, and there were excellent opportunities in e-commerce, logistics, and in financial services and bilateral trade.

On the double taxation agreement India wanted a level playing field. Luxembourg was keen to protect its interests too, especially since bilateral trade between the two countries had slumped dramatically since 2004 – from $100 million to less than $12 million. This was more difficult and, politically, he sensed that India was still playing for time, holding out for the Mittal bid for Arcelor to go through unhindered.

Looking tired, Krecké nevertheless felt comfortable that he had the key points covered, and together with support from Luxembourg's man in Delhi, Ambassador Paul Steinmetz, he was well set to achieve his diplomatic goals in India's political capital. Just as an added precaution, his advisers had called one of India's PR gurus, Dr Niren Suchanti, chairman and CEO of the Pressman Group, to guide him through potential hazards.

Krecké got the customary diplomatic fast-track clearance and walked through the VIP lounge to the chauffeur-driven white Mercedes. On its passenger-side wing the Luxembourg flag fluttered gently in the early morning breeze. Forty minutes later, the minister stepped from the car outside the entrance to the Oberoi hotel on Dr Zakir Hussain Marg, overlooking the lush greens of Delhi Golf Club and minutes away from government ministries and Connaught Place. Krecké was just about to go inside when he noticed a red light coming towards him out of the darkness. It was a television camera, and it was homing in on him. Next to the cameraman was the tenacious Shailly Chopra, one of the anchors for NDTV Profit, the leading Indian English-language TV channel focused on business. Chopra is smart and aggressive and goes to great lengths to be the first to get a story, especially ahead of great business-channel rival CNBC TV18.

Krecké got both barrels.

'Minister Krecké, good morning, and welcome to India,' Chopra began. 'I would like to interview you for the breakfast programme today. Is your government out to stop Mittal Steel bidding for Arcelor? There is a lot of ill feeling about this in our country and your friend Kamal Nath is eager to speak about this with you.'

Krecké, although well used to the media spotlight, was caught off guard. Welcome to India? It was a conspiracy! Who had tipped off the local media that he was arriving in New Delhi? Who knew which hotel he was staying at? Security had broken down. It must have been the Indian government, or was it Mittal? he asked himself. But how did Mittal know of his schedule? Was there a mole in the home camp?

He quickly recovered his poise, and smiled at his assailant. 'I hope you will appreciate that I do not give interviews at two-thirty in the morning, especially after a nine-hour flight. But I will be happy to speak to you later in the day,' the minister added, tactfully.

'I totally understand but I would like to talk to you now, exclusively, because a lot of people will be watching this.'

'We can arrange to do this later through the embassy,' Krecké repeated.

Chopra had a scoop, and no way was she letting go. 'Minister Krecké, there is a lot ill feeling in India right now about the way Mittal Steel is being treated over the Arcelor bid,' she persisted. 'It looks like political intervention, bordering on racism. What are you going to do about it?'

Krecké decided this was not the time to dodge the issue. In fact, it could be a useful trailer for the remainder of his two-day trip. 'I am here because Luxembourg has strong political and economic ties with India and we want this to continue by agreeing a double taxation agreement,' he said.

'As for my friend Kamal Nath, I will allay his fears. We are not seeking to intervene in any current takeover bid, as I will explain to ministers in your government in the next two days.' He then rolled out the key messages on the real reasons for the new takeover law and rammed home the point that the shareholders of Arcelor would decide on Lakshmi Mittal's bid.

'I want people in India to understand that this is not a racial issue,' Krecké insisted. 'It is, however, an emotional issue for the people of Luxembourg. In the nineteen-eighties the steel industry was in dire straits and the government had to rescue Arbed, the predecessor company to Arcelor. It was the biggest employer. The taxpayers had to participate in a "solidarity tax" so today they feel like "moral" shareholders. We, the government, have to protect jobs and investment in our tiny country.'

Chopra was not going to be fobbed off with a history lesson and tried to push harder, but Krecké needed sleep. 'I will speak more about this in the next two days, so if you don't mind I would like to take some rest,' the minister said, and pushed on into the hotel.

All the early morning TV news programmes picked up on the interview. India's five prime-time business channels were leading with the news of Krecké 's arrival and his comments made outside the Oberoi. Print journalists and photographers were excited, and interview requests were now piling into the Luxembourg embassy. Krecké knew that the media would be parked outside his meetings with Kamal Nath and Palaniappan Chidambaram. He badly needed to exert some control. He called for Dr Suchanti, the fifty-six-year-old PR veteran, to provide it.

Suchanti was frank. Krecké had to hold a solo press conference. Such was the intensity of media interest, there was no way he could get away with a few set-piece one-to-ones with favoured reporters. It would simply antagonise the rest of the media, he counselled. In any case, most of the media were picking up well on Krecké's key messages. 'Let's keep reinforcing these messages,' Suchanti said. Krecké asked him to organise a press conference at the Oberoi later that day while he went to meet Kamal Nath and Chidambaram. Behind the comforting ministry walls he felt he was back on track and in pursuit of his double taxation avoidance treaty.

Security had been stepped up so that only bona fide journalists were allowed into the press conferences later that day. Lakshmi Mittal's local PR team, the business diary of the *Hindu* revealed, were for once on the outside and unable to look in so they attempted to plant questions on journalists. At Krecké's solo conference back at the Oberoi, they tried to persuade them to take in tape-recorders to find out what was being said. Most, but not all, declined to do so. As the paper reported, 'Corporate wars are no less than regular warfare, where early information about the opponent's plans helps strategise better.'

'Luxembourg will look at Mittal Steel's bid from the shareholders' point of view,' Krecké told a press conference after meeting Kamal Nath. 'We have appointed JPMorgan and have sought their financial advice, after which we will decide.' He also said that the Luxembourg regulators would probably wait until the takeover law was in place before they decided on Mittal's bid – although the two issues were not related, he added.

'The issue is not of L.N. Mittal,' Nath agreed, 'but there is an important question of national treatment.'

Next day the English-language and Hindu press were full of headlines about Krecké. 'New Law Not to Block Mittal Bid'. 'Mittal Bid a Matter for Shareholders'. Krecké's key messages had finally hit home. Kamal Nath told the media, 'Krecké assured me that it is not the issue of India. Luxembourg is a shareholder in Arcelor. Luxembourg's reaction is as shareholders and should not be taken as a reaction on the nationality of the person making the bid.'

As Krecké waited in the departure lounge for his flight back to Luxembourg he caught the news on a TV monitor. On the streets of Paris students were still protesting against the liberalisation of the labour laws and global free trade, occupying the Sorbonne, fighting the riot police and burning cars on the chic, tree-lined boulevards near the Eiffel Tower. Krecké could not help but smile at another story, showing him shaking hands with Nath. 'It was kiss-and-make-up time,' said the newscaster. Here was a moment for a battle-scarred politician to savour. I have never had such coverage, Krecké told himself. In past visits to India, his PR staff had struggled to get him a single interview. But how would the wider coverage be received by Arcelor and in the Luxembourg media?

When he arrived back in Luxembourg, the daily *Tageblatt* had its own views. It said Krecké had been 'a victim of political blackmail' by India.

Monday 3 April

Kensington Palace Gardens

As he sipped his espresso at the breakfast table in the conservatory, Romain Zaleski was immediately taken by Lakshmi Mittal. He liked the man's openness and candid approach, such a sharp contrast to his customary dealings with Italians. Zaleski had been in London over the weekend talking to rare-carpet dealers and had agreed, following the call from Yoel Zaoui, to prolong his stay so as to see Mittal. He had also heard stories of the Mittal art collection, and he couldn't wait to feast his eyes on it.

'Why are you buying Arcelor's shares at over thirty euros when I have made a perfectly good offer of twenty-eight?' Mittal asked.

Zaleski paused, wishing to remain neutral. His blue eyes met with the piercing brown eyes of the Mittal chief. 'It's very simple,' the Frenchman said, looking characteristically impish. 'Arcelor is a very good company and I believe we will make money on our investment.'

'I want you to help me,' Mittal said.

Zaleski was stunned by Mittal's frankness in asking for help from somebody who was investing heavily in the other side. He smiled. He said again: 'Arcelor is a very good company and we will make money on our investment.'

As they broke from the breakfast table, Zaleski's eye caught the Van Gogh on the corridor wall ahead of him. He raved about it to his host.

'But you haven't seen my Picasso,' Mittal said. 'Let me show you.'

Zaleski was no lover of Picasso, but he kept that to himself. As he entered the Mittal picture gallery he stopped in his tracks. On the wall was a Picasso in vivid red brushwork. 'This is fascinating,' he told Mittal. 'Picasso never normally used red. It's my favourite colour.' Zaleski was warming even more to his host.

What Zaleski did not tell Mittal was that he had been asked by Gonzalo Urquijo to join the Arcelor board. He had refused, explaining, 'I wish to remain independent.' He did not want to become an insider, which would restrict his room for manoeuvre as an active investor. When this was reported back, canny Joseph Kinsch, only too aware of Zaleski's history, suddenly felt rather uneasy. You could never quite accuse Romain Zaleski of changing sides because Romain Zaleski was always resolutely on his own side. Kinsch called Urquijo into his office and told him, 'From now on, whenever you speak to that man *I* want to know about it.'

Zaleski was on the move again. On 7 April his investment company, visiting Shougang Steel in China, sank a further €500 million into buying Arcelor shares. The company was now sitting on 23.33 million shares in Arcelor, some 2.11 per cent of the company. He decided to keep on buying.

Tuesday 4 April

Arcelor headquarters, Avenue de la Liberté

'This is a necessary step to ensure Dofasco is maintained inside Arcelor as a valuable asset and to stop its steel-making technology ending up with another company.' The formal announcement from Arcelor headquarters was a three-pronged attack on Mittal.

Of the three, Scott Simpson's carefully crafted *stichting* got top billing. Even though neither Arcelor nor Dofasco had significant operations in the Netherlands, the Strategic Steel Stichting was now formed. It had a three-man board of directors that had no control over the management, but it could block the sale of Dofasco. Subject to the discretion of the Arcelor board the *stichting* would dissolve in five years. Over in Hamilton, Ontario, Don Pether had never heard of a *stichting* and immediately did some research. He soon found the Gucci case and discovered the name Scott Simpson. He wondered quite how independent the board of the Strategic Steel Stichting might be, given that Arcelor's in-house lawyer Frederik Van Bladel was one of its directors. Dollé and Kinsch were convinced that Mittal could not buy Arcelor without selling Dofasco to finance the acquisition. 'The *stichting* will make Arcelor immune from takeover for the next five years,' Chairman Kinsch said boldly.

Arcelor's second defence initiative was designed to keep its share-holders on-side. It was increasing the dividend it was paying in 2006 to €1.85 a share, up from the €1.25 it had announced earlier and a massive headline-grabbing 185 per cent increase on the €0.65 it had paid out in 2005.

There was more. To really woo the shareholders Arcelor said it was returning a large sum of money to them in a share buy-back. For the first time in its history the company would offer to buy shares, and at a decent price, from its shareholders, especially those who might be wavering towards Mittal. For those who wanted to tender only some of their shares, it meant a large dollop of cash in the pocket while still retaining an interest in a highly profitable company. This was Michael Zaoui's initiative, but he had had to work overtime to convince Kinsch to open the Arcelor cash box. 'Your company is generating so much cash flow, so here is some-thing we can do on our own to make shareholders happier while we look for a third-party offer.'

'How much did you have in mind, Mr Zaoui?' Kinsch asked.

'In the region of five billion euros. It's a great defence measure.'

Kinsch smiled. 'You bankers are always telling clients to give away their money, but I must remind you that it is not *your* money, Mr Zaoui.'

'It's not yours either, Mr Chairman,' Zaoui said.

Kinsch succumbed.

'Announce the buy-back, but do not put a date on it,' Zaoui advised. That way the shareholders, cash-starved for so long, would be kept on side. The Arcelor statement duly announced that the buy-back would happen 'sometime during the year after the with-drawal or failure of the Mittal Steel offer'.

The breakingviews.com verdict on the *stichting* was abrupt: 'So much for [Arcelor's] promised value-based defence. Arcelor has cre-ated a potent poison pill.' Thanks to the *stichting*, if Mittal continued his attack in the face of this obstruction, Arcelor shareholders would not be able to make a straight comparison of value and strategy between the two companies. 'Instead they would have to worry about whether Mittal would be weighed down by the €3.8 billion Canadian steel maker.'

But all at Arcelor were cock-a-hoop at the great big Dutch

roadblock erected in Mittal's path. At a roadshow in Luxembourg Guy Dollé was asked, 'How do you think ThyssenKrupp is going to react to the *stichting*?' In front of three hundred people he replied: 'If I was ThyssenKrupp I would be hesitating between hanging myself and cutting my wrists.'

Berkeley Square House

'Wow, this *stichting* is a very smart move,' said Yoel Zaoui, looking at the worried faces in the Mittal Steel boardroom. The buy-back, with its vague timetable, was equally smart. He recognised his brother's signature. When this was all over he would call Michael and congratulate him. 'But the Dutch trust really doesn't move the needle over to them,' he reassured them. 'They are being very clever, very creative and very determined, but it's not in the shareholders' interests to tie up Dofasco like that. There will be a backlash.'

Aditya Mittal picked up the triple challenge hurled in Mittal Steel's path by Arcelor with typical confidence. First, the buy-back. 'By adopting a defence on redistributing cash Arcelor is tying its hands for the future,' he told the financial daily *Les Échos*. 'If the bid does not go ahead, it will find itself with an excessively high net debt – we estimate at €11 billion, for an operating profit of only €5.5 billion in 2006! It is amputating its growth potential by the same amount and compromising its capacity to be one of the future leaders in the sector.'

Now that the *stichting* prevented Mittal from offloading Dofasco to ThyssenKrupp would they have to sell some of their American plant to keep the competition authorities in the States pacified? the paper asked. Aditya explained that they had already lodged anti-trust documents with the US authorities but could not comment further. 'It is not clear that keeping Dofasco is in the best interests of shareholders. The proof: if the bid becomes a friendly one, would a sale become possible? We need to know: either Dofasco is a good asset or it's not.'

Like his father, he completely ruled out raising the bid. 'Our offer has already been raised from €28.20 per share on announcement to €32 today, thanks to the rise in the price of Mittal Steel shares, which account for 75 per cent of the payment. This natural rise is likely to continue since our shares are still undervalued. Some experts believe they still have upside potential of 35 per cent or more.'

Lakshmi Mittal took his media blitz to Luxembourg and an interview with the magazine *Télécran* that appeared on 5 April.

'How is your relationship with Jean-Claude Juncker?' he was asked.

'I don't want to comment on that,' Mittal dodged. 'We have had many contacts with politicians during the last eight weeks. I have followed the discussion about Luxembourg's takeover law in the press. I'm very happy about the way the discussion was conducted and especially glad that the politics have not been influenced by special interests.'

'Today in the *Financial Times* Prime Minister Juncker is quoted as having said he is opposed to hostile takeovers.'

'I agree with him,' Mittal said. 'We don't like hostile takeovers, either. We said that we would like to sit at the table together with Arcelor to talk about a successful merger.' Again he emphasised that there would be no job cuts, that a new company would have its headquarters in Luxembourg and that he would honour all Arcelor investment plans in the country.

Then he was pitched the billion-euro question. 'Mr Mittal, when will your takeover bid officially open?' It still had not cleared all the regulators.

'We are counting on the regulatory authority opening the transaction in the second half of April. Then the shareholders will have thirty to thirty-five working days to come to the right decision. I am confident that the right decision will be made. I am not even thinking of a different outcome.'

26

Paris

With 'Sauvignon' way out front in the Arcelor Stakes and Guy Dollé ready to pin a metaphorical rosette on Alexey Mordashov's bull-like chest, a new white knight veered into the race out of nowhere. It had come courtesy of JPMorgan Chase in Paris, but it was not French. It spoke German. Pierre Servan-Schreiber christened the new arrival 'Sweet'. It came from Düsseldorf and it was one of the most famous companies in the whole of Western Europe. Its real name was ThyssenKrupp. The very same ThyssenKrupp that Lakshmi Mittal thought he had locked into a legal deal over Dofasco, removing it as a potential white knight for Arcelor, was now riding to the rescue of the Luxembourg company.

The late entry of 'Sweet' over the Easter break caught everyone in the Arcelor camp by surprise, especially Guy Dollé, and for good reason. First, Thyssen and Arcelor had fought ferociously for the hand of Dofasco. Then came Mittal's backdoor Dofasco deal with Ekkehard Schulz, and now the Germans were ring-fenced in Arcelor's *stichting*, which left them totally marginalised and distinctly irritated.

But the double-dealing and corporate shenanigans were about to rise to new heights in a dark swath of confidentiality agreements locked away in the Paris office of Skadden, Arps.

The German approach had been engineered through some initial stealth work conducted by both Schulz and Dr Gerhard Cromme, chairman of the supervisory board of ThyssenKrupp AG, the conglomerate's parent. Shortly before Easter Schulz had discovered that Joseph Kinsch was on a much needed golfing holiday in the Balearic Islands. Such was the urgency of Schulz's mission that he had flown to see him and on the nineteenth tee had broached the idea of the two groups coming together as an elegant way of resolving their different problems. Schulz told Kinsch that he thought the *stichting* was an outrage and so did the market, but given that he could now do nothing about it, a merger between their two companies would enable Arcelor to fend off Mittal and dump Mordashov, whose company was hard to value, while Thyssen, no longer marginalised, could still emerge with a share of Dofasco and a joint route into the USA as part of an all-powerful world-leading steel group. Arcelor and ThyssenKrupp combined would be a true champion, he said, merging the best industrial know-how and technology Old Europe could offer in the brave new world.

Smaller and even less nimble than Arcelor, Thyssen's track record in the consolidation game had suggested it was a non-runner. In all respects Arcelor was the superior company. But for Kinsch, brought up in Germany, married to a German and originally apprenticed in the German steel industry with Arbed, there was an immediate and understandable sense of ethnic togetherness. ThyssenKrupp was still a great brand to be associated with, and he admired the Germanic pride in their technology. In parallel, Cromme had used his high-level contacts at JPMorgan Chase in Paris, where he was on first-name terms with the chairman. The Luxembourg government was also receptive to an all-European tie-up, with Jean-Claude Juncker, the ultimate Euro-enthusiast, quite open to a bit of lobbying from his neighbours.

There was less enthusiasm among the banking advisers, except for Morgan Stanley, who saw the opportunity to hit the glory trail; the others were caught up in the other white-squire and white-knight talks, which, with the exception of Mordashov, were going nowhere. Even discussions with the last bright hope, 'Cabernet' – Companhia Siderúrgica Nacional (CSN), the second-biggest steel company in Brazil and a major competitor of Arcelor Brazil – were stalled because of the international ambitions of Benjamin Steinbruch, the chairman and managing director, who had become too demanding.

Like most of the white knights he had become greedy, wanting too big a slice of Arcelor.

Kinsch returned to Luxembourg and stopped the clock on the 'Sauvignon' negotiations. For Merrill Lynch, leading the Mordashov talks, it was galling to have to sit and watch as Michael Zaoui and Morgan Stanley, alongside Pierre Servan-Schreiber, Scott Simpson and Michel Wurth, sat down to talk with ThyssenKrupp. The negotiators camped over Easter at the Paris offices of Skadden, Arps, but the talks were anything but sweet. The fast-track nature of the discussions threw up a mountain of problems, not least the fact that Arcelor and Thyssen would have to get rid of some major assets if they were not to breach EU competition rules. So massive were the anti-trust issues that Thyssen and Arcelor, with advisers, decided to call on Competition Commissioner Neelie Kroes to test the water.

'If it's a drop-dead answer, there is no point continuing the negotiations,' Servan-Schreiber advised as the party left by private jet for Brussels.

As the minibus with tinted windows carrying the Arcelor–Thyssen delegation approached the headquarters of the Directorate General for Competition at 70 rue Joseph II, the driver slowed to take instructions.

'We should be cautious,' Ekkehard Schulz said nervously. 'I think the German contingent should exit first and go into the building alone, while the Luxembourg group should go round the block so that we are not seen arriving together.'

The Germans got out and entered the building quickly. The minibus did another circuit, then stopped and waited for twenty minutes.

'This is just like a spy movie,' Servan-Schreiber joked to Dollé as the van headed back to Neelie Kroes's office.

While they waited for their passes to be issued and to be called to see the commissioner, Dollé took out his magnetic pencil and held it against one of the steel stanchions in the new glass and steel building. 'Arcelor steel,' he said, smiling at Servan-Schreiber.

Servan-Schreiber was amazed.

The smile vanished from Guy Dollé's face as a young man in a khaki jacket came racing over.

'Mr Dollé, I am from *La Tribune*. 'May I ask what you're doing here today?'

'I am here to present to officials, as I frequently do in my business,' Dollé replied without blinking, as he grabbed his security pass and moved towards the lift.

The journalist took a look at the signing-in log. Under 'Visiting' it had Dollé's signature next to 'N. Kroes'.

The Arcelor–Thyssen presentation was in full swing when a secretary tiptoed into Neelie Kroes's office and gave her a note. The competition chief read it, then looked up at Guy Dollé.

'There is a journalist from the EU press corps who wants to know why you are here,' she smiled.

'I think we should proceed with the presentation,' Dollé replied diplomatically, but inside he was cursing. Somebody was telegraphing his every move.

Even though the discussions with Kroes were about the principle rather than the detail of a merger, it soon became clear that in order not to fall foul of competition rules a combined Arcelor–ThyssenKrupp group would probably have to divest itself of most of its overlapping businesses in Europe, the bulk of each partner's activities. Another major problem was that ThyssenKrupp was not just a steel company, but one of the world's biggest technology groups with nearly 188,000 employees worldwide working in steel, in components for mechanical engineering and the automotive industry, elevators and escalators, in materials trading and services, with sales of more than €47 billion in 2005/6. For a merger with Arcelor to work, ThyssenKrupp would have to put its steel assets into a separate company before merging. This they agreed to do.

However, the German company was ultimately controlled by two foundations with very long names, one for Thyssen and one for Krupp – the famous armaments company that had hardwared the Nazis – which had merged to form the mighty ThyssenKrupp conglomerate in 1999. Run by very old men and not known for dynamo decision-making, the two foundations were reluctant to see their controlling stakes diluted by the Arcelor deal. For Arcelor's part, compared to the Mordashov deal a Thyssen tie-up seemed to offer them little industrial benefit, but the fact that they decided to carry

on negotiating to try and find a deal was testament to their desperation and to their concern that valuing SeverStal was a major obstacle
on the Russian front.

Back in Paris the ThyssenKrupp talks dragged on, as both sides
tried to sort out the potential competition problems, haggling over
which bits of their empires they were prepared to hive off, and to
come up with a model that would both work and be more attractive
to shareholders than Mittal's offer. To the Arcelor team it began to
seem that it was all one-way traffic, with ThyssenKrupp giving very
little and expecting Arcelor to bend to their every demand. Haggling
became niggling. And that was before they had even got to the price.

Meanwhile, nothing was happening on the SeverStal front, which
made Guy Dollé and Alexey Mordashov increasingly frustrated.

As the days wore on the Thyssen negotiations were becoming so
slow that Servan-Schreiber began to get suspicious. Maybe fatigue
and negotiating numbness were clouding his judgement, but during
one of the breaks he said to Scott Simpson: 'Maybe this is all a front,
a torpedo launched by Mittal in order to waste our time.'

Simpson wasn't so sure that Mittal and Schulz were working some
clandestine back channel, but of one thing he had no doubt: 'These
people are monsters to negotiate with.'

They raised their concerns with Kinsch. 'Let's keep going,' the
chairman said.

So the negotiators pressed on. Although they still had not agreed
a value on ThyssenKrupp's steel assets they were finally within sight
of inking a deal that offered more than Mittal's opening bid, and
which would create a brand-new European global steel champion –
Arcelor–ThyssenKrupp.

Then Ekkehard Schulz called another meeting. It happened in a
hotel in the spa city of Aachen, once known as Aix-la-Chapelle, the
spa city near Aachen and the medieval capital of the great Frankish
empire-builder Charlemagne. As soon as Dollé and Kinsch entered
the room, they sensed that Schulz was not going to follow in the old
king's footsteps. As François Henrot, Rothschild's adviser to
Thyssen, got to his feet he looked nervous, as though he was about
to hyperventilate. He said he wanted an additional option.

What option?

His client wanted more shares in Arcelor. In fact, ThyssenKrupp wanted to take control of Arcelor for shares alone, without putting any cash premium on the table.

'We don't want to get into a bidding fight with Mittal,' Henrot said. If there was a cash component for Arcelor they would get into a war with Mittal, who had more firepower than they had, and they didn't want to run the risk of losing everything.

Arcelor's advisers, waiting in adjoining rooms, could not believe it.

'What are they doing, dragging us down Rose Alley?' Michael Zaoui fumed.

'They want the earth,' Scott Simpson agreed. 'It's not going to fly.'

The talking was over. ThyssenKrupp pulled out.

Why had they set their demands so unrealistically high? Was it really a fear of getting into a scrap with Mittal, or were the Germans, as Pierre Servan-Schreiber had suggested, a torpedo launched from Berkeley Square House to waste Arcelor's time in finding a counter-bidding saviour?

Guy Dollé felt he had been stabbed in the back, first by the EU's bureaucratic competition hoops and then by the over-demanding Germans. And he had seen valuable days snatched from his grasp just as Arcelor had been inching towards a deal with SeverStal. He raced back to Marc Pandraud and his number two Emmanuel Hasbanian at Merrill Lynch, cursing the lost time. Mittal would not be held up by the regulators and the Skadden, Arps lawyers for ever. It was time to return to Alexey Mordashov, and fast.

Romain Zaleski, displaying a card-player's timing, had just increased his stake in Arcelor. He now owned 3.63 per cent of the company's shares.

Thursday 20 April

Mittal Steel Gandrange, Lorraine

It was now twelve weeks since Mittal had announced his deal, and although the charm offensive was going well and the investor road-shows, especially those in France organised by Laurent Meyer of Société Générale, were promising, he was privately becoming increasingly frustrated by the delay in opening his offer to Arcelor shareholders. Every time he saw Pierre-Yves Chabert he asked him, 'When are we going to open?'

'A couple of weeks more,' Chabert said.

'That's what you said two weeks ago,' Mittal reminded him, with a smile that was not as warm as usual.

Chabert hoped he was right, but Skadden, Arps were playing a blinder on the bedbug front. When the Securities and Exchange Commission in Washington had asked Chabert for a pro-forma presentation of accounts for both companies and insisted that the Arcelor material must come directly from the company and not from publicly available sources, he had called Pierre Servan-Schreiber for help. He sent him a detailed email.

'Can you be more exact on what information you need?' Servan-Schreiber responded.

Chabert sensed Servan-Schreiber was being obstructive and went back to the SEC and asked if he could use publicly available information on Arcelor. It took the SEC two weeks to respond, and when it did, the US regulator said: 'Have they said no?'

'They haven't said no and they haven't said yes,' Chabert replied.

Chabert was told to go back to Servan-Schreiber, setting out in even more detail the information that the SEC was insisting on. After a suitable delay, he responded. He would agree to provide the information, on two conditions: 'First, that Mittal Steel does not in any way imply that Arcelor is approving or agreeing what you are offering for the company.'

Chabert agreed.

'Second,' Servan-Schreiber said, 'Mittal must pay the cost for providing the financials.'

'How much will that cost?' Chabert asked.

'I will have to ask the auditors.' Chabert could hear the smile in his opponent's voice.

Two weeks later Servan-Schreiber called Chabert. 'The accountants say that to produce the information in the form you want it will take six months and cost twenty million dollars.'

This was clearly bullshit, but Chabert was now desperate. He went back to the SEC, which this time finally allowed him to use publicly available information. This one query had eaten up six weeks. Multiply that across every jurisdiction, and a nightmare could be unfolding. Although not for Pierre Servan-Schreiber. From his side of things, he told Scott Simpson, 'this deal is a lawyer's wet dream'.

The bedbugs were now getting right under Lakshmi Mittal's skin, which was why he had escaped to his favourite environment, a steel plant, to show a gang of thirty French journalists just how he had turned it around. Mittal had bought Gandrange from Guy Dollé and Usinor in 1999. Then it was loss-making, and its employees lived under constant threat of redundancy and closure. 'Standing here in 2006, I am happy to say that this is no longer the case,' Mittal told them. It was now one of Europe's leading producers of wire rod and other products used extensively in the automotive, construction and engineering industries. 'We can be quite precise about the impact of our offer for Arcelor,' he went on. 'At the close of business last night the cumulative increase in the market capitalisation since the announcement of our deal was around 11.5 billion euros. Arcelor shareholders will be asking themselves – where does that value go without Mittal?'

Even though the political tide was beginning to turn his way – the day before he had had encouraging discussions with the Belgian Prime Minister Guy Verhofstadt and the two minister presidents of the Flemish and Walloon regions, where Arcelor had plants – and today he had the Gandrange union rep Marcel Thill on hand to tell the journalists just how much happier the workforce was under Mittal than it had been under Guy Dollé, there was something unusually hesitant about Mittal's performance.

A gastric bug had attacked his stomach. He had thrown up in the bathroom and had barely made it to the lectern, which he was now gripping hard. Philip Gawith was terrified that he was going to keel over, thereby turning a great media opportunity to quash Dollé's accusations about Mittal running the plant into the ground into a gift for Arcelor. Somehow he made it to the end. 'Let me finish by saying that you find us in good spirits.'

Nicola Davidson's spirits were on a knife-edge.

'We look forward to posting our offer document – and we remain very determined to succeed in this project. I now look forward to answering any questions you might have,' he concluded.

After just a few, Davidson leapt in and took Mittal back to the car.

There was no chance he would be able to lead a plant tour. She told him to stay put while she went to sort something out.

Ten minutes later, as she was just about to explain the change in the tour arrangements to the journalists, photographers and cameramen, she noticed a familiar figure striding towards them in a white hard-hat. 'Mr Mittal can now lead your tour,' she told them, looking at him quizzically. Somehow he had made a startling recovery. He proceeded to lead the party on a two-hour forensic visit to the plant.

Now back in England, both Mittals were having strange encounters. Control Risks Group told Lakshmi that somebody had been eavesdropping on Mittal Steel phone calls. The phones were now being swept regularly for bugs, and the spooks were advising that all staff be very careful about using their mobiles. They were not to give out their numbers to anybody they were not one hundred per cent sure of.

Climbing into his car one day, Mittal told Carlos, his driver of twelve years: 'Keep an eye out for a blue BMW. I have been told that we are being followed.' Although they never spotted the BMW, this battle was fast beginning to resemble one of his favourite James Bond movies.

Meanwhile, Aditya had received an intriguing invitation to dinner at Gordon Ramsay at Claridges, and was sitting in a private dining room waiting for his companion when he spilt his glass of red wine. Damn, he thought, he will think I'm nervous. A waiter was mopping up around him when in walked the Luxembourg justice minister, Luc Frieden.

27

Thursday 20 April

London

In hostile takeover battles the defender often seeks to put the predator under the microscope, sometimes with surprising results – and even better if a third party joins in the same intrusive game. Arcelor had begun to focus heavily on what it perceived to be a weak link in Mittal's armoury – his corporate governance. And for once it found it had allies from unexpected quarters.

First came Colette Neuville, the feisty Frenchwoman who was always championing shareholders' rights from her office in the picturesque cathedral town of Chartres, about a hundred kilometres south-west of Paris. Neuville was president of the French minority shareholder rights group known by its French acronym, ADAM, who held just one share in Arcelor – enough to cause trouble – but this time she was challenging Mittal Steel executives to a face-to-face meeting, hitting out on three major points. 'Cut the Mittal family's dual voting rights, improve the terms of the offer for Arcelor, and do something about the lack of a detailed plan for the merger of the two companies,' she told them.

Ms Neuville said her members wanted none of the family's double voting rights and argued for the conventional route of one vote per share, like most European companies. Sudhir Maheshwari listened intently, pointing out, 'The company is proposing to extend the board if it wins, but that is all it is prepared to give way on.'

Within days of Ms Neuville's comments, Arcelor got another lift to its morale, this time from John Plender, one of the *Financial Times*'s most respected columnists, who revealed that three of the five independent non-executive directors of Mittal Steel had financial links to the company's chairman and founder.

'The news comes at a sensitive time for the company, in the middle of a hostile takeover bid for Arcelor,' Plender commented in a lengthy investigative article. Narayanan Vaghul chaired Mittal Steel's audit committee and sat on the board's remuneration and nominations committees. The nominations committee was responsible for developing, monitoring and reviewing the governance principles at Mittal Steel. Vaghul was also the chairman of ICICI Bank, of which Lakshmi Mittal was a director. Next, Plender focused on one Andrés Rozental. The former Mexican diplomat chaired Mittal Steel's remuneration and nominations committees and sat on the audit committee. Mr Rozental was also president of the Mexican Council of Foreign Relations, which listed Mittal Steel as a benefactor.

Third was Muni Krishna T. Reddy. He too sat on the audit and nominations committees and was a director of Intercommercial Bank of Trinidad, which was part-owned by Lakshmi Mittal.

Plender acknowledged that the three men met fully the established criteria of independence, and stated that Mittal Steel's governance practices were not significantly different from those required by domestic companies under standards laid down by the New York stock exchange, where Mittal Steel was listed. But, he said, 'whatever the box-ticking position on independence, Mittal Steel is open to accusations of cronyism in the boardroom'.

Not resting there, Plender trawled through Mittal Steel's voluminous filings on the US Securities and Exchange Commission website. There he found the company's articles of association and its governance disclosures, which suggested that its existing governance arrangements – which Mittal Steel said would remain in place after the takeover – raised questions that might worry investors. Plender maintained that any change in the family's double-voting privileges meant little in practice, because the powers conferred on outside shareholders in Mittal Steel's articles of association would remain academic as long at Mr Mittal retained a voting majority. 'Even if he reduced his voting control to below 50 per cent, the board can still prevent such items from appearing on the agenda if it believes that to do so "would be detrimental to the vital interests of the company". The articles contain no definition of vital interest. So the directors have limitless latitude in exercising their discretion. Other powers conferred on outside shareholders by the articles, such as those relating to the appointment and dismissal of directors, are similarly valueless if Mr Mittal chooses to exercise his voting power against them.'

Plender conceded that the family model of governance was familiar to European investors and the model worked well because there was no divorce between ownership and control of the kind that plagued companies with dispersed ownership. 'Yet the outside investors' share of the bounty is at the discretion of the inside shareholders unless there are protections in law and in the company's governance rules to prevent the insiders extracting private benefits of control at outside shareholders' expense.'

Plender now turned his microscope on to Mittal Steel accounts. 'At first sight the picture is acceptable,' he said, but under closer examination it pointed to Mittal Steel as a Dutch holding company with no business of its own because all the assets were in operating subsidiaries. 'Yet the Mittal website on corporate governance says nothing about whether subsidiaries have to apply and enforce the listed parent's governance rules, what governance information has to be disclosed to the board by the operating companies, and what rights the non-executives have to extract information from the subsidiaries. The management board rules are described as being those of Mittal Steel International NV, not those of the quoted parent company, Mittal Steel NV.'

When the *FT* raised these questions with Mittal Steel a spokesperson admitted that a mistake had been made and there was no such company as Mittal Steel International. The rules were Mittal Steel's.

Finally, Plender examined Mittal Steel's different categories of shares. It was unusual in having two different classes of directors – 'A' and 'C', he explained. The A directors were Lakshmi Mittal, who combined the role of chairman and chief executive, Aditya and Lakshmi's daughter Vanisha, both active in the business, who were elected for four-year terms. The five non-executives were class C directors, with more limited rights to represent the company. 'They are unquestionably poor relations, serving for one-year renewable terms. In effect, they serve at Mr Mittal's pleasure,' Plender commented.

In Luxembourg and in particular in the Arcelor boardroom, Plender's article brought whoops of joy. An influential third party who was underlining their very own concerns in public would be far more effective than their own pleas.

Lakshmi Mittal shrugged off accusations of cronyism, but it got him thinking.

Like an army, Aditya Mittal was marching on his stomach. This time he was in a discreetly upmarket restaurant in Milan, and once more waiting to have dinner with Luc Frieden. Eventually the justice minister arrived, looking like the Spy Who Came in from the Cold. Even though he had the backing of Jean-Claude Juncker to keep covert channels of communication with Mittal open – following Thierry d'Argent's dictum that the government's interests would not always be the same as those of Arcelor – Frieden was so nervous, he confided to Aditya, that in his diary he pencilled in their dinners as 'meeting with American university friends'. It was true, both he and Aditya had been at American universities and had accents to match, but they had never known one another. At another dinner in another leading European city, one of Frieden's old Harvard chums was present: Pierre-Yves Chabert.

In all, the American university friends had six clandestine dinners together.

For both sides it was the chance to explain their business and political cultures to one another and to gauge current thinking with no notes taken. It was also another opportunity for Chabert to remind Frieden that Luxembourg would regret at its leisure a negative takeover law passed in haste.

Sunday 23 April

IISI director's spring board meeting, Barcelona

The fashionable seaside Hotel Arts, close by the Barcelona yachting marina and the city's beach, was the favourite venue for all conferences in the Catalan capital. Everyone knew that the real daylight business was done around the side tables in the first-floor lounge and bar or on the sun-kissed verandas that looked out towards the Mediterranean. At night, it was paella and Rioja, followed by a visit for suits on the loose to the many lap-dancing bars around the marina.

Lap-dancing was the last thing on the mind of the International Iron and Steel Institute chairman Guy Dollé as he stepped on to the podium to present trophies and prizes to the winners of the 2005 steeluniversity.org challenge. Steeluniversity, run by IISI with the University of Liverpool, provided e-learning resources on steel technologies for students and 'steel industry supply chain employees'. The irony was not lost on Dollé that the trophies he was now handing out to the steel stars of the future had been crafted by the apprentices of ThyssenKrupp.

Irony was not a word on Lakshmi Mittal's mind at this moment, but confrontation was, as he set his sights on Professor Dr Ulrich Middelmann, vice chairman of the executive board of Thyssen-Krupp. 'There is mistrust between our two companies,' Mittal told him. Middelmann stumbled out what sounded like a half-apology 'for any misunderstandings'. Mittal stared him down, remembering the Thyssen family motto, 'Virtue Transcends Riches', but did not push it further. He felt betrayed, especially by Schulz, with whom he had also had words, but he knew that ThyssenKrupp was a divided camp, split between those who, like Schulz, were of the company's quest-for-riches tendency, and others, the 'Virtue' wing, that did not want to betray the deal they had with Mittal for Dofasco.

Mittal knew for sure now that Arcelor must be talking to any and every steel company that might come and save it from him, even those who had promised to support Mittal Steel when he had called them back in January, just before he had announced his opening offer for Arcelor. One potential white knight worried him in particular, a keen young entrepreneur that Mittal had had his eye on for some time, for whom a merger, or more, with Arcelor would be a big leg-up on to steel's top table.

'Alexey,' Mittal greeted Mordashov. 'You know that completing this transaction with Arcelor is very important to us – it is why we have been pursuing it for so long.'

'Of course,' Mordashov said.

'Good, then I hope you will not obstruct me,' replied Mittal, getting straight to the point.

Mordashov smiled and said: 'Lakshmi, Arcelor is too big for SeverStal.'

Mittal nodded.

Then Mordashov added: 'At the same time, I will also have to take my business decision.'

Although he had not attended the SeverStal opening ceremony in Cherepovets, news had filtered back to Dollé that SeverStal, and particularly the company's director of strategy Vadim Makov, were now more open to bringing in all their assets to Arcelor to strike a deal. There was also a more reasoned approach on valuation, Dollé was told. It looked as if Marc Pandraud's tactics of patient tenacity were working, Dollé thought, as he took his seat in the hotel restaurant, but Makov – who was out on the beach sunning himself with Dollé's fixer Alain Davezac – was the day-to-day hands-on man. He needed confirmation from the man who mattered, the owner Alexey Mordashov, who was now approaching his table at a measured gait.

'Alexey, welcome. I understand that you are more favourably disposed to bringing all of SeverStal's assets into a transaction with Arcelor,' Dollé said enquiringly as the young Russian sat down opposite him. 'I gather too that we may have more of a meeting of minds on the valuation of your company.'

'I am fully prepared to go down this route in our joint interests,' the Russian confirmed. 'But we need to get some momentum back into the discussions. It would be good to pre-empt Mittal before his formal offer is posted.' Mordashov was fishing for a reaction that might tell him SeverStal was still the only game in town.

'Despite the other discussions we are holding,' Dollé told him, 'you are still my preferred option – if we can get the terms right.'

Mordashov smiled, and they shook hands.

After lunch as he made his way to his room, Guy Dollé reminded himself that the intransigent Russian had cost him two and a half months of vital negotiating time. But it was a price worth paying if he could sprint for the deal he yearned for in order to outwit Lakshmi Mittal.

*

Mittal, meanwhile, was involved in a bizarre argument with Vladimir Lissin. During a break in the proceedings of the IISI board meeting in Barcelona, the NLMK boss had brought with him a special Russian cake to share with his fellow delegates. He was dividing it up among a large smiling group of steelmen when Lakshmi Mittal came along.

'Can I have a piece of that cake?' Mittal asked, but he wasn't smiling.

'Of course,' Lissin said, 'it is for everybody.'

'I think I should have a piece because it is like my offer for Arcelor, for everybody,' Mittal told him, taking the cake.

Lissin looked uneasy.

'My offer is for the benefit of the whole industry,' Mittal persisted.

Lissin was starting to look irritated. Nobody was smiling now.

'I want you to get out of my way on Arcelor,' Mittal told him, clearly annoyed by Lissin going public in his desire to buy 15 per cent of the Luxembourg company.

Lissin stood his ground, but he looked upset. He was being attacked in public, belittled in front of his peers.

28

Friday 28 April

Luxexpo conference centre, Kirchberg, Luxembourg

Arcelor's annual general meeting was always a grand affair, but this year there was a heightened buzz around the registration desks in the Luxexpo foyer. More than three hundred shareholders and accredited observers had come not just to hear the usual progress reports and financials from around the empire, but also to find out from the mouth of Joseph Kinsch the progress on Arcelor's fightback against Mittal Steel.

There was a touch of Cecil B. De Mille about the setting for the event. A glitzy video presentation on a panoramic screen with fast-moving dialogue and vivid pictures, portraying Arcelor people and technology at work, courtesy of Publicis, kept people entertained. Light music spilled out from hidden speakers around the large auditorium as shareholders took their seats, clutching their electronic voting equipment and earphones for simultaneous translations of a show that was traditionally conducted in French. The side walls of the hall were draped in deep blue and there was matching theatre-style seating, split by two aisles. A phalanx of print journalists, paparazzi and broadcast cameramen jostled as Chairman Kinsch, Guy Dollé and the senior executives now took their seats, set a metre apart on a spotlit stage that ran almost the full width of the auditorium. Every one of them was sporting an 'I love Arcelor' lapel badge.

Joseph Kinsch took command of the proceedings with his usual consummate skill, flanked by a chirpy-looking Dollé, a serious-looking Wurth, a smiling Urquijo and a placid Roland Junck. On Kinsch's far right was Schmit, the government representative on the board who also acted as a scrutiniser when it came to the electronic voting. All the directors were up for re-election, but the DG members were not involved in the count.

The mood on the podium was distinctly cheerful. Kinsch did not look like a man who was about to face a vote of confidence – along with his deputy, José Ramón Álvarez Rendueles – the first time his rule had ever been challenged. But Kinsch was facing flak from across the Atlantic from Institutional Shareholder Services, a Rockville, Maryland-based shareholder voting and corporate governance adviser to more than a hundred firms who were share-holders in Arcelor. Explaining its opposition to the re-election of the chairman and deputy chairman, ISS had stated publicly, 'Opposing the nominees is the most appropriate measure for shareholders to show their displeasure at the company's recent actions.'

The French shareholder rights group ADAM was more hard-line, requesting that the resolutions for renewing sixteen directors, including the chairman and his deputy, be voted down. And this was in spite of Arcelor's 'value creation plan', announced the previ-ous month, which had worked wonders with other disgruntled shareholders. The plan committed Arcelor to delivering gross oper-ating revenues of €7 billion a year, which would lead to a more progressive dividend policy boosted by a big jump in cash flow, pre-dicted to be of the order of €4.4 billion per year for the next three years. Arcelor also threw in €2.2 billion, expected to result from the integration of Dofasco.

These were all strong defence themes to stave off the Indian predator.

If the balance sheet looked more than robust, Arcelor was still shooting itself in the foot on the communications front. That day Sarah Laitner, Brussels correspondent of the *Financial Times*, had taken the company to task for a short video that had just appeared on its website. It showed Daniel Bouton, the chairman and CEO of Société Générale, speaking in the most complimentary terms about Arcelor. It had been filmed in 2003 when Bouton had still been on the Arcelor board as one of the main independent non-executives. Just before the video ended a voice-over added that the banker was now 'acting against the company' by offering to provide €8 billion to support Mittal. 'Arcelor clearly has not learnt the lesson,' Laitner wrote. 'The video gimmick has simply reinforced the impression it is pretty desperate.'

The chairman was not to be deterred. 'We are talking about weapons to stop Mittal,' Kinsch promised the AGM. 'We have got lots of ideas we are reflecting on.'

The value plan was the latest initiative in the Arcelor armoury, designed to fire up interest in a high-performing company from new institutional investors and hedge funds, some of whom were present in the room for the first time. It was working well, and more and more investors were seeking to pile into the stock, recognising that Arcelor had been seriously undervalued. Even more comforting to Kinsch, Dollé and the rest, it was now three months since Mittal had made his intentions known, but he was still bogged down by the bedbug letters and was no closer to opening his offer.

In some international quarters Scott Simpson's moral justification for the *stichting* – that Mittal should use his own assets to fund his offer, not Arcelor's – had not gone down well. Critics said it was a poison pill designed to scupper the Mittal offer and they had come to the AGM to voice their opposition. Chief among them was Colette Neuville of ADAM.

'On behalf of my members I want you to submit the Dofasco defence strategy for shareholder approval,' she had demanded in a letter to Kinsch the week before the annual gathering. 'We also want to rule out the possibility of Arcelor issuing new shares without shareholder approval.'

In reply, Kinsch declined to consider either point. 'Any decision taken by the board is always in the company's interest and in the interest of maintaining Arcelor's share value,' the chairman responded in a letter that had mysteriously found its way to the *Wall Street Journal*. Now he returned to the theme. 'The board is not going to use its power to issue new shares within the framework of the authorised share capital in order to dilute the stake of existing shareholders,' he insisted. There was a caveat: 'If such an issuance was to be planned, it would only be run in order to create value for shareholders, and within the framework of an industrial project.'

The meeting lasted nearly two and a half hours. Kinsch, the Silver

Fox, stormed through, polite when he had to be, firm when necessary, and generally upbeat about Arcelor's ability to fend off Lakshmi Mittal. Dollé gave a very assured review of the group businesses and Urquijo rattled through the strong financial results.

Now it was time for the AGM to cast its vote on the chairman. Hedge fund Atticus Capital, a leading shareholder, didn't want him; ADAM wanted to see the back of him, and Institutional Shareholder Services were calling for his head. The shareholders began to register their votes.

Buoyed by the impressive company results, all the directors were voted back in, but it was the chairman's vote that was the most eagerly awaited. As it flashed up on the screen they could see that 75.7 per cent of the shareholders present had voted to keep him, with a fifth against. He took the vote in his stride. 'Today's vote was a plebiscite,' Kinsch told reporters grandly.

'We take encouragement from the meeting that the shareholders have expressed confidence in Arcelor's business model.'

'This shows that shareholders believe that the board is defending their interests,' Guy Dollé added.

With gastric juices flowing and 'goody bag' – including a gift, corporate literature and an 'I love Arcelor' badge – in hand, the shareholders raced for another hall one floor down to enjoy Arcelor's finest champagne and gorge on a buffet spread including French, Italian, Chinese and even Indian cuisine, followed by a trip to the laden cheese and dessert trolleys.

Colette Neuville preferred a diet of healthy realism on the Kinsch vote, pointing out that only 33 per cent of the company's shareholders had taken part in it. 'The directors have let themselves be blinded,' she said. 'In a takeover more than 50 per cent of the shareholders always decide.'

And where were the big shareholders? Romain Zaleski, now sitting on 4.3 per cent, was nowhere to be seen.

'We're seeking talks with him,' Kinsch confirmed, as he lit up with a much needed Maryland. The chairman realised that Romain was not sticking to the script. The original idea had been that he should stop at around 3 per cent.

29

Hotel Gritti Palace, Venice

Romain Zaleski and his wife arrived in Venice for what promised to be a very agreeable weekend, relaxing in the palatial marble surroundings of one of Venice's very best hotels and mingling next day with the great and the good at the opening of François Pinault's new museum further up the Grand Canal at the Palazzo Grassi.

Zaleski knew that Lakshmi and Usha Mittal were also in town for the opening-night party for nine hundred VIP guests and, no doubt, Mittal would find time to catch up with Arcelor's biggest single shareholder. Zaleski did not have long to wait. Lakshmi called him. Not only was he in Venice, he was staying in the same hotel. 'I am in suite one-five-six,' Mittal said. 'Don't bother to go the reception desk, come straight up.'

Over coffee and mineral water Mittal asked his guest a simple question: 'Tell me, what do I have to do to win this battle?' – trying to mask his deep sense of frustration over Arcelor's unbending responses and at the snail-like pace of obtaining regulatory approval for his bid documentation.

'Make Mittal Steel a real company with one category of share,' Zaleski counselled. 'And answer the critics of your corporate governance by being prepared to reduce your stake in the combined business to below 50 per cent.'

Mittal took it on the chin. 'I may have to issue more shares in this deal, which could dilute my holding to around 45 per cent.'

Zaleski knew exactly how Mittal was feeling. His many battles with the Italian business and legal communities had taught him the need for patience. The battle for Arcelor would be like a marathon rubber of bridge in Verona, where Zaleski often played. It was always a game full of bluff and counter-bluff, before the winning hand arrived. Verona was also where the balcony scene in *Romeo and Juliet* took place, and it was here that Zaleski drew an analogy.

'Lakshmi, you have to think of Arcelor as a beautiful woman. Woo her, serenade her, and be prepared to pay more for her hand,' he grinned.

Thursday 4 May

Arcelor headquarters, Avenue de la Liberté

Guy Dollé and Joseph Kinsch had just suffered a massive disappoint-ment. The 'European Parliament and Council Directive 2004/25/CE', the takeover directive, had passed into Luxembourg law. One of the major planks in Arcelor's defence was now gone. None of the poison-pill amendments penned by Servan-Schreiber and the professors, or by Michel Wurth's Chamber of Commerce, had made it. The new law was neutral. Pragmatism and Luxembourg's realisation of keeping its place in the world had won the day – maybe even a few good dinners had helped. Chairman Kinsch had particular cause to feel let down by Luc Frieden and his American-educated, pan-European ways. Frieden's father had worked for Arbed.

'Parliament makes the law, but *he* made the proposal,' Kinsch told Dollé. 'I had a different approach from his solution, one that favoured Arcelor.' But Kinsch's view was already consigned to his-tory. The battle was now swinging back to the offer value and an industrial plan.

'We've got to get the momentum back into the "Sauvignon" nego-tiations,' Emmanuel Hasbanian told his Merrill Lynch boss, Marc Pandraud.

'We have a good chance now that "Sauvignon" is being much more realistic,' Pandraud replied.

The two-and-a-half-month delay caused by Mordashov's

intransigence on valuations, followed by the hold-up caused by the sudden intervention of the Thyssen talks, meant that the Merrill Lynch bankers needed to put their collective foot on the accelerator and keep it there. Mittal was closing. Nicolas Vallorz, Arcelor's 'split rock' equivalent to Sudhir Maheshwari, was seeing greedy white knights and squires slip back into the mist, so there was added pressure from inside the chateau to stitch a deal.

After a series of negotiations, which had taken them to Barcelona, Dresden, Vienna, New York, Moscow, then back to Luxembourg, the Arcelor and SeverStal negotiating teams had at last begun to close in on an agreed shape for the transaction. In essence, Arcelor would issue new shares enabling the Russian company to take a 32 per cent stake in the combined entity, just 1 per cent below the threshold that would have triggered a full bid under Arcelor's by-laws, which would have been too challenging for the Russian.

In return, SeverStal would combine its steel businesses, its iron ore and coal mines and related infrastructure. Synergies would yield more than €4 billion in operational savings and enable the merged companies to produce 70 million tonnes of crude steel annually, taking Guy Dollé and Arcelor back to the top spot.

Tuesday 9 May

The Lanesborough Hotel, Hyde Park Corner, London

There was a heavyweight crowd waiting in the foyer. Sudhir Maheshwari, Yoel Zaoui, Richard Gnodde, Jeremy Fletcher, Nicola Davidson, Philip Gawith and the rest of the Mittal battle team kept gazing out through the open doors. Aditya Mittal arrived first. He looked pensive and tired as he appeared, clutching a few sheets of paper, and switched off his phone. Apart from Wilbur Ross, who skipped in looking gnomic and planted kisses on Nicola Davidson's cheeks, there was a distinct tension. The hotel was stuffed with journalists, Peter Marsh to the fore, and financial analysts tinkling their coffee cups or thumbing out text messages. As the TV crews went through final checks on the inside, a lone press photographer on the pavement outside maintained his expectant beat.

Seconds later, the man himself came through the doors. Lakshmi Mittal looked calm, greeting everybody with a smile as though he was walking into his favourite club. His smile was deceptive. He had come to play hardball with Arcelor.

'Ladies and gentlemen, thank you for agreeing to join us at short notice,' he said, opening up the press conference. 'As you know, we have said from the beginning that we would prefer to have a friendly transaction with Arcelor.'

For the past ten days he had been trying to persuade Joseph Kinsch to come to a meeting to discuss the improvements he was prepared to make to his offer. There was nothing doing. Kinsch, guided by Michael Zaoui, had responded on 4 May, saying that he was not ruling out the possibility of discussions 'under appropriate circumstances', but that the Arcelor board and management believed that his offer was wholly inadequate, had significant concerns relating to the valuation of Mittal Steel's shares, and questioned the merits of the proposed combination of the two companies. Kinsch also considered that Mittal's industrial plan, which now ran to a monumental hundred pages, did not 'contain the specific' – that is financial – 'elements of a business plan, nor does it justify the strategic logic of the combination'.

Furthermore, Kinsch said, there was a precondition to any meeting. Arcelor would need to receive Mittal Steel's business plan – containing much more sensitive and confidential financial information on Mittal Steel's actual and projected company performance than an industrial plan – for a detailed review. Mittal had refused. 'Sharing a business plan at this time raises significant regulatory issues,' he told Kinsch. 'The level of detail and disclosure we have provided in this area already is unprecedented.'

'He says his business plan is confidential,' Kinsch reported to Michael Zaoui.

'Excuse me!' Zaoui was becoming exasperated at what he saw as Mittal dragging his feet. 'How can it be confidential if he wants to sit down and discuss merging with us? Tell him that we still do not know enough about his business beyond what a few analysts write. Once we see his business plan we can study it and decide if it forms the basis for a meeting.'

Mittal had finally lost patience playing at round and round the house with Chairman Kinsch, telling him: 'On May the ninth I shall make public these exchanges in compliance with regulatory requirements and issue a press release that explains how, despite several attempts, we have been unsuccessful in engaging Arcelor in constructive dialogue.' Once his offer opened he would bypass the board and issue his prospectus directly to Arcelor's shareholders.

'Let me outline some of the improvements we proposed to Arcelor,' Mittal told the conference. 'We suggested enlarging the Mittal Steel board to fourteen members, with Mittal Steel and Arcelor equally represented with six members each, plus two further independent directors. We proposed a management board of six people, with Mittal Steel and Arcelor equally represented. We proposed moving to a one-share one-vote principle. And we also said that in the context of a recommended transaction, Mittal Steel would be prepared to revise the value of its offer.'

'Why should Arcelor need a business plan to assess the value of Mittal Steel's shares?' he asked. 'Our shares are listed on the New York stock exchange and Euronext in Amsterdam, enjoy great liquidity, and are widely followed by investors and analysts. One does not assess the value of these shares by looking at a business plan. We hope that this is not another pretext not to engage in discussions with us or to put another roadblock in the way of this combination.'

Wilbur Ross took the microphone. Nobody but Arcelor had questioned the industrial logic of putting the two companies together, he said. 'There has been an increase of ten billion euros in the value of these two companies since the announcement of our offer. That reflects a favourable market response. Ten billion euros is a pretty powerful report card on this deal. Against that backdrop, in not entering into a dialogue with Mittal Steel, despite our improved amendments, one has to question in whose interests the Arcelor board is working – their own or their shareholders'? They are acting more like court jesters than fiduciaries for the shareholders.'

Peter Marsh asked by how much Mittal Steel might be prepared to raise its offer. Lakshmi Mittal peered over his glasses and smiled. 'Peter, I think that is a question that Arcelor should be asking us.'

Mittal had one more announcement to make before flying off to his company's AGM in Rotterdam. 'In the context of the steady evolution of the corporate governance of Mittal Steel, Mr François Pinault has today agreed to join the board.' He paused, waiting for it to sink in. 'As you all know, Mr Pinault is one of France's most successful and respected business leaders. His wide knowledge of European business will be a great asset to Mittal Steel as it builds its business.'

Out of the friendship that had begun at Anne Méaux's dinners, fuelled by Pinault's shame at the xenophobic remarks made by Arcelor and the French political elite, including his friend Jacques Chirac, Lakshmi Mittal now had a key to the door of the French business establishment. Mittal's legitimacy on mainland Europe had just received a massive boost. Pinault's Mittal directorship was his only board appointment with a company in which he did not have significant business interests. Accusations of cronyism on the part of the Mittal board would now be undermined. Anne Méaux looked on, satisfied at a job very well done.

Her close friend Michael Zaoui was, unusually, taken completely by surprise. He detected Yoel's hand in there somewhere, too. When this was all over he vowed to congratulate his brother on a masterstroke.

'This is a great coup,' Zaoui admitted to Scott Simpson. 'Pinault is highly respected, he's a great investor, he is a wonderful businessman, he is a great person and there is no downside whatever in having him join the Mittal board.'

Oh my God! Simpson thought quietly to himself when he heard the news. Simpson, who, like Michael Zaoui, had worked so closely with Pinault, was astonished that his Gucci white knight had broken ranks to join Mittal. This was worse than the Pope transferring to Canterbury. This was a very bad day for Arcelor.

Never one to miss a chance to enter enemy territory, Mittal arrived in Miami on 11 May to give a presentation to the Merrill Lynch Global Mining, Metals and Steel Conference. Rather dryly, it was entitled 'The New Steel Paradigm and Future Challenges', but it ended with a slide on which appeared these words: 'The steel industry is very fragmented, much more fragmented than some key suppliers like iron ore companies. And much more fragmented than some key customers, automotive companies, for example. It's very important for us to be much more consolidated in the future, not just on a regional basis but also on an intercontinental basis.'

He then flashed up on screen the source of the quotation: 'Guy Dollé – CNN interview, May 2005'.

He returned to London to find that Yoel Zaoui was pressing him and Aditya to attend a strategy meeting. The Goldman Sachs adviser had a proposition for them.

'I think it is time that you considered raising the offer, and giving some ground on corporate governance,' Zaoui advised. 'None of us wants this fight to go on until next year and it's time to put an end to all this. It's a great deal, but you gotta pay more.'

Mittal listened.

'Psychologically, this is the right time,' Zaoui said.

Mittal nodded. His intelligence was telling him that Arcelor was busy talking to white knights. He just wasn't sure which one was going to come charging over the hill.

'How much will we have to increase by?' Lakshmi Mittal asked. 'What should be our new terms?'

Zaoui gave him a figure.

'If you will excuse us, Adit and I need to discuss.'

Father and son took themselves off to a different room. They were to stay there an hour.

30

The Cavendish Conference Centre, Duchess Mews, London

No wonder Lakshmi Mittal was the most relaxed show in town. After nearly four months his offer was now live. In a landmark ruling the SEC in Washington had said that Dofasco corralled in a *stichting* was not a problem for Mittal, as long as he divested himself of another North American asset. Another major plank of Arcelor's defence had gone. And now, after all the delaying bedbug letters from Pierre Servan-Schreiber and Scott Simpson to Pierre-Yves Chabert had at last been debugged, the Luxembourg regulator had, along with all the other European regulators, agreed the previous day that Mittal could now send out his prospectus to the Arcelor shareholders.

Servan-Schreiber would always argue that Arcelor's lawyers had 'won' in the sense that they had achieved their aim of severely delaying Mittal, but they had not 'saved' Arcelor. It would be down to the bankers to get the most they could out of Mittal, who was still undervaluing the Luxembourg company. But with his offer in play Mittal had decided it was time to go proactive. He told the conference that he was upping his offer for Arcelor.

'Today's developments are the most important since we announced the offer on 27 January,' he began. He was increasing his offer to €37.74 in cash for each Arcelor share, an eye-watering 34 per cent over the launch offer and a 70 per cent increase over Arcelor's closing price of 26 January, the day before his offer launch. The revised offer for all outstanding Arcelor ordinary shares and convertible bonds valued Arcelor at €25.8 billion. Shareholders could take either full cash or a mix-and-match of Mittal shares and cash. In addition to the improvements he had announced on 9 May of one-share one-vote and an equal balance of directors in a combined company, Mittal had also agreed that if the deal went through then his family's stake in the combined entity would be around 45 per cent in share capital and voting rights. 'Today, following our opening offer yesterday, is the right time to announce this and take it to the shareholders.'

He batted away a suggestion that such a dramatically increased offer was a sign of desperation. 'This revised offer is evidence of my determination to move this transaction to a satisfactory conclusion without further delay.'

So why had he reduced his family's shares and voting power to under 50 per cent when it was something he had said he was not willing to do? Peter Marsh asked.

'Our family is very forward-looking,' Mittal said. 'I have never ruled out one-share one-vote. We are always ready to embrace change in the interests of this deal and the consolidation of the steel industry.' He also promised that the combined company headquarters would be in Luxembourg.

Mittal had listened to Yoel Zaoui, who had told him to raise the share offer to €37. He had listened to François Pinault and Romain Zaleski on his family's voting rights. But would Arcelor be listening?

That morning he had called Joseph Kinsch. 'I explained to him that we were improving the value of our offer and corporate governance and asking if we could meet,' Mittal told the press conference. 'He explained to me very patiently that he has a board meeting on Sunday and he will get back to me after that. Maybe he is delaying until then in the hope that a great many shareholders will call him between now and then so they can have a value discussion.' He smiled at the likelihood of the chairman wanting that to happen.

Mittal felt that there was a groundswell for his deal. The Belgian government was now supporting it; the government of Luxembourg and the French government were saying the shareholders should decide. Even that great guardian of the grammar of business, Thierry Breton himself, was saying that he would favour neither one side nor the other. Everybody, it seemed, was with the share-holders now.

In the revised offer Mittal Steel was also dropping its solitary condition – that of requesting a minimum acceptance to its offer of 50 per cent of all Arcelor shareholders. This struck at the heart of Arcelor's unsuccessful attempts to influence the shape of the new Luxembourg takeover law. By insisting on a 50 per cent minimum acceptance for all takeovers, the law would have limited Mittal's option to waive his condition after the closing date for acceptances. That would have meant that shareholders would have been irrevocably locked in without knowing whether Mittal had won full control, once the closing date had passed. In the dynamics of a hostile takeover that would have left shareholders with no chance to change their minds.

The new offer would be open for thirty days. Shareholders had until 29 June to accept it.

'Look,' Mittal said, relaxing visibly, 'this is the most compelling offer you have ever seen.'

'That's right,' someone called out, 'but even last time it seemed you were saying it was a very compelling offer.'

'Last time I said it was the *best* offer,' Mittal corrected him, the trademark beam beginning to break on to his face. 'Now it is a most compelling offer. With a compelling offer you are compelled to accept. With the best offer you have a chance to better it.'

Villa d'Este, Lake Como

Built by a fiery marquis for his ballerina mistress in the sixteenth century, Villa d'Este now boasted George Clooney as a regular guest, as well as pomegranate body treatments – 'the most fabulous in the world'. It was indeed *un hôtel mythique*. Edward VIII was photographed there with Wallis Simpson for the first time after his abdication. Marlene Dietrich came to Villa d'Este to hide from the world in 1949, and spent most of her days on a boat touring the beautiful blue lake wearing a large black hat. It was also here that Alfred Hitchcock wandered the grounds, with its endless flights of marble steps, fountains, temples and angelic statues and imagined his first movie, *The Pleasure Garden*. Inside, the papal red carpet, voluptuous velvet drapes and the Empire-style beds crested with lyres provided a stark contrast to the BlackBerrys, iPods and all the other hi-tech playthings of a Morgan Stanley investor conference.

Michael Zaoui was enjoying a mid-morning cappuccino and a Hoyo de Monterrey Habana on his balcony overlooking the lake before returning to the fray. On his way back down he saw a TV screen at the bottom of a staircase. It was tuned to Bloomberg, the leading financial and business news channel. He almost passed it by, but something stopped him.

Lakshmi Mittal's improved offer was being reported. Zaoui stood open-mouthed in front of the screen. Arcelor shares had soared 12.7 per cent, reaching €35.15, this time a lower price than Mittal's offer.

What the hell has he done that for? What we asked for was his business plan, Zaoui fumed. He made his excuses to his colleagues and went to call Kinsch. He gave him his advice on how Arcelor should respond to Mittal's improved offer: 'Total silence'.

In Kinsch's office it was a different story. Benoît d'Angelin and Bernard Oppetit of hedge fund Centaurus Capital had come to see the chairman. Centaurus had been upping its stake in Arcelor and was still supportive, but ever since the *stichting* they had become increasingly concerned that Arcelor was riding roughshod over its shareholders.

'We have always said very clearly, you guys have done a very good job, OK, and we have supported you,' d'Angelin began, 'but when we saw Guy Dollé back in early February he promised us that you would not ignore shareholders' wishes and thwart the Mittal bid. And then you did the *stichting*.'

Kinsch raised his hand for d'Angelin to stop. Gonzalo Urquijo, who was also in the room, began to look uneasy.

'I hope you understand one thing, young man,' Kinsch said. 'Arcelor is a Luxembourg company.'

'We do understand that – it's why we wanted to see you,' d'Angelin said. 'Very few people realise it is a Luxembourg company.'

'If you understand it is a Luxembourg company,' Kinsch continued, clenching a cigarette in his hand, 'you will also understand that

I have all the powers. And Guy Dollé and others, they don't have any power. In a Luxembourg company it is the chairman of the board who has the power. The CEO runs the show, but he is not in charge. He is not even a member of the board.'

The Centaurus pair were stunned by Kinsch's portrayal of a CEO who had forged Arcelor as just an engineer.

When he arrived back in London, d'Angelin was still reeling from the dressing-down. His allegiance was beginning to be stretched. He put in a call to an office on Canary Wharf.

'Hi, this is Jeremy Fletcher's PA. How may I help you?'

Sunday 21 May, noon

Arcelor boardroom, Avenue de la Liberté

The timing of Lakshmi Mittal's improved offer had seemed uncanny to Dollé and Kinsch. On Wednesday 17 May, the day before Mittal had officially opened his bid to the markets, they had been in Moscow with Gonzalo Urquijo, Alain Davezac and their lawyers, applying the finishing touches to their deal with SeverStal. Alexey Mordashov was on the verge of signing a contract. The news of Mittal's raised offer had blown the doors off the SeverStal deal. Now the terms of that agreement on which the Arcelor board was about to vote would have to be redrafted to make it more attractive than Mittal's latest offer.

Joseph Kinsch was not alone in thinking there was a mole at work in Arcelor, tipping Mittal off on the company's every move. Reports had appeared in the local Luxembourg press that seemed to include word-for-word accounts of top-secret strategy meetings that had taken place inside the Skadden Room just down the corridor from Kinsch's own office. Two Luxembourger journalists on the country's two main dailies had been taken off the story for writing 'pro-Mittal' articles. As the Arcelor directors assembled in the boardroom, Arcelor's security spooks Kroll Inc. had already introduced the technology to stop people texting and using mobile phones. Photocopying of board papers was now strictly controlled, a task given only to a few trusted staff. These were handed out just minutes before the meeting. Even though Arcelor's white knights were mentioned by codenames only, Mittal must have got wind of 'Sauvignon', now edging ahead of 'Cabernet'. So from where was that wind blowing? Guy Dollé and the French looked in the direction of the Spanish for culprits, and the Spanish shot back accusing glances at the French. Maybe it was the Belgians. Joseph Kinsch and his Luxembourgers looked at everyone. The truth was that Arcelor was riddled with moles.

Updating the board on the negotiations, Guy Dollé was passionate that a deal with Mordashov could still be achieved. 'Arcelor has within its grasp the opportunity to exploit Brazil's and Russia's low-cost production, two of the fastest-growing economies in the world.' But there was more to his passion than industrial logic.

Aware of how close the SeverStal deal was, Kinsch advised his board that they should soften their stance slightly towards Mittal, but play for time. After the meeting he issued a statement: 'We shall examine the contents of Mittal Steel's offer as soon as it is approved by the CSSF [Commission de Surveillance du Secteur Financier],' it said. 'After regulatory approval, Arcelor's management will then report back to the board. Arcelor needs to be able to assess the industrial merits as well as the value of the Mittal shares offered in exchange.'

That should give plenty of time to get the revised SeverStal deal in place.

Kinsch was asked if the board would accept or reject Mittal's new offer. The chairman, as wily as ever, gave no indication. 'The board has also reiterated the management board's mandate to present it with all options which are in the interests of all stakeholders.' He said that Arcelor had been right to reject Mittal's initial approach. 'The new offer by Mittal Steel demonstrates the pertinence of the positions taken by the board since January 29.'

'Why did you break with stock market customs and raise your price so early?' *La Tribune* asked Lakshmi Mittal, sensing his timing might be driven by inside information on Arcelor's defence strategy.

'This procedure has been going on for four months. We didn't want to put it off any longer,' he said. 'If we had revised the price before it was approved by the stock market authorities, it would

have run the risk of making their work even longer. We had also contacted Arcelor a month ago and we saw no signs of progress towards
a friendly dialogue. So we preferred to address their shareholders
directly, by right away giving them a complete offer that they couldn't
refuse. It's now time to close this operation and start working
together.'

'Arcelor keeps coming up with new defensive moves. What new
rejoinder are you expecting from them?'

'I cannot believe that a responsible management would deprive
its shareholders of such a fine offer,' Mittal continued, 'and its
employees of such a growth opportunity, and weaken their company through purely defensive actions.' He was fully expecting to
secure more than 50 per cent of Arcelor shares, he said, and could not
believe that any white knight could possibly offer a better deal.

'Do you know Romain Zaleski, the Franco-Italian businessman,
who has now bought 5 per cent of Arcelor's capital?' the interviewer
asked.

Mittal paused and smiled politely. 'It is not appropriate at this
stage for us to comment on any eventual contacts with Arcelor shareholders.'

That evening, Alexey Mordashov and his wife checked in to their
$1500-a-night suite at the Hôtel Le Royal. Vadim Makov had also
checked in his bags. Kinsch and Dollé joined them for dinner in the
hotel's restaurant, La Pomme Cannelle, and reported on the outcome of the board meeting. Mordashov was relaxed. The door was
still open.

'But the terms will have to be changed so as to more than match
Mittal's revised offer,' Dollé explained.

More tough talking lay ahead, but now that Mittal had posted his
offer and was free of roadblocks, the clock was ticking fast in the race
for Arcelor.

31

Arcelor boardroom, Avenue de la Liberté, Luxembourg City

As the Arcelor negotiators took their seats with Mordashov's team at the round table in the management boardroom, they knew they had a problem. Lakshmi Mittal's increased cash component taking his offer to €7.6 billion meant that Arcelor had to at least match it. They were offering a buy-back and special dividend worth €5 billion so they had a €2 billion shortfall.

Alexey Mordashov was reluctant to put cash into the transaction. Apart from his steel assets, he had included the iron ore and coal mines and related infrastructure, but these were highly illiquid assets and difficult to value. He had also put in Rouge Steel, the US steel-maker, and Lucchini in Italy. The negotiating teams worked on comparisons with the Russian companies Evraz Steel, of which Roman Abramovich was a shareholder, and Vladimir Lissin's NLMK, which were both listed in London.

As the negotiations dragged on, Gonzalo Urquijo and Philippe Capron finally convinced Mordashov that he should contribute an additional €1.25 billion in cash. In return, SeverStal would get 32 per cent of the combined group, equating to 295 million new shares valued at €44 each, totalling around €13 billion. Under the terms of the deal, the Russian company would not be able to buy any additional shares for four years, because that would effectively trigger a takeover, and would not be entitled to sell any part of its holding for five years. SeverStal would be allowed six directors on a newly constituted board of eighteen, and Mordashov would become president of the strategy committee, with Kinsch seeing out the rest of his two-year tenure as chairman and Dollé retaining his CEO role.

This new deal would enable Arcelor now to distribute a Mittal-matching €7.6 billion to shareholders who sold back their shares at €44 a share, an attractive proposition for hedge funds and especially people like Romain Zaleski, whose share-buying showed no sign of abating. But as the negotiators began to nail down the final contract details, it was the issue of shareholder loyalty that was now bothering Pierre Servan-Schreiber.

'We will have to put this to the shareholders,' he said. 'We have had very direct threats from the investment community. We can't just shove this down their throats, because we're going to get an enormous push-back.'

Mordashov reacted furiously. He stood up, and so did his advisers. Many of them were ex-McKinsey people, some of whom had worked with Bill Scotting, and followed the Russian everywhere like a line of ducks. 'If this goes to Arcelor shareholders, I am leaving this room now and you will never see me again,' Mordashov said. 'I have been talking to you for weeks on the basis that you can give me a 30 per cent shareholding without resorting to shareholders, and now you say this. Why are you reneging?'

Servan-Schreiber looked at Scott Simpson and nodded. 'We'd like a time out.'

The lawyers retreated quickly to the Skadden Room. 'Politically we have to take this to the shareholders,' Servan-Schreiber said to his colleague. 'But if the deal going through depends on a shareholder vote and a two-thirds majority, then Mordashov won't buy.' For a few minutes they brainstormed desperately, terrified that Mordashov and his entourage might already be storming out of the chateau. Then Servan-Schreiber came up with a variation. 'What we *could* do is say to shareholders that the deal is done unless you want us to *un*do it.'

They returned to the meeting.

'It would be a bit like a referendum,' Servan-Schreiber explained to the Russians, 'which is different from authorising the deal.'

Mordashov, Makov and the McKinsey ducklings looked interested.

'At an EGM we will state the deal is done but if more than 50 per cent of the shares vote against it, then we'll wind it down and we'll give the 140-million-euro break-of-contract fee to Mr Mordashov.'

What, asked one of the Russians, was a typical turn-out at an Arcelor general meeting?

'The highest is 35 per cent,' Servan-Schreiber confided.

Mordashov smiled. 'I like this referendum much better,' he said.

Emannuel Hasbanian of Merrill Lynch was working in an adjacent room when Nicolas Vallorz, Arcelor's coordinator on the white-squires initiative, burst in with a serious look on his face. 'Why are you not in the discussion next door?' he asked. 'They are proposing a negative vote principle on the SeverStal deal.'

'That's one stupid idea,' said Hasbanian, and promptly called his boss Marc Pandraud in Paris. Pandraud had just finished a call with Guy Dollé in which he had told him that a negative vote would get slammed by the financial markets.

'The trouble with lawyers is that they have no understanding of how sophisticated investors behave and think,' said Hasbanian. 'You will inspire a lot of antagonism among shareholders if you go through with this idea. It is going to look like you are trying to railroad a decision in your favour. Merrill Lynch will not put its name to this,' he added, almost in tears.

Kinsch asked Michael Zaoui for guidance. He was much more robust than Hasbanian. 'Everybody knows that Arcelor can issue 30 per cent of its shares without reference to shareholders, period,' he said. He could also see a strategic rationale for the negative vote. It might compel Mittal to do better. 'It's consistent with the governance of a large public company where the board makes decisions and then asks the shareholders to show up and vote against if they feel the board has made a mistake. My judgement is that a large number of shareholders will show up for a decision of this importance.'

'Are you sure you want to do this?' the Deutsche Bank adviser Brett Olsher asked Guy Dollé. 'Why put a 50 per cent restriction on it? Why not just have a straight shareholder vote to vote it down?'

Dollé saw it much more simply. A deal with SeverStal was a dream come true, and the directorate general would recommend it to the board.

Lakshmi Mittal, meanwhile, was walking into the George V in Paris for a second secret meeting with Jeannot Krecké. Both men were working overtime, keeping all channels open.

Ascension Day, Thursday 25 May, 3 p.m.

Arcelor boardroom

Joseph Kinsch had called for a board meeting on what was a public holiday throughout Europe because he did not want to delay a decision on the SeverStal transaction until the customary Sunday. Presenting the deal to the board was Guy Dollé's finest hour. He went through its merits in detail, including the complex maths involved in understanding the valuation of the Russian company's assets at €44 per share, bettering Mittal's revised offer.

By 4 p.m. the board had rubber-stamped the SeverStal transaction, the negative vote and the break fee. The vote was unanimous.

Kinsch now invited Alexey Mordashov to the boardroom to address the directors. The Russian talked enthusiastically about the merger and repeatedly thanked the board for giving him the opportunity to talk to them. At one point emotion got the better of him, and his eyes watered as he spoke in that grand gilded shrine to Luxembourg's finest men of steel, all staring down at the new boy from Cherepovets.

Even though the Merrill Lynch bankers were still opposed to the negative vote, there was a sense of relief among most of the advisers as they prepared for the contract-signing in the board room. A genuine comradely spirit emerged as they mingled with the directors and their new Russian partners. Then, news spread that it was Philippe Capron's forty-seventh birthday that day. An extra celebration was called for. But the catering staff were away celebrating the public holiday. There would be no five-course dinner tonight. Instead, a makeshift team managed to drum up a spaghetti supper, washed down with Arcelor's finest red. Then a giant dish of yoghurt was paraded in with a solitary flickering candle, as the assembly sang 'Happy Birthday' to Capron in French and Russian.

The opera-loving Guy Dollé had cause to sing louder than most.

The deal with SeverStal meant that he would succeed Kinsch as chairman of Arcelor after all. The succession, which had been all set up in a cosy deal and already sanctioned by the board before the unwanted intrusion of Lakshmi Mittal, could go ahead as planned. Chairman Dollé could then retire, as he had always dreamed, as boss of the biggest steel company the world had ever known.

32

Berkeley Square House, London

Lakshmi Mittal sat at his desk and took a few minutes to reflect before calling Aditya. Arcelor had announced its deal with SeverStal just an hour before, and Mittal felt like a boxer elegantly ahead on points in a fifteen-round title fight who is suddenly knocked to the ground by a crunching body punch out of nowhere in round twelve. Frazier had just nailed Ali.

'I think we have lost this deal,' he had told Usha over breakfast. She smiled at him and said, 'You mustn't worry. Maybe this will be good for us.' Although he showed few signs of stress she knew the toll the battle was taking on her husband and her son, not to mention all the others involved in the deal.

Mittal took a deep breath, refocused and dialled Aditya. He was in America doing investor roadshows with Julien Onillon. 'Adit,' he said simply, 'I think we have lost the battle for Arcelor.' He sketched in the SeverStal deal. 'I have had a conference call with Yoel and Sudhir and today we will be working here together on our options, then when you get back tomorrow the whole team will meet.'

Flying down to Boston from New York in the plane normally chartered by Tony Blair, Julien Onillon had never seen the irrepressible Aditya look so deflated. The mood was not helped by the fact that there were only five passengers on the flight. If it had not been for the hum of the engines, the silence would have been deafening.

As soon as Nicola Davidson walked into Lakshmi Mittal's office he could tell that she had heard the news too. The office was filling up with Mittal staff and advisers who all looked as though they had experienced the death of a cherished friend.

Mittal smiled at Davidson. 'Nicola, you mustn't be so down.'

'But, Mr Mittal, all these months of work,' she said, 'all for nothing.'

'Nicola,' he said, changing the subject, 'somebody said I would have to be, I think the word was "stoyc", over this. I cannot find what it means, this *stoyc*.' His dictionary lay open on his desk.

'Oh,' Davidson said, 'you mean stoic.'

'Yes, but what does it mean?'

'It means somebody who accepts disappointments and difficulties, or pain, without complaining. Someone who just puts up with whatever is thrown at them.'

'Oh,' Mittal said, furrowing his brow. 'I don't think that's me, do you?'

2 p.m.

Avenue de la Liberté, Luxembourg City

'Mr Mordashov is a true European, who speaks German and English,' Joseph Kinsch said, announcing the deal triumphantly in front of 'my friend' the Russian ambassador to Luxembourg. Dollé, as pretender to the Arcelor throne, looked equally elated. 'Arcelor and SeverStal share an industrial vision,' the chairman went on. 'We have known each other for years and had always planned to forge closer links.'

In Moscow, the local media saw the deal as a victory for Mordashov's Kremlin-friendly tactics. Earlier in the month he had met Putin at the presidential retreat in the Black Sea resort of Sochi, where the President had given the SeverStal leader the nod to transfer his assets to an international company. It had also not escaped Kremlinologists that Mordashov had been Putin's electoral agent in 2004 and had also been closely involved in Russia's bid to join the World Trade Organisation, one of Mr Putin's pet projects. Cynics, on the other hand, suggested Mordashov had found a neat way to get his assets out of Russia.

'I am taking a big risk and paying a high price,' Mordashov retorted.

José María Aristrain, Arcelor's second-biggest shareholder, saw it differently. 'SeverStal is coming through the kitchen door, not the main entrance,' he told *Les Échos*, adding that Mittal 'is too tight and must offer a much higher price'. He was not the only one who was unhappy with Arcelor's handiwork. Bernard Oppetit of Centaurus had described the SeverStal 50 per cent negative vote as 'the Chernobyl of corporate governance'. Benoît d'Angelin flew out to Luxembourg to protest to Kinsch. Once again, d'Angelin got no joy from the chairman. Taking a cab back to the airport, he got talking to the driver. 'What do you think about Arcelor and Mittal and SeverStal?'

'You know what, I was dead against that Indian guy,' the cabbie said. 'It's our company – no way is an Indian guy going to take our company. But you know what, now I'd rather go for a clear deal with an Indian than do a murky deal with a Russian.' So dramatic was this battle for Luxembourgers that everybody in the country, from supermarket shelf-stackers to the secretaries in the Prime Minister's office, had a view.

That morning, when Alexey Mordashov arrived at Arcelor's auditorium, it was packed with three hundred and fifty senior managers from all over the company's empire. Three times a year Dollé brought them together to provide an all-day briefing on what was happening across the different business segments, and there would be workshops to discuss technology and the latest market trends. There was always a heavy French contingent from his home province of Lorraine.

This time they had also come to hear a presentation from Mordashov about the SeverStal deal, but as Guy Dollé entered the room the managers rose spontaneously en masse and cheered and applauded him to the podium. In spite of all his failings on the media front, it was a sign of the affection and respect in which he was held by his colleagues. Joseph Kinsch would never have got the same response. A smile broke on to Dollé's face. At times abrupt, abrasive and antagonistic, he was visibly moved.

Listening to Mordashov was *not* a moving experience. The presentation he gave was long-winded and the slides were too cluttered with detail. It was not an auspicious start for the managers' new

Russian partner. Mordashov appeared both leaden and authoritarian. It might have gone down well in Cherepovets, but in Luxembourg it made his audience feel deeply uneasy. The cameraman filming him to make a DVD promoting the brave new alliance with SeverStal realised that it was going to take some savage editing.

World Bridge Championships, Verona

Relaxing after finishing twenty-first in the senior section, Romain Zaleski was enjoying being back in the game he loved, after a thirty-year gap. His partner was the accomplished player Albert Faigenbaum, who was also head of the World Bridge Federation. Zaleski's enjoyment was interrupted by a call from Milan.

'News is just breaking that Arcelor is about to acquire SeverStal,' said the caller, Marco Cobianchi, a journalist from *Panorama*, the weekly Italian business and politics magazine with a readership of just under three million. 'In return, Alexey Mordashov will get a 32 per cent stake and they are still going ahead with the buy-back, after which it seems the Russian could end up with 38 per cent and become president.' Relishing his chance to chide Zaleski, sensing that the Midas touch was about to desert the Frenchman, he added: 'This time you will lose.'

'I most certainly will not lose,' Zaleski told Cobianchi coldly. 'Wait and see. This deal is not in the interests of shareholders, and they will not back it, believe me.'

Saturday 27 May, 2 p.m.

Goldman Sachs, Peterborough Court, Fleet Street, London

The rain was sluicing down out of grey skies as thirty-five members of Mittal's core team arrived at Goldman Sachs's office, formerly home of the *Daily Telegraph*, to try and come up with a defence against Arcelor's SeverStal deal. For the first time in the campaign Lakshmi Mittal had to be reactive rather than proactive. Nobody was quite sure how to handle it.

That morning, Aditya Mittal had opened his *Financial Times* to a picture of Mordashov, Kinsch and Dollé in a three-way handshake. He felt for his father – That's the wrong guy they have in the picture!

The mood in the room was as bleak as the weather outside. When Lakshmi Mittal turned up, though, he surprised everybody, including his own son, by saying, 'This is going to be a very good day.' As far as he was concerned, there was going to be nothing *stoyc* about his response to Arcelor.

'This is not some *stichting*,' Yoel Zaoui began, 'this is serious. Mordashov is going to get hold of 38 per cent of Arcelor's capital and yet the valuation of SeverStal is not transparent. Then there is this bizarre 50 per cent negative vote.'

'Getting to 50 per cent is impossible,' Aditya said. 'I mean, the highest voting in Arcelor's history is 35. And just to make the hurdle even higher, they insist that if you are going to vote at their AGMs you must register and not trade your shares for five days in advance of the meeting. If you're a hedge fund that's a significant financial bet you're taking.'

'What price corporate democracy?' Jeremy Fletcher wondered. 'They have fought this whole battle on French dirigiste principles with Kinsch telling Dollé, "find some way of scuppering the Mittal deal."'

'If *we* are not acceptable, why would a Russian oligarch be acceptable to the governments of France, Spain, Luxembourg and Belgium?' Adrian Coates asked. It was exactly the kind of shareholder democracy that Putin might approve of.

Spiro Youakim found himself in a very difficult position. He had worked as an adviser to SeverStal and knew Mordashov well. Even though he had had no contact with the Russian since he had signed to Mittal's advisory team, he felt compelled to speak. 'Alexey is a very reasonable man,' Youakim said. 'He is not an oligarch, he is a value-buyer. But I do think Arcelor have totally misread how their shareholders will react.'

'If he is such a reasonable man, why don't you call your friend Alexey and ask him to withdraw?' Coates snapped.

'I am not even going to dignify that remark with an answer,' Youakim shot back.

The Mittal team was wobbling. Sudhir called them to order.
'How are we going to resolve this?' Aditya Mittal asked.

'Following our meetings yesterday,' Lakshmi said, 'I believe there
is a glimmer of hope.' He handed over to Shahriar Tadjbakhsh and
Pierre-Yves Chabert, who circulated the draft of a letter they had
been working on overnight. To be sent on behalf of Arcelor's shareholders, it was addressed to Joseph Kinsch.

> We have noted your proposal to seek shareholder approval for
> the transaction (and the related share issue), and the
> procedure proposed for seeking such approval, namely an
> assumed approval unless 50 per cent of the issued share
> capital of Arcelor objects to the transaction at a shareholders'
> meeting to be held on June 30. We note in this respect that
> attendance rates at Arcelor shareholders' meetings have never
> in the past exceeded 35 per cent.
>
> We would like to have the proposed SeverStal combination
> proposed to and approved by shareholders in a manner
> consistent with widely followed procedures across Europe and
> in accordance with best corporate governance practices . . .
> allowing shareholders a meaningful opportunity to choose
> between the SeverStal and Mittal Steel transactions.
>
> To this effect the shareholders hereby request, in
> accordance with Article 70 of Luxembourg law dated August
> 10, 1915, on companies, the convening of a shareholders'
> meeting to be held within 30 days from the date of this letter.

Chabert had penned it in his Paris office on the rue de Tilsitt the
previous afternoon. It had gone through several drafts, each one
emailed back and forth between Yoel Zaoui, Sudhir Maheshwari
and Shahriar Tadjbakhsh, then back to him for more honing. Initially
it had been a lot more aggressive, informing the Arcelor board that
there was a risk of personal liability for them if they did not agree to
a meeting. This final version was much softer and more surgically
skilful. It was not calling for the rejection of Mordashov's deal, just
asking for a level playing field. The dig about corporate governance
was particularly pleasing to Lakshmi Mittal. But who was going to
sign the letter for it to have any effect?

'The Arcelor by-laws say that if the shareholders, who hold in aggregate more than 20 per cent of the issued share capital, call for a meeting, then the company has no option but to hold it,' Tadjbakhsh explained.

Aditya Mittal was not so sure. 'What do we achieve by getting 20 per cent to sign? Their AGM is calling for a 50 per cent vote.' In addition, shareholders were notoriously reluctant to sign petitions or reveal themselves as activist protest voters.

'We have arranged the letter in such a way that all those signing it will have no idea who the other signatories are,' Chabert explained. 'We have had so much support for our offer from the shareholders that I think we can do it.'

It would not be easy. In addition to getting past 20 per cent, there was another challenge: to get this meeting held before Arcelor's meeting of 30 June, and allow the statutory thirty days' notice, the letter would have to be delivered to Kinsch by the end of 30 May. And to make the task even tougher, it was a bank holiday weekend in the United States and across Europe. Shareholders would be hard to come by.

It was time to hit the phones. The team was once more working as one. One of the first people Jeremy Fletcher called was Benoît d'Angelin at Centaurus Capital, which had now increased its stake in Arcelor to €600 million.

During the course of the day, orchestrated by Tadjbakhsh they made hundreds of calls – Spiro Youakim alone made more than seventy. They cajoled, persuaded and answered shareholder fears that they would be seen to be acting illegally in concert and might be sued or incur some form of liability if they signed. Some calls lasted two hours. One moment, they could be talking to someone who held a hundred thousand shares; the next, to someone who had six million.

By midnight on 28 May they had only 8 per cent of shareholders agreeing to sign the letter. These included Centaurus and the French postal service, La Poste.

The phone calls continued.

Sunday 28 May

Shougang steel mill, China

Romain Zaleski, on a fact-finding business visit, accompanied by other members of the board of Carlo Tassara International including his daughter Hélène, was deep in conversation with his Chinese hosts when he received a message. Please would he call Yoel Zaoui.

Zaoui asked if he would sign the shareholder letter. Zaleski said he would come straight back to him.

'You must sign,' Hélène Zaleski urged her father.

If Zaleski, with his 5 per cent holding in Arcelor, would sign the letter it would add considerable weight to the cause.

'I will not sign,' Zaleski told Zaoui. 'It's not important and I have no obligation. The real battle is the share buy-back. It will transfer cash out of Arcelor without increasing its value. We have to stop it. If it goes ahead Mordashov will be too strong and you will have no chance left. Let's get the priorities right.'

Yoel Zaoui reported back to Lakshmi Mittal.

'We have to see Zaleski urgently,' Mittal said. If he could not get Zaleski to sign the letter he sensed that he was prepared to support him in other ways. 'Find out when he is back from China.'

Zaoui secured the first mutually convenient date – late afternoon on 8 June at Zaleski's San Felice residence.

Over the long weekend, the Goldman team worked at their phones. As the news of the SeverStal deal had sunk in, anguish at the way Arcelor was behaving grew. The signatures began to come in. Eight per cent became 15 per cent, then 18. And not only did the shareholders have to sign – they had to get bank statements of their securities accounts, just in case they were asked to produce them, confirming that they had the right number of shares that they were indicating in the letter.

If Lakshmi Mittal was disappointed with Zaleski's refusal he did not let it show. He took encouragement from Zaleski's use of the words 'We have to stop it', with emphasis on the 'We' as he waited inside the business centre at Stuttgart airport. His jet, engine still warm, was parked outside.

He did not have a copy of the shareholder letter with him. Mittal knew that it was dangerous to wave pieces of paper in José María Aristrain's direction. When they had first met in Madrid back in February, Aditya had bounded in like Tigger and handed Aristrain a piece of paper, saying, 'Please sign to support our offer.' It had taken all of Lakshmi's diplomatic skills to stop the Spaniard walking out. 'Let's start the meeting again,' he had said gently. Since Madrid, Aristrain had met Mittal at Kensington Palace Gardens. He was visiting London with a view to moving his family there for greater safety. The two men talked regularly, Aristrain reminding Mittal often that he had to raise his offer.

Aristrain had revealed that he was growing increasingly frustrated with the Arcelor board, which he felt was being denied key information. From Aristrain's one-step-removed perspective, Kinsch and Dollé, especially Dollé, seemed obsessed with Mordashov to the extent of saddling the company with a badly structured deal which would hand Arcelor to him, served on the chateau's finest porcelain. They were running Arcelor like a fiefdom and Aristrain thought his board representative was just following Kinsch's orders. Ramón Hermosilla Martín had certainly been a favourite of the chairman. Aristrain replaced him. Weeks later he fired the successor, another lawyer. Now as Aristrain greeted Mittal warmly, his newly appointed board rep Antoine Spillmann accompanied him. Unlike the others, forty-three-year-old Spillmann was not a lawyer but a former banker, and now a partner in a wealth and asset management company called Bruellan, based in Geneva. Multilingual and suave and with fashionably greying temples, Spillmann was also a self-confessed 'deal junkie'.

Mittal explained the shareholder letter initiative to Aristrain. 'All it is calling for is a meeting to discuss our offer and the SeverStal offer.'

'I don't like the way Arcelor is treating you,' Aristrain said. 'You do not say somebody is your enemy and slam the door in their face until you have at least heard their offer. I would like to support you. Please show me the letter.'

Mittal confessed that he did not have a copy. He explained that he had not wished to be presumptuous. Aristrain smiled at the stealth diplomat.

'Let me have my office fax it to you here and to your lawyers,' Mittal suggested.

An hour later José María Aristrain had added his signature. As he handed the letter to Mittal, he said, 'This does not mean that I am endorsing your offer. You must pay a higher premium for Arcelor.' And then he added, 'You must also stop the share buy-back.'

On his return flight to London, Lakshmi Mittal reflected that on the share buy-back Arcelor's two largest individual shareholders were singing from the same hymn sheet.

By Monday Mittal's team was edging towards the magic 20 per cent. Just to be sure, they kept calling Arcelor's shareholders. By the end of Tuesday they had spoken to two-thirds of them. Hedge fund Atticus and Fidelity, one of America's biggest investment banks, joined the revolt and agreed to sign. Suddenly the ranks had swelled to 30 per cent. They contacted every one of them again to reconfirm that they were happy for the letter to go. Aditya Mittal was no longer sceptical. Here were 30 per cent of Arcelor's shareholders lodging their protest when no more than 35 per cent had ever showed up at a meeting.

Just before midnight on Tuesday 30 May the shareholder letter – which went out on Goldman Sachs headed paper, with supporting signatures, each one on a separate sheet – was put into a PDF and emailed to Mittal's Luxembourg lawyer Alex Schmit. He printed it off, and one of his colleagues rushed by car round to Avenue de la Liberté. There was always a security guard on duty. He would take it in and put it on the desk of Chairman Kinsch. It was important that the package be handed in personally and signed for as proof of delivery.

An hour later Pierre-Yves Chabert's mobile rang. 'There's nobody here!' said a troubled female voice. It was Schmit's colleague. She was standing on the pavement outside Arcelor. 'The guard must be asleep or something.'

'OK,' Chabert said, thinking fast. 'Post it through the letterbox, and then prepare another set for delivery at six a.m. this morning.'

They had missed the deadline. Although the letter might not achieve anything in itself, it would crystallise the issues for the investors looking on uncertainly at Arcelor's negative-vote tactic to force through the SeverStal deal.

33

'This is criminal,' Kinsch shouted. As soon as he read the letter he had asked his bankers and lawyers to check the signatures against the names on Arcelor's share register. They could not match them all up. 'Mittal has not secured even 20 per cent of bona fide shareholders, let alone 30,' the chairman railed. Kinsch suspected that hedge funds friendly to Mittal had been doing a spot of 'stock-lending' of their clients' Arcelor shares so that ownership rights transferred across to the borrower, giving them the right to vote at shareholder meetings.

'It's a disgrace,' Michael Zaoui agreed when he saw the letter. What on earth could Yoel be thinking of? This was a very unusual move. This wasn't his style. He was dying to call his brother right then and there and ask him, but he knew the vow-of-silence rule. 'We knocked them back with a fairly spectacular punch on SeverStal and they are retaliating, but that is no justification for this,' he continued, looking baffled. 'The best you can say is that they are in a panic, they have acted out of desperation, they didn't have the time to check all the signatures and the holdings, and they didn't know this was borrowed stock.'

'There is nothing "best" about this,' Kinsch said, putting his banker straight. 'We need to do something about it.'

The chairman was looking businesslike, wearing a well cut wide-weave grey suit, pale-blue and white striped shirt and a pale-blue tie with diagonal brown stripes, but as he sat down to write a letter to all those who had signed, demanding that they prove themselves to be beneficial or real owners of the shares, his hand was shaking. Neither was his mood improved by seeing José María Aristrain's signature.

Kinsch had more than once remarked: 'I had high esteem for his father, he was an industrial man, he built up Aceralia, but this one, he only has one advantage – being the son of his father' – echoing Guy Dollé's attitude towards Aditya Mittal. Ever since Antoine Spillmann had been representing Aristrain Jr, Kinsch had noticed a certain unwelcome belligerence creeping into the Spaniard's attitude.

As Joseph Kinsch wrote on in his lofty office just feet from the great Arcelor boardroom, where the stern steel baron portraits gazed down on an acreage of empty mahogany table skirted by forty-three microphones, he consumed a number of cigarettes. For a moment it looked as though the Silver Fox might vanish into his own smoke.

Within hours the *Wall Street Journal* had splashed the Goldman Sachs shareholder letter on its website and dubbed it, with pulp-fiction aplomb, 'The Dirty Thirty Letter'.

Dirty or not, Mittal's communications team now went into overdrive to shoot down the SeverStal deal. A series of cartoons showing shareholders blindfolded, gagged or lost in a maze of Arcelor's making appeared in newspapers across Europe with the slogan: 'Arcelor shareholders – you have the right to be properly informed.' In the Mittal speaker notes the communications team was instructed: 'Please mention this to your journalists, but ensure that the information is an off-record briefing point: 196 million shares have called for an EGM to discuss both deals . . . [but only] 191 million shares voted for the re-election of Kinsch. At the time Kinsch said: "I consider today's vote as a vote of confidence, a real mandate."'

Meanwhile, Nicola Davidson had put together a ninety-six-page dossier of hostile press reaction from Europe and North America. 'Arcelor's planned merger with SeverStal is an affront to shareholder democracy' was the breakingviews.com verdict, but some of the most vitriolic reaction came from the French press. 'The SeverStal merger is claimed to value Arcelor at €44, but the announcement on Friday led to a fall in the share price to €33,' said *La Tribune*; 'So much for creating shareholder value.' 'Alexey Mordashov, good businessman that he is, is acquiring his SeverStal shares in dubious circumstances,' *Le Figaro* commented.

Colette Neuville of the French shareholder rights group ADAM
was incensed. 'All the brouhaha to protect Danone from the
American Cowboy,* and now Western Europe's steel industry is
being allowed to fall into Russian clutches, when it is plain for all to
see what Putin has done with the gas sector.' Vladimir Katoutine,
analyst at Aton Capital's brokerage division, told *Libération* darkly:
'Mordashov might be Wunderkind, but I still don't know how one
can end up running 12.5 billion worth of assets. Mordashov privatised SeverStal in his own name, but very little is known about the
matter.'

Kamal Nath, India's commerce and industry minister, once again
accused Arcelor and its host governments of playing the race card.
"When the Russian offer came nobody made any comment and that
seemed very strange to me. So was it a question of a takeover or was
it a question of Mittal being Indian?"

The *Toronto Star*, with great Canadian understatement, headlined: 'Arcelor Muddies Waters with Complex Move.' Guy Dollé
might have told the paper that the deal was a breakthrough for his
company, 'creating a truly extraordinary growth platform for
investors and a much better choice for our shareholders', but it was
not surprising that the employees at Dofasco were feeling a little
dazed. The very day the SeverStal deal was unveiled, Arcelor
announced that Jacques Chabanier, a former senior vice president
at Usinor, was replacing Dofasco CEO Don Pether, the man who
had guided the Hamilton firm through some of its most turbulent
years.

Chabanier, who had headed Usinor's stainless-steel operations in
the United States, had been most recently in charge of Arcelor's
strategic alliance with Nippon Steel of Japan. 'I know more or less
everybody in every plant within Arcelor,' Chabanier told Naomi
Powell of the *Hamilton Spectator*. 'I think what I really have is an ability to connect Hamilton with this big animal which is Arcelor. I used
to say that whatever the problem is, there is somebody within
Arcelor who knows a solution. The only problem is to find the guy
who knows the solution.'

---

* PepsiCo.

The big problem for the steel-makers of Dofasco was which animal they were really working for. Dofasco might have been beginning to integrate with Arcelor – itself the prey of Lakshmi Mittal – but it was now governed by the trustees of an obscure Dutch *stichting*, with its eventual fate possibly being decided by Mordashov in Moscow. Many yearned for the days when life was simple.

Taking pot shots at the Russian was Wilbur Ross. 'There are serious questions in the minds of Western institutions as to how good it is to have a Russian oligarch in charge of this company,' he salvoed. 'What if Putin decides he doesn't like Mr Mordashov any more? What happens to the company and the steel assets?' Next, he stalked on to the pages of the *International Herald Tribune*, saying that shareholders should have the chance to indicate whether they preferred Mr Mordashov or Mr Mittal – 'not management meeting in a broom closet'.

On 29 May Alexey Mordashov had flown in to London for a round of roadshows organised by his investment banking adviser ABN Amro. He was in upbeat mood, but he was not being too careful about his future role in the company. At one of the roadshows he alarmed some investors by referring to himself as the 'Prince of Steel' and suggesting that once Kinsch and Dollé had shuffled off he would become the industry's king. The news leaked out as he was giving an interview to counter all the negative press coverage to Peter Marsh of the *Financial Times*.

On the controversial 50 per cent negative vote, he said, 'I was not involved in deciding the mechanism for how shareholders should vote on this issue. The [Arcelor] board has the right to issue shares to outside people such as myself, without putting the matter to any kind of vote by shareholders. Existing investors in Arcelor have known about this aspect for some time. Therefore it is strange to see shareholders complaining now.'

Mordashov insisted that the valuation of his assets at €14 billion was realistic, claiming that '95 per cent of the figures are audited' and that the tie-up with Arcelor was not a hasty marriage of convenience – 'I first met Guy Dollé in 1996.' Neither had he needed to get Vladimir Putin's permission to merge with Arcelor. 'It is a very big exaggeration to say I am a friend of Mr Putin,' Mordashov insisted, even though back in March he had accompanied his leader to a summit meeting in China. 'SeverStal is a private company . . . answerable to our shareholders,' he said. 'SeverStal discussed the idea of a merger with Arcelor with the Russian government. People in the government were very positive and supportive. But there was no sense we had to get permission.'

Marsh then pressed him on another major shareholder criticism, that Mordashov's 32 per cent share deal, rising eventually to 38 per cent of Arcelor, was a neat way of bypassing Luxembourg's exchange regulations that stipulated that once an investor reached a threshold of 33 per cent he was obliged to make a full bid for that company. 'Do you feel any obligation to make a full bid?' Marsh asked him.

'The figure would go up to 38 per cent, assuming the share buy-back by Arcelor goes ahead as planned. I will not participate in the share buy-back,' Mordashov said. 'I have no intention of increasing my stake in the new company through buying shares. Also, I would not be allowed under the regulations. Because my initial stake, taken in an active way, will be less than 33 per cent I am not obliged to initiate a takeover bid. The fact that my share will be going up to 38 per cent is due not to my action but the actions of others through the share buy-back. I am taking a "passive" stance on the buy-back. Because of this, the stipulation related to the 33 per cent share threshold does not apply, and I am not obliged to make a bid. Also, I have no plans to make a takeover.'

It was a typically competent and unwavering performance from Mordashov, trying to distance himself from any games that Arcelor was playing – and concealing any concerns at those they might be playing with him. But however resolute he looked, he was a man beginning to swim against the tide.

Lakshmi Mittal, meanwhile, had taken more legal advice from Pierre-Yves Chabert, who confirmed that the Arcelor board could be liable if it ignored the 'Dirty Thirty' letter. In the Mittal communications team speaker notes dated 1 June was this entry:

Only for your BACKGROUND information:

The Arcelor Board may be liable

- In the event that the Arcelor Board chooses to ignore the letter sent by the 30% shareholder base, the Board may be liable.
- Under Luxembourg law the only way that the Board can be sued is through a specially convened meeting.
- To call such a meeting you need 20% of the shareholder base.
- Arcelor may have previously thought they were immune to this, but now there is a group of 30% which have demonstrated their displeasure.
- The possibility of litigation looks less remote if the Board continues to ignore their fiduciary duties and ignores the request from this 30% to hold a meeting to vote on the way the SeverStal transaction should be approved.
- In such an event, the Board members would be personally liable.

It may never have been attributable to Mittal, but the personal lia-bility threat that had been omitted from the Dirty Thirty letter and now leaked fast to Luxembourg was designed to rattle the nerves of Arcelor's resolutely compliant board like never before.

Having shaken them up, Lakshmi Mittal's next move was to be altogether more conciliatory.

34

Friday 2 June

Avenue de la Liberté

Joseph Kinsch called Arcelor's local external legal adviser Philippe Hoss along with Pierre Servan-Schreiber into his office. He now referred to them and Scott Simpson as the three musketeers, with Michael Zaoui as D'Artagnan. The Chairman was holding a piece of paper in his hand. 'I received this letter from Mr Mittal, and I want you to read it and tell me what you think,' he said. The lawyers sat and read it. Mittal was offering a similar management and ownership structure to the one Arcelor had agreed with SeverStal. Not only that, he had sent his business plan including guidance on Mittal Steel's 2006 earnings and a proposal for an eighteen-member board with twelve independent directors and a commitment that the Mittal family would vote its shares in accordance with the board's recommendations.

Servan-Schreiber spoke first. 'Mr Chairman, we are lawyers. Shouldn't you be discussing this first with your financial advisers?'

'I do not trust them, Pierre, so I wish that this would stay amongst ourselves.'

Servan-Schreiber was astonished, even though distrust and paranoia were par for the course during takeover battles. 'Mr Chairman, much as I take pride in what I do, I am not going to be able to advise you on valuation and other strategic matters.'

'But what do you think we should do, Pierre?' Kinsch was insistent. He wanted a non-banking response first.

'It looks to me, Mr Chairman, as if he has provided everything that we have asked for,' Servan-Schreiber said. 'I think you must sit down and talk to him.'

Kinsch nodded as if to say, that's what I thought you would tell me. There was no denying that Mittal's offer was now the better one. Kinsch was to sit on the letter for several days.

Lakshmi Mittal's advisers had been dead against him sending the letter to Kinsch. They said he was giving too much ground when he did not need to. But after all these months he just wanted to get the deal done. He also sensed that the other side was showing signs of battle-weariness. They must be considering they were virtually giving Arcelor away to SeverStal. Both sides were fighting themselves to a standstill. Something had to give.

'We have to make this approach because we are not making any progress,' Mittal told Yoel Zaoui. 'We are a two and half times larger company than SeverStal, and yet with what we are now offering we are getting only 10 per cent more of the equity. How can any board member support the SeverStal deal?'

By offering yet more concessions he would put the stone-walling Arcelor board in a difficult position, with its shareholders increasingly restless if it chose not to come to the table. But it also offered the board a face-saver. In the wake of yet more concessions and in the interests of shareholder democracy, a top-class per-fumery could be seen fraternising with a maker of cheap eau de cologne.

'They won't be expecting it,' Aditya said, backing his father. 'We have turned the tables.'

'I don't think the board will listen,' Zaoui argued.

Lakshmi Mittal smiled. 'They will have no choice.'

The same day he wrote to Kinsch, Mittal received a letter from Neelie Kroes. The European Competition Commissioner had ruled. There were no competition issues preventing the coming together of Mittal Steel and Arcelor. Another roadblock Arcelor had hoped for to stop Mittal in its tracks had not materialised.

Michael Zaoui had been through Lakshmi Mittal's business plan line by line, as had the rest of the bankers and lawyers. 'It's a lot more optimistic than what we had anticipated in our analysis of

Mittal Steel,' he advised Joseph Kinsch. 'We need to ask them a lot of questions and find out where this upside comes from.'

'You think now we must talk to him?' Kinsch asked, reluctantly. There was an inevitability about the Mittals' persistence, patience and pragmatism. While Kinsch still clung to his Not for Sale sign, Lakshmi Mittal knew that if the price was right the deal would always get done.

'Yes,' Zaoui nodded. 'Now it is time to talk. Thank him for his plan and say you would like the two sides to meet to discuss a number of questions that you have arising from it.'

Even though Kinsch's resistance was ebbing, like some of his board he still hoped that Mordashov, his 'true European', would carry the day thanks to the 50 per cent negative vote. If Mittal won, Kinsch feared for the future of Guy Dollé. With Mordashov on board, Guy could still be chairman of Arcelor until he too retired, just as they had always planned. Under Mittal that dream would be shattered.

Kinsch agreed to write back to Lakshmi Mittal.

35

Carlo Tassara steelworks, Val Camonica, Brescia

Guy Dollé was genuinely impressed by Romain Zaleski's steel-works. It was the first time he had been there. He went round deep in conversation with the staff, complimenting them every step of the way. He was in his element. Afterwards, when with Gonzalo Urquijo he presented the SeverStal deal to Zaleski and Mario Cocchi, it was a different story.

Zaleski already knew that Urquijo was a skilful CFO, but what of Dollé? He had heard much – and much of it, conflicting. The CEO explained everything there was to know about the deal with Mordashov and why it was a much better deal than Mittal's. It was all good competent stuff, but when Dollé spoke he avoided all eye contact with Zaleski, who felt as though he was being treated as somebody who knew nothing about steel. It was a mistake, but he let it pass. Most important to Zaleski was seeing the passion and the vision of those wanting to do business with him. But where was Guy Dollé's? As Dollé monotoned on, he seemed to have left his at home. Zaleski did not like the buy-back or the 50 per cent negative vote required to overturn the SeverStal deal, but he still thought Arcelor was an excellent company. What he was not so sure of was in whose hands it would prosper most – Dollé's, Mordashov's or Mittal's? Romain Zaleski was still a free agent, perhaps more than Lakshmi Mittal had thought.

Zaleski drove Dollé back to the airport. Perhaps he would unwind in the car. But there was no change. Clasping the wheel, Zaleski thought, Here are two fellow Frenchmen, two steelmen, who both went to the École Polytechnique, and yet it seems there is nothing in common between us.

6.30 p.m.

Le Cercle Interallié, 33 rue du Faubourg Saint Honoré, Paris

Le Cercle Interallié, just along from the Élysée Palace, was a great venue for a coming-of-age party. A thousand guests were milling happily about in the exotic gardens of one of Paris's most prestigious clubs, founded in 1917 exclusively for politicians, diplomats, business leaders and judges in the vast mansion once owned by Henri de Rothschild.

Anne Méaux was celebrating eighteen years of Image 7, and everybody who was an A-list somebody was there. Mere celebrities without invitations found an excuse to be out of town. Jacques Chirac was not there and nor was his fellow economic patriot Thierry Breton, but French culture minister Renaud Donnedieu de Vabres was more than happy to drink Méaux's champagne. His was not the only head to turn as two guests arrived – surprisingly, together – elegantly surfing the photographers en route. Yoel and Michael Zaoui had just had coffee at the George V. Given the state of the deal, about which they had not talked, they had discussed coming separately.

'That's crazy,' Michael had said. 'We're brothers for God's sake, going to the same do. Let's share a cab.'

Michael kissed Anne Méaux on both cheeks, complimented her on 'another stunning dress', and went off to mingle. François Pinault caught him early.

'Michael, good to see you. You know this deal will keep going up.'

'That's the general idea,' Michael laughed, nodding to the businessman.

He didn't notice that Anne Méaux had reappeared at his side. 'Michael, there's somebody I want you to talk to,' she said, taking him by the elbow to a quiet corner of the garden.

'Hello, Michael, it's good to meet you,' Aditya Mittal said. It was the first time they had ever met. After months of both working in their respective vacuums and with no face-to-face communication with the other side, the atmosphere was initially strange as they shifted to the terrace steps, watched by many pairs of eyes.

'Having worked so closely with Yoel, I feel like I know you, Michael,' Aditya continued. They began talking about children. Michael's two were almost grown up; Aditya was expecting his first the following month.

'Your life will change for ever, for the better,' Michael Zaoui promised him. As they talked he found he was surprised by the younger Mittal. He was not the arrogant, brash son that Guy Dollé could never refer to by name. He was polite, amusing, warm and very, very sharp. A nice combination.

'I know we can't talk about the deal in detail,' Aditya began.

'I have no mandate from the company to do anything,' Michael Zaoui said.

'Our offer really is the best deal in town and I hope that the Arcelor board will give it proper consideration,' Aditya said.

'There is a time for war and a time for peace,' Zaoui replied enigmatically. 'We felt that you were very hostile, that you made a bid without consultation, and that has coloured our side's perception of your side.'

'It was never our intention to engage in an all-out war,' Aditya said.

After twenty minutes the two men parted. Aditya, Yoel Zaoui and Shahriar Tadjbakhsh went off to a Chinese restaurant to plan their next strategy.

'It's clear that our best shot is to propose to shareholders that they vote against the buy-back offer,' Aditya said.

'It's a massive ask,' said Tadjbakhsh.

'But if it works it will derail the SeverStal deal,' Aditya argued.

Arcelor and its advisers would never expect that their cash-starved shareholders would vote against a special dividend of this magnitude.

Thursday 8 June, 11 a.m.

Sheraton Hotel Business Centre, Brussels Airport

Roland Junck was nervous. He had chosen the venue carefully. Brussels was where the Arcelor jet was based, so its appearance on the tarmac would not raise eyebrows. If this first meeting between two sides who had been fighting a bitter war became public knowledge it would put even more media and market pressure on Arcelor, and Arcelor was under enough pressure as it was. Even its own staff, beyond the inner circle and key advisers, had been kept in the dark. Junck's calm exterior crumbled as soon as he entered the Sheraton's foyer. Right in front of him was a big hoarding welcoming delegates to a conference of Arcelor's top Belgian management.

'Show them straight up,' Junck told the desk and walked briskly to the suite he had reserved.

As Aditya Mittal entered the building with Bill Scotting, his father's words filled his head. 'Adit – go and convince these guys. Everything is on you now.'

Aditya was his normal relaxed self as he shook hands with Junck, but for the first few minutes the body language between the three men was awkward after months of tough fighting. Junck called it 'the war'. 'Don't worry,' they laughed, 'we left our guns at the door.' Even though Arcelor, and particularly Guy Dollé, was still publicly pursuing the deal with SeverStal, there was no hostility as the three men settled down to the business of getting a feeling for each other's company. Following Lakshmi Mittal's concessions to Kinsch, they focused on all the issues raised in Mittal Steel's industrial plan, which now ran to more than two hundred pages, and his business plan. They talked about each other's growth targets, the shape and future of a combined group, where Mittal's synergies would come from, where on the steel cycle they both were, as well as a raft of technical questions to do with procurement, distribution, discounting, fabrication facilities and knowledge-sharing.

The men parted, and agreed to meet again. Aditya Mittal could tell his father that he had the distinct impression from Junck that things were beginning to flow their way.

Gruppo Lucchini headquarters, Via Oberdan, Brescia

Romain Zaleski and Mario Cocchi were received by Giuseppe Lucchini, the titular head of Italy's second-largest steel group, who had recently sold a controlling stake to Alexey Mordashov in a deal that had brought great relief to Lucchini's bankers while adding 3.5 million tonnes of finished steel to SeverStal's capacity. Zaleski was relieved that the Lucchini sale had gone so well since Banca Lombarda, where he held a 2 per cent stake, had been one of the creditor banks.

Mordashov as the new owner was also paying a visit to the Lucchini plant, accompanied by Vadim Makov and Thomas Ver-aszto, his aggressive Austrian chief financial officer. Mordashov, anxious to maximise his time in Italy and clinch the support of Carlo Tassara's chief in the Arcelor fight, had asked Giuseppe Lucchini if he could arrange a meeting with Zaleski. The septuagenarian bil-lionaire had his own reasons for wanting to meet the young Russian, since they both had a heavily vested interest in Arcelor's future.

After a visit around the plant, they retreated to the Lucchini pri-vate residence for lunch. Mordashov was in expansive mood, arms wide, talking about his grand design for SeverStal and Arcelor. But he was so obsessed with his blue-sky vision that, just like Guy Dollé two days before, he was studiously avoiding all eye contact with Zaleski. Mordashov left it to other members of his SeverStal entourage to find out exactly where Zaleski stood – would he sup-port them or was he in the Mittal Steel camp?

Veraszto opened up with a characteristically fast ball. 'What do you want from this deal?'

Zaleski paused, glanced at Cocchi, and responded, 'Look, I invested in Arcelor because I am confident about the future of the business. I am very relaxed and I shall stay invested.' He was not going to be suckered into pinning his favours to anybody just yet.

He was also becoming irritated by Mordashov's pontificating. Whether the self-crowned 'King of Steel' was showboating, or just showing off, Romain Zaleski did not care for it. He admired people who listened as much as they spoke.

He looked at his watch and rose from the table. 'Gentlemen, Mario and I have an urgent appointment back in Milan. If you will kindly excuse us.' As they left, Zaleski shook the Russian's hand politely and said, 'May I compliment you on your acquisition of Lucchini. I hope you have big success – with or without Arcelor.'

Returning to Giuseppe's Lucchini's dining room, Mordashov said: 'That seemed to go well.'

'Alexey,' Makov was heard to say, 'you understood nothing.'

As far as Romain Zaleski was concerned Alexey Mordashov had his head in the clouds.

4 p.m.

San Felice, Milan

Lakshmi Mittal and Yoel Zaoui arrived at Linate Airport to find Milan still basking in a warm early summer's day. The four-kilometre journey to the white lattice gate of the Zaleski residence took less than fifteen minutes. As Romain Zaleski welcomed them, Mittal was impressed by the contrast between the grandeur of Zaleski's religious artworks and the almost ascetic simplicity of the rest of the house. Rumour had it that after each successful raid, Zaleski would give thanks to God by purchasing a major religious work for his stockpile.

Zaleski and Mario Cocchi showed Mittal and Zaoui to a small terrace, which looked out on to a pretty, narrow garden with a small marble fountain in the middle. Over soft drinks, Zaleski got to the point quickly.

'The real battle is about the buy-back,' he said. 'We have to stop it because it will make Mordashov too strong. If we don't, you will have little chance of succeeding.'

The point had not been lost on Mittal or Zaoui. The whole transaction could finish up with a complex ending, with Mordashov at 38 per cent and Mittal Steel around 40 per cent or more, but leaving neither with effective control. That's why Zaleski's holding was a crucial swing factor.

'Can you increase your offer for a second time?' Cocchi chimed in.

'Mr Zaleski, I will not increase,' Mittal said sharply. 'We talked in Venice. You gave me advice. I have done all the things you have asked in restructuring the bid. I am even prepared to own less than 50 per cent of the combined company. Now I need your support.'

Zaleski rose and took Cocchi aside.

'We have to help him,' Zaleski told his colleague. Cocchi nodded. They quickly returned to the terrace.

'You can count on our support, ' Zaleski told his visitors.

The Sheraton Hotel Business Centre, Brussels Airport

Roland Junck, Aditya Mittal and Bill Scotting had talked for six hours, at the end of which they agreed to talk some more. As they left the hotel they walked straight into a group of Italian steelmen who were also coming out of a meeting. Junck recognised some of them. For an awkward moment the three of them stood there, as the Italians looked first at him and then at Aditya, then smiled knowingly at each other.

As he took the jet to Luxembourg, Junck reflected that Arcelor and Mittal did have different histories and approaches. Mittal travelled down narrow avenues to targets at great speed. Arcelor operated on a broader front after all due consideration. Mittal was instinctive, Arcelor pragmatic. But both companies did have a very similar vision, and he believed that they could learn from each other. He ordered and mulled over his thoughts on the short flight home.

At seven that evening Junck walked into Avenue de la Liberté and met the Arcelor DG. 'It was very promising,' Junck told them. 'I think, on the basis of the talks I had today, that there is more than enough common ground for us to carry on talking. We have agreed to meet again in Brussels next week, June 30, and I think that Michel and Gonzalo should be there with me so we can talk about all the issues.'

Guy Dollé, who had fought so hard to keep Arcelor out of Mittal's hands, could not believe that his colleagues were making overtures to the enemy. He shook his head and had just one comment. 'I think Roland is suffering from Stockholm Syndrome.'

*

On Sunday 11 June the Arcelor board met to discuss Lakshmi Mittal's revised offer, Mittal Steel's business plan and the Dirty Thirty letter, 'representing or claiming to represent some 30 per cent of Arcelor capital'. Chairman Kinsch steered his directors towards the inevitable: 'Mittal Steel's offer is inadequate from the financial point of view as it continues to undervalue Arcelor.' He had taken Michael Zaoui's advice that Arcelor shareholders should not tender into Mittal's offer. Zaoui knew there was more to come from the Mittal coffers. Kinsch still insisted that Arcelor was not up for sale, but it was up for a merger with Mordashov.

'The SeverStal transaction will create the world's steel champion and the most profitable steel company,' the chairman told his board, 'and our shareholders should back it at the meeting scheduled for June 30.'

In Kinsch's view the Junck–Aditya Mittal meeting had confirmed once again 'that Mittal Steel's strategy is mainly volume-driven while Arcelor's is margin-driven. As a result of these diverging business models, the synergies generated by the proposed combination of Mittal Steel and Arcelor are on the low side compared to those generated by recent large steel-sector mergers and compared to those generated by the proposed merger of Arcelor and SeverStal.'

To Guy Dollé sitting opposite him, this was music even sweeter than *The Magic Flute*. What was not so sweet was that Kinsch was advising the board that it should mandate the general management board to meet with Mittal 'to review the improvements that Mittal Steel offered to make to its current offer'.

Kinsch was covering himself against accusations being orchestrated by the Mittal spin machine that his board was acting unlawfully in going for the SeverStal offer. 'Neither the SeverStal transaction nor the way it is structured violates any law or any provision of the corporate charter,' the chairman insisted. 'By approving the SeverStal transaction I am certain that we acted not only lawfully, but also in the best interests of Arcelor, its stakeholders and shareholders.' The heads around the table nodded. 'In fact in the absence of the SeverStal proposal, Mittal Steel would not have improved its offer.' The chairman was well aware, too, that the proposed negative vote needed to overturn the SeverStal deal was getting negative feedback, even from its own advisers. 'The 50 per cent level for a rejection of this transaction is designed to encourage shareholder participation,' Kinsch went on, announcing that there would be 'a communication campaign' to ensure 'that shareholders massively participate at the June 30 meeting and vote in favour of SeverStal'.

Antoine Spillmann, attending his first meeting on behalf of the increasingly disgruntled José María Aristrain, begged to differ.

'Mr Spillmann,' Chairman Kinsch reminded him, 'on this board we have a tradition of unanimity.' Kinsch put all matters to the board, including setting the share buy-back price, due for ratification on 21 June, at €44.

The meeting lasted five hours, but the end result was as always. The vote was unanimous.

Tuesday 13 June

Avenue de la Liberté, Luxembourg City

Joseph Kinsch issued a convening notice to the 30 June EGM to be held at the Luxexpo at 11 a.m. The agenda had just two items. Number one: 'Review of Mittal Steel's public exchange offer on all of Arcelor's shares and convertible bonds'. Second: 'Consultation as to the contribution by Alexey A. Mordashov of all of his economic interests in the SeverStal steel business (including SeverStal North America) as well as SeverStal Resources (iron ore and coal) and of his stake in Lucchini and €1.25 billion in cash (the "SeverStal Transaction") to Arcelor pursuant to the conditions described in an information document addressed to the shareholders'.

Shareholders could vote in one of two ways: to maintain the option offered by the SeverStal transaction; or they could vote against it.

As Shahriar Tadjbakhsh read through the four-page document he was alerted by a paragraph tucked away at the bottom of page two. It said: 'If the SeverStal option is maintained, the shareholders remain free to tender their shares (or not) to Mittal Steel's offer. The SeverStal Transaction will become null and void if, at the end of its offer, Mittal Steel holds more than 50 per cent of Arcelor's share capital, taking into account shares issued or to be issued in connection with the SeverStal Transaction.'

He got out his calculator. What he discovered certainly did not pass Philip Gawith's smell test. Arcelor was up to its obstructionist tricks. Tadjbakhsh explained the small-print deception to Lakshmi Mittal and Sudhir Maheshwari, but he also said it gave them the opportunity to highlight it to a significant shareholder who was also a member of Arcelor's board.

'It is time for you to call Mr Spillmann,' Mittal suggested.

Over in Luxembourg Georges Schmit of the Ministy of Economy and Foreign Trade was having his doubts about the government's stance on the SeverStal deal. 'The PM is leaning too far out of the window towards Moscow,' he told Jeannot Krecké. 'The deal is not structured properly. We are giving the Russian too much in return for a deal where we could end up being sidelined and find the head-quarters in Moscow.'

'Georges, this game is not over, believe me,' Krecké said. 'I have a sense that Lakshmi will be back with an improved offer.' Schmit noted the first-name terms. In fact, Krecké was in almost daily contact with Mittal by mobile. 'I detect from his tone that here is a man who has that greatest quality of all, perseverance. He will be back with a higher offer that Arcelor and SeverStal will find hard to beat.'

'If that happens, Minister, and we remain the domicile for the merged business, we still have our national champion, but what do we do with our shares? Do we sell or keep them to retain a seat at the board table?'

'We sell half and take the one-billion-euro profit and pump it into the diversification of the economy. Politically that will be very acceptable.'

'Will the PM buy that?' Schmit asked.

'He knows it could be our only option at the end of the day.'

Wednesday 14 June

San Felice, Milan

Romain Zaleski decided it was time to play trumps. In a short state-ment, Carlo Tassara International announced that it would vote against the massive shareholder buy-back scheme, which now stood at €6.5 billion, although it was careful to state that its decision did not necessarily indicate how it would vote at the shareholders' EGM. This was classic Zaleski bridge play, still keeping the parties in the dark as to his real end game.

'The buy-back is a very negative move and not in the interests of shareholders,' the statement said, pointedly. 'It will lead to a change of control in Arcelor's capital without any obligation for SeverStal to launch a takeover offer. The share buy-back is a transfer of cash from Arcelor to its shareholders, without any value creation.'

Zaleski knew that the international media would seize on the statement. The *Financial Times* said it was the first indication that a large influential shareholder was opposing the board and speculated that smaller investors were planning to do the same.

He followed up the statement with an interview on Bloomberg TV. 'The buy-back will destroy shareholder value,' he told his interviewer. 'It will protect Arcelor from takeover bids and it will affect its share price.'

There was the commercial nub. If the buy-back went ahead, Zaleski, sitting on a 5 per cent holding in Arcelor acquired at an average cost of around €32, could see the value of his shares heading sharply south. He called on other shareholders to follow his example. It was a panic point for all investors, especially the hedge funds, who might now take their profits and dump their Arcelor stock.

The Carlo Tassara announcement caused ructions at Arcelor. Kinsch had been right to be suspicious of Zaleski. He immediately sent BNP Paribas into action, who pleaded with Zaleski to reconsider his decision. Gonzalo Urquijo called him with a similar request. 'I am in a difficult position talking to you,' the Spaniard confided to Zaleski. 'My colleagues in Luxembourg think I have let the wolf in through the front door.'

'Cancel the shareholder meeting on the buy-back on June 21,' Zaleski demanded, sticking to his principled view about value destruction for shareholders. To ease his conscience, spurred on no doubt by a sense of divine guidance, he then promptly arranged to repay BNP Paribas its original €1 billion loan with refinancing arranged through the Italian banking community.

He had also been true to his promise to Lakshmi Mittal. He

increased his shareholding in Arcelor to 7.4 per cent. He was now the Luxembourg company's single biggest shareholder.

Saturday 17 June, 10 a.m.

Bruellan Wealth Management, 2 rue S.-Thalberg, Geneva

'Arcelor had 614 million shares outstanding at the end of 2005, and they propose to issue an extra 295 million shares to Mordashov,' Shahriar Tadjbakhsh began, sitting with Sudhir Maheshwari in the Geneva office of Antoine Spillmann, 'so he would hold a little over 32 per cent of the diluted share capital. Then there's the proposal to buy back up to 148 million shares, which would take Mordashov's stake in Arcelor to more than 38 per cent, since he will not have tendered shares into the share buy-back.'

'OK,' Spillmann said, 'I'm with you.'

'Right,' Tadjbakhsh continued. 'From Mittal's perspective, as we have to secure 50 per cent of the fully diluted shares to win and to have the SeverStal deal come undone, it means that we have to win in the tender offer 50 per cent of the sum of 614 + 295 – i.e. 455 million shares. We have to get 455 million shares out of the 614 million outstanding, since the Mordashov shares will not be outstanding at the time the tender is due to close, and even if they have been issued, it is clear that Mordashov will not tender them to us. That means we have to get 74 per cent – 445 million out of 614 – of the outstanding shares in the tender. In effect Arcelor has unilaterally raised the bar from the traditional 50 per cent to an unreasonably high level.'

Maheshwari nodded in agreement.

'It gets worse,' Tadjbakhsh said. 'If you consider that, say, 10 per cent of the float is in the hands of those adamantly opposed to Mittal – that's sixty-one million shares – that means the threshold we have to cross in effect goes from 74 to 82 per cent. Factor in the prospect of the share buy-back, which will tend to keep more shareholders away from the Mittal offer, and the bar goes even higher.'

In other words, Arcelor was rigging it so Mittal could never win outright. And there was another problem Tadjbakhsh had identified. 'Mittal could "win" the tender, say, by getting 50 per cent of the 614 million outstanding shares, but with Arcelor on automatic pilot to issue 295 million shares to Mordashov, Mittal's shareholding would be diluted down to 34 per cent, giving Mordashov 32 per cent with the remaining 34 made up of other shareholders.'

'A three-way standoff,' said Spillmann, who had not spotted the devil lurking in the fine print.

'Correct,' Tadjbakhsh said. Having Spillmann and therefore Aristrain on Mittal's side was crucial now. He was the largest individual shareholder with a seat on the board.

For two hours Maheshwari and Tadjbakhsh took Spillmann through Mittal's business and industrial plans, but he was fixated on the wording of the convening notice. 'They have included this passage without any reference whatsoever to the board,' he said, looking insulted. 'If this gets through we will end up with the worst of all worlds – no overall control.'

It was heading for noon when the three men drove the short distance to Geneva's Noga Hilton overlooking the lake and its famous fountain. Inside the hotel's Chinese restaurant they met José María Aristrain.

'Who chose the restaurant?' Aristrain said in an aside to Spillmann.

'They did,' Spillmann began, but before he could say any more Lakshmi Mittal arrived.

Mittal was in the mood for a Chinese lunch. As they pondered the menu, Tadjbakhsh, Maheshwari and Spillmann précised their meeting. Aristrain interrupted suddenly: 'My business is a family business, something you understand only too well, Lakshmi. The Spanish shareholders, the Aceralia people, have been cast aside by Arcelor.' Where Zaleski was very calculating, Aristrain was emotional.

'It is the shareholders who own a company. Management are merely stewards,' Mittal said, trotting out a favourite line. 'The Arcelor board is not taking the right decision in refusing to listen to us. They have been talking to everybody except us. We have been ready to start a dialogue since day one.'

Aristrain nodded and switched tack. 'This is not first and foremost about money,' he said, 'although until now there has been no cash distribution to shareholders.'

'I know the industrial logic of my deal is going to be the best for all the shareholders,' Mittal told him, swinging back to his text, 'but if they decide to go with Mordashov, that is their choice, but they must have the chance to vote properly on transparent options.'

Aristrain agreed, but he wasn't any more taken with the many-paged menu than he was with Joseph Kinsch's convening notice.

'I am sorry,' he admitted, 'but I do not like Chinese food.'

Lakshmi Mittal called the waiter over. 'Please, would you bring Mr Aristrain a plate of cheese?'

After their contrasting lunches the two men shook hands. As they parted, José María Aristrain said to Lakshmi Mittal: 'You have my support.' But that support was not a blank cheque for Mittal. What the Spaniard meant was that he was supporting a level playing field where the Arcelor board could evaluate the Mordashov and Mittal deals side by side.

Jeannot Krecké called Alexey Mordashov on his mobile. The Russian sounded down and the minister agreed to meet him. They sat on the sun-drenched terrace drinking coffee at the Hôtel Le Royal for an hour. Krecké saw a deep disappointment in the Russian's demeanour.

In spite of steadfast support from Guy Dollé and some others, Mordashov felt that the body language from Arcelor and for that matter the government was not what it had been. He even suspected that he was being used as a stalking horse by Arcelor just to get Mittal to ramp up his price. Even so he had booked the full suite of offices on the basement floors of the hotel, and deposited a group of advisers including the investment banking teams from ABN Amro and Allen & Overy, the London law firm, working on plans for a new counter-offer. The astute Russian knew that while the battle was going Mittal's way rather than his, he was determined to try and reverse things.

'Do you think it's all over?' Mordashov asked. 'I have a sense that there are factions within Arcelor who don't want me. I just need your support, Minister.'

Krecké found it difficult to respond, even though he wanted to help. He promised to call Mordashov later in the day, after he had spoken with his prime minister. Jean-Claude Juncker was at his private residence but when he heard how disappointed Mordashov was, he agreed to see this Russian who had so impressed him. 'Get in your car and bring him over,' he ordered.

In the early afternoon Krecké collected Mordashov and they drove to meet Juncker, but after two hours of tea all they could offer the Russian was sympathy. They could not interfere on his behalf.

Alexey Mordashov, however, still had cards to play, and that evening he boarded a plane and flew out of Luxembourg.

The food was far more to José María's Aristrain's liking on Sunday 18 June at Le Chat-Botté, the famous restaurant at the Hôtel Beau Rivage, one of the fanciest in Geneva, suitably decorated with tapestries, sculpture and rich upholstery, and with a polite and correct staff serving some of the best food in the city. While he and Antoine Spillmann waited in a private dining room for their guests to arrive, Aristrain feasted his eyes on the menu, which included 'a delicate *filet* of perch from Lake Geneva'. Who needed monosodium glutamate?

Aristrain was just mulling over his choices when Alexey Mordashov and Vadim Makov walked in. He had invited them because he had a proposition to offer that he believed would make the SeverStal deal more palatable to shareholders and the market.

'SeverStal coming together with Arcelor is a good idea, but I have never seen such a badly structured deal,' he began. He still could not decide between Mittal and Mordashov and he wanted the Russian to sign up to something that was comparable to what Mittal Steel had on the table. Then the board would have a free and fair choice. Over a leisurely lunch Aristrain's deal-junkie Spillmann sketched out a new proposal to their guests.

36

Monday 19 June

Avenue de la Liberté

Joseph Kinsch's correspondence file made most interesting reading. Now, to the Dirty Thirty and Mittal's missive of 2 June the chairman of the board could add another. It was from José María Aristrain. 'The proposed purchase of SeverStal has been structured in a way that sends confusing signals to Arcelor's shareholders,' it began. Kinsch grabbed a cigarette. 'Consequently, we believe the transaction should be structured differently. SeverStal should be purchased through the combination of cash, shares and convertible shares.' In Aristrain's package Mordashov would be given €7 billon in cash and a combination of shares and convertible shares to be agreed between SeverStal and Arcelor. In return, Mordashov would use all the €7 billon received to buy Arcelor shares in the marketplace. 'This commitment will be honoured at the prevailing market price, up to a maximum of €50 per share. It is understood that Mr Mordashov will not exceed the threshold of 33.3 per cent of Arcelor's fully diluted share capital. We understand that it is essential to also include in the new proposition an exit strategy in case Mittal Steel ends up with control.'

With this improved deal in place, Aristrain wrote, SeverStal no longer needed or required any special rights of corporate governance, and Arcelor's existing by-laws and corporate governance rules should remain in force. 'Having discussed these matters with Mr Mordashov, we believe he has a good understanding of the above suggestions. I am kindly suggesting that these proposals be added on to the agenda of the forthcoming meeting on June 21.'

Kinsch shook his head at Aristrain's pay-off: 'We would like to inform you that the content of this letter will be released to the press within two days of the next board meeting.'

The 21 June meeting, due to vote on the share buy-back, now looked like a potential disaster. Even if Aristrain's plan was not an improvement on the SeverStal deal as far as Kinsch was concerned and was too little too late, it was symptomatic of the increasing shareholder backlash led by the defecting Zaleski, the biggest single shareholder in Arcelor. The Wallonian region, the third-biggest shareholder, was also against the buy-back. Kinsch rang round his board members. No quorum was required at the meeting and Arcelor needed a two-thirds majority to succeed. But if its record for shareholder voting was 35 per cent, a minority of little more than 10 per cent could defeat the proposal. Given the enthusiasm with which cash-starved shareholders had greeted the buy-back when it had been announced, it was remarkable that they were now willing to vote down a €6.5 billion pay-out. Arcelor's claim that the buy-back and its proposed merger with SeverStal were separate was not winning anybody over any more. In investors' minds the two were closely linked as a device to thwart Mittal.

Defeat was out of the question, Kinsch told his board. Later that day he put out a press release postponing the meeting: 'In light of the current discussions between the management of Arcelor and Mittal Steel, and in order not to impair any solution for the future of Arcelor, the board of directors has resolved to withdraw the convening of the extraordinary general meeting of June 21. Shares blocked in order to allow participation at that meeting in person or by proxy can be unblocked immediately.'

In a defiant sentence it added, 'The board reserves the right to convene an extraordinary general shareholders' meeting in order to allow its shareholders to decide on such distribution [the buy-back] in case the unsolicited offer by Mittal Steel is not successful.' But this was window-dressing. By simply postponing a vote, Kinsch and his board had just lost another argument: that Arcelor was the true guardian of shareholder rights.

If Zaleski was delighted, Aristrain was livid that his revised SeverStal deal was not now going to be discussed at all. He demanded that Arcelor abandon its plan to issue shares to

Mordashov and called on Kinsch and Dollé to resign. They should 'come out of Arcelor'; they represented the 'old way' of running public companies, where shareholders' views were ignored.

There was no way that Joseph Kinsch was going to respond to that demand. Nor was there any indication from Arcelor that it was going to cancel the vote on 30 June to approve the SeverStal deal.

37

World Steel Dynamics Success Conference, New York

In the steel business the Annual Steel Success Conference organised by World Steel Dynamics was Mecca. Every year they turned up in their droves. For the twenty-first such conference WSD had chosen as its theme 'Steel's New Game: Bigger Bets – Bigger Jackpots'. Over three days, here was the chance for twelve hundred delegates to network, size up the opposition, start and quash rumours, scope a deal or hawk a résumé. But mostly they spoke in the bars and corridors and off-piste parties about one deal above all others. It was steel's only game right now, where the bets and the jackpot were getting bigger by the day.

It was in great anticipation that the steelmen took their seats in the main auditorium at the Sheraton New York Hotel & Towers on 7th Avenue and 53rd Street for the conference's top-of-the-bill event, the address of the 'highlight speaker'. When WSD managing partners Peter Marcus and Karlis Kirsis had been planning the conference, they wanted a speaker who challenged accepted ideas and practices and was not afraid to cause intellectual and sometimes emotional turmoil. Traditionally the conference loved a speaker who was an outsider and who could turn things on their head to take the industry forward. There had been only one choice as to who would take the role this year.

What nobody knew was that, just a few hours before, the star of the show had lost his voice. Lakshmi Mittal had flown into New York's private Teterboro Airport the previous day from Boston, where he had done a roadshow. High above the Hudson River, he did not bother to glance up from his BlackBerry and admire the over-familiar view. Throughout the journey he had been emailing Aditya for progress on the talks he was having at Brussels Airport with Roland Junck, Michel Wurth and Gonzalo Urquijo to hammer out a memorandum of understanding between himself and Arcelor. It was now their fourth meeting since 8 June and it looked promising, Aditya was telling him.

But Mittal, dressed in a light-grey Armani suit, was not going to give the fellow passenger sitting right next to him any inkling that the deal he had been chasing for months across four continents was now within a fingertip of being sealed. Nelson D. Schwartz, senior writer at *Fortune* magazine, was riding shotgun with Mittal for a major feature he was writing called 'Emperor of Steel', which was one up the scale from Mordashov, whose ambition was to go from Crown Prince to King. Being a good journo, Schwartz was prodding. He knew that Mittal would never have let him fly if he had been about to lose. The amount of time Lakshmi was putting in on his BlackBerry meant something was about to happen.

'I don't know what will happen,' he told Schwartz. 'Arcelor is still fighting.'

On landing, he lunched with editors from the *Wall Street Journal* and then held more roadshows with investors. That evening he had attended the conference's welcome cocktail party, which he was sponsoring. When he arrived everybody clustered around him, bursting to talk. And now with a major speech to make he had woken up at 4 a.m. unable to speak. He was terrified he would not be able to give it. He called Usha for help. His voice was barely above a whisper and she couldn't hear him.

'Listen,' he croaked, 'I cannot speak.'

'Get some salt and gargle with salt water until the pharmacy opens,' she told him.

Gargle in one hand, speech in the other, Mittal hoped for the best when the time came. He looked at his watch. It was now 6 a.m. He had just over four hours to try and find a voice.

As he rose to give his address Mittal looked around the serried ranks of steel's major players. There were many familiar faces, including most of Arcelor's potential white knights. His brother Vinod was also there and so too was Spiro Youakim. Predictably enough, his speech was entitled 'Building a Sustainable Model for the Future'.

'All congratulations must go to the organisers Peter and Karlis for turning this event into an important day in the diaries of all steel executives,' Mittal said. He did not recognise the voice as his own, but it was a voice. He prayed it would get him through. He paused, until he felt his audience metaphorically tiptoe closer to the microphone. 'The congratulations, of course, do not end there,' he continued. 'We must surely also congratulate them for the hat-trick they have managed to pull off – getting Guy Dollé, Alexey Mordashov and myself into the same room on the same day.'

Lakshmi Mittal relaxed visibly. He had the crowd with him. The speech that followed was measured, reiterating that his 1998 vision of steel having to go global to survive had been the correct one, 'not because I was proved right, but because it is what was necessary for the long-term health of the industry'. He also took his chance to nail some myths once and for all. 'If we agree – and I hope we do – on the benefits of scale for the health of the indus-try, the other important question to address is whether steel companies should specialise in one particular type of produc-tion – for example, higher-quality versus more commodity-type steel.

'It is entirely normal for large multinational companies to make a variety of products tailored for different markets and demands,' Mittal told them. 'Mass car manufacturers like Toyota and VW are happy to own luxury brands like Lexus and Audi. No one would suggest that a company like Ford, or Coke or Unilever should have to choose between one market and the other. The same, naturally, applies to Mittal Steel.'

For Guy Dollé this was all too galling, as Mittal ended with a ral-lying call to the industry in which 'demand trends are positive and continuing consolidation is taking us towards the stability we desire. Most exciting, though, is that I still believe we are in the early stages of this renaissance.'

After coffee Mittal went off to do another roadshow with New York investors while the conference delegates broke off into various panel discussions. Alexey Mordashov took his place on panel 1, 'International Steel Game: Chess without Checkmate'. Even though Kinsch had rejected Aristrain's revised deal, he was in no mood to countenance a Mittal victory over Arcelor. There was still the negative vote to come on 30 June, which was stacked in his favour, and he still had Guy Dollé's backing. The previous evening Dollé and Alain Davezac had had a meeting with Mordashov and Vadim Makov at which Dollé had rammed home that Arcelor was now under mounting pressure from dissident shareholders like the ADAM group and the hedge funds, who increasingly saw a Mittal takeover as more attractive than the complicated SeverStal swap. 'Just tell us what we have to do to make our deal stick,' Makov had said. The Russians still reckoned they could fashion an offer that would beat Mittal.

'Arcelor/SeverStal is going to become a very balanced company with a strong presence in Europe, the best market. It will also have a strong presence in Brazil and Russia,' Mordashov told the conference, citing a lower cost of production and future growth in the steel market. 'This is going to be a strong and unbeatable combination by far. Arcelor/SeverStal should grow in the future to maintain our leading position in the steel world.'

Mordashov impressed his listeners. He was youthful, clean-cut and clearly somebody going somewhere fast. SeverStal would be as good an industrial fit with Arcelor as Mittal, and in many ways better, he told them. 'It's the best-value proposition in terms of price, in terms of corporate governance, in terms of cost of execution because it's friendly.'

But, unlike Mittal's, Mordashov's English lacked fluidity and made his vision less compelling and not so easy to understand. Also, Lakshmi had the track record. The bar-room juries assembled. Mittal had picked up a perfect 10. Mordashov could only muster a doughty 8. Ultimately, the steelmen said, Mordashov's company could not be valued accurately and he was too close to Putin to do business with. Neither did he do jokes.

Later in the morning Mordashov picked up the prestigious Steel Vision Award. But still the top prize eluded him. How many moves did he have left to make to achieve his vision of turning himself from white knight into King of Steel?

Guy Dollé was the luncheon speaker. His theme was positive consolidation in steel. 'At Arcelor, value before volume is our motto,' he said, theming his remarks. 'That is to say: size matters, but that cannot be the sole strategic *raison d'être*. This is a value-driven industry.'

What he went on to deliver was a manifesto for Arcelor; a point-by-point rebuttal of the Mittal creed. 'There is room for many animals in the new Garden of Eden of the steel industry,' Dollé continued, 'some of them small, highly focused, some others large and even gigantic. But all of them, and especially the big ones, should be guided by the idea that value and not size comes first . . . As a large and global player, Arcelor has a more balanced strategy, based on capturing growth opportunities in developing markets, as well as keeping our profitability in mature markets. In both cases, Arcelor balances specialities and commodities for the sole purpose of delivering value. This is the way to enhance the new interest that investors are showing for our industry. This is "the Arcelor way".'

By the time Dollé had finished many who had heard him felt they had been listening to a sermon. When Peter Marcus asked him if he would take questions – the conference routinely asked its star speakers the toughest questions it could, most of them lobbed by Marcus – Dollé refused point-blank. Even the most generous of judges would have been hard-pushed to give him more than a 5.

With all three players in the Arcelor/Mittal/SeverStal drama in the same building, journalists were following every whiff of a possible development. When pressed, Guy Dollé admitted, 'There have been lots of high-level meetings between the senior executives of Arcelor and Mittal over the last few days. The two companies are still not complementary.' Dollé knew that he was running out of time. He had heard from Urquijo that talks with Aditya Mittal were much more advanced than he had hoped, although a deal was still not struck. Journalists asked Dollé if he had any plans to meet with Lakshmi Mittal. 'No,' he said, adding, 'The SeverStal transaction will be improved to take account of shareholders' concerns.'

But had he really done enough to persuade Mordashov? Alexey was not a man who liked taking backward steps.

*

At three that afternoon Lakshmi Mittal took the elevator to one of the Sheraton's smaller suites. He had had his staff book it, but not in his name. Secrecy, and delicacy, at this point were very important. He walked alone and quickly. Detained by roadshow investors, he was running fifteen minutes behind schedule. This next meeting was not one he had wanted to be late for. He opened the door and walked in. There was only one other person in the room. He was sitting sipping a glass of water.

'Guy, I am very sorry I am late,' Mittal said, extending his hand. After a moment's reflection Dollé took it. It was the first time the two men had spoken properly since the dinner of Friday 13 January. For a moment it felt as if the air had been sucked from the room.

Joseph Kinsch was still pushing hard for Dollé to stay on and work on the integration of the new company. He felt a sense of responsibility for a man who had moulded Arcelor, and had asked Mittal to persuade him to stay. Dollé's wife Michele was also urging him to remain with Arcelor – for financial reasons and for his reputation in the industry.

As he sat down to talk, Lakshmi Mittal was not convinced that he and Dollé could ever work together after all that had happened between them, but if that's what it took to cement a deal, then so be it.

Their conversation began haltingly. 'Let's forget what has happened,' Mittal said. 'I am sorry if I have hurt you in any way. Nothing was meant to be personal, it was part of the negotiation.'

Dollé apologised too, but he was really saying sorry to himself. How he wished that he had not made the 'monkey money' remarks, even though he insisted to that day that it was not what he had meant. He had been naive not to realise that the Anglo-Saxon press would gleefully use the words to haunt, taunt and ridicule him.

'You have been a great leader for Arcelor,' Mittal told Dollé. 'I would like you to stay on as CEO of our new company.'

'I will think about it,' Dollé replied, but he had already made up his mind. The Arcelor he knew and loved was slipping into the past. But if Mordashov could still manage to pull it off, and take the company from under the nose of Mittal, then that would be different.

On the way to the airport Dollé's mobile rang. It was Gonzalo Urquijo. Kinsch had decided that an investor visit to Cherepovets would happen, as planned, on 22 June. Dollé's spirits soared, only to be dashed. The visit was on, but the agenda had changed.

Guy Dollé slumped into his seat in the swish confines of the Bombardier Global Express long-range VIP jet that Arcelor had hired for the flight back to Europe. He was shattered. His body ached and his mind was numb, having been pummelled by words. Alongside him were Alain Davezac, Martine Hue, Rémi Boyer and Jean-Yves Naouri. He had told them of Mittal's offer. Dollé loyalists all, they had been thrilled that the same hand would be on the tiller even if the ship was bigger and sailing under a new name.

'Of course you are going to accept,' they said.

'Of course I am not,' Dollé replied. 'How can I work with him and the son?'

As the food and wine began to flow the mood changed from grimly realist to almost demob happy. Suddenly Naouri could bear sitting down no longer. He leapt to his feet and started to recite.

> *'Et que faudrait-il faire?*
> *Chercher un protecteur puissant, prendre un patron,*
> *Et comme un lierre obscur qui circonvient un tronc*
> *Et s'en fait un tuteur en lui léchant l'écorce,*
> *Grimper par ruse au lieu de s'élever par force?'*
> *Non merci.*

Dollé recognised the speech that Cyrano de Bergerac makes in Act II, Scene VIII, in response to his close friend and fellow soldier Le Bret, who, worried that Cyrano's principles will ruin his career, says: 'Oh! Lay aside that pride of musketeer. Fortune and Glory wait you!'

Cheered on by his colleagues, Naouri went on with his party piece:

> *And what should one do?*
> *Seek a protector, choose a patron,*
> *And like the crawling ivy round a tree*
> *That licks the bark to gain the trunk's support,*
> *Climb high by creeping ruse instead of force?*
> *No thank you.*

Naouri sat down as suddenly as he had stood up, to hearty applause. As the Arcelor plane sped on Guy Dollé wore a smile of resignation on his face. Just as Cyrano had said, he would live according to his ideals. He had no interest in making friends with unworthy men.

As Dollé slept, a news release flashed up on SeverStal's website: 'SeverStal announces today that it has proposed to the Board of Directors of Arcelor, the world's number one steel company, that is substantially improve the terms of their merger agreement announced on May 26, 2006. The proposal is in response to investor feedback provided by Arcelor's shareholders over the course of the last several weeks.'

Mordashov was lowering his shareholding from 32 per cent of Arcelor to 25, improving his offer to shareholders by €2 billion. He was also undertaking not to acquire more than 33 per cent of Arcelor's shares without submitting a public takeover bid for the entire group. and he had given up all claims to chair the strategic committee. Instead, 'Mr Mordashov will be free to vote his shares in line with normal shareholder practice.'

'I have taken careful note of all the investor feedback and believe that this enhanced proposal meets their requirements,' Mordashov announced. 'The improved terms create outstanding value to shareholders and reflect my continuing belief in the industrial logic of combining these two superb companies into the global steel champion'.

Meanwhile, the talks between Arcelor and Mittal Steel continued. There was a rumour going around that a new proposal from Lakshmi Mittal was likely to value Arcelor above €40 a share.

Later that day, Pierre Servan-Schreiber was working on legal aspects of the memorandum of understanding when his sonar bleep ringtone interrupted him. It was Jean-Louis Lantenois from the French regulator AMF, who was calling from Copenhagen, where all the market regulators were having their annual general meeting.

'We are suspending trading on all markets for Arcelor shares,' he said.

'What?' Servan-Schreiber could not believe what he was hearing. 'But you can't do that.'

'We are doing that.'

'What are you trying to do – kill us?' The regulators must have had one too many glasses of champagne. The suspension was unprecedented. 'You can only suspend trading if either there is information about Mittal or Arcelor that is about to be released and you want to give time for it to go across the markets, which is not the case,' Servan-Schreiber told him, 'or you can suspend when there is erratic and irrational behaviour on the markets, which is not the case either. So on what grounds are you suspending?'

'Pending a clear solution,' Lantenois said. If the regulators were baffled as to what was going on between the competing Mittal and Mordashov offers, what hope was there for the investors? Uncertainty led to false markets and misleading share prices. Lantenois was adamant. Servan-Schreiber felt he had a gun to his head.

'The situation is now too confusing,' the regulator concluded, and with that the line went dead.

38

Wednesday 21 June, 6 p.m.

Brussels International Airport

As soon as his Gulfstream touched down and drew to a halt in the private sector of the airport, Lakshmi Mittal could see Joseph Kinsch pacing up and down outside smoking a cigarette. Following Aditya, who could now do the route blindfold, he went through the small immigration and security office and then across the parking lot to the business centre.

In minutes the two men were face to face across a table. Shorn of their dragoons of external bankers, lawyers and PR advisers, the game was now down to the two men who had the ultimate power to seal the deal. The fixed expression on Kinsch's face told Mittal that the chairman, accompanied by his second, Gonzalo Urquijo, was not here just to bow down to industrial logic and market forces. He was going to be tough.

'I appreciate the concessions you have made, especially on the governance, Mr Mittal,' Kinsch said, 'but your improved offer still does not value Arcelor highly enough. You must pay more.'

'We could go to thirty-nine euros,' Lakshmi Mittal replied.

'At least forty,' Kinsch countered.

Neither man would budge. The price would have to wait.

Mittal accepted readily that the merged company should be head-quartered in Luxembourg. Ever the operator, he had come to realise during the course of the battle that the Grand Duchy was a very good place to be politically, and in Jean-Claude Juncker it had a premier whose address book was the key to the inside of Europe's political firmament. No longer would he be on the outside looking in. But what was this new company to be called?

'It has to be MittalArcelor,' Lakshmi insisted.

'ArcelorMittal,' said Kinsch, sternly. 'Our name in Europe is better known than yours.'

All four men argued back and forth, as in a doubles match where neither side could put the ball away. Then Kinsch's flinty eyes twinkled as his gaze alighted on Aditya. 'I thought *you* would appreciate "AM" more than "MA",' he said.

'What?' Aditya said incredulously. 'Are you dyslexic?'

'AM are your initials,' the chairman reminded him, 'and I am sure that one day this company will be yours.'

Kinsch had broken the ice. The meeting ended at 10 p.m. Four hours was a long time for the chairman to go without a cigarette.

'Tomorrow,' he said, flaming up outside, 'I will put what we have discussed to my management board.'

After hearing Kinsch's report on his meeting with Lakshmi Mittal the Arcelor management had little choice but to announce that an emergency board meeting would be held on Sunday 25 June, 'to take a decision regarding the latest proposals from Mittal Steel and Mr Mordashov'. However, the EGM for 30 June, where the 50 per cent shareholder vote would be needed to see off Mordashov, would still go ahead.

Shareholders hoping to see off the negative SeverStal and believing they were at last winning were warned to be careful by breakingviews.com. 'If a genuine auction develops, Arcelor shareholders will be delighted. But officially the board is still pursuing a mechanism for approving the SeverStal transaction that is as democratic as the pigs in *Animal Farm*. Until shareholders are given a fair choice between the two proposals, they must not drop their guard.'

Thursday 22 June

SeverStal, Cherepovets, Russia

SeverStal's home city was no place to be in June. The mosquitoes were so bad that the hundred visiting investors and analysts could not leave the company hospitality chalets to tour the plant. The place was also crawling with the Kalashnikov-toting security guards who had escorted them in an armoured convoy from the airport. Nothing much seemed to have changed since Jeremy Fletcher's eviction from the Soviet steel plant.

Alexey Mordashov welcomed his guests. 'SeverStal's problem is that nobody knows us. We must make a much greater effort to ensure that people can see our true value, which is why we have invited you here today.' He may have looked calm, but underneath he was seething. On arrival he had greeted Roland Junck thus: 'We feel that Arcelor has given up on us. You have not given us the support that we need to make a merger with Arcelor happen.'

'I am here to support you now,' Junck replied. He had indeed come to support Mordashov and SeverStal, but not in an alliance with Arcelor. Joseph Kinsch still had a lot of respect for the Russian who had shown him such deference. He still wanted the world to know that Alexey was the coming man of steel.

As Mordashov watched Junck go though his slides, extolling the virtues of the Russian company, there was something very familiar about them. Then he realised. They were the same ones that Junck had used at the end of May in Moscow at a conference organised by Peter Marcus, another Mordashov fan, on the evolution of steel. Then as now, Junck wanted to show how SeverStal was not opaque and secretive but was a company with an international reputation. 'It has a global future in the consolidation of steel,' he told the visitors. But there was also something different about this presentation. Junck had removed all the slides that argued Arcelor and SeverStal should merge to become lead players in the consolidation game at the expense of Mittal. With Mittal's offer now heading towards the final memorandum of understanding, Arcelor had to be seen to be neutral.

Kinsch had decided, with Mittal's blessing, that the visit to Cherepovets should go ahead to help put SeverStal on the map, to save Mordashov's face, and to save him from the wrath of Putin.

That afternoon Vadim Makov buttonholed Roland Junck. 'Our deal with you can still happen,' he said. 'We will bring in other Russian steel companies to invest and raise the offer higher than Mittal's.'

'Vadim, don't you see that if you did that you would end up losing control of Arcelor to somebody else?' Junck also knew that it was not just about money. Making Arcelor's potential white knight even more Russian would scare off investors once and for all. But Makov was insistent. New partners would be found. To Roland Junck SeverStal's desperation was now obvious.

Friday 23 June, noon

Club Grand-Ducal de Luxembourg

Unusually, Joseph Kinsch had not brought his golf clubs. Instead of looking forward to a leisurely round he had come to tell Alexey Mordashov that in his opinion the chances of a deal with SeverStal were dead. The chairman was blunt. 'The shareholders are no longer convinced that there can be any positive construct with SeverStal.'

Mordashov looked crestfallen. 'We had a deal. We shook hands.'

Kinsch had been around too long to get involved in the emotional side of breaking unpleasant news. When it came to family and close friends, he was an emotional man, but where business was concerned he was, like Lakshmi Mittal, completely unsentimental. 'I have my doubts about the valuation of SeverStal because it's a Russian company with mining activities which is not publicly listed, and it is very difficult to make an exact valuation of your assets,' he explained. 'We had our teams make a valuation but I don't know whether it was a good valuation or not – nobody knows.'

Mordashov said he was prepared to revise his offer again, to make concessions.

'Mr Mittal has already made a great many concessions,' Kinsch replied. The brothers Zaoui had already met to iron out the last technical details of a deal. Much as Kinsch liked Mordashov and admired his good manners, he knew the tide was flowing hard against the Russian. Shareholders were now the dominant players in the game. They would decide.

Mordashov vowed that, having come this far, he would not give up.

Guy Dollé, meanwhile, was all for giving up. In spite of Mittal's

request to stay on and the fact that the memorandum of understanding stated that he would remain as CEO, Dollé knew that with
Lakshmi Mittal as president he would never fulfil his cherished
dream of becoming chairman.

Kinsch brought the two men together in his office.

'Guy, the merger of the two companies can best be handled by
you,' he said, desperately fighting for a role for Dollé.

Dollé began to vacillate. Perhaps he might stay on. Mittal suggested that Dollé might take a role as consultant on the merger, but
the Frenchman's indecision had begun to get on his nerves. In this
life you either did something, or you didn't.

Saturday 24 June, 8 p.m.

The Waterside Inn, Bray, Berkshire

Perched on the banks of the River Thames 'like a sparkling petit
four', Michel Roux's three-Michelin-star restaurant was famed for its
world-class cuisine and tranquil setting. But Aditya Mittal was feeling far from tranquil. He should have been inside celebrating his
cousin's twenty-first with eleven friends. But Aditya's chair was
empty. He was outside in the car park, the only place he could get a
signal on his two mobile phones and vent his feelings fully.

'The deal is off,' he shouted into one of them. 'Look – we did this
deal in good faith with you, Roland and Michel, the lawyers, everybody. We agreed all the conditions. Mr Kinsch and Mr Mittal signed
the memorandum of understanding. And now you're telling me this!
There is no deal. Forget it.' Earlier that evening Lakshmi Mittal had
emailed the memo to everybody, with the message tag: 'Thanks to
every one of you who got us to this stage.'

With Arcelor's board due to meet the next day at noon to decide
between the Mittal and Mordashov offers, Aditya had heard a rumour:
the Russian, armed with a new line of credit from ABN Amro and
encouraged by some members of the Arcelor board and senior management, was about to come back with a new partial offer for Arcelor as
a more palatable alternative to overall effective control. If Mordashov
did that, the board would also have to consider it at its meeting.

Confronting Gonzalo Urquijo on the other end of the line, Aditya now knew that it was more than just a rumour. There was still an active 'anti-Mittal' cell working to the wire to swing Arcelor to Russia. Any pleasure he had derived from another rumour – that Guy Dollé was going to leave the company – had vanished. Mordashov had now got €22 billion in cash and shares.

'There is no way we are going to let you torpedo our deal by giving a slice of Arcelor to SeverStal,' he told Urquijo. The idea of both Mittal and Mordashov having big stakes but no control had been a recurring nightmare. Having also talked to his father, he knew that Lakshmi was dead set against.

Next, Aditya got a call from Yoel Zaoui. 'There are circumstances in which you could accept a partial offer,' he advised; but he didn't get very far in explaining them to Aditya, who was indignant at Arcelor's brinkmanship. 'No way,' he told Zaoui. 'As far as I am concerned a partial deal is bullshit. The deal is off.' If Arcelor wanted to play that game, Aditya told Urquijo in another call, they would see what real brinkmanship was like, and hung up on him. Going to the wire in the final throes was typical of a big takeover fight. Who would blink first? Aditya Mittal rejoined his friends in the restaurant.

Next morning at 9.30 a.m. Gonzalo Urquijo called Aditya back: 'Are you sure that your offer is off?'

'It's still off,' Aditya insisted.

Urquijo called again. There would be no new partial deals with Mordashov. The original SeverStal offer would go to the board.

'Then, our deal is back on.'

39

Arcelor boardroom, Avenue de la Liberté

Joseph Kinsch opened the board meeting as he always did, quietly and precisely, but this time the mood was tense. As well as the eighteen board members and Guy Dollé's DG there were so many advisers from the nine banks and the legal team in the room that every seat was taken. 'There is one outcome which is not possible today,' Kinsch said, 'and that is a combination between Mittal Steel and SeverStal and Arcelor. I would like to ask our advisers, the investment bankers, and also the legal advisers to present the two different models and compare them. After we have seen all the presentations and we have had all the discussions on the legal, commercial and governance questions of each offer, I will then ask the members of the management and the advisers to leave the room, and the board will come to its decision.'

As the presentations began Guy Dollé kept asking himself: Why would Alexey not list his company in London, like I told him? If he had just done that we would not be here now.

Mittal had now increased his offer to €40.40 a share. Michael Zaoui had always had the figure of €40 in his head as the target he was aiming at. He had never raised it with Kinsch because the chairman was adamant, as he always had been, that Arcelor, his company, was not for sale. Kinsch talked instead about Mittal or Mordashov 'acquiring assets'. Whatever the terminology and whatever the outcome of the meeting, Zaoui knew that in reality Joseph Kinsch was going to lose effective control of his company because as Michael was fond of saying, 'When the flashy number starts flashing you've got to think about *selling* your assets.'

But which way would the board go – Mittal's bigger offer whereby he would take the company, or a lesser 'merger' with SeverStal whereby the succession would pass from Kinsch to Dollé but power would effectively shift to Mordashov and Cherepovets?

As Antoine Spillmann listened, he knew that José María Aristrain had made up his mind. Fellow board member John Castegnaro, the Socialist Party MP representing the steel country of the south, was gloomy at the thought of having to choose between the Russian and the Indian. They are asking us to make a choice between two devils, he thought.

Noon

18–19 Kensington Palace Gardens

The whole Mittal gang were there clinking their champagne glasses, talking over the great times they had had in the last five months and the still greater times to come. Yoel Zaoui was relaxed, more Ben Stiller than Al Pacino. The Goldman Sachs advisers Shahriar Tadjbakhsh, Lisa Rabbe, Gilberto Pozzi and Richard Gnodde mingled with bankers Fletcher, Coates and Spiro Youakim, Philip Gawith and the Maitland communications team, Anne Méaux, Pierre-Yves Chabert and Laurent Meyer who had flown over from Paris, and Mittal's in-house warriors led by the ringmaster, Sudhir Maheshwari, who had kept the whole show on the road. The film crew that had been shadowing Mittal every step of the way was also there, cameras turning, hoping for a sparky aside from Wilbur Ross. And as ever Nicola Davidson was dashing about, making sure that everything was just so, no detail however small escaping her forensic gaze.

A board meeting had just finished at a large table set up inside the house, with screens so that everybody could see coverage of any developments from Avenue de la Liberté reported on Bloomberg, while the board reviewed the campaign and put down markers for the future of a big new company. Other screens were in place for

England's World Cup match against Ecuador, which was due to kick off in Stuttgart at 4 p.m. If England won they were through to the quarter-finals. Hopefully by then Mittal would have already posted his own victory. Outside in the garden on this day that all in the Mittal team hoped they would remember for the right reasons, a buffet lunch was being arranged with typical Mittal efficiency on an expanse of white linen tablecloths.

There was no doubt that Mittal's team had become stronger and stronger as the battle had dragged on, even though some of them looked a little older and were showing signs of wear and tear. Firm friendships had been formed. None of them had worked on a deal this big or this complex and brutal. No one had gone off-message or strayed from Lakshmi Mittal's vision on the industrial logic of his deal. As he had said at the outset, everybody in the team would know everything that was going on at all times. 'I have never before worked with a client where I knew a hundred per cent of what they were thinking,' Yoel Zaoui said. 'Lots of clients claim to be great listeners,' Jeremy Fletcher agreed, 'but Lakshmi is the only person I have met who really listens to what his advisers are telling him.' As somebody else said: 'This battle is where the BlackBerry came of age as a key communications tool. While we knew what was going on at all times, Arcelor were queuing up for the pay-phone.'

As the wine waiters cruised through the crowd, the mood in the Mittal house and gardens was not triumphalist. The team was confident they had done enough to win, but they were not going overboard. They were demob-nervous. Lakshmi Mittal, surrounded by his family, wandered among his advisers, shaking hands and smiling as he pretty much had since the beginning. A slight greying of his sideburns and a few more lines at the corners of his eyes were the only signs of the continual strain and pressure that he had been under for five months. Aditya was there, relaxed, glass in hand, still looking seventeen years old.

Lakshmi checked his watch. Would it be him or Mordashov? Even though he was in the box seat with a signed memorandum of understanding, the Arcelor board could still go with the Russian.

Mordashov was with Makov and the crew in the Hôtel Le Royal, still working away at their laptops and hoping to put more last-ditch money on the table. Even if the board backed Mittal today, there was still the EGM of 30 June to try and sway shareholders away from endorsing the Indian's offer. Fifty per cent would still have to vote against the SeverStal deal to blow his hopes out of the water.

Outside the Arcelor boardroom Philippe Capron, other external advisers and Arcelor's M&A team were camped out in side offices or pacing the long marble corridors like expectant fathers. Two hours, three hours went by. Whenever anybody came out of the meeting they grabbed them for news.

There was none.

The board had been in session for four hours when Alexey Mordashov stepped out on to the balcony of the Royal Suite at the Hôtel Le Royal to take the afternoon air. He could hear shouting and singing coming from down below. Groups mainly of men were running down the street waving flags. It was the city's Portuguese community heading for the bars, getting in the mood for their country's match that evening against the Netherlands. Whoever won that game would play the winner of England v. Ecuador in the quarter-finals. Russia had not even made it to the tournament, Mordashov reflected. To see Serbia and Montenegro there and not his country devalued the tournament in his eyes, but that disappointment would be more than made up for if he won Arcelor. What a prize to take home to Putin. He was counting on Guy Dollé to fight his corner.

At 3 p.m. the great double doors to the Arcelor boardroom flew open and Guy Dollé marched out and away down the corridor to his office, frustrated more than ever that he as CEO was not a member of the board and had no vote.

All the advisers followed him, then fanned out into various parts of the building. Some were talking animatedly, others staring down at the floor. Pierre Servan-Schreiber went to stretch his legs outside. There at the large wooden back gates of the chateau's courtyard a crowd of journalists and photographers was getting increasingly restless. One of them he recognised: Julien Ponthus, Reuters' man from Brussels who had now been standing out there for five hours.

'What's going on?' he asked Servan-Schreiber. 'We haven't seen anybody from the communications department.' Servan-Schreiber was stunned. If Arcelor treated journalists like that, no wonder it got a bad press. The least they should have done was come out from time to time and thank the journalists for their patience. Servan-Schreiber told Ponthus that the presentations were done and Kinsch had ordered everyone but the directors to leave. 'Now we need to sit alone,' the chairman had said.

'How long will it take?' Ponthus asked. 'Who's going to win?

Servan-Schreiber shrugged to both questions. There was no way he was going to do the job of the Arcelor communications department. And also, he did not know the answer to either.

There was still no news.

The boardroom doors of Arcelor clamped shut once more. The chairman and his directors would now decide the company's future.

Tea was being served at 18–19 Kensington Palace Gardens when a great cheer went up. Those not already glued to screens rushed over to see what was happening. Could it be true? It *was* true. David Beckham had just put England into the lead 'with a long-overdue piece of free-kick magic'.

There was still no news from inside the chateau. Lakshmi Mittal wondered what was taking the Arcelor board so long. 'The longest board meeting *we* ever had was one and a half hours,' he said. Sitting in his office, Guy Dollé was wondering the same thing. Both at Arcelor and Kensington Palace Gardens nerves were beginning to fray.

At a quarter to seven Joseph Kinsch finally called an end to the debate. He told the board that he was going to ask each member in turn to voice their preference. Even Prince Guillaume, the Grand Duke's brother, would be called upon to speak.

Shortly after seven Julien Ponthus, still camped outside the Arcelor chateau, saw a ministerial car coming towards the gates. Inside was Jeannot Krecké. Ponthus and other journalists began to run towards the car. Ministers never turned up unless they sensed an opportunity to comment on something momentous. At the same time his BlackBerry alerted him. He checked the screen. It was an email from the Arcelor communications team.

At about the same time Lakshmi Mittal put down his phone and walked quietly back to rejoin his guests, gathering his thoughts as he did so.

'I have just spoken to Mr Kinsch,' he began. All talking stopped, glasses were gripped with stem-breaking intensity. 'He has told me that the Arcelor board is recommending our offer.' Mittal sounded and looked for a moment as though he was giving a funeral address, but then his face broke into a big beaming smile. He saw his team's shoulders relax. He could see their reaction about to burst through the dam of expectation, which had been keeping their feelings at bay all day. All hell broke loose.

'In the end, the vote was unanimous,' he said, over the din of celebration.

At Avenue de la Liberté all the directors had gone home, but there was a din of a different kind. The whirr and rip of shredding machines could be heard down the empty corridors. It was an ignominious end for a tiger.

40

Monday 26 June, 2 p.m.

Avenue de la Liberté

All of Luxembourg awaited the arrival of Lakshmi Mittal, including Monsieur Shrek.

'On both sides of the courtyard all the HQ secretaries were lined up, wearing saris, made up with kohl and with a big red spot on their foreheads, causing some of them to squint. Each had a basket under her arm, ready to throw petals in a gesture of welcome. I have to say that while this get-up favoured the more Mediterranean types – Juan's PA suddenly looked a lot more attractive to me – it didn't do very much for the sturdy wenches of Taxembourg, for whom a rather more Viking style – furs and helmets adorned with horns – would have been more flattering.'

The truth was more prosaic. After the bloodiest takeover in recent times there was still a skirmish to be fought: 'the battle of the chairs'.

Nicola Davidson had been calling Arcelor repeatedly with the same question: 'Mr Mittal would like it if Aditya could have a seat on the stage too.' The chairman's answer was always the same: 'Only if Mr Dollé also has a chair.'

Guy Dollé always said the same, when Kinsch asked him if he would go up and share the stage: 'No.'

As the world's media filed into Arcelor's majestic home, there were just two *Mastermind* leather chairs on the stage – one for Kinsch and one for Lakshmi Mittal. There was no seat for Aditya.

Lakshmi Mittal arrived for the press conference looking every inch the happy bridegroom. After a particularly gruelling courtship that had started with insults, he had ended up with a very satisfactory marriage of convenience.

Joseph Kinsch walked guardedly across to the podium to deliver his speech. The chairman was looking gaunt. He placed his glasses on his nose and began in French: 'I would like to extend a particularly warm welcome to Mr Mittal and his family to Luxembourg – his father, Mrs Mittal, of course, his son, son-in-law, his daughter and daughter-in-law.' All were sitting in the front row. Guy Dollé was sitting on the bride's side, watching the future slip away from him as he heard his chairman utter the words he hoped he would never hear: Arcelor and Mittal were coming together.

'We are pleased to note that Mittal Steel has taken our arguments on board, increasing its offer and with a new industrial model and improved governance,' Kinsch said. Mittal's deal-winning €40.4 a share 'values the company at 25.4 billion euros, a 50 per cent improvement on January and the first offer. Corporate governance will be based on the Arcelor model with only one class of shares. The company's headquarters and operational head office will be in Luxembourg,' the chairman added proudly. The senior management would be drawn equally from the two companies and the new ArcelorMittal board would also be equally balanced. Mittal would become president of the company and Kinsch would remain chairman until 2007. 'The day I leave here Mr Mittal will become chairman of the company.'

Somebody had asked Kinsch how it felt becoming chairman of the biggest steel company in the world. 'I have always been the chairman of the biggest steel company in the world,' he said imperiously.

Guy Dollé would leave the company sooner, once a new CEO had been appointed. He had his principles; what he did not have was Kinsch's ultimate survival instinct.

'The task ahead of us is challenging indeed,' Kinsch said. But he could not hide his true feelings, adding, 'For while the challenge will be enormously stimulating, it will also be very difficult – far more difficult than would be a gradual merger of companies with the same profile.'

'This is a seminal day for the steel industry,' Lakshmi Mittal responded. Not only that – his family had a 43 per cent stake in the world's largest steel company, 'a giant with a massive footprint on every continent'. The new company would dwarf other steel-makers, he said, controlling close to 10 per cent of world steel production, churning out 120 million tonnes of crude steel a year and employing more than 320,000 people. It would have a total market capitalisation of $46 billion, and combining operations should save $1.6 billion in synergies.

At a final offer price of €40.4 a share the Arcelor defence team could justifiably say it had massively increased shareholder value on Mittal's opening offer. It had been, as Michael Zaoui had prom-ised Joseph Kinsch back in February, 'the mother of all defences'. It would go down in corporate history. Equally, Mittal's winning price was still almost €4 short of Julien Onillon's valuation of Arcelor way back in December 2005 when the Mittals had identified it as a takeover target. So everyone was happy with what was now dressed up as a 'merger', with the exception of Guy Dollé as he watched by far the biggest shareholder, and in effect the new owner of the com-pany, go back to his chair.

When Mittal sat down, he beckoned Aditya to the stage to answer some of the follow-up questions. But instead of answering them, then returning to his seat in the front row, he stayed put. Kinsch did not look amused. Chair or no chair, Aditya remained determinedly on stage alongside his father, as he had throughout the battle. No, he was not going to become CEO, he said, stu-diously avoiding looking at Dollé. 'None of the management positions have been decided.'

This was all too much for Dollé. His face fell into his hands and he was heard muttering, 'How could you be so bloody naive?' Kinsch should have realised. The only way that 'the son' was going to be kept off that stage was by cuffing his ankles to his chair.

'This is a marriage of reason,' Kinsch said, 'let's hope it will end as a marriage of hearts.'

'We've been trying to persuade the bride for the past five months that we love her and that she should accept the marriage proposal,' Mittal joked, turning to the chairman. 'We are hoping for a very happy marriage.'

As soon as the conference was over and the Mittal family were ushered into Arcelor's premier dining room for their first taste of the chateau's legendary cuisine, Guy Dollé fled, refusing to answer any questions. How he must have wished that he had been given a magic flute rather than a magic pencil to aid him in the fight for his beloved Arcelor. Throughout the battle he had been fearless, but patience and a judicious silence at key moments had deserted him from day one.

Despite his agreement with Arcelor, Mittal knew that the SeverStal plan, due to be discussed at the EGM on 30 June, was legally binding, and that shareholders could still back the Russian deal instead unless those representing 50 per cent of Arcelor's capital rejected the proposal during the meeting and tendered their shares to Mittal. And if he could raise the funds there was nothing to stop Mordashov from coming back with a massive new cash offer to top Mittal. And now, on the evening of a momentous day, Lakshmi Mittal discovered that he was at the centre of a brand-new political storm heading in from the east.

That night the Kremlin was in a fury. It threatened tit-for-tat reprisals against Western firms hoping to invest in Russia. Konstantin Simonov, director of the Centre for Current Politics in Moscow, said it would be a 'symmetric response. If you are allowed to buy Russian assets, you should help Russian companies buy Western assets. The Kremlin thought the SeverStal merger was signed and completed, so this is a very unpleasant surprise for them. It comes at a very bad time, just as the government is considering what sectors of the economy should be blocked to foreigners under the new law on strategic sectors.'

Putin stayed silent, leaving the energy minister Viktor Khristenko to wade in at the unfairness of it all. Mordashov too allowed others to speak for him. SeverStal's deputy chief Gregory Mason announced that the company was considering whether to sue Arcelor for breach of contract, adding that SeverStal was expecting to get the €140 million break-of-contract fee from Arcelor. Had Arcelor used SeverStal as a foil to push up Mittal's bid by 40 per cent? he was asked.

'I can't comment on whether they used us,' said Mason, 'but the fact is we made a good last offer, and they didn't even have the courtesy to discuss it.'

Tuesday 27 June, noon

Restaurant Clairefontaine, Luxembourg City

Located on one of the city's most idyllic squares in the heart of the business district, Clairefontaine was used to discreetly welcoming high-profile visitors including government ministers, businessmen, foreign dignitaries and those just on the prowl for some good old understated luxury. Reservations were essential. The waiters primped and put the finishing touches to the best table in the house as they waited for the arrival of Lakshmi and Aditya Mittal.

Within minutes the Mittals were joined by Minister Frieden and a new friend – none other than Jean-Claude Juncker. He was smiling so broadly when he arrived that his head looked in danger of dividing into two. But then, he did have a double celebration. Not only would his government net €400 million from cashing in some shares following the Mittal deal, while still keeping 3 per cent in the new company, the Prime Minister had just won the 2006 International Charlemagne Prize, 'in recognition of his role as a driving force and key player' in the integration of Europe.

With the press excluded, the four men sat down to a menu devised by Clairefontaine's Falstaffian chef and owner, the alliteratively named Tony Tintinger. When they re-emerged they could not dodge the cameras. Luc Frieden shook hands formally with the Mittals, but Juncker took a pace forward, reached up and put one arm and then another around Lakshmi Mittal's broad shoulders and hugged him. Mittal looked a little startled at finding himself in the embrace of a man who in the depths of the previous winter would have been happy to cast him into the dungeons of Senningen Castle, where they had had their first meeting on 31 January. Now, as they stood there in the summer sunshine Juncker wasn't finished. It was the turn of Aditya, shorter than Juncker, to disappear into the prime ministerial embrace. This must be what they meant by *la bénédiction du gouvernement*. When Luc Decker, Jeannot Krecké's press attaché, saw the pictures he sighed: Why on earth did he have to do that? This was a political embrace too far.

*

Warmed by the fine wine and the foie gras, Juncker stood to address the Parliament. He no longer talked of hostile takeovers he did not understand, but of mergers and marriages. He thanked Krecké, Frieden and Georges Schmit for bringing the government's ship home. In a long speech he said that it was never his intention when he spoke back on 31 January to give the impression that Luxembourg 'is a nation that is impenetrable, a closed shop, a grocery store that rolls down its blinds and looks after none but itself. We are an open country, we like to trade with the rest of the world, to engage in industrial politics including and in particular steel politics.'

Lakshmi Mittal, he said, was an intelligent man, a worthy man, a man who commanded respect but who had learned the Luxembourg way of doing things and had dropped 'excessive' demands. Although the government was asking Parliament to back its support of the Mittal offer, Juncker also praised Alexey Mordashov and hoped that ArcelorMittal would 'maintain extremely close relations with the Russian steel industry and in particular with SeverStal'.

Mordashov still hoped that after the meeting of 30 June those close relations would take the form of a deal between Arcelor and SeverStal. He was not in the mood to retreat to Cherepovets. He would have taken comfort from a series of full-page advertisements, pre-booked by Arcelor before the Mittal deal and aimed at shareholders, that now appeared in the international press encouraging the fight against Mittal. It was claimed that the deal with Mittal had been so last-minute that it had been too late to pull the ads. Whether or not that was true, it suited some at Arcelor to keep the anti-Mittal profile going as long as possible to help SeverStal.

Then a rumour began to swell across Europe's media. SeverStal was teaming up with Roman Abramovich, a shareholder in Evraz Steel, to offer a bigger, Mittal-busting, bid for Arcelor.

Evraz was failing to return all calls.

41

Friday 30 June, 11 a.m.

Luxexpo Centre, Kirchberg, Luxembourg

On that bright summer's day more than four hundred shareholders and accredited observers arrived for the shareholders' extraordinary meeting. It was an unusually high turn-out. Around the podium Kinsch and members of the DG gathered and chatted among themselves. As they took to the stage all but one were wearing their 'I love Arcelor' badges. Guy Dollé's lapel had no badge. He had dispatched that emotion to history. He was moving on.

As the cameras flashed, the panoramic screen behind the podium produced a dramatic backdrop of moving pictures of steel while Urquijo played the Spanish waiter, dispensing glasses of water to Dollé, Junck and Wurth. Georges Schmit and Antoine Spillmann sat to their right, and would act as scrutinisers for the vote.

'I want to remind the audience today that throughout this battle our sole concern and passion has been to defend the Arcelor model, and this we have done,' Kinsch said as he began an impassioned speech that lasted almost an hour. 'None of this would have been possible without the management's fighting spirit, led by Guy Dollé,' he added, to applause from the audience. 'We have created more than twelve billion euros in value for our shareholders. I do not wish to appear triumphant, but let me tell you – this stock market battle will go down in history.' SeverStal was never used as bait in order to increase Mittal's price, he insisted. 'It was Mittal's offer which served as the catalyst to stimulate the alliance with SeverStal.' He paid tribute to Alexey Mordashov. 'I wish him and his group the best of luck.'

As Kinsch took questions from the floor, he appeared surprised to see a Luxembourg representative of Carlo Tassara International come to the microphone.

'Mr Chairman, as the representative for the single largest shareholder in Arcelor, I feel it is right that we should be one of those scrutinising the vote.'

Kinsch smiled and invited the Luxembourger to join the podium alongside Schmit and Spillmann. 'Satisfied, Madame Neuville?' he said cheekily.

Neuville could not miss an opportunity to hit back at Kinsch. 'What happens if the three scrutinisers disagree? Will we have to rely on a two-to-one majority vote?' There was laughter from the audience as the Frenchwoman, dressed in white, returned to her seat.

Despite two hours of questions from the floor, Kinsch with his polished diplomacy and customary politeness parried those demanding explanations of Arcelor's apparent about-turn from outright hostility to its arch-rival Mittal Steel to backing a deal with it. Some investors complained that they had been ill informed about the board's use of poison-pill defences and questioned its actions.

Colette Neuville came back to the microphone: 'How have we reached such an imbroglio that we have to vote on a project that has been abandoned?' she said, getting in another dig at the chairman. There was applause as she sat down.

'I am aware of the fact that the period we have just experienced seems lacking in clarity in spite of all our efforts to justify our actions,' Kinsch replied. 'Believe me, all the options were examined.'

As he waited for the result, he prayed that his words of 11 June would not return to haunt him: 'The 50 per cent level for a rejection of this transaction is designed to encourage shareholder participation.'

A record 57.94 per cent of all Arcelor's shareholders attending had just thrown out the SeverStal deal. Guy Dollé's company of perfumers had been hoisted on its own petard. Alexey Mordashov was now in full retreat to Cherepovets.

As Lakshmi Mittal enjoyed some time with his wife Usha and looked forward to becoming a grandfather for the first time, his army of advisers was dispersing. For most of them this had been a 'destination deal'. There would never be another as big, as complex or as hostile. And for most of them this was the first time they could tell their families and friends exactly what it was they had been up to for the last five months. What they talked about most was not the size of the deal, the billions of euros, the racism, the double-dealing and the long hours, but the almost wartime camaraderie that existed amongst all on the Mittal team. Spiro Youakim was not alone when he said: 'If Lakshmi called me up and said I want to do another deal, I would be round at Berkeley Square House in five minutes.'

But for Mittal, this deal was not a destination but a work in progress. He did not have time to bask in victory. He still had only 10 per cent of the world's steel production and he wanted to be the first to produce 200 million tonnes a year. There was more to do in China, and a brand-new steel mill to be built in India, his very first in his homeland. The Andrew Carnegie of his day, he had still not finished creating 'the finest steel institution the world has ever seen'.

He would start by making friends with those who for five months had been his enemies.

Back in her elegantly chaotic office in Paris Anne Méaux put away her Mittal files and smiled at a large full-colour photomontage she had prepared but never used in the victorious campaign. It showed a grinning Lakshmi Mittal dressed in a beret and stripy jersey and carrying a baguette under his arm. The balloon from his mouth said: 'Do you like me any better now?'

Postscript

In India the delight at Mittal's victory was palpable. The commerce and industry minister, Kamal Nath, who had had a good war, pronounced: 'There is a new economic architecture and countries that have had a different mindset will now have to accept that India is going to be a major player in the new global architecture.' Finance minister Palaniappan Chidambaram chipped in: 'We are happy and proud that an Indian-born entrepreneur is the biggest steel-maker in the world.'

A month after the battle was over, Lakshmi Mittal's year was complete. He became a grandfather, when Aditya and Megha had their first child, a daughter Sanaya. In December 2006 the *Financial Times* named Lakshmi Mittal its 'Person of the Year'.

The thirteen banks that advised both sides on the deal banked, between them, $200 million in fees. Mittal's total adviser bill for the banking, legal, lobbying and communications work required to acquire Arcelor amounted to $188 million – a million dollars a day, according to the first annual report of the new company.

Romain Zaleski, too, was happy and proud of his role in the whole story, as were the salerooms and dealers in religious art. He had made a profit of around €1 billion on the transaction. He accepted Lakshmi Mittal's invitation to a seat on the board of ArcelorMittal, joining fellow billionaires José María Aristrain, François Pinault and Wilbur Ross.

The other billionaire in our story, Alexey Mordashov, had a year of mixed fortunes, but it got better as it wore on. In November 2006 he decided to do what Guy Dollé had long urged him to do – he listed SeverStal on the London stock exchange. In one of the largest and most successful offerings in London by a Russian company, SeverStal, advised by Spiro Youakim and Citigroup, raised over $1 billion through a placement of just over 9 per cent of its total issued share capital. The year 2006 also saw SeverStal adopt international best practice on corporate governance, including the appointment of independent non-executives to the board. Financially, by the end of the third quarter of 2007 SeverStal was forging ahead. It reported revenues of $11.2 billion, 23 per cent higher than the corresponding nine-month period the year before, and posted an operating profit of $2.02 billion, up 44 per cent, while its net profit of $1.32 billion was up 60 per cent.

Given his position as one of Russia's leading steel producers and his arrival on the international stage, it was fitting that Mordashov was appointed Russia's honorary consul to Luxembourg. As a spokesman put it, 'Mr Mordashov has moved on.'

The Germans won no prizes. Late in 2006 ThyssenKrupp issued proceedings against Mittal in the District Court in Rotterdam, accusing him of breaching their letter of agreement. The 'Virtue Transcends Riches' company wanted to secure the release of Dofasco from the *stichting* and 'allow its sale to ThyssenKrupp'. It was suing Mittal for not breaking the foundation, even though he had twice attempted to get the *stichting* dissolved only for its directors to refuse, preventing any sale. In January 2007 the court threw out ThyssenKrupp's petition, saying that Mittal Steel could not be expected to 'do more than it has already done in order to seek dissolution of the *stichting*'. Instead, Mittal is still trying to sell a plant at Sparrows Point in America, and Dofasco, protected by its *stichting*, continues to merge into ArcelorMittal.

ThyssenKrupp decided that steel mergers were not its favourite occupation, and instead to invest $4 billion in building its own plant in the USA.

In April 2007 Lakshmi Mittal was once again top of the *Sunday Times* Rich List, with a fortune of £19.2 billion, up from £14.8 billion the previous year, and way ahead of second-placed Roman Abramovich at £10.8 billion. According to the Rich List compiler Philip Beresford: 'The Mittals will receive at least £413 million in dividends from the new group in 2007. A separate investment portfolio is valued at £570 million.'

The money merry-go-round was working at full speed for others too. In writing this book we discovered that on 5 June 2006 a transfer of some €50 million reached a new bank account at Bank of New York in Manhattan. The account and transfer had been set up by the finance department at Arcelor. In takeover battles where there is the likelihood of a change of ownership, the senior management have to ensure the peace of mind of their key staff – the 'defenders' – regardless of the outcome of the fight. Arcelor had devised a 'golden parachute' scheme, common in business, where senior managers could be compensated, even if not fired or forced to accept a new position under a new owner. For any member of the DG the scheme guaranteed four times his or her salary, but to be capped at normal retirement age. Nine members of the executive committee were entitled to three times their salaries, and fifteen other managers involved in the defence could claim double. The bank transfer was deposited into an 'escrow' account, where the money was legally held by a third party pending the fulfilment of a contract. As a Bank of New York official succinctly put it: 'When you have a parachute, you are strongly advised not to rely on somebody else to pull the cord.'

Because Guy Dollé was so close to retirement, he picked up only one year and three months' money.

In the year since the Arcelor victory, when Mittal was named by *Time* magazine as one of the world's '100 Most Influential People', there were signs that he was beginning to win over even the hardest of Gallic hearts: in September 2007 he was appointed a non-executive director of the French aeronautical company EADS, the parent company of Airbus.

In October he presented a rare bronze Indian statue to the Guimet Museum in Paris: 'The creation of the world's leading steel company signifies a long-term and very serious commitment from both the company and myself personally to France, its people and its economy.' Standing at his side was President Nicolas Sarkozy, who only in May had commented that because of the Arcelor–Mittal deal French industrialists 'now had to bow to Indian industrialists so as to

get a good price for steel'. Now Sarkozy had changed his tune, in
public at least, telling Mittal: 'A year ago you were not welcome in
most of France, but that has changed.' At that moment a smiling
Jacques Chirac entered and shook Mittal by the hand. 'Now all of
France welcomes you,' Sarkozy said.

Rumour had it that Mittal was even being considered for a Légion
d'Honneur, an award that Anne Méaux was given shortly after the
Arcelor takeover was completed in recognition of her contribution to
public life and the fact that she had not sold any butter to the
Germans. Meanwhile, France's former Minister of Finance,
Economy and Industry Thierry Breton took his talents to the cradle
of free-market capitalism, and is now a senior lecturer in business
administration at the Harvard Business School.

In Luxembourg, ministers Krecké and Frieden topped the polls
in June 2007 in the annual *politbarometer* of the newspaper *Tageblatt*,
both scoring 69 per cent of the vote. The previous year they had
been placed sixth and fourth, respectively.

But not everyone was so happy about the way the fight had been
conducted, especially on the subject of stock-lending, which featured in the Dirty Thirty letter. John Plender of the *Financial Times*
opened up a fierce debate by recommending European stock market
regulators take a close look at the transparency of stock-lending in
European shareholder rebellions. If such rebellion as the Dirty
Thirty had happened in the US, Plender said, highly detailed chapter and verse would have had to be supplied in filings to the
Securities and Exchange Commission. The message from the
Mittal–Arcelor fight, he concluded, was that in Europe permitting
hedge funds and other investment institutions with very different
objectives to dictate the structure of a global industry was highly
questionable 'in the absence of more sunlight'.

Goldman Sachs was outraged. Managing director Lucas van Praag
wrote to the *FT*, claiming that Plender was being 'seriously misleading'. In his letter of 11 July 2006 van Praag said: 'The fact that
the cover letter sent to Arcelor's board bore no single address is neither questionable nor unusual, since it did not come from any one
entity but was a communication from some 60 different shareholding
institutions, who independently provided their details as signed

attachments to the letter. And, while many of these institutions' names are handwritten, their identity and the information about their respective holdings is completely legible.

'Together the signatories represented almost 30 per cent of Arcelor's capital; and, notwithstanding suggestions to the contrary, to our knowledge there has been no evidence indicating that they collectively spoke for less than that percentage.' Arcelor, van Praag insisted, had provided 'no information to support this allegation' that the letter was signed by less than 20 per cent.

Many faces from Arcelor are still to be seen at ArcelorMittal. Michel Wurth and Gonzalo Urquijo are both members of the group management board, responsible for the day-to-day running of the company and advising the board.

Roland Junck was appointed the first CEO of ArcelorMittal, but in July 2007 he left the company and is now a consultant. Of his sudden departure a press statement said: 'Mr Junck had particular responsibility for integration, which is now successfully operationally completed, ahead of schedule.' Lakshmi Mittal replaced him as CEO. Junck retains a link with the company through his new position as a board member of Arcelor China Holding S. a. r. l., a subsidiary of ArcelorMittal.

Martine Hue and Philippe Capron also departed, Hue to Publicis as an investor relations consultant and Capron to be chief financial officer at Vivendi, the communications, games, music and media conglomerate, in Paris. Alain Davezac is now executive vice president in charge of strategic planning and mergers and acquisitions for the Indian steel company Essar, which has operations in Canada, the United States, the Middle East and Asia. His office is in Berkeley Square, virtually next door to the Mittals.

In May 2008 Joseph Kinsch, who had succeeded in preserving the Arcelor industrial model, retired to the greens of the Club Grand-Ducal de Luxembourg and was succeeded as chairman of ArcelorMittal by Lakshmi Mittal. A statue of Kinsch is still to be erected in honour of his contribution to the Luxembourg steel industry.

Guy Dollé divides his time between Luxembourg, Paris and a holiday home near Dunkirk and sits on the board of Gaz de France.

On the ArcelorMittal merger he says: 'The jury is still out. In mergers of this size it takes five to ten years to say if they have been
successful or not.' Market observers were also split as to whether the
steel industry could maintain heady annual growth rates of 6 per
cent. What are Dollé's feelings towards Mittal? 'Which one?' he
smiles. 'Lakshmi Mittal is a great man of steel.'

The market has already voted. In the first nine months of 2007
ArcelorMittal's EBITDA (earnings before interest, taxes, deprecia-
tion and amortisation) stood at $14.6 billion, 30 per cent higher than
2006, with its shares trading at around $72 (€50). No new acquisitions
were foreseen, Lakshmi Mittal told us. It was time to concentrate on
organic growth and efficiency, he said, and then proceeded to make
thirty acquisitions in 2007.

Nippon Steel was alarmed, and hired Michael Zaoui's Morgan
Stanley to help it put its defences in place in case Mittal came for
it next. Posco of South Korea also felt it could be 'in play' to Mittal and
went hunting for investment banking advisers to help in the event
of an attack from ArcelorMittal. In December 2007 Mittal bought
Argentina's largest steel distributor, M.T. Majdalani y Cia. SA.

Elsewhere, the consolidation of steel continued, with Tata Steel
of India snapping up Britain's Corus, beating off the avaricious
Brazilian group CVRD, which had been one of Arcelor's potential
white squires. CVRD then changed its name to Vale and went for
a possible consolidation deal with Xstrata, the London-listed international mining giant. Meanwhile, China's annual steel production
topped 500 million tonnes.

In January 2008 Mittal announced that he was going to close the
steel plant at Gandrange, scene of his dramatic press tour in April
2006. Trade unions and politicians in France and Luxembourg
started a campaign to protect the six hundred jobs, from the thou-
sand-strong workforce, that they alleged would go at the plant.
ArcelorMittal pledged: '[It] intends to fully honour its social responsibility during the implementation of this reorganisation project.'

In the same month the company announced record 2007 trading
results with EBITDA of $19.4 billion, up 27 per cent year-on-year,
and net income of $10.4 billion, a 30 per cent increase on 2006. In
February 2008 the company repurchased 679,633 shares at €45.80

each in a buy-back which netted investors and shareholders more than €31 million.

To celebrate the winning of Arcelor a 'completion party' was organised, a traditional event to mark the end of takeover battles. With most companies this would amount to champagne and sandwiches. Too mundane. Something grander would be needed to celebrate the history-making deal. Basing it on a movie theme, this party was called Mittal's 111 – reflecting the number of people who had worked on Project Olympus. They had toyed with the idea of holding the party at the Parthenon in Athens but opted instead for Brocket Hall, a stately home in Hertfordshire. In the autumn of 2006 the 111 guests were greeted on the red carpet by Marilyn Monroe and James Dean look-alikes and huge *Ocean's Eleven*-style posters of Lakshmi Mittal's face superimposed on to the body of Frank Sinatra and Aditya's on to Dean Martin's. After dinner and speeches there was an Oscar ceremony to reward key members of the team, and the whole event was kicked off with a huge display of silver fireworks accompanied by Mr Mittal's favourite James Bond theme tune, the one from *Goldfinger*.

Acknowledgements and the Players

We would like to thank our agent Mark Lucas for his unflappability and his belief in this project and for showing us early on how to fashion a story that would captivate others as much as it captivated us.

This would not have been such a good read without the astute judgement and talent of Steve Guise our editor at Little, Brown, our desk editor Iain Hunt, and many others who have backed us every step of the way and helped us keep it crisp.

We would like to thank especially Nicola Davidson, vice president for corporate communications at ArcelorMittal for her generosity with her time and for arranging so many important introductions for us. In Luxembourg Patrick Seyler, general manager, international affairs, ArcelorMittal, Luc Decker, press officer to the Minister of Economy, and Guy Schuller, press officer to the Prime Minister of Luxembourg, Jean-Claude Juncker, gave us their valuable perspective and pointed us in many right directions. Without the help of these four people many doors would have stayed closed.

We would also like to thank Jan Cornelis, internal and external communications manager at ArcelorMittal Ghent, for a fascinating tour of the magnificent steelworks there and giving us a feel of how this great alloy is made. Equally, we thank Rachel Mitchell at ArcelorMittal in London, who arranged it for us and was such good company. In Ontario, Canada, Naomi Powell, steel correspondent of the *Hamilton Spectator*, provided invaluable insights into the Dofasco end of the story, while in New York, Peter F. Marcus, managing partner of World Steel Dynamics, gave us the low-down on steel and what motivates the men who make it. In India we are grateful to Dr

Niren Suchanti, chairman and CEO of the Pressman Group, for his take on Jeannot Krecké's visit to the country.

No book is possible without its unsung heroes. Alexandra Westberg provided us with invaluable research, Bernard Compagnon technical advice and guidance, while Juliet Roberts in Luxembourg not only translated interviews but afforded us great hospitality and a memorable curry. In all our visits to Berkeley Square House we developed a special affection for ArcelorMittal's discreetly affable Portuguese butler Manuel Gonçalves, for his green tea and his cappuccinos – with the initials 'AM' stencilled in chocolate on the top – and for explaining to us the difference between a pantry and a kitchen. We pay tribute to Laurent Fery, *maître d'hotel* at Arcelor, for some sumptuous dining at Avenue de la Liberté. We also wish to thank Jean-Luc Pignier, revenue manager of Hôtel Le Royal, Luxembourg City, who showed us where billionaires like to rest their heads.

As in all writing, seeing is believing, which is why we would like to thank Miranda Counsell at Connected Pictures in London and Alain Goniva at ArcelorMittal in Luxembourg for raiding their archives to bring us footage of some of the major events in this story. Stefan Schwarz, deputy of corporate communications at ArcelorMittal in London, was also very helpful to us. Equally we could not have done this without our team of heroic interview transcribers: Claire Bastin, James Delaney, Julie Field and Marian Stapley, who spent a great many more hours than is healthy on our tapes.

We would also like to thank those that we are unable to name for their courage in coming forward to talk to us. We would equally like to acknowledge and name those who refused many, many requests to engage in conversation: SeverStal and ThyssenKrupp.

Tim Bouquet – I would like to thank good friends and fellow authors John Preston, Simon Brett, Kate Mosse and Greg Mosse for their belief that I would make it into print, especially when I doubted it myself. I would like to thank Byron for guiding me through the complexities of the business jungle. I also salute Edward Milward-Oliver for his patience in waiting for me to come out of it! Thank you too to Peter Clayton for his generous and sound advice. A very special appreciation goes to Russell Twisk. If he had not sent me out to track a fox I would not be writing this now.

But most of all, this book is a tribute to my wife Sarah and my children Ella and Milo for their unwavering love and support and their good humour and great patience as I grappled with a strange new vocabulary of poison pills, bedbug letters, white knights, black knights and steel products long and flat.

Byron Ousey – I would like to thank my colleagues at Gavin Anderson, especially Richard Constant and Fergus Wylie, for their encouragement. My two sons, Jonathan and Benjamin, aware of my advancing years, were wonderfully supportive and cajoling, during my more stressful moments.

Finally, my return to writing would not have been possible without the care and thoughtfulness of Marcia, my partner. Without her 2005 Christmas present to me – the creative writing course at West Dean College – I would not have had the delight of meeting Tim and this book would not have been written.

Lastly, we would like to list and thank sincerely all those who talked to us and told us the story:

The Players

The Steel Makers
Mittal Steel
Lakshmi Mittal *Chairman and Chief Executive Officer*
Aditya Mittal *Chief Financial Officer*
Sudhir Maheshwari *Managing Director, Business Development and Treasury*
Nicola Davidson *General Manager Corporate Communications*
Malay Mukherjee *Member of Group Management Board*
Bikham Agarwal *Executive Vice-President (Finance)*
Julien Onillon *Director of Investor Relations*
Bill Scotting *Director of Continuous Improvement*
Roland Verstappen *Director, Government Affairs*
And from the board
Wilbur Ross Jr *(W. L. Ross & Co.)*

Arcelor
Joseph Kinsch *Chairman*
Guy Dollé *Chief Executive Officer*
Michel Wurth *Deputy Chief Executive Officer*
Gonzalo Urquijo *Chief Financial Officer*
Roland Junck *Member of Group Management Board*
Philippe Capron *Director of Financial Affairs*
Alain Davezac *Senior Vice-President*
Frederik Van Bladel *Legal Counsel*
Martine Hue *Head of Investor Relations*
Patrick Seyler *Head of Corporate Communications*
Rémi Boyer *Executive Secretary*
And from the board
John Castegnaro *Député, Luxembourg Chamber of Deputies*
Antoine Spillmann *(Executive Partner Bruellan Wealth Management, Geneva) representing Corporación JMAC BV*

Dofasco
Don Pether *Chief Executive Officer*

The Bankers
Goldman Sachs
Richard J. Gnodde *Co Chief Executive Officer*
Yoel Zaoui *Head of Investment Banking, Europe*
Shahriar Tadjbakhsh *Managing Director, Head of French Mergers and Acquisitions*
Gilberto Pozzi *Managing Director, Investment Banking Division*
Lisa Rabbe *Executive Director, Government Affairs*

Morgan Stanley
Michael Zaoui *Chairman of European Mergers and Acquisitions*
Bernard Gault *Managing Director, Investment Banking Division*

Credit Suisse
Jeremy Fletcher *Managing Director, Investment Banking Division*

HSBC
Adrian Coates *Managing Director, Metals and Mining*

Citigroup Global Markets Limited
Spiro Youakim *Director, European Metals and Mining*

Société Générale
Laurent Meyer *Managing Director, Corporate and Investment Banking*

Deutsche Bank
Brett Olsher *Co-Global Head of Industry Coverage and Natural Resources*

BNP Paribas
Christophe Moulin *Managing Director, Corporate Finance*

Merrill Lynch
Marc Pandraud *President, Merrill Lynch France*
Emmanuel Hasbanian *Managing Director, Mergers and Acquisitions (France)*

JPMorgan Chase
Thierry d'Argent *Managing Director (France)*

The Lawyers
Cleary Gottlieb Steen & Hamilton
Pierre-Yves Chabert *Avocat au Bureau de Paris*

Skadden, Arps, Slate, Meagher and Flom
Pierre Servan-Schreiber *Avocat aux Bureaux de Paris et New York*
Scott Simpson *Partner (London)*

Elvinger, Hoss and Prussen (Luxembourg)
Philippe Hoss *Partner*

Dechert (Luxembourg)
Marc Seimetz *Partner*

The Shareholders
The Government of Luxembourg
Jeannot Krecké *Minister of Economy and Foreign Trade*
Luc Frieden *Budget Minister and Minister of Justice*

Carlo Tassara International
Romain Zaleski *Presidente*

Centaurus Capital
Benoît d'Angelin *Managing Director*

The PR advisers
The Maitland Consultancy
Philip Gawith *Partner and Senior Consultant*
Lydia Pretzlik *Partner and Senior Consultant*

Image 7
Anne Méaux *President*

Publicis
Jean Yves-Naouri *Executive Vice-President*

Index